ROGUE'S GAMBIT

TRIALS OF THE AEGIS

BOOK TWO

AARON HODGES

ABOUT THE AUTHOR

Aaron Hodges was born in 1989 in the small town of Whakatane, New Zealand. He studied for five years at the University of Auckland, completing a Bachelors of Science in Biology and Geography, and a Masters of Environmental Engineering. After working as an environmental consultant for two years, he grew tired of office work and decided to quit his job in 2014 and see the world. One year later, he published his first novel - Stormwielder.

FOLLOW AARON HODGES...

And receive TWO FREE novels and a short story!

https://aaronhodgesauthor.com/newsletter

ALSO BY AARON HODGES

Trials of the Aegis

Book 1: Warden's Justice

Book 2: Rogue's Gambit

The Sword of Light

Book 1: Stormwielder

Book 2: Firestorm

Book 3: Soul Blade

The Legend of the Gods

Book 1: Oathbreaker

Book 2: Shield of Winter

Book 3: Dawn of War

The Knights of Alana

Book 1: Daughter of Fate

Book 2: Queen of Vengeance

Book 3: Crown of Chaos

The Evolution Gene

Book 1: Reborn

Book 2: Havoc

Book 3: Carnage

Descendants of the Fall

Book 1: Warbringer

Book 2: Wrath of the Forgotten

Book 3: Age of Gods

Book 4: Dreams of Fury

The Alfurian Chronicles

Book 1: Defiant

Book 2: Guardian

Book 3: Conquest

The Swords of Heaven and Hell

Book 1: Darkstrider

Book 2: Voidlight

The Four Circles

Book 1: Help! My Wizard Mentor Had A Heart Attack And Now I'm Being Chased By A Horde Of Giant Spiders!

The Untamed Isles

The Path Awakens

The Kingdom of Fresia

1

The nights were cool in Tah'raus. Even with winter's departure and the arrival of spring, the winds came howling in from the ocean to suck the warmth from the broad avenues of the capital. Then there was the rain, constant and heavy, it fell almost horizontally with the force of the breeze, so that the water found you even beneath awnings and canopies.

But after two months in the city, Kaila Dwyn didn't mind. At least the wind dispersed the stench of urine and rotting garbage that hung about the slums. Sometimes she would even stand atop of the seawalls and look over the raging waters of the bay, bracing against the wind and the rain, and wonder what lay beyond.

Tonight, however, she had a different task.

The sun had set hours ago, but the marketplace remained busy. This city was never quiet; its streets rumbled at all hours with the passage of carriages and the bellowing of hawkers. Hundreds of little lanterns kept the darkness at bay; each lit by a tiny shard of the crystal known as agimet.

The crystals were vital to Tah'raus. Their magic powered everything from the lanterns to the strange, horseless machines that carried men and women through the capital's streets.

Noblewomen wore it as jewellery, bragging how the light inside —*atar* it was called—enhanced the hue of their skin. Even the nobleman approaching hurriedly along the path towards her wore an agimet powered timepiece on his wrist. They had become popular amongst the nobility since the agimet revolution two decades ago, apparently.

The sight of it had the blood pulsing in Kaila's ears. In Tah'raus, the crystals had created a life of abundance and pleasure for the Fresian nobility, but elsewhere in the kingdom they were forbidden—dark things used by the Elysian enemy for their vile magics. Kaila's father had mined it from the depths beneath a volcanic mount. Day after day, he had risked his life to deliver it to the Wardens, those noble heroes who fought the enemy; the only ones worthy of such power.

Or so they had been told.

Lies, all of it—a tale to perpetuate the subservience in the Dominances, so they would not claim a small measure of power for themselves.

Speaking of which…

…adopting the vacant-eyed expression of a noblewoman, Kaila stepped into the path of the approaching man. While not overly large, he still had at least fifty pounds on her, and she inevitably came off second worst in the subsequent collision. The papers she'd been carrying went flying as she was knocked from her feet, and the cry of pain as her elbow collided with the pavement was only partly feigned.

"*Oh!*"

Her assailant wore a horrified look as he gawked at her sprawled on the ground.

"Terribly sorry, miss!" he gasped. Regaining his composure, he knelt to help her up. "Are you all right?"

His concern seemed genuine, which matched what Kaila already knew about her mark. She'd spent the past couple months in the capital learning to be a thief under the watchful eye of her mentor, Theron—but this was her first time taking point.

Her target was Eamon Stadwit, a nobleman from a small town on the Vermillion Coast who had recently come into an Earlship. Public accounts had labelled him a compassionate ruler, apparently even substituting his workers' stipends from his own purse last winter after a poor harvest. Not that the capital considered this to be a *positive* thing—the records had been scathing about the breach in protocol.

More importantly, he was a bachelor, and word was that he had come to the capital in search of a bride. His sights would be set on a Daughter of the Magisterium. Chosen for their beauty and intellect, then trained in commerce and politics, Daughters were groomed to be the perfect wife to the nobility. Engagement to a Daughter would change the fortunes of even the most mediocre earl overnight.

But of course, the chances of that happening for a man of Eamon's station were slim to none. About the same chance, in fact, as colliding with a Daughter in the middle of a crowded marketplace. All of which was to say, this encounter was entirely by her design. As were the papers Kaila had flung so dramatically into the air. They drifted down around them as she clutched her arm with a wince.

"I'm fine, I think," she murmured, adopting a dainty tone as he help her to her feet. "I'm so sorry. I didn't see you there at all."

"Quite all right," Eamon said. "My fault for not looking where I was walking. Here, let me help you with these."

Kaila watched as he bent to gather the papers, noting the widening of his eyes as he spied the seal of the Magisterium. He stilled, hand extended for the next paper, before recovering himself and finishing the task. As he handed back the papers, his fluster was replaced by a broad smile.

Like a hound on the prowl, Kaila thought to herself as she accepted them. Her hands were trembling so badly she almost dropped them again.

"Oh sorry, I…gosh…" she stammered, "this city…is it always so *busy?*"

"Oh, dear." Eamon's smile softened, the lines crinkling around his eyes. "You're new here, aren't you, Miss…"

"Eliza Wrenn," she lied, adopting the name of her childhood rival. The girl might be an *actual* Daughter by now, for all Kaila knew. She drew no small amount of pleasure at the thought of ruining the girl's reputation.

"Eliza," Eamon repeated the name as though committing it to memory. "I am Earl Eamon Stadwit of the Vermillion Coast. Please, I fear my father's clumsiness did not skip a generation. Here, let us sit a moment in this fine establishment." He gestured to the frosted windows of a nearby cafe. "I will buy you a drink and we can settle our nerves before continuing on our way."

"Oh, *thank you,*" Kaila gushed. She added a little crackle to her voice, like she was bordering on tears. She thought it a little over the top, but apparently these noblemen loved to act the hero.

Smiling, Eamon looped his arm through hers and led her into the little shop. Warmth swallowed them up—every restaurant in Tah'raus worthy of the name had one of the latest heaters, little black boxes powered by agimet that put out the heat of a small furnace. There were many such machines in the capital now. Devices for cooking, others for cooling food and beverages, and still more for cutting and drilling and lifting—even some to pump water through pipes to the houses of the nobility. An age of wonder had dawned over the capital—for some at least.

And all of it built on the backs of men like her father.

No wonder the Magisterium ruled with such an iron fist. Every town and village in the kingdom, no matter how small, had at least one Sister. It was they who tutored the children of Fresia, teaching them their false histories and instilling their sense of duty to the crown. Those who failed to learn their lessons were cast aside, consigned to latrine duties or sent to the frontlines to fight. The Sisters even governed at local levels, administering paperwork for the nobility and sitting in judgement in the courts of the Magisterium. One couldn't even travel the roads of Fresia without permission from a Sister.

Removing her coat, Kaila sat at a little table in the glass window while Eamon waved down a waiter and ordered a bottle of Brensheld red. Kaila accepted the glass with a smile, before Eamon offered his own for a toast.

"To Eliza," he said over the *clink* of crystal, "may your endeavours in our glorious capital bear fruit."

Kaila studied Eamon over the rim of her glass as she followed his lead. He was handsome enough, she supposed, with a square chin and dark hair. Sure, there was more fat on his bones than muscle, but a girl could certainly do worse. The wine was tasty, and deep as they were in the merchant's quarter, it was no small flex of his wealth.

Unfortunately for Eamon, Kaila had no interest in a pairing —and she certainly had nothing to do with the Daughters of the Magisterium. Sure, she *looked* the part. The rich foods of the capital had turned the scrawny mountain girl into a woman grown, and beneath her coat she wore a long satin dress that Theron had found for her. Dyed emerald green to match her eyes, it hugged her newfound curves. The lace-trimmed sleeves were the latest fashion, though they would hinder her ability to draw the dagger in her boot. The plunging neckline finished the look, revealing the gold collar of a Daughter that had been hidden by her coat.

But it was all fake. Just like the papers, the dress was part of the perfect trap she and Theron had set for the ill-fated nobleman. And from the direction of his gaze, he had already taken the bait.

The success should have given Kaila some semblance of joy. All her hard work these past weeks was finally paying off. Some satisfaction, at the very least. But the finer emotions had abandoned Kaila months ago, swept away by her rage. She was consumed with a singular purpose, one that filled her every waking thought, following her even to her dreams.

Revenge.

Revenge on men like Eamon Stadwit, who could walk through the streets of Tah'raus without blinking an eye to the extravagance, without a single care for the blood shed for this opulence. The blood of men like her father, who had toiled and sacrificed to make a better world for his daughter, only for his efforts to be leeched away by this diseased capital, the so-called jewel of human civilisation.

Tah'raus.

All her life, Kaila had read stories of its wonder. How the capital led the war against the Elysian, uniting humanity beneath one banner. Metals and grain and meat, wood and cloth and minerals; every town and city and Dominance sent all they could spare—and more—to Tah'raus, so they could feed and clothe and arm the soldiers of Fresia.

But only a fraction ever made it to the frontier. Instead, men like Eamon Stadwit had grown rich from the labour of the masses. Lavish feasts that could have fed her entire village were commonplace, while the markets overflowed with goods that would never travel anywhere close to a soldier's stomach. The nobility made no secret of their riches, adorning themselves in expensive silks and lounging in grand mansions along the seawall.

It was enough to make a girl downright *murderous.*

Kaila took another sip of her wine, letting it linger on her tongue, before carefully setting down the glass. She glanced at Eamon through her lashes, giving him a hesitant smile. "Can I be honest with you, Earl Stadwit?"

"Please, call me Eamon," he replied gracefully, "and of course you can, my dear."

The wine was strong and Kaila could already feel it warming

her cheeks. "I fear I am ill-suited to Tah'raus." She made a show of lowering her eyes to the table. "I come from a small village in the Iron Pinnacles. I had heard stories of the capital, of course, but nothing our Sister taught us could prepare me for the reality."

It was the truth, in a roundabout kind of fashion. *The best lies are those sprinkled with fact*, Theron liked to say.

Eamon lapped it up. "You're a brave woman, Eliza," he said. "I too am new to the city. It is certainly a harsh place compared with my village in the south." Smiling, he reached across the table and took her hand. Kaila suppressed a shudder at the clammy touch of his skin. "Maybe those of us from the small places of Fresia should join forces."

"Oh," she murmured, her eyes growing wide, "you think so?"

Eamon nodded earnestly. "Of course. We could benefit each other greatly. I have some influence here, and…" He hesitated, looking sheepish. "I'll admit, I caught a glimpse of your papers in the street. You are…"

She lowered her eyes. "A Daughter," she admitted, "at least, so they tell me. The other girls mostly come from the larger cities. I…"

"Let me be your ally," Eamon said quickly, overeager now. "I can help you, Eliza. And together…" His grin broadened. "Together we could be a force to be reckoned with, don't you think?" He squeezed her fingers.

Keeping her eyes on the table, Kaila let the words hang between them, before slowly lifting her head to meet his gaze. A shy smile touched her lips.

"Oh, Eamon," she breathed. "You have no idea what it means to hear that." She averted her eyes. "I've felt quite lost since I arrived."

"Well, you don't have to feel that way anymore," Eamon said warmly, both his hands enveloping hers now. "Come, why don't we dine together? Not here," he added quickly as she glanced around for the waiter. "There is much for us to discuss. Sensitive matters. I can have my servants prepare a banquet if that would be agreeable?"

"Yes." She smiled, allowing a little glimmer of excitement to shine through her mask. "I think that would be *most* agreeable."

The poor man almost looked surprised, as though he couldn't quite believe his good fortune. Had Eamon been wiser, he might have trusted his instincts. A Daughter, the ticket to a life of status far above his simple Earlship, had quite literally fallen into his lap.

Alas, Eamon was like all the other noblemen she'd helped Theron scam in the past two months—greed dwarfed any sense of decency he might possess. It never seemed to matter how much they had, it was never enough for men like him. They always needed more.

She almost allowed herself to feel remorse as he paid the bill, then brought her coat. She pulled it on, grateful for its warmth. Her dress offered little protection from the elements, despite the small fortune it had cost Theron. The wind howled through the cafe as Eamon opened the door. Kaila braced herself as she stepped into the street, pausing to wait for him to follow. As they moved into the throng, she glimpsed a familiar face. Theron. His dark eyes met her own before fading back into the crowd.

Kaila's stomach twisted as her mind went to all the other looks he had given her—the teasing glances in the cave, the frightful concern after their battle with the Warden, and the heat that night when she had come to him in the ruins…

…gritting her teeth, she shoved the memories deep down inside. That was over now. Whatever brief romance they'd shared in the mountains had been swallowed by her rage. Instead, she linked arms with Eamon and flashed the man a smile, allowing him to take the lead.

They made their way through the narrow avenues of the marketplace, eventually passing into the broader Sutton Street, where the windows were filled with jewellery and precious gems. Amongst the gold and silver and platinum, agimet pieces shone with the radiance of *atar*. Kaila had a piece of the crystal in her own pocket, but it was different to these. The humans cut and polished their crystals, so they shone with a brilliant, unnatural white. Elysian like herself thought of them as broken because they couldn't be used for their magic—at least not without terrible consequences.

Her own crystal was untouched by human tools and its glow was softer. You could almost see the colours within, shifting from ocean-blue to moss-green to fire-red. And when Kaila held it in her hands, she saw the fabric of the universe.

But that power came at a cost. Just taking the crystal from her pocket would fill her veins with the *atar* inside. Then the silver light would shine from her eyes, marking her as Elysian. One of the enemy. Some Elysian could hide themselves—those Theron called Weavers—but neither she nor Theron possessed that ability.

Instead, their Gift was to move the universe around them. It made them powerful in their own right, but the way their eyes lit up like the twin moons, not exactly subtle. And in the capital, drawing unwanted attention as an Elysian was as good as placing the hangman's noose around your own neck. The city crawled with Wardens—those unnatural soldiers of the Magisterium, whose black armour protected them from the magic of the Elysian. Though they had been less visible in recent weeks…

It was a relief when they moved on from Sutton Street, entering a more residential section of the city. Walls hemmed them in on either side, tall and unadorned, interrupted only by heavy iron gates set in deep alcoves. If you had never been inside, the casual observer might believe that behind those walls were the same squalid flats found all throughout the city—the kingdom, in fact.

But Kaila knew from experience the grandeur concealed within; great manors of granite and marble, imperial staircases and lush gardens fed from water pipes only the powerful could afford. The king and his closest allies might be comfortable displaying their wealth with their mansions built atop the coastal wall, but they had the direct protection of the Magisterium. Most others chose strong walls and anonymity to guard them against a jealous public.

Not that they had anyone fooled. Just a glimpse was enough to know this was a preserve of the powerful. Here the streets were swept clean each dawn and dusk and the trees lining the pavement were freshly trimmed. And they were empty. In the slums, children ran barefoot day and night through streets littered with refuse, and elderly huddled forgotten in the alleyways, no longer of value to their noble overlords. Those were the parts of the city she had frequented these last weeks. She had no choice. Only in those forgotten, neglected tenements could her kind survive.

Elysian. The Gifted. *The enemy.*

What a joke. The truth was, most of them just wanted to *survive.* If the Magisterium would just leave them alone, most would be content to forget their cursed magic and pass as regular citizens.

But not her, not anymore. Kaila's father had taught her to meet an enemy with blade in hand.

And the Magisterium was her enemy.

The Stadwit family manor was a short distance and their stroll soon came to an end. Kaila cast a glance over her shoulder as Eamon banged on the iron door. The night had grown darker, the agimet lanterns sparser away from the bustling marketplace, and she caught no sign of Theron amidst the shadows. That was probably for the best as the gate swung open and a pair of guards stepped out to survey the street. They seemed the sort that took their job seriously. Many in the capital were just as indoctrinated by the Magisterium as those in her own village. Kaila almost pitied them.

It wouldn't stop her from killing every last one of them though, if she had to.

Inside the gate, a path of crushed white stone led through a lush garden lit by the brilliant white of agimet lanterns. The scent of roses and jasmine washed over Kaila as Eamon led her between the bushes, up to the manor itself, where six marble steps led to doors of oak. A servant held them open as they approached, beckoning them inside with a bow. As they entered, he followed close on their heels, taking both their coats.

"Prepare the parlour, Charles," Eamon announced. "Daughter Eliza will be joining me for dinner."

The servant raised his eyebrows in surprise, before sweeping into another bow—deeper this time—and racing off, leaving them alone in the entrance hall. Kaila took the opportunity to survey her surroundings. Now she was inside, her job became simple—locate the safe where the family kept most of their physical wealth. Unfortunately, though Eamon was a minor earl, the manor was impressively large. Granite floors gleamed under the light of an enormous chandelier, while tapestries depicting several great battles between humans and Elysian adorned the walls. Flowers, probably from their own gardens, had been set around the room, filling the air with their rich scent, while a broad staircase led to the upper floors. If the manor followed traditional capital design, the sleeping quarters would be located there.

"Shall we?" Eamon asked, gesturing to the door through which the servant had disappeared.

Kaila struggled to supress a sigh. He would want to dine and politely discuss the terms of an engagement. No doubt he would have lots to say about how he could offer her life of comfort and luxury—while she used her contacts and status as a Daughter to leverage his own endeavours, maybe even destroy a few of his rivals.

But now she was inside…Kaila found her patience wearing thin. It was time she put their game plan in action. Theron wouldn't mind if she skipped a few steps...probably. Moving in close to the man, she tilted her head back with a smile.

"I thought you might show me around your lovely manor

first, Eamon," she said breathlessly, laying a hand on his chest. "Perhaps…upstairs?" The safe was most likely to be in his private chambers.

A gasp caught in Eamon's throat as his pulse began to race beneath her fingers. He was young for his rank, a few years past twenty, and far too naïve to hear the warning sirens sounding. Suddenly, he wasn't thinking about politics, but her dress and all the other things it offered. Nodding, he took Kaila's hand and all but dragged her towards the stairs.

She found herself smiling as they ascended. What had Theron been so worried about? This seduction business wasn't that hard, after all. Sure, impersonating a Daughter was a capital crime—but so was just existing as an Elysian, so what did she care?

Several portraits lined the hallway at the top of the stairs—Eamon's ancestors, judging by the resemblance. Plush woollen carpets muffled their footsteps and the air was warm. She spied the squat black outline of an agimet heater as they made their way along the corridor. The glow of the lanterns had been dimmed, and in the shadows, Kaila could almost imagine it was someone else's hand she held.

Arriving at a set of double doors, Eamon opened them with a flourish. "My personal chambers," he said, voice hoarse as he gestured for her to enter.

Within, Kaila's eyes were drawn to the enormous four-poster bed. Piled high with cushions and draped in violet curtains, she wondered at the absurdity of it. What need did one man have for such opulence, when a single cot achieved the same comfort? Just the fur rug at the foot of the bed could have served as a bed in a pinch.

But Kaila said nothing of her inner thoughts, crossing instead to a pair of glass and iron doors that opened onto the balcony. The night was crisp as she stepped outside, the thin silk of her dress offering zero protection from the chill. Below were the gardens of the manor, cast silver in the moonlight. She scanned the shadows. When she saw no sign of movement, she touched a finger to the agimet concealed inside the cuff of her dress—one of three small crystals concealed on her person.

Standing with her back to the noble, Eamon didn't notice the faint glow that appeared in her eyes. The world shimmered, before a thousand lights appeared in the garden. *Soullights.* Everything in the universe had one. The Gift of the Elysian allowed her kind to see and manipulate them. At that moment, all she needed was the *atarsight.* If Theron was waiting in the gardens below as planned, she would see his *soullight.* Unfortunately, there was no sign of him.

"You'll catch a cold, my dear," Eamon said softly from behind Kaila.

Her skin crawled as his lips brushed against her ear and she felt the weight of his hands on her hips.

Goddamnit Theron, where are you?

He was meant to help with this part! Though, she'd counted only two guards on the gate. That, plus the manservant…the odds weren't terrible.

Making the decision herself, Kaila released her crystal, allowing its power to fade from her veins before turning to face Eamon.

"It's beautiful," she whispered, leaning into him briefly before pulling back, her eyes darting to the bedroom. "Would you… would you…"

Eamon's eyes were dark with desire. He loomed over her, a rough thumb lifting her chin as he leaned down. She suppressed a scream as he pressed his lips to hers. He tasted like meat and old cigars. It took all her self-control not to shove him away.

Instead, as they broke apart, Kaila pushed him back into the bedroom. Her heart was pounding now—not from any kind of attraction, but trepidation for what she was about to do. Turning, she tried to close the doors of the balcony behind them. If she could do this quietly—

Rough hands seized Kaila around the waist and dragged her

away from the doors. In the privacy of his bedroom, the polite Eamon from the marketplace had been replaced with a beast.

"Come, my dear," Eamon rasped, pressing himself against her. His eyes were huge in the gloom. Kaila did shudder this time as his fingers traced a path up her thigh. "Let me show you." Eyes flickering closed, he leaned down to kiss her again.

Nope. That was it. Doors open or closed, *that was far enough.*

Kaila hit him with her power.

2

Crouched amidst the sprawling roots of a gomero tree, Theron watched as the nobleman gestured Kaila through the iron gate of the Stadwit property. Pride swelled in his chest. So far, her first solo job had gone off without a hitch. And this was no simple smash and grab. It was risky to impersonate a Daughter, but two months in Tah'raus had left little of the naïve young woman he'd first met in the Iron Pinnacles. Kaila might still struggle with her powers, but she'd taken quickly to the life of a rogue.

Even so, he wasn't about to let her walk into the lion's den without backup. His fingers traced the hilt of the dagger sheathed on his belt, checking it was loose, before he rose and stepped into the street. As he did so, a rough voice spoke from the shadows.

"Theron, fancy seeing you here."

He tensed, swinging around as a figure detached itself from a nearby wall. He didn't draw the knife—or his agimet. *Yet.* If a stranger knew his name, this was not a chance encounter, and noise would draw the attention of the Stadwit guards.

A man emerged from the darkness. His face was rough and criss-crossed with scars, their pale streaks covered only partially by an untamed beard. Worst of all was the bulbous nose, which looked to have been broken one time too many.

"Sorry," Theron spoke in a whisper, eyes narrowed as he studied the interloper, "but I don't believe I know you."

The thug shifted closer, a faint light appearing in his eyes. *Atar.* Theron's fingers twitched towards the pocket where he kept his largest crystal. He preferred to avoid conflict with his kind, but not all followed the Elysian code.

"Been a long time," the man grunted. He had the broad, muscular shoulders of a brawler and wore a patched and stained leather jerkin. "The boss wants a word with you."

A chill crept down Theron's spine. *Ambrose.* He'd been avoiding the Weaver since his return. He owed the crime lord a fairly substantial amount of coin, and while he'd returned with five large pieces of agimet, split between two Movers the fortune hadn't gone far. He'd hoped to avoid the tailor for a few months yet.

"Garrick," he grunted, recognising the man at last. He wasn't wearing his own face. His boss was a Weaver who could change the appearance of his followers. "You piss off Ambrose or something with that nose?"

Garrick scowled. He was a Bruiser—meaning his scowls were usually reserved for people whose face *he* was about to rearrange.

"I mean it, Theron. Ambrose isn't happy you returned without telling him. He wants to see you—*now.*"

"I'm a little busy, if you couldn't tell," Theron replied, gesturing over his shoulder.

Garrick's eyes flickered to the manor, then back to Theron. "From what I saw, your friend had the situation well in hand."

"You don't know her like I do."

The Bruiser sighed. "Look, we can do this one of two ways, Theron."

Slipping his hand into his pocket, Theron clenched his crystal and drew in a whiff of *atar.* "You think you can take me, Garrick?"

Shielded by the broad roots of the gomero tree, the guards wouldn't notice the light. But the large man just crossed his arms and glowered. Standing head and shoulders above Theron, it was a sound rebuttal. Snorting, he threw up his hands.

"*Fine*," he hissed, "but let's make it quick, okay?"

Garrick grunted and turned away, sliding into the shadows. As Theron followed, he released his crystal. A prickling sensation crept across his skin, turning sharp as the last of the *atar* in his veins dissipated. He gritted his teeth against the pain. *Withdrawal.* It was the aftereffect of using a broken crystal—something generally advised against unless you were looking for a quick and messy death. He had only done it to save Kaila's life back in the Iron Pinnacles. Kaila didn't know—and if he had any choice in the matter, it would stay that way.

Garrick led him back the way Kaila had come earlier. They went several blocks, arriving again at the outskirts of the merchant quarter, where he was led to the front of a dress store.

"Inside," the Bruiser rumbled.

Theron raised an eyebrow. "One of his?"

The Bruiser glowered but didn't answer. Theron took it as a suggestion to hurry up. The unmistakable screech of a mechanical buzzer came from somewhere inside the building as he entered and Theron cringed. Honestly, what was wrong with a good old-fashioned bell? At least they didn't use the broken agimet that powered everything else in this blasted city.

His stomach twisted with the familiar hunger for *atar*. His hand twitched towards his pocket and the hidden agimet crystal. Elysian used *atar* to power their Gift—in his and Kaila's case, allowing them to shift things with nothing more than a thought. Bruisers like Garrick, on the other hand, used *atar* to fortify their own bodies, granting themselves enough power to punch through solid stone. But *atar* itself was external; the natural energy of the world, it gathered organically at locations known as nexus points. His ancestors had built their cities around these points—settlements like their fallen capital, Iselador and even

Tah'raus itself—though the Magisterium would deny that until their dying day.

But a nexus point alone was not enough. Agimet was needed as a vessel to channel and store *atar*. But only in its natural form. Breaking or cutting the crystals attuned them to the nexus, turning them from natural vessels into a churning cauldron of power. Perfect if you were powering the great machines created by humanity—deadly if you were a soft and fragile Elysian. Trying to draw from the broken crystals had seen the death of many of his people.

Theron clenched his fists. The result wasn't much better for those like himself who survived. *Atar addiction.* So far, it hadn't crippled him, but it grew worse each time he used his Gift. And here in this twisted capital, surrounded by all those corrupted shards...he could feel them calling to him, fuelling the need. Ordinary agimet dulled the desire, at least for a time, but could not sate it.

Drawing in a breath, Theron forced the cravings down. He had to be careful. Ambrose wasn't someone you crossed. The Weaver had been a part of the Elysian underground for as long as most could remember, and his image only grew with each passing year. He had ears and eyes everywhere nowadays, fingers in every pot. Nothing happened in Tah'raus without him finding out. It was a wonder Theron had managed to keep his return secret for this long.

As he entered, the only inhabitants to greet him were mannequins. Each wore what Theron assumed to be the latest in Fresian fashion. He wasn't exactly well-versed on the subject. Ambrose was a different matter. Clothing was the official side of his business. He probably owned half the fashion brands in the city at this point. You were as likely to hear his name from the lips of the nobility as you were the Elysian underground.

Footsteps approached from the back of the shop as the tailor himself appeared. Ambrose Braider was a small man, with narrow shoulders and a slim face—or at least, that was the appearance he presented to the world. Being a Weaver, you could never really know. He appeared to be alone, but this too could be an illusion. There could be any number of bodyguards in the shop, concealed by the man's illusions.

Ambrose's hair was slicked back, and a hint of mascara shaded his obsidian eyes. He wore a tuxedo tonight, though his bowtie was undone and he was busy rolling up his sleeves, as if he'd just finished with some fancy engagement involving fruity cocktails and dancing.

"Ambrose!" Theron exclaimed, throwing out his arms. "Just the man I've been looking—"

Thwack!

Ambrose hit hard for a man of his size. The right hook caught Theron in the cheek and spun him from his feet. He clutched at the nearest mannequin for support.

"Trickster's fists, where'd you learn to punch like that?" he cursed, steadying himself and pressing a hand to his cheek. It smarted where the man had struck.

"Two months, Theron?" the tailor said, his voice almost conversational. This time instead of a fist, he laid a hand on Theron's shoulder. "You don't write. You don't drop by the store and say hello." His voice hardened, fingers digging into Theron's flesh. "*You don't bring me my gold.*"

Everything went black.

There was no flash, no flickering of the lanterns as warning; just sudden, absolute darkness. Theron's skin crawled, but he maintained his calm. It was only an illusion woven by Ambrose's Gift. Unfortunately, the knowledge was not as comforting as one might hope.

"There were some unexpected snags in my plan," he replied, attempting a grin. "You know how it is, bribing these Magisterium officials. Half of what they give you is useless, false, or outdated. It took me months to find the right—"

An uppercut lifted him to his toes and sent him reeling backwards. There was no recovery this time as he crashed into a mannequin and the pair of them went down in a pile of limbs. Footsteps followed, then a hard leather boot on his throat.

"Where is my money, Theron?"

"Like I said, there were complications," Theron gasped as Ambrose pressed down on his windpipe.

The buzzer on the front door sounded before Ambrose could respond. "Everything okay in here, boss?" It was Garrick.

"*Just fine*, thank you, Garrick," Ambrose replied in a hard voice. "What did I tell you about interrupting? Do I have to add warts next?"

"No, boss. Sorry, boss."

Still on the ground, Theron chuckled as the door thumped closed again. "You need better henchmen, Ambrose," he croaked. "I caught onto Garrick's tail an hour ago."

"Oh? Then pray tell me, why are we here, Theron?" Ambrose's tone remained miffed. Not good.

"How about you let me up and we have a civilised conversation?"

"How about you tell me where the hoard of agimet you promised is?"

Theron swallowed. "The haul wasn't as…lucrative as I'd hoped," he said quickly. "I meant to come see you, I really did, it's just, I've been working so hard since getting back, trying to come up with enough to repay you—"

A sharp kick to the ribs silenced Theron. Gasping, he doubled up on the floor. Red flashed, and when his vision returned, everything was upside down. Ambrose leaned over him, eyes burning with the fire of *atar*.

"You know how many people warned me not to trust you when you came asking?" he said softly. "A promise from Theron isn't worth the threads of that filthy trenchcoat he wears, they claimed." The room began to rotate, slowly at first, then faster. Theron's gut churned. "But *oh no*, I told them. I know the boy. He wouldn't betray me. Not Ambrose, the man who first picked him up off the streets. Gave him agimet, gave him a *purpose*."

Even with his eyes closed, the illusions crawled their way inside his brain, making his ears ring and his head spin. Groaning, Theron fumbled for his pocket, but he couldn't find the agimet. *Where is it!* A dull *thunk* came from somewhere nearby. *The crystal!* He grasped for it, but there was no longer telling up from down, real from false.

Abruptly, the world resolved itself. Theron found himself on his knees, a fallen mannequin alongside him. He almost vomited right there on the floor of the shop, but Ambrose loomed in his fine tuxedo, the agimet he'd dropped resting in his hand.

"You didn't have anything of this calibre before," he mused, eyes finding Theron's. "You found the town after all, didn't you? Don't tell me you've been holding out on me."

Despite the crystal in his hand, Ambrose's eyes had returned to their usual obsidian. The joy of being a Weaver; they could conceal the glint of *atar* with an illusion. Ambrose had begun his career selling weavings to Elysian who wished to live normal lives. That was how they had first met.

"If I'd made my fortune, do you think I would risk pissing you off?" Theron croaked, rubbing his throat as he sat up. "Like I said, there were complications."

"What happened?"

"A Warden."

Ambrose raised his eyebrows. "And you're still alive? That *is* a miracle."

"It's a long story."

"You'll have to tell me it sometime. For now, I'll settle for the rest of my agimet?"

"'That's it," Theron lied. "Turns out, they didn't store it in the town. I scavenged that from the mine itself, but the rest had already been moved. By the time I worked out what they'd done, the Warden was onto me."

"You couldn't track down the shipment?"

"There was a storm." *And a girl.*

"I see." Ambrose was still studying the crystal, but finally he let out a sigh. "I must say, I'm disappointed, Theron. I expected more from you."

"I'm sorry, Ambrose," Theron murmured. His fingers twitched, the cravings clawing their way up from inside of him. If Ambrose took the crystal… "I'll get you your money," he continued quickly. "You know I'm good for it."

Ambrose only grunted. Reaching into his pocket, he drew out a clothe sack and tossed it at Theron's feet. It chimed as it landed. Frowning, Theron pulled open the drawstrings. The shimmer of gold came from inside. His frown deepened as he looked up at the tailor.

"I'm not sure you know how debts work."

Letting out a sigh, the tailor sat himself on the counter of the shop. "I have a job for you."

That set Theron's hackles to tingling. He'd known the Weaver a long time. Ambrose had taken pity on him when he'd been just a child wandering the streets of Tah'raus and come begging for a weaving. The tailor had been a minor player back then, kinder and a thousand-fold less grouchy. But that didn't make them anything close to friends. If Ambrose was offering him a job, it wasn't out of the goodness of his heart.

"Ah," he said cautiously, "what kind of job?"

"The kind that repays large debts owed by ungrateful orphans."

"I'm not an orphan," Theron grumbled. "So, it's dangerous?"

A thin smile stretched the man's lips. "You always were astute."

"No thanks, then." Theron flashed his trademark grin.

Ambrose's face darkened. "Since when do you shirk at a little danger?"

"Haven't you heard? I have an apprentice now. Gotta think about her safety, don't I?"

"I see." Ambrose levered himself off the counter. "Unfortunately, it was not a request."

Theron clenched his fists. This had gone on long enough. Anything could have happened back at the manor. He needed to get back in case Kaila needed his help, like she had in Iselador…

"I'll have your money by the end of the week, Ambrose."

The Weaver stared back. "What about my interest?"

"Interest?"

"And penalty fees," Ambrose continued, a smirk gracing his lips. "Considering it has been *a year*, plus the stringing me around, all up I figure you owe me…oh, let's say three times what you borrowed."

"*What?*" Theron's heart practically tore itself out of his chest. "Ambrose, be reasonable—"

"Oh, I think I am being *quite reasonable*," the tailor growled. As he spoke, the crystal in his hands flashed. *Atar* reappeared in his eyes, burning through the illusion. The room darkened and a sense of dread fell over Theron, tingling in the base of his skull. Ambrose seemed to grow larger as he closed the gap with Theron. "Had anyone else vanished for a year with my money," he continued, "I would have strung them up in Soul Square for all to see."

Suddenly Ambrose *towered* over Theron. The walls closed in around him and the air grew thin. *Hot.* His lungs heaved, screaming as he found he couldn't breathe. Even knowing it was illusion, Theron couldn't keep from trembling. Sweat beaded his brow, but somehow he managed to hold his ground.

"Ah, yes, well," he gasped, eyes tearing up from the strain of getting out the words. "When you put it that way…ah, when do we start?"

There was no sound, no sense of movement, but the world abruptly returned to normal.

"Knew you'd come around." Ambrose wore a pleasant smile as he clapped Theron on the shoulder. "I always could count on you."

Theron swallowed, his heart still palpitating. "I, ah, I can choose my own team?"

The tailor frowned. "Since when do you work with others?"

Shaking off the last effects of the illusion, Theron shrugged. "People change."

Ambrose snorted. "People don't change." He waved a hand. "But bring your apprentice, if you wish. So long as she doesn't get in our way."

Theron nodded. "She won't," he hesitated then, eyeing the tailor, unsure how much he should press. "So what's the job?"

"A simple impersonation, a little seduction—nothing you can't handle."

"That's not exactly my usual MO," Theron replied carefully. "I'm a Mover, not a Weaver."

"The man you are to impersonate hasn't been seen in the capital in almost twenty years, when he was just a child," Ambrose said quietly.

"Still, a Psionic then…"

"I have faith your natural charm will be sufficient," Ambrose growled. "Now, there's a time, name and address in the bag. I will meet you there tomorrow."

Theron's frown only grew. A job like this…even if a Weaver wasn't necessary, it sounded well outside his area of expertise. He looked from the Weaver to the sack of gold. There was a small fortune inside.

"How do you know I won't run?"

"Take a look at the name."

Reaching into the bag, Theron pulled out the scrap of paper he found inside.

What…is this?

One glance at the name had his stomach tying itself in knots. His skin prickled as blood pulsed in his ears. Trembling, he met the tailor's obsidian gaze.

"How long have you known?"

A smirk crossed the crime lord's lips. "So you'll do it?"

Theron swallowed. He wasn't sure what Ambrose had planned, whether he was seeking wealth, or power, or if this was part of some larger plot. But it didn't matter. He was an addict now, his every waking moment consumed by desire—and pain. What did he care for any of that? What did he care for *anything?*

Avenge me, brother…

A smile graced his lips. "With pleasure."

"Good." Ambrose held out Theron's crystal. The glow of its *atar* was depleted, but Theron accepted it gratefully. "*Do not* be late." His eyes flashed bright with *atar*.

And then he vanished.

Rude, Theron thought, glancing at his crystal. Ambrose would have plenty of agimet concealed on his person, but he'd drained Theron's nearly dry out of sheer spite. Muttering a curse, he returned to the street, where Garrit had already disappeared. He made straight for the manor. He'd been gone almost an hour. Surely not enough time for Kaila to get into trouble. She was probably still deep in negotiations over a glass of fine wine and plate of pheasant.

He was back outside the gates within minutes. The street was still, light still shining from beneath the iron gates. Everything was normal.

Theron had just let out a sigh of relief when, with a mighty *roar*, the roof of the Stadwit manor exploded outwards into the street.

<hr>

KAILA DIDN'T HIT THE EARL *THAT* HARD. OR AT LEAST, SHE didn't *mean* to hit him hard. Unfortunately, she'd only had these powers for a couple of months, and getting the *proportionality* of things right when it came to her Gift was still…troubling.

All of which was to say, when she grasped Eamon's *soullight* and pushed him away, he didn't so much as *move*, as *flew* across the room with enough force to smash through the wooden canopy of his bed. The resulting crash was loud enough to be heard all the way from the street, even had the balcony doors been closed.

"Trickster's balls," she muttered, adopting one of Theron's favourite curses.

She glanced at the door as distant shouts carried from somewhere below. Groaning, Eamon was still trying to pick himself up from the ruin of his bed. He froze, though, when he looked up and found her standing over him, eyes blazing with the power of an Elysian.

"What in the name of the First Matron," he cried, gaping.

Her jaw hardened, fingers tightening into tiny balls. It was the First Matron who had started all of this a thousand years ago. *T'iana.* In the lost city of Iselador, the slave mechanist had turned against her Elysian masters and stolen an artefact of great power—the Aegis. With its magic, she had freed the human slaves and led them in a rebellion against their former masters.

Or at least, that was the Magisterium's story. Kaila had stood in the ruins of Iselador and looked upon the statue of T'iana. Queen, the Elysian had called her then. A thousand years later, they still cursed her as the Great Betrayer.

Striding to the door of the bedroom, Kaila slid home the locking bolt. Hopefully that would delay the guards a few minutes. Behind her, Eamon made a *thump* as he rolled from the bed and crawled towards the balcony. Kaila stepped around the ruin of the bed to cut off his retreat. Whimpering, he flopped onto his back and gaped up at her.

"Pl…please," he moaned. Blood ran from his nose, staining his silk shirt red. "I didn't mean…I won't…what do you want?"

Kaila bore down on him, eyes burning as she clenched her piece of agimet. "Your safe," she snarled. "Where is it?"

Much of a noble's wealth was stored in vaults protected by the Magisterium, but not all of it. They always had a safe or two of their own. *Spending money* they called it. Only, in a world where most considered an extra days ration chip a blessing, their *spending money* was enough to purchase a small hamlet.

"Yes, yes, of course, here!" Fumbling for his belt, Eamon tossed his purse at her feet. "There, that's everything!"

It made a gentle chiming sound as it landed. Her jaw hardened. Trust a nobleman's greed to run deeper than his good sense. Sniffing, she flicked a finger. Gestures weren't technically necessary for her Gift, but she found they helped her focus. Plus, they added some style.

A brilliant white lit the room, spilling from her eyes. Eamon gave a strangled cry as her power lifted him into the air. He kicked and thrashed and tried to scream, but drawing a thread of *atar* from her crystal, Kaila wrapped it around the node of lights she hoped was his throat and drew it tight. The only sound that emerged from his mouth was a strangled squeak.

"Do you think I'm stupid?" she hissed, stepping closer. Twin needles of pain stabbed at the base of her skull from the effort of maintaining the two threads of *atar*—one holding the earl aloft, the other squeezing his windpipe. She had seen Theron manage dozens at once, but he'd had over a decade of practice.

The fear on Eamon's face turned to panic. Spittle frothed at his lips as he thrashed, eyes bulging, veins popping in his forehead. Meaty hands batted at the unseen fingers curled around his throat.

He wouldn't find them. Rage allowed Kaila to suppress the pain as she firmed her magic's grip. She'd been practicing this technique for weeks now, ever since Theron had shown her that *soullights* were not just a single light, but a collection of many. If she was careful, Kaila could direct her Gift against just a few of them, rather than the whole.

And if she *wasn't* careful, well, it wasn't like the world would miss one more dead nobleman.

"Now, the safe—"

Crash!

Kaila spun as the door to the bedchamber tore open, emitting two guards and the servant from earlier. The three men stumbled to a halt when they saw Kaila standing amidst the ruin of the bed, eyes burning with the cursed magic of the enemy. The four of them stared at one another for a long moment.

Then, her concentration broken, a *thump* came from behind Kaila as Eamon crashed to the ground. The nobleman wheezed, finally managed to suck in a breath. Unfortunately, he wasted it on speech.

"*Quickly, men!*" he rasped, "It's one of *them!* Get it!"

Kaila raised an eyebrow—and her dagger, which she slid from her boot—as the guards and servant shifted nervously on their feet. "You sure you want to do this, guys?"

The whisper of steel swords being drawn was her only answer, before the men began spreading out in a half-circle to bar her exit. A snarl drew her attention back to Eamon as he regained his feet. He had gathered the broken bed poster and wielded it now like a club.

"You're in for it now, devil," he said. "I should have smelt the corruption on you from the start. Come, lads, the Magisterium will reward us handsomely for the head of a blasphemer."

Kaila's lips tightened, her rage slipping free of its cage. Drawing a crystal from her pocket, she held it in her left hand, dagger in her right. A smile crossed her lips.

"All right then. Who's first?"

Unfortunately, Eamon and his men were smart enough not to take the bait. Instead of coming at her one at a time, they charged together, screaming and swinging their weapons. It made the job of her staying alive a great deal more difficult.

"Trickster damn you, Theron, where are you?" she gasped as Eamon swung for her skull. The man seemed particularly agitated, as if her impersonation had been some personal afront against his name.

Kaila ducked the makeshift club and lashed out with her Gift, striking his *soullight* and hurling him backwards. He was not her only foe, however, and even as she delt with the earl, pain tore across her bicep as one of the guards scored her with his sword. Only the second man stumbling into his comrade's path and throwing off his swing saved her from a deeper wound.

Even so, she cursed and scrambled back—straight into the arms of the manservant. He had no weapon, but hurled himself at her bravely, wrapping Kaila in a bear hug and squeezing tight. She gasped, straining against his wiry strength. Footsteps approached from behind—Eamon—while the guards advanced.

The thump of panic began in Kaila's heart. Her eyes darted from one man to another. Arms trapped, she couldn't bring her dagger to bear. She gritted her teeth, fingers tight around the crystal. It was her only chance.

The men raised their weapons. No time for a complicated working—or even a simple one. Kaila drew on her crystal until she felt the *atar* inside of her, swelling, crawling, *burning* to escape. Normally, she spun the energy into threads. Now, however, she unleashed it all at once.

The world turned white, lit by the brilliant flash of her eyes, and then everything Kaila had bottled within burst outwards. Energy raced from her in a wave, entangling every *soullight* it touched.

Eamon and his staff screamed as they were swept up.

They weren't the only things, though.

The bed was the next to be caught in her power. It was torn from the ground, hurled away from Kaila, along with a chest of drawers and the closet. The floor beneath her feet followed, then the high ceilings, and finally the walls; they tore apart before her eyes, disintegrating in the maelstrom she had unleashed, as some parts were pulled in one direction, others thrust up, down, and every which way.

In an instant, every person and object within a fifteen-foot radius of Kaila was torn to shreds.

The light in her crystal flickered and died. Darkness descended on the manor. Kaila found herself suddenly falling. Thankfully, the floor below remained untouched, and Kaila had practiced falling quite a bit these past few weeks. Her feet crumpled as they struck, sending Kaila into a roll that carried her halfway across the room before striking a fallen cabinet.

Cursing beneath her breath, she lay there clutching her shoulder where the guard had cut her. But she couldn't linger long. Blood was seeping through her fingers and what she'd just done would draw the city watch—and the Wardens—to the manor like flies to a corpse.

Gritting her teeth, she levered herself to her feet. Stars burst before her eyes and she swayed as the first after-effects of her power touched her. Usually it wasn't so bad, but when she overdid it—like channelling an entire crystal in a single pulse—there tended to be repercussions. A shard of pain sliced through her head, like a nail being driven deep into her brain. Darkness swirled at the edges of her vision. She clenched her teeth, clinging to consciousness. She couldn't afford weakness now.

Struggling to pierce the darkness, she looked for Eamon and his cronies. Surely, they couldn't have survived that. But one of the first lessons she'd learned in this new life was to never count an enemy dead without verification. Nothing moved amidst the darkness, but that didn't mean she was safe.

Light appeared. The glow of a lantern, approaching from the corridor outside. Kaila tensed, reaching for her dagger before realising she had lost it in the fall. The crystal in her hand was empty, but—

A man appeared in the doorway. Kaila was gathering herself to leap at him, when he lifted the lantern and its glow lit his face.

"Where the hell have you been?" she gasped at Theron.

The thief raised an eyebrow as he surveyed the chamber. By his light, she counted the messy remains of four bodies—two of which were plastered against the walls above. *Good.* At least she knew they were dead.

"I thought we agreed this would be a *quiet* job?"

"Don't look at me like that!" she cried, standing in the ruin of what had been the earl's bedroom a few minutes earlier. "What happened to you?"

Theron was still studying the scene, but now he turned to her with a grimace. "Sorry, something came up."

"You were meant to be here."

He nodded. There was a soft, wet sound as one of the bodies peeled off the wall and toppled to the ground. It was Eamon, though there wasn't much left of his face after what her power had done to him. Blood began to pool on the floorboards. Theron wandered over to the dead man.

"Was all this really necessary?" he asked, wrinkling his nose.

"Does it matter?" Kaila snapped, allowing the bitterness to creep into her voice. "He was one of *them*."

He didn't approve. She could tell. Too bad. Kaila wasn't about to apologize. Her mercy was all worn out. These people had turned herself and everyone she had ever known into slaves, good only to dig their crystals and grow their food. The world suffered while men like Eamon grew fat off their labour. That one, undeniable truth had carved the last scraps of empathy from Kaila's soul. Only anger remained. It was all she needed.

"You know most nobles have no idea what goes on in places like Elgoss. The Magisterium likes it that way. Easier to control the flow of information."

"They don't know because they don't *want* to know," Kaila said shortly. "Now, are we going to rob this place or wait around for the city watch to arrive?"

Theron sighed. "Don't suppose you got the location of his safe before you went all fire and brimstone on the poor bastards?"

"He was strangely uncooperative on the topic."

Theron grunted. Pulling a crystal from his pocket, he offered it to her. "How about a top-up?"

She raised an eyebrow, surprised to see Theron's agimet was as empty as her own. Usually he was careful with his *atar*, having survived most of his life off scraps of crystal much smaller than the ones they now possessed. Just exactly what *had* he been up to?

The flicker of lanterns appeared in the broken windows. No

time for questions. The force of her magic had scattered debris across half the neighbourhood. It was only a matter of time before they had company in the form of a shiny metal man. And neither of them were in the condition to take on a Warden just now.

Gripping Theron's agimet in one hand and hers in the other, Kaila closed her eyes. Tah'raus had been built over a powerful nexus that would naturally charge the crystals over the next twelve hours. But they didn't have twelve hours.

Fortunately, Kaila had a second ability, one that marked her heritage as not just Elysian, but a Warden as well. The Magisterium's personal soldiers possessed the ability to charge agimet without waiting for the nexus to do it for them—though they'd kept that fact a secret for hundreds of years. A Warden had even invited Kaila to join their order after he'd seen her power. Of course, that same man had killed her father and hunted her for days through the mountains, so she had killed him instead.

Now Kaila stretched her mind into the world. Colours flickered, shifting and changing, becoming the vortex that was the nexus. A few tendrils lingered about the agimet in her hands, but it would take hours yet for them to gather enough force to cross the crystal barrier. Instead, Kaila acted as a catalyst, grasping the tendrils and dragging them into the crystals.

Light flickered against her eyelids and opening her eyes, she offered the now glowing agimet to Theron.

"Anything else you'd like while I'm at it?" she asked in a teasing voice.

"Keep a watch on the street," Theron grunted, ignoring the jest. "I'll find the safe."

A knot tied around Kaila's stomach as Theron stepped around her. She shook herself. This was not the time to get sentimental. Theron was a practiced hand with his *atarsight*. If there were any hidden compartments in the walls, he would find them.

"There," he said, pointing at a painting of the earl on the wall in the room above.

With a flick of his hand, the portrait flew off to the side, revealing an iron door. Metal groaned as his eyes burned brighter, followed by the rending of wood and steel. Kaila leapt backwards as the safe tore from the wall and crashed down at their feet. It struck with enough force to break several boards. The floor groaned ominously beneath them.

"Care to do the honours?" Theron asked. "Maybe this time you can practice a bit of subtly and crack the lock."

She scowled at him before drawing on her freshly charged crystal. The *soullight* of the safe appeared, expanding as she focused, revealing the thousand little lights that made up the greater whole. It was…complicated. She started moving lights, more to see what happened than with any real hope of cracking the lock yet.

"Are you going to tell me where you were?" she asked as she worked.

"It seems we've been offered a job."

"A job? I thought *this* was the job."

"This is a different kind of job. To repay a favour, so to speak."

Kaila paused, recalling something he'd said in the mountains all those weeks ago. "You owe someone money, don't you?"

"I like to think of it as *we* owe someone money. You know, since you're the one that got in my way back in Elgoss."

Snorting, she returned her attention to the safe, but the distraction had made her lose track of the threads. Her patience at an end, she snarled and sucked more *atar* from her crystal. Brute force it would have to be. The locking mechanism screamed and twisted, before with a final *twang*, the door tore off its hinges and hurtled through the hole in the ceiling, disappearing into the night sky.

"Hope that doesn't land on anyone," Theron muttered,

studying the sky before returning his gaze to the safe. "I thought you were trying for subtle."

"I did."

"Your crystal is half empty again."

Kaila rolled her eyes. "So? I can recharge it, remember? I don't need to be efficient like you."

"Until you find yourself in a place without a nexus to charge from," he replied with a sigh. "Very well, grab the gold and let's get out of here. The Wardens won't be far away."

Removing his jacket, he turned it inside out so it formed a bag and offered it to her. Crouching beside the safe, Kaila was pleasantly surprised to find a small hoard of gold and precious gems. No agimet, but given it would be cut for human use anyway, that didn't bother them.

A few minutes later, loaded down with their new riches, the pair of thieves fled through the rear garden of the Stadwit estate. Shouts came from the front of the house, but there was no sign of pursuit as they clambered over the high concrete walls and slipped into the night.

"So, what exactly is this new job?" Kaila asked when they were several blocks away and headed for their current safe house.

"Not sure exactly."

"You don't *know?*" Kaila exclaimed.

"That's the beauty of borrowing money from a mob boss. You don't really get to ask questions."

"That's just *great.*"

Theron rolled his eyes. "It did come with a few perks," he said, tossing her a burlap sack.

She caught it with a frown. Inside, she found almost as much gold as they'd just stolen from Eamon. She raised an eyebrow.

"I thought you were the one who owed money."

"I think gold lost all meaning to Ambrose years ago. These days he trades more in favours."

She pursed her lips. The gold shifted inside the sack,

revealing a card with writing on it. She plucked it from the shifting coins.

"This says we have to meet someone at the Falkenrath manor," she said, eyes widening as she read the last part. *"Tomorrow!"*

"Oh, right, did I not mention that part?" Theron grinned. "Guess we better go and enjoy some of tonight's winnings, hadn't we? Knowing Ambrose, tomorrow is probably just the start."

Whistling a tune to himself, he wandered down the street in the direction of the merchant quarter, while Kaila called after him.

"The start of what, Theron? *The start of what?*"

3

Midday found the pair of them lounging in the back of a carriage, parked up on some side street in the richest part of the capital, where the nobles didn't just live in manors, but veritable mansions set atop the coastal seawall. She and Theron had spent most of the night and half the morning in various marketplaces, spending the coin Ambrose had given him on new clothes and chests and odds and ends, all of which had been loaded into this rented carriage. He'd even visited a barber and changed out of his favourite overcoat into a double-breasted burgundy coat with matching leggings—a combination that was downright garish even to Kaila's limited tastes.

Now though, as the hours ticked by and the sun crept past its zenith, Kaila found herself growing impatient. Theron lay across the front seat where the driver typically sat, feet hanging out the window and a fedora placed over his face to block out the sun. She knew he wasn't sleeping, though he was doing a good job of feigning it.

"What are we waiting for?" she asked at last.

"Ha?" he grumbled, lifting the hat to peek out the window at her. She was meant to be keeping watch on the mouth of the alley. Frowning, he glanced from Kaila to the sky. "Do you think it's two hours past midday yet?"

"The note said one."

"Not what I asked."

Kaila snorted, before relenting and looking to the sun. "Yeah, I'd say it's about two past."

"Good. Let's wait a little longer, just to be sure."

True to his word, he drew the fedora back over his eyes and a few seconds later, began to snore. Grinding her teeth, Kaila marched to the mouth of the alley and looked out. There was already another carriage in the street, parked outside what had to be one of the largest mansions in the city—judging by how it towered over its neighbours. Unlike minor nobles like the Stadwits, these families felt no need to conceal their wealth behind plain stone walls. Massive windows watched the street from the second storey, while marble statues lined the balustrades of the third storey balcony. Flanked by tall marble columns, a broad stairway led down to the road.

The Falkenrath mansion, the note had said. Something about the name tugged at her memory.

Certainly, its grandeur was another hole in the stories she'd been told as a girl. Tah'raus was meant to be a frugal city, its people sacrificing wealth and beauty in solidarity with the rest of Fresia. Sister Eurador had even shown them drawings of the squat, ugly buildings that were meant to line the streets, and of the hard-working men and women with dirt on their faces.

And those places did exist here. Not everyone got to share in the wealth plundered from the Dominances. Crammed between these wealthy neighbourhoods were the slums of the labour class, where men and women toiled twelve hours a day in factories and warehouses, processing the wealth of a kingdom for their noble masters. Those were the images the Sisters spread through the kingdom, so the Dominances would believe all of Fresia carried the burden of their duty together.

Kaila's fingers were just tightening around the crystal in her pocket when the whirring of an agimet-powered machine started up behind her. She turned to find Theron manoeuvring the carriage through the narrow alley. Scowling, she waited until the last second to step aside and let him pass. The thief whistled a merry tune to himself as he directed the contraption into the street.

Shaking her head, Kaila followed as he brought the vehicle to a stop behind the other with a practiced hand. Stepping down from the driver's seat, he made a show of brushing the lint from his coat before adopting a haughty look Kaila had come to know as his impression of a nobleman.

Bang!

Kaila's heart lurched as the double doors of the mansion crashed open on the stairs above, emitting an older man dressed in a finely tailored suit. His face mottled red with anger, he swung back as a second man filled the doorway.

"…never in all my years…" he stormed, shaking his fist, "…your lord will hear of my displeasure…" he trailed off midsentence as he turned and finally noticed the pair standing in the street below.

"Sir, please…" the second man, this one dressed in the plain white uniform of a servant, chased him down the stairs, but also stumbled to a stop when he saw the visitors below.

The nobleman was the first to recover his wits. "Master Falkenrath, I presume?" The words were polite, but his tone carried the threat of a hound snapping at the limits of its chain.

"Theron," Kaila hissed beneath her breath, eyes darting from the men to her companion, "what in the *hell* is going on?"

"No time to explain. You're my personal servant. Quick, get the bags," he muttered through a smile, before throwing out his hands and exclaiming: "*Good sir!* Why, you must be the one and only Ambrose Braider!"

Kaila was left standing dumbly in the street as Theron leapt to intercept the finely dressed nobleman, who had now reached the bottom of the stairs. Ambrose glared at the Elysian thief with eyes as hard as chipped obsidian.

"I am not accustomed to waiting, Master Falkenrath," Ambrose said, his voice now like frost.

"Yes, yes, of course!" Theron gasped. Sometime in the past few seconds, his suit had come eschew. "I am so *dreadfully* sorry. Traffic at the gates, you must understand, but I am here now!" He paused, glancing over his shoulder at Kaila. "What are you waiting for girl? *Get the bags!*"

Kaila startled at his tone before recovering her senses. She climbed onto the roof of the carriage to retrieve the first bundle while the two continued their discussion.

"Master Falkenrath, you did not leave so much as a message with your servant to expect my arrival," Ambrose said harshly. "I have been waiting for well over an hour. I do not care that your father commands the forces of our good kingdom. This is simply unacceptable."

A chill crept down Kaila's spine as she overheard the words. Crouched atop the carriage, she slowly turned to look at the three men below.

Everything clicked into place.

Falkenrath.

As in, *Leonardo Falkenrath.* General Iron Hand. Twenty years ago, her father had served under his banner. Theron couldn't possibly be posing as the man—he was far too young to pass for the seventy-year-old general...

...but his son.

Suddenly, her scalp was tingling. A dozen choice words that would have made her own father blush leapt to her mind, but she bit them back. Theron was impersonating the son of one of the most powerful men in the kingdom.

What the hell was he thinking?

"Ambrose, what are you saying?" Theron exclaimed. "*Of course* I sent word! Surely my family servant has ensured your comfort while you waited?" He swung on the last man.

Frozen on the steps of the house, the servant looked like a deer facing a pair of lions. "Ah, sir…I'm afraid…I didn't…"

"You received the letters warning of my arrival, did you not?" Theron pressed, removing his hat and advancing on the poor servant.

"Sir…"

"Surely no servant of my family would leave the famed Ambrose Braider waiting in discomfort while his master navigated in haste the twisted streets of this cursed city?"

"Sir, we don't…I didn't have ice…I must—"

"*No ice?*" Theron stormed, swinging back to Ambrose. "Sir, truly, I had no idea our household in the capital had fallen into such disarray. Please, if you would come inside—"

"My time is a valuable commodity, Master Falkenrath," Ambrose interrupted. "I took this appointment as a favour to your father. I have other engagements I cannot possibly defer."

"Another date then?" Theron clasped his hands in a beseeching manner.

"I am afraid my next available appointment is not for *at least* another six months."

Theron's hands fell to his side, a look of defeat upon his lips. "I see."

"Yes, quite," Ambrose replied, lifting his nose with a sniff. "You may talk to my secretary if you wish to arrange it. In the meantime, I must be going."

As he stepped around a now forlorn-looking Theron, a man appeared from inside the other carriage, drawing out a set of iron stairs as he did so. Ambrose marched up them and disappeared behind the curtained windows, while the servant drew back the stairs and closed the door. The whirring of gears followed as the driver took his seat up front and directed the machine out into the street.

Theron and the servant stood on the steps, staring after the departing vehicle. Frozen with a bag of clothing clutched to her chest, Kaila was still struggling to work out what *the hell* was going on. Wasn't *Ambrose* the one Theron owed money to?

"What is your name, sir?" Theron said suddenly, his face growing dark.

"Sir, please, you have to believe me, I have served your family loyally—"

"I said what is your name?"

"Scott Turnsbougher, sir," the servant whispered, bowing his head.

"Well, *Mr Turnsbougher*, you will pack your things and leave immediately," Theron snarled, his voice cold. "Your services are no longer necessary."

"Please, Master Falkenrath, I have a family…"

"You should have thought of them before neglecting your duties to *my* family." He turned away, dismissing the man with a wave of his hand.

The servant hung his head. He knew he was defeated. Kaila actually felt sorry for the man as he trudged up the steps to the mansion.

"You going to stand there staring all day?"

Startled, she swung around to find Theron grinning at her.

"What the hell was that all about?" she asked. With no one watching, she tossed the bag she held unceremoniously to the street and clambered down after it.

Theron had the look of a toddler who'd just got his hands on a glass of ale. "Well…" he said, extending a hand towards the mansion. "Why don't you join me for a drink in the home of General Iron Hand, and I'll tell you all about it?"

———

THERON REFUSED TO SAY ANYTHING MORE ABOUT HIS SCHEME until the servant packed his things and left. Only as the door closed on the forlorn looking man did he finally turn to Kaila with a grin.

"About that drink?"

Kaila followed him through the manor, their footsteps echoing softly against the marble floors. Despite her weeks in the capital, Kaila had never seen anything like this place. Each room was more extravagant than the last. Agimet chandeliers adorned the high ceilings, while velvet tapestries covered the walls. They passed through an enormous dining hall, where a long table sat empty, though the glasses and serving plates in the cabinet didn't have so much as a whiff of dust on them.

Her guilt deepened at the sight, but Theron pressed on, guiding them through a library filled with towering shelves, where the aroma of polished wood and old books lingered on her nose. From there, they passed through a room with an entire wall made of glass. Her mind cringed at the sheer extravagance of it, especially as it seemed to exist solely to look out over a large pool of water outside. Neither the pool nor the glass wall served any real purpose from what she could tell, though the labours it must have taken to create and maintain them...

Finally, Theron led her up a spiral staircase to a sitting room, where a large bay window looked out over the waters of the bay. The air was heavy with the scent of sea salt and warm with the afternoon sun. He gestured for her to take a seat while he strode to a dark wooden cabinet in the corner.

Kaila cast her eye over her options, mindful this room alone was larger than the entire flat she had shared with her father. Directly in front of the window was an armchair upholstered in emerald green, while to her left sat a chaise lounger of soft velvet. Nearest to her was a low, plain settee. She slid onto its cushions as Theron emerged from the cabinet with a decanter and a bottle.

"Hmm, I forget if this was a good year," he muttered, studying the label.

"What is it?"

"Ar'imes red," he replied, "I'm sure it must be. Iron Hands wouldn't keep a bad year lying around, surely."

Setting the decanter on the small wooden table between the

sofas, Theron drew his knife and set about removing the wax seal. Kaila watched on, her frustration growing with each passing moment. The rumble of waves as they struck the seawall carried from outside, while somewhere overhead a gull squawked. Freeing the cork at last, Theron began pouring the violet liquid into the decanter.

"*Theron*," she hissed at last, unable to contain herself any longer, "what the *hell* are we doing here?"

A familiar smile on his lips, Theron did not respond immediately. Instead, he removed three long-stemmed glasses from the cabinet and poured the two of them a measure from the decanter. He held one out to Kaila with an expectant look. Grating her teeth, she accepted it, well aware the thief would only answer her questions when he was good and ready.

He then raised his glass for her to chink in the custom of the nobility. Only then did they drink. Kaila had to admit, the wine had a rich flavour, with a note of something sweet…cherry, maybe?

"To the king's good health," Theron said as he drank.

Kaila almost spat out her wine. "*What?*"

Theron tisked. "What's the first thing I taught you about a con?" he said. "Live the part. We're nobility now. We have to act like it, even when no one's around."

Rolling her eyes, Kaila muttered something about the king under her breath that at least related to his health, before taking another sip. It really was quite good.

"So what was all that about?" she asked, eying Theron as he sprawled sideways in the armchair. "*Really* about," she added pointedly when he opened his mouth in what she was sure would be another tall tale.

Closing his mouth, Theron regarded her a moment. "Diversion."

"Come again?"

"The secret to every good magician, my dear," he explained. "Think about it—put yourself in the place of that servant. If we had simply shown up on your doorstep one day, claiming to be the son of your liege lord, what would *you* do?"

Kaila pursed her lips. "I guess I'd be a little suspicious."

"Exactly. At the very least, you'd ask questions. Maybe send a few letters. Ambrose can buy a lot of lips, but if even a whisper of what we're doing here reaches the general, its game over." He shrugged. "So I gave our good friend Scott Turnsbougher something else to worry about—like a very angry, *very powerful* man pacing his parlour for two hours. Poor sap, his nerves were probably shot long before we showed up and made him look a fool."

"So…instead of asking *who the hell are you*," Kaila surmised, "he was too busy trying to figure out how *he* could have messed up so badly in the first place."

"Exactly!" Theron said, grinning over the rim of his glass. "He didn't even think to consider the whole thing might be a setup."

"So Ambrose was in on the whole thing?"

The loud *bang* of a door somewhere downstairs interrupted their conversation. They exchanged a glance as further *thumping* noises continued through the house, before Theron managed to respond.

"Ah, not exactly."

"*Theron! Where are you hiding?*"

"Ambrose!" Theron cried as the nobleman from earlier appeared in the doorway to the sitting room, his face beet-red with anger. "So glad you could make it! Look, I even poured a glass of your favourite—the Ar'imes red, right?"

"You bastard son of the Trickster," Ambrose snarled, advancing on the Mover, "do you know how long I've been planning this…" he trailed off, eyes narrowing on the bottle on the table. "Is that a 72?"

"Ha?" Theron glanced at the bottle. "Oh, yeah, I couldn't remember if that was a good year, but I figured the old man wouldn't keep the rotten stuff around."

Ambrose swallowed visibly. "That…that bottle alone is worth more than your entire debt to me."

Kaila perked up. "How much is that exactly?"

The nobleman ignored her as Theron frowned. "Including the interest?"

Ambrose nodded.

"Trickster's balls," Theron muttered. With a theatrical sigh, he poured the third glass and offered it to Ambrose. "Well, waste not want not, I guess?"

There was still a slight twist to Ambrose's lips, as though he was struggling to maintain his anger in the face of Theron's unyielding cheer, but after a prolonged pause he accepted the glass and sank onto the last sofa with a groan.

"Trickster's balls indeed," Ambrose muttered with a shake of his head. Sipping the wine, he exhaled, seeming to take a moment to savour the experience—before returning his gaze to Theron.

"Well, care to explain what that was all about?"

Kaila snorted. The wine had already gone to her head and she was unable to contain her laughter. "Diversion."

The older man's eyes snapped to her, his brow creasing into a scowl. "Did I say you could speak, *girl*."

Kaila bristled at his tone. "Excuse—"

Ambrose snapped his fingers.

It was like someone had turned off the world. Theron and the tailor and the manor, all of it vanished, leaving only a world of white. Even the sound of the waves against the seawall quieted. She tried to scream, only to realise she had no mouth, no body at all. It was as though someone had torn her consciousness from her body and hurled it into the void.

Could an Elysian *do* that?

Panic was just beginning to take hold when the world came rushing back. The scream tore belatedly from her throat as Kaila found herself back in the folds of the sofa. Gasping, she pushed herself up and fumbled for the agimet in her pocket. Theron stood over her, one hand extended, eyes burning with the glow of *atar*. Beyond him, Ambrose had half-risen from his chair.

"That's enough," Theron growled.

"I have already stopped," the tailor replied with a smirk.

Theron's eyes darted to Kaila and lingered on her. She swallowed at the intensity she saw there, her mouth suddenly parched.

"Do what you want with me, Ambrose," he said at last, lowering his hand. "But touch her again and I'll tear you limb from limb."

The tailor smiled at his words, but as he held Theron's gaze, it slowly slipped from his lips. "Very well, Theron," he said softly, "but if she's to be a part of this job, I expect you *both* to follow my orders and bide by my rules. Can you do that?"

The Mover grimaced, his eyes flicking to Kaila. "What do you think, Kaila?"

"Don't have much choice, do we?'

Theron snorted. "There you have it, Ambrose. Good enough for you?"

The tailor just scowled and took another sip of his wine. "Very well," he said, his eyes shifting around the room. "What happened to the servant?"

"He left."

"At least your antics were good for something," Ambrose muttered. "Maybe this entire thing won't immediately go tits up like last time."

"I resent the suggestion the Ripley job was my fault."

"You dropped our mark off a five-storey rooftop!"

"It was self-defence!"

Kaila looked from one man to the other as they bickered, a frown growing on her forehead. They were squabbling like a pair of children while they sat in the manor of the most powerful general in Fresia, drinking his wine, putting their feet on the furniture…

"*Excuse me!*" the words burst from her in a rush, her patience

—always thin—worn past breaking point. "But would someone like to explain what this 'job' is actually about—sometime this century, preferably?"

The pair fell silent, turning as one to stare at her. Ambrose still wore that slightly irked expression on his lips, as though he found it distasteful just to sit in her presence. He hadn't even asked Kaila for her name or what she could do. She was clearly secondary to whatever he was planning with Theron, an inconvenience he would suffer, so long as it kept the Mover on side.

Conversely, Theron looked like a fox that had gotten into the hen house. His eyes glittered as he turned to the other man. "Yes, Ambrose, what *is* this job you've been planning? It must be important, if you're willing to involve *yourself.*"

"It is," Ambrose said, rising from the sofa. Taking the decanter, he refilled his glass before wandering to the window. He stared out across the bay for a minute, swirling the scarlet liquid in his glass before downing it in one gulp. "In fact, this will be the most important job any Elysian has undertaken since the Great Betrayal."

Now it was Theron's turn to chuckle. "That's a little dramatic, don't you think? Come on, Ambrose, just tell us, what's the score?"

Turning from the window, Ambrose caught them both in the darkness of his eyes. "The king is dying."

Silence.

"*What?*" Kaila and Theron exclaimed together.

Ambrose clasped his hands behind his back. "His heart, apparently," he said softly. "The physicians say it will give in before the year is done. So far, he has managed to keep this knowledge from the public, but it will not be long now before it filters out."

Blood pulsed in Kaila's skull as the words sank in. She had to make a conscious effort just to exhale. Her hands shook, threatening to spill the precious wine on the lush woollen rug. The glass rattled as she placed it on the table and then used both hands to grasp the sofa beneath her, as though by doing so she could keep the entire world from spinning.

The king was dying?

It wasn't so much the news as what in the *hell* did this job have to do with the King of Fresia?

"You can't actually be thinking…" Theron started.

"When he dies, Matron Eliana Frye will be forced to step aside," Ambrose spoke over the top of the thief. "Neither heir has a partner. Whichever is the first to correct that oversight is likely to inherit the throne."

Silence. Kaila looked from the tailor to Theron, trying to understand what she was missing.

"So you are then," Theron muttered with a shake of his head. His voice remained calm, as though they were speaking about the weather, not pulling a con over the most powerful figures in the Magisterium.

"The son doesn't want any part in the throne," Ambrose continued as though he hadn't heard Theron.

Theron raised his eyebrows at that. "What kind of madman would refuse a crown?"

"I've heard a few rumours about the boy. He left the Magisterium a few years ago, after he came of age."

"Brave," Theron muttered, tapping a finger to his chin, "though I suppose when you're a prince, you can afford a bit of foolishness."

"*Sorry,*" Kaila interjected, her voice rising several notes above her usual soprano, "but how does *any of this* have *anything* to do with us?"

Theron and Ambrose exchanged a glance.

"Would you like to tell her, or should I?" Ambrose asked pointedly.

Theron sighed. "It's an old plan we came up with years ago." He turned to Ambrose. "Though without any intention of ever enacting it, of course."

"Only because we didn't think the opportunity would come around so quickly."

Pursing his lips, Theron looked thoughtful. "We'll still need a Psionic, even with my charm doing the heavy lifting."

Ambrose snorted. "Who did you have in mind?"

"Quintin."

"He's retired," Ambrose said.

Theron chuckled. "Let me deal with his so-called retirement," he paused. "I might have to make some promises."

"Like what?" Ambrose's voice dripped with suspicion.

"Weavings."

The tailor's face hardened. "My work does not come cheap, Theron."

"Don't I know it," Theron replied. "But we need him. He's the only one who could pull off a job this delicate."

"*Pull off what?*" Kaila growled.

Theron chuckled. "The last time the Magisterium changed leadership, it was a bloodbath," Theron replied. "Several powerful nobles and even a fair few Daughters ended up dead— a few at the hands of our old friend the Reaper, actually. Most think the pair who eventually became our king and Matron had a hand in the deaths, but no one could ever prove it." He leaned forward in his recliner. "But that's not the important part. The important thing is that for months, no one held the Aegis."

Kaila blinked. "The Aegis?"

"Yes, the Aegis," Theron said sarcastically. "You know, the artefact humanity stole from our people centuries ago?"

"I'm familiar with it," Kaila snapped. "But what does the Aegis have to do with anything?"

The Aegis was a magical device stolen by the First Matron T'iana when she'd led the first human uprising. Its power was wielded jointly by the king and his Matron, just as they divided the rule of Fresia between them. The Matron oversaw matters of religion—the Magisterium along with its Sisters and Daughters, while the king dictated the laws of the land and commanded his Wardens and generals.

"Because we're going to steal it, girl," Ambrose growled.

"*What?*"

"I can see from the stupefied look on your face that you approve."

Kaila shook her head. "You're mad. Why…"

She couldn't even vocalise the ridiculousness of what they were suggesting. Going after merchants and the occasional minor noble was one thing, but the Magisterium itself? That was true insanity. The power of the king and his Matron were absolute. To cross them was suicidal.

"Why would you take that risk?"

There was a moment of hesitation between the two as they shared a glance.

"The Aegis is the greatest treasure our people have ever known," it was Ambrose that eventually answered.

Narrowing her eyes, Kaila stared at Theron. When he did not meet her gaze, she knew. "There's something more, isn't there?"

"Yes—" Theron began.

"Don't," Ambrose cut him off.

"If she's to be a part of this, Ambrose, she deserves to know."

"Know *what?*" Kaila snarled.

There was another long moment as Theron held Ambrose's gaze, until finally the tailor sighed and waved a hand.

"Thank you," Theron sighed, his eyes turning to Kaila. "How much do you actually know about the Aegis? About what it does?"

Kaila frowned. "Not…not much," she murmured. "Elysian artefacts weren't exactly top of the curriculum in Sister Eurador's classroom."

"I bet," Ambrose grumbled.

"Ignore our grumpy friend," Theron interjected. "The truth

is, no one knows exactly what the Aegis is. All we have are stories."

Kaila blinked. "Stories?"

Theron nodded. "Stories about where our people came from."

Suddenly Kaila's throat was parched. "What do you mean —*came from*."

Theron continued as though he had not heard her. "These stories claim the Aegis was a powerful talisman, capable of folding space—much like a Jumper." Jumpers were a kind of Elysian that could teleport short distances. "But without any limitations. It could transport its wielder between kingdoms, continents, even different worlds."

Kaila swallowed. "You're saying…you believe we're not from this world?"

"It explains why T'iana's betrayal," Ambrose added his thoughts, "and her *theft*, brought about the fall of our civilisation."

"Without the Aegis, we were separated from our home world," Theron continued. "Trapped and outnumbered by humanity, our defeat was only a matter of time." He paused. "Or so the story goes."

There was a pounding like drums in Kaila's ears as she looked from one man to the other. Any moment she expected them to burst into laughter, but neither cracked, and at last she shook her head.

"So all this," she rasped, "you're planning to risk *everything* based on an old story that might not—*probably isn't*—even true?"

Drinking deeply from his glass, Theron set it on the table and shrugged. "If it's not, then we'll still have stolen the Magisterium's most important talisman right out from under their noses. I'd say that's a pretty decent second prize, wouldn't you?"

"But *how?*" Kaila gasped. "It doesn't matter if the Aegis would make us *gods*—a hundred Wardens guard the Sanctum.

We barely managed to defeat one in Iselador. Just how exactly were you planning to steal it?"

"Weren't you listening, girl?" Ambrose growled. "The king is dying. He needs a heir—one supported by both the Magisterium and the nobility—or he risks his legacy going up in flames. Whoever replaces him will *inherit* the power of the Aegis."

"Which brings us to the truly beautiful part of the plan," Theron chipped in. "The part so outrageous, not even the most cunning of the Sisters will suspect it." He grinned. "We're going to put an Elysian imposter on the Fresian throne."

Theron was right—it was so outrageous all Kaila could do was sit and gape at them.

"The son does not want the throne," Ambrose continued through her shock, "but his sister, Jenna Frye would like nothing more than to wear her mother's crown."

Kaila stared at the tailor, then at Theron. Theron, who had spent most of the morning decorating himself as a noble, cutting and combing his hair, trimming his beard, buying new clothes, all so he could impersonate the son of a powerful general...

"You're saying..."

"The king and his Matron rule together," Theron said quietly, his eyes on Ambrose. "So what's our timeframe?"

"The physicians gave the king three months," the older man replied. "If we haven't secured the succession by the Summer Gala, we risk the contest being thrown wide open."

"Three months," Theron grunted, "not much time."

"You've always had a way with woman—I trust you'll manage."

Theron shrugged, before turning to Kaila, as though expecting her input. She was still gawking at the pair, not quite sure whether to laugh at the joke or *scream* at the terror of it all.

"You can't be serious?"

Shaking his head, Ambrose turned to Theron. "I thought you said she was bright."

His tone roused Kaila's anger. "It'll never work!" she

snapped. "You can't possibly think you'll fool the entire Magisterium with what, a few fancy suits?"

"I do it every day, girl," Ambrose growled.

"And when word reaches the general about his son suddenly living it up in the capital?"

"For that, old Iron Hands would actually have to leave the frontlines," it was Theron who answered, his voice strangely bitter.

Kaila wasn't having any of it. "What about the son then?" she demanded. "What happens when he decides to visit the capital, only to find some doppelganger already here in his place?"

Silence answered her words. The pair exchanged another of those meaningful looks. Kaila was surprised they couldn't hear her teeth grinding.

"What now?" she snapped. "What is it you're not saying *this time*?"

"The son already knows," Theron said softly.

Kaila's heart just about stopped in her chest. "What?"

"He already knows, Kaila," Theron murmured. "In fact, he's right here helping us." He paused, staring at her as though waiting for a response, but Kaila could only muster a look of utter confusion. Letting out a sigh, he shook his head. "You remember the story I told you? About my sister?"

She nodded silently, blood thundering in her ears.

"It was General Iron Hands who killed her," he said quietly. "Our father."

———

KAILA SAT ON THE EDGE OF THE STRANGE POOL, LISTENING TO the distant rumbling of the city streets. The night was dark—one of those rare times when both moons hid behind the curve of the world, but the glow of agimet beneath the water set the patio alight.

Ripples raced across the surface as she touched her toes to the water. She wondered at the luxury of it. A pool. Not for bathing or raising fish, but the sheer luxury of it. To dip your feet on a warm summer night. Meanwhile, men like her father shivered in the snowy mountains with barely a piece of coal for warmth.

Normally, the thought would have driven her into a mindless rage. But not tonight. Tonight, her mind was already full.

Because we're going to steal it, girl.

They were mad. That was the only explanation. They were going to throw their lives away, and for what? Some vague hope of another world, a paradise where their kind lived their lives free of the Magisterium? Her fingers tightened on the granite lip of the pool. For just one second, Kaila allowed herself to imagine what that would be like. To be free of her torment and the fear.

For just a second, she felt something inside, a warmth almost like hope…

…and then she remembered all that stood between them, the Magisterium and its Wardens, the dark walls of the dome that loomed over the city. Pain, deep and aching, filled her chest and she doubled over, a sob escaping her lips.

She couldn't live for hope. Hope would kill her in this world, fool her into believing things could be better and then stab her through the gut and leave her to die alone in the dark.

I want them to hurt.

The plan was madness, but it would give her something else she had wanted since the day Theron had led her through the gates of the capital and she had seen the truth—the chance to fight back.

We're going to put an Elysian imposter on the Fresian throne.

That act alone, it would be worth more than any stolen arte-fact, more than all the gold and agimet in the vaults of the Sanctum. It would put a chink in the Magisterium's aura of invincibility, show others that they were fallible.

Soft footsteps approached, and she looked around to see Theron standing in the *atarlight.* "You were quiet in there."

"I didn't think Ambrose wanted my opinion."

She had instinctively disliked the tailor. He was too much like *them.* Polished, arrogant. He had looked down on Kaila from the moment he'd laid eyes on her, like she wasn't worthy of his attention. And she still wasn't sure what *he* got out of all this. From what Theron had told her, he was already powerful in his own right, the tendrils of his empire stretching through not only the Elysian underground, but much of the noble houses as well. Why would a man like that be willing to risk everything on such a gamble?

The thief snorted. "Since when did you let something like that stop you?"

Kaila found she could not meet the thief's eyes.

It was General Iron Hands who killed her. Our father.

Her gaze was drawn out across the bay, where the lights of a single fishing ship fought against the currents. Despite the calm air, the waters were violent this night, churning as white-capped waves rumbled in from the distant ocean.

"Why didn't you tell me?" she said at last. "About your father?"

Theron let out a sigh. He removed his shoes before sitting on the ledge next to her and dipping his toes into the pool. His eyes followed her gaze and they watched the ship struggle for a time in silence.

"Maybe I didn't want to see that look in your eyes," he said at last.

"What look?"

"The look that says how *sorry* you are for me."

"Theron…"

"*Don't,*" he interrupted. The smile he flashed her took the bite out of his tone. "It's okay. It's just, my father isn't something I talk about, *ever.*"

Kaila swallowed. She could understand how he felt. Her father's death was still a gaping wound in her soul. She couldn't imagine the hurt of seeing him turn against her. The last thing she would want was to be reminded of it. But even so…

"Okay, Theron," she said, "but now we're sitting here in his palace. You can't just pretend that's normal. I need to know the rest of the story. You get that, right?"

"I know," he sighed, but his eyes remained distant. "It's just… where to start?"

"How about with your sister?"

"Freya," Theron breathed, a smile touching his lips. "She was always adventurous. She couldn't wait to get out and see the world one day." His smile faltered. "After her Trials."

"The agimet…"

"She didn't know," he rasped. "No one did. Not even our father suspected until she picked up that stone."

Kaila swallowed the lump that struggled to choke her. "What…what happened next?"

"She didn't even try to run." Theron's eyes never left the water at their feet. "She just stood there looking at our father as though expecting him…" His voice cracked. "It wasn't until the Warden grabbed her that I think she realised he wasn't going to help her."

"And then?"

"They hanged her," he croaked. "Our mother too—after my father accused her of adultery."

Kaila shivered. It was a common story. When a child was discovered to be Elysian, their parents were retested with agimet as well, and if neither was revealed to possess the Gift, the blame was laid upon the mother.

At least Kaila had been spared that horror. She had never known her mother—her father had told her she'd died fighting on the frontlines. But that had been a lie. The woman might even still be alive, though her father did not know who she was—only that she had saved him from a group of enemy soldiers and then nursed him back to health. Months later, she had reappeared long enough to pass him a newborn child.

Kaila yearned to know more about the mysterious woman. There were too many things about her own Gift that still didn't make sense—like how she possessed the powers of an Elysian *and* the Wardens, or why she had not been able to use the crystal in her Trial of Agimet. But those answers would have to wait for another day.

"And…what about you?" she said instead to Theron.

"I was watching," he whispered. "Hiding where I shouldn't have been. I'll never forget the look on her face when they put the noose around her neck." He shook his head. "There was still *atar* in her eyes when she saw me. I don't know how she knew to use her Gift, but somehow…" he trailed off, his jaw clenched.

"What did she do?"

A smile touched his lips. "Freya was a Muse," he said. "She used her Gift to speak to me in my mind. She told me to run." His jaw hardened. "So I did."

Kaila shivered as she imagined the scene; the young Theron hidden away, watching as his father murdered his sister, the silver eyed girl telling him to run.

"And your father?"

He shrugged. "He sent soldiers out to find me. My Gift wouldn't develop until years later, but Bermish was a large city, even back then. I hid until the hunt died down, and eventually smuggled myself aboard some wagons heading for the capital."

"And you?" she asked, still confused by that part, why Theron could pretend to be himself.

Theron smiled. "I became my father's dirty little secret," he laughed, the sound harsh in the darkness. "He could pretend my sister wasn't his, but all I ever heard growing up was how much I looked like my father. So after I disappeared, he spread a story about a sickness that had befallen me. Later, I became a recluse, never leaving the walls of his citadel in Bermish." Shaking his head, Theron rose with a groan and stretched his arms towards the sky. "Until today, that is."

Kaila rose slowly to join him. She still had one question—she just wasn't sure whether she should ask it. Theron must have seen the look on her face though, as he arched an eyebrow.

"Go on, spit it out," he said, the familiar grin returning to his face.

"Why choose the Falkenraths?" she asked. "Ambrose could make himself out to be anyone, right? Any of the noble families. So why you?"

Theron smiled. "That's easy—because he *can't* pretend to be anyone. At least, not if he's going anywhere near the Sanctum and the Wardens inside."

Kaila frowned. "Their armour protects them from illusions as well?"

"Kind of," Theron replied. "You remember what it felt like, when he used a weaving on you?

Shuddering, Kaila nodded as she recalled the feeling of nothingness. "It definitely didn't *feel* like an illusion."

"Because as far as your body was concerned, it wasn't," Theron replied. "I've seen men claw out their own eyes trying to escape his *illusions.*"

"And this is the man you decided to borrow money from?" Kaila asked, even as she made a mental note to never cross the tailor.

"Not my point," Theron muttered. "My point is his Gift works by convincing *you* that what you're seeing—and every other sense—is real. We've found it can still work on Wardens, but only for a short time. It's like their armour's protection forces the weaving to work extra hard to convince them its real."

Kaila's eyes widened in understanding. "So it uses up too much *atar?*"

"Exactly. A crystal that should have lasted hours can be used up in a matter of minutes around a Warden."

Kaila pursed her lips. It made sense. The Gift worked strangely around Wardens. When she'd tried to move the Warden in Elgoss, the power had recoiled back on her instead, hurling her out a sixth story window. She wondered in what other strange ways the other Gifts might interact with the black armour.

"Any other questions?" Theron said when she hadn't spoken for several long seconds.

Finding his eyes on her, Kaila looked away. She drew in a breath, considering everything he had told her. About his father, and the Aegis, and the plan. It was a lot, all of it. A terrible risk for all of them, but if it worked, if they succeeded...

"Okay," she said at last, "crazy as all this is...I'm in." She hesitated. "Only...*is* there a part for me in all this? Or am I just meant to play your house servant for the next few months. Serve your drinks, clean the latrines?" She wrinkled her nose. "I know I'm new at all this, but please, I want to help."

He grimaced when she looked at him again. "Are you sure you want this, Kaila? If things go badly—and that's likely—the Magisterium isn't going to let this pass. If they discover what we're doing, they'll come after us with everything they have. Nowhere in Fresia will be safe."

"I don't care," Kaila murmured. "All I've wanted since the day we got to Tah'raus was to fight back. So if you're going to spit in the face of the Magisterium, I want to be a part of it. For dad. For Caellum, and everyone else they've hurt."

Theron looked like he would say something more, but he seemed to reconsider, looking out over the bay again instead. The fishing ship had almost reached the port. No doubt its crew would be relieved to spend a night in a safe birth. If only such a thing existed for people like them.

"There is one thing," Theron said softly.

Her heart lifted. "What?"

"The son."

The budding hope stuttered in her chest. "But Ambrose said—"

"I know what he said."

"You think he's wrong?"

"I think there's a lot at stake," Theron replied, "and I'm not going to gamble our future on a nobleman turning down the throne when the time comes."

"So what do you want *me* to do?"

"Study him like you did with Eamon. Find out everything there is to know about this prince, so if he decides to make a play for the crown, we'll be ready. Think you can handle that?"

Kaila nodded. It wasn't much, but at least it was *something*. And Theron was right. The prince was too much of a loose end to leave to the Trickster's games.

"Good," Theron said with a smile. "Now come on, we'd better get you settled in the servants quarters—that latrine isn't going to clean itself..." He trailed off as Kaila drew *atar* from her crystal and fixed him with the glare that had torn the roof from the Stadwit manor. "I mean, I'm sure we can find you a guest room somewhere."

4

Quintin woke to the soft *tick-ticking* of the clocktower, just as he did every morning. Eyes still closed, he lay there a while, imagining the great contraption somewhere above his head, its slender hands counting through the minutes of the day. Its face was limestone, the pale stone reflecting the glow of *agimet* within to illuminate the hour for late night drunks and early labourers alike. The silver casing had lost its sheen long ago, tarnished to a sickly green in the salt laden air, but the inner mechanisms were sealed with quartz, protecting the *atar*-powered machinery that kept the brass hands moving.

Tick, tock.

In his mind's eye, Quintin imagined the hands growing closer to the hour, the pulleys shifting, the hammer rising above the bell, preparing to announce the start of another day…

Tick, tock, CLANG!

Letting out a groan, Quintin rose and crossed the loft to his window. From his vantage point in the tower, he watched the fog seep across the bay. The dense cloud muffled the sounds of waking, the crying of children and soothing coos of mothers, the grumble of men and the rattle of steel wheels on concrete streets.

CLANG!

Slowly, the sun peeked its fiery head above the slate rooftops and the mists burned away. The stillness remained though, and with it the putrid rot of dead fish and other less sanitary wastes. It seemed this would be one of those rare days where the winds did not reach the capital. Unfortunate for anyone with a nose.

CLANG!

Quintin listened as the night's quiet slowly came to an end. Not just with the chiming of the clock or the rumble of carriages, but the buzzing in his mind. They weren't voices like the Sisters taught humanity about his kind. Psionics didn't read minds, but instead the little vibrations given off by a person's *soullight*.

CLANG!

Though when he cast the threads of his power over the city, there were patterns. At this time of morning, a note of fatigue hung about Tah'raus as its denizens woke to the ringing of the great clock. It was a low tone, not sorrowful, but haunting. It rolled across the city like the unbroken waves in the harbour.

CLANG!

As the sun struck higher in the sky, other pulses joined the gentle awakening. Here, the rapid, uneven shriek of passion, there the furious crackling of a parent disciplining an unruly child; the swirl of sorrow was quick to follow as tears began. He could not have picked the exact moment of its change, but suddenly fatigue had given way to the chaotic buzz of a city in flux.

CLANG!

On the sixth chime, the bell fell silent. Quintin sensed other minds coming awake below. His girls. He spent a minute considering what he sensed from each. Max had had a nightmare she was still trying to shake. Her mind was confused, her tune rising and falling without rhyme or reason. So very like Max.

Beside her, Jasmine was her sister's opposite in every way, serene, like peace personified, calming as she reached out to sooth her younger sibling.

Quintin smiled, satisfied he could leave the pair to their morning routine. They knew what tasks they must complete before setting off for their morning lessons. It still made Quintin nervous, sending them to be tutored by a Sister. What if they said something wrong? Let on about who and what they really were? And yet, it was a necessary camouflage. People took note of children wandering the city during the hours of class. Elysian trying to live in plain sight couldn't afford that kind of attention. Besides, they were *kids*. They needed to spend time with others their age—even if it was under the malevolent watch of a Sister.

Though with Jasmine due to sit the Trials this year, that would soon have to change.

Soon, but not just yet. For now, he could give them this little slice of normality, to live among other humans, in a community, before his inheritance forced them to uproot their lives and flee. After their mother…he owed them that much.

Just as he owed the good people of Tah'raus his Gift— whether they realised it or not.

He was different from other Elysian in that way. Quintin didn't subscribe to the Magisterium's way of seeing the world— divided down strict lines. Human and Elysian. Nor had he succumbed to hatred like so many others of his kind; those who saw persecution by an all-powerful system and decided all who benefited from that system were their enemy. As if the everyday citizens of Tah'raus had any more say in how the Magisterium ran the kingdom than the Gifted they strung from the gallows.

Yes, it would be easy to see the hatred on the faces of his Fresian neighbours and think they deserved retribution. Unless you were Psionic and could sense the emotion behind the mob— what it was that drove them to cheer the violence.

It wasn't hatred. It wasn't even anger.

It was fear.

Fear of the unknown. Of what the Gifted could do to them. Even of the Magisterium, who punished those who spoke out against their teachings with the same brutality they used against the Elysian.

And once you knew they were afraid, well, it is hard to hate a man for that.

And so Quintin had resolved to use what power he had to put a little more joy into the world. To make the lives of his neighbours a little easier. So maybe, just maybe, they could be a little less afraid. That was his mission this morning, like every other morning.

But where to start?

Leaving the clocktower, he entered the streets of Tah'raus. He went on foot, disliking the feel of the agimet powered carriages. The lanterns and various other devices worn by the Fresians were bad enough without blinding his *atarsight* with the harsh glow of a carriage. At least the sheer quantity of cut crystals in the city these days meant his own tiny gemstone went unnoticed. He wore tinted glasses, designed to camouflage the use of his powers. They didn't work for larger workings, unfortunately, but they served for his purpose that morning.

He found his first good deed in Fountain Square, where a dozen crystals lit the dancing waters of the T'iana Fountain. A statue of the First Matron stood on a plinth in the centre, surrounded by battling images of Wardens and their Elysian enemy. The depiction of T'iana of course omitted any suggestion she herself may have been Elysian. That was a secret the Magisterium had been sure to burn from their records centuries ago.

The pair who drew Quintin's attention were arguing beside the fountain. Merchants most likely, judging by their clothing and the heavy purse the man wore on his belt. The woman was unleashing her fury upon the man, whose face was growing redder by the minute. A quick listen of their inner emotions, however, revealed a higher pitch concealed beneath the angry discordance.

Pain. Doubt. *Fear.*

Quintin could have tisked. Silly humans. Fear, again? So often it was the source of their misfortune, causing strife where simple communication could have resolved their problems. Unfortunately, it was easier to say nothing than what they really needed.

Except the truth had a habit of coming out regardless, and the more you tried to contain it, the more likely it was to come bursting forth in a rush of anger. Then they wouldn't say what they *really* wanted…

…unless someone gave them a nudge.

Stretching out his power, Quintin grasped the low tones of the man's grief, the isolation and sense of impending doom. Like most men, he had sensed the gulf growing between himself and his partner, but feared to speak up, in case he made it worse. Which counterintuitively, *had* in fact made the situation worse. It was past time he spoke his piece.

It was almost painful, watching him try and contain the emotion, the way his face twitched and shook, before the mask cracked. A cry rasped its way up from the pit of his throat as the tears burst forth, the words he'd been holding in so long spilling out.

"I'm sorry, Margary, I love you! But these last few months, it felt like I was losing you, so I guess I pulled away, even though I didn't want to, even though I don't want to lose you, I pulled away because I was afraid and I love you, please, do you think… do you think we can fix this…"

He trailed off as Quintin allowed his influence to fade. The magic didn't last after he withdrew, but the words remained. The man gaped at his wife, as though unable to believe he'd spoken.

The woman, too, looked shocked. Eyes wide, her face drained of colour, she stood for several heartbeats. Quintin gave her a little push, diminishing her anger and warming the melodies of her heart that had grown cold through the months of pain. A tear streaked her cheek.

"Oh, Tomas," she breathed, throwing her arms around his

neck, "of course I want to try! I just…I've missed you! You work so hard in that factory, I never see you, and after we lost…after I couldn't…"

They were both crying now, whispering to each other while the crowd took a wide birth around them. Quintin allowed himself a smile. Who knew if the pair would work things out, or if absent his magic they would revert to harsh silences and harsher words. But he had given them a chance.

Stepping through the crowd, he brushed past the embracing couple, fingers darting out to detach the man's purse. Payment for his services—nothing was free in life, after all. Whistling to himself, he went on his way, already searching for his next good deed.

Instead, his Gift brushed against a familiar mind among the crowd. It was easy to pick out, for unlike the chorus of emotion that were most minds, this individual hummed with a single sensation. *Excitement.* It was not a natural state, but rather the mind of someone who had trained to resist a Psionic's intrusion.

Theron.

When he turned, Quintin wasn't surprised to find the man standing behind him—though he was surprised to find him in company.

"Theron," he said, "well met."

They clasped hands, the man grinning with a gladness Quintin could tell was genuine, even through the shield behind which Theron hid his true emotions. Then he turned to the woman at his friend's side. She was young, not yet past her second decade, with long black hair and emerald eyes that studied him with unmasked suspicion. Unlike Theron, her emotions were an open book. There was no fear in this one— despite her calm exterior, her *soullight* shrieked with a harsh rage.

"And well met to you as well, young miss," he said, meeting her gaze without flinching. "The name is Quintin Orpheus."

"Kaila Dwyn," she replied somewhat hesitantly.

Quintin inclined his head. "And how did you come to be in the company of this scoundrel, Kaila Dwyn?"

The young woman blinked, her eyes flickering to Theron and then back to him.

"Hey now…" Theron spluttered.

"Oh you know," Kaila interrupted, apparently catching on as a smile tugged at her lips, "he came barging into my hometown with some grand plan to rob the Magisterium. Then everything fell to bits and I had to bail him out."

"Excuse me—"

"Sounds like Theron," Quintin said with a laugh. "Come on, let's see if we can find someplace more private to talk."

Theron and the young woman nodded and they moved off, emerging eventually onto a broad avenue which circled the park at the centre of the merchant quarter. They had to wait for a break in the traffic to cross—the new agimet powered carriages were densest in this part of the city, especially in the early hours. Once amidst the spruce and pine trees, however, the rumble of wheels and clang of tools faded into the background. They found a bench and sat, and Theron gave Kaila a look.

"Mind if we have a moment?"

She raised an eyebrow, but shrugged and rose again. Quintin watched her wander away across the grass, curious.

"I like this one," he said at last, turning his gaze to Theron.

The man's *soullight* still hummed with the same excitement as earlier. It was somewhat galling for a Psionic like Quintin to be unable to read the man. Though in this case, he couldn't complain. Quintin had been the one to teach Theron the skill, after all.

"It's not like that," Theron replied.

"No?" Did he detect a hint for red in Theron's cheeks?

"Not anymore," the Mover grunted.

Quintin chuckled. "Ah, so it's like *that*." His lips twitched. "A wise young woman, in that case."

Theron scowled. "Not what I came to talk about," he said. "I have a job."

"Ah, well, in that case, you know I'm retired."

Theron snorted. "I think the couple back in Fountain Square would disagree."

"I misspoke. I don't do *your* kind of job any longer."

"And what kind of job would that be, old friend?"

Quintin lifted an eyebrow. "The kind that draw unwanted attention and leave chaos in their wake."

"Ah," Theron murmured.

"Ah indeed."

"Well, I tried," Theron said, rising with a groan.

"That's it?" Quintin looked up in surprise. "No pleading or promises of treasure to convince me to join you?"

The damned thief actually had the nerve to shrug. "Ambrose will be disappointed."

"Ambrose is involved?"

"You said you didn't want to be involved."

"I don't," Quintin snapped. "But I have to think about the girls, now that Claire…"

He trailed off. The words hung between them, the pain left unspoken. They were both Elysian. Gifted, they called themselves. How could they not? Otherwise, they would have to call it a curse. They all had stories like his own. Husbands and wives, brothers and sisters, children and parents; sooner or later, you lost someone to the Wardens.

Or they got you.

Quintin tapped his fingers lightly against the bench. His gaze drifted from Theron to where Kaila stood in the distance, arms cross, brow furrowed as she glared at passersby. Even without *atar,* he could almost hear the rage roiling within her.

"The girl," he said softly, "who is she really?"

"A Mover, like me," Theron said, following Quintin's gaze. He paused before continuing, "She grew up in Elgoss. An agimet mining town."

Quintin's head whipped around. "You mean you really found it?"

"Yeah. Unfortunately, it didn't go exactly as planned."

"Does it ever?" Quintin muttered. He considered pressing the matter further, but there were other matters to discuss.

"You owe Ambrose money, don't you?" he asked instead. "That's why you're doing a job for him."

"*With* him."

"Sure. So what's he got you doing—some nobleman's vault, or another caravan job?"

"No," Theron murmured, his eyes still on Kaila. "We're going after the Magisterium."

"Please tell me you're joking…"

"The king is dying."

The words were like a Binder's explosion going off. Suddenly his ears were ringing, drowning out all other sound. Theron loomed over him, his face grim, gaze distant.

"Then the Aegis…"

"Ambrose wants to make a play for it, yeah."

His heart pulsated. Theron wasn't talking about just any job. He was talking about *the* job. The heist every Elysian for a thousand years had dreamed of pulling off. "You'll be walking right into the lion's den, Theron."

"I know," the Mover grimaced. "Why do you think I want the best Psionic in the city at my side?"

A shiver shot down his spine. He'd told Theron no—and for good reason. He couldn't risk something happening to him, not for pointless things like gold or gems or power.

But this job wasn't about that. This was about humanity and the Elysian, the agony of their shared history, and whether that would also be their future—or if there was another path, a way for them to escape the Magisterium's persecution.

"I get why you'd want no part in this," Theron said quietly, "you have to protect your girls." He hesitated. "That's why I had

Ambrose agree to perform two weavings—one for each of their Trials."

Goosebumps crept across Quintin's scalp. What Theron was suggesting was risky. An inferior weaving might not be enough to hide the silver glow in an Elysian's eyes. And often there was a Warden present at Trials, in case an Elysian was discovered. A truly skilled Weaver was needed to convince one of them—and only then for a short time.

But of all the Weavers in the city, Ambrose Braider was the best.

He swallowed, considering what the offer meant. His girls could remain in the city, pass their Trials and grow up to be normal citizens of Fresia. Sure, they would still be beholden to the Magisterium, but that was a great deal more than most Elysian could hope for.

Then there was the matter of the Aegis. Rumours abounded about that ancient talisman, but there was little in the way of verified information. He looked again at Theron. His friend *had* changed. There was a tension in Theron. He wore the same easy smile as always, but there was a frailty to it, like brittle glass that might shatter at any moment.

"Say I'm interested," he said softly, "but first, I want to know why. Putting your faith in myth and legend isn't exactly your kind of job, Theron. So why are *you* doing this?"

The Mover shrugged. "Like you said, I owe Ambrose money."

"No, it's more than that."

Theron wouldn't look at him. Quintin pursed his lips. It wasn't like the Mover to let anyone force him to do anything. So instead of arguing, he rose with a groan.

Surprise registered on Theron's face. "Where are you going?"

"If you won't tell me the truth, I can't work with you." He turned to walk away.

"The girl," Theron's voice was soft as he spoke. "Do you

know what she said to me, back in Iselador, when she first learned the truth about T'iana?"

"What?" Quintin asked, glancing back.

"That it has to mean something," Theron said. "These powers we have. That there has to be a reason for them."

Quintin held the man's gaze, before puffing out his cheeks and exhaling. "Well then," he murmured, letting his thoughts settle. His eyes were drawn to the girl. She had taken a seat on the grass, watching the distant traffic as it rumbled along the avenue. "So what's her part in all this?"

There was a pause before Theron replied. "She's my apprentice."

Strange. He was still lying, or at the least, holding something back. Even unable to read his emotions, Quintin could tell that much.

"She's full of anger, Theron. You realise that?"

He shrugged. "Yeah, a few nights ago she blew up the Stadwit manor. I read the signs."

"That was *her?* From the mess, I thought it must have been a Binder! Just how much agimet did you steal from that town?"

Theron chuckled. "She might be a little rough around the edges, but she's got talent."

"Do you mind if I talk to her?" he asked.

"Why?"

"You and Ambrose I know, Theron, even if the tailor likes to pretend he's something else." He turned his eyes on Kaila. "But I'd like to know who *she* is if we're going to be working together."

Theron's eyebrows shot up into his mop of blonde hair. "Then you'll take the job?"

"We'll see," Quintin said.

Then he rose and approached the young woman whose *soul-light* had replaced the serenity of the garden with jarring chords of rage.

KAILA LOOKED UP AS A SHADOW FELL ACROSS HER FACE. SHE'D found a spot of soft grass where the sun shone through the branches, warming the spring air. She had slept poorly in the feather bed of the Falkenrath guestroom and her eyes must have slid closed, for she didn't hear the footsteps approaching. She was surprised to find the Psionic, Quintin, standing over her.

Immediately she was on guard. She had felt what a Psionic was capable of—the Warden they had fought in Iselador had possessed the same powers. She would never forget that feeling of emptiness as he walked towards her. Not anger, or fear, or hatred, just…nothing.

Quintin, however, wore a smile as he gazed down at her. "You're angry."

She opened her mouth to spit a denial, but one glance in the Psionic's hazel eyes and the words died in her throat. Tears threatened instead as the pain rose within. Her eyes prickled, but she clenched her teeth and shoved it back down, determined not to show her weakness—even if this man could read her mind like a book.

"Do you have a problem with that?" she said finally.

"If I did, I doubt there'd be an Elysian left in this city I could work alongside," Quintin replied, arching an eyebrow.

Kaila sat up and brushed a few stray leaves from her dress. "So why are you here?" she asked, her tone colder than she intended.

"Because of what else I sensed inside of you."

Her face hardened. She didn't like the thought of him poking around in her mind. "And what emotion is that?"

Letting out a groan, Quintin lowered himself to the grass alongside her. For a moment, his gaze looked through the trees, out across the park to where carriages rumbled and people walked back and forth along the avenue.

"Hatred," he said at last, though his eyes did not flicker from the distant traffic.

Again that trembling inside, a sudden rushing to her skull,

like there was too much blood for her body. A quiet thunder rumbled in her ears as she looked at Quintin.

"I would have thought most Elysian had that one as well."

"Most," Quintin agreed, "though you might be surprised at the human capacity for forgiveness."

"Except we're not human," she sneered, unable to contain herself. "Not to them."

He finally turned then, taking her in with those hazel eyes of his. Eyes that could see right into the depths of her soul.

"Do you know why the Magisterium has spread that lie?"

Clenching her jaw, Kaila shook her head.

"Because it makes the rest easier," he said. "To believe their other lies. To *hate*." He seemed to contemplate the words for a while. "It *would* make it easier, wouldn't it? If it were true and we really were another species. If we didn't know that some of them are innocent."

"But they're *not* innocent!" Kaila spat, the words tearing from her before she could stop them. "They're a part of all this! The Magisterium, the lies! *All of them!*"

Panting, she glared at Quintin, fingers clawing up the grass, her entire body taut with rage.

Quintin said nothing, just watched her, and slowly her anger trickled away, exposing the pain.

"All of them?" he asked. "Even the ones who toil day in and day out in the factories for a measly ration chip? Even the physicians and the nurses that help the sick and injured in their clinics? Even the children?"

Closing her eyes, Kaila shook her head. "But they…they…" The words wouldn't come. "They hate us."

"No, they *fear us*," Quintin said softly. His eyes were on the people again. "Out of ignorance, maybe, but look closer the next time you're amongst them and they speak of the Elysian. They're afraid, Kaila. Just like you were once afraid."

A lump lodged in her throat. "Why are you telling me this?"

"Because anger can be useful. It can inspire us, drive us. But hatred is a poison that will destroy us all if left unchecked."

"Even if they deserve it?"

"If you really believe that, Kaila, you're as lost as they are." Rising, he looked down at her with those strange eyes. "Something I've learned in all my years; people are rarely what they seem."

"We don't all have the luxury of spying on other people's thoughts," Kaila snapped, her anger creeping through again.

"No," Quintin replied, and she could see the sadness in his eyes. "Perhaps the world would be a better place if they could." He offered her his hand.

She studied it suspiciously. "I thought you couldn't work with hatred."

A smile crossed his lips. "Maybe I've decided to make an exception."

She frowned, but took his hand and he lifted her to her feet. They wandered back to where Theron waited, still sitting on the wooden bench. His eyebrows lifted at their approach.

"So this is what it feels like to be on the outside," he murmured, rising to greet them. He actually looked nervous as he glanced from her to Quintin. Kaila could count on one hand the number of times she'd seen him flustered. "So…"

Now it was Theron's turn to endure the Psionic's hazel gaze. He handled it better than Kaila had—or at least, it seemed that way as Quintin finally let out a sigh.

"I'll do it," he said. "Just give me the day to put things in order."

"Really?" Theron looked genuinely surprised as he turned to Kaila. "What did you say to him?"

She just shrugged. In truth, she was still trying to figure that out herself—and what Quintin had been trying to say. The thought of *not* hating the people of Tah'raus was incomprehensible to her.

"She reminded me of the path we're all on," Quintin said

quietly, "the one my girls will take if things don't change." He seemed to consider his next words carefully. "A life of bitterness and pain and hatred. If there's any chance we can change that, however remote, then I have to take it. For them."

Theron was silent as he watched the older man. "I think I understand."

"Good," Quintin replied, "so when do we start?"

Theron grinned. "That's the beauty of it. We already have!"

"Of course you have."

5

Repositioning herself on the concrete edge for what had to be the hundredth time that day, Kaila took another peek through the strange device Theron had called a spyglass. It confirmed the crown prince of Fresia was still seated safely at his desk. Gritting her teeth, she rose and paced another lap of the rooftop.

She had found this little nook on her first day scouting his apartment, after revising every document and note Ambrose's people had collected about the prince. Which wasn't much, just that Rohan had left the Magisterium the day after his Trials, moving to the merchant quarter to live alone. He only had a few servants and no personal guards—though the building boasted a platoon that kept watch day and night.

But despite her early success, a week had now passed and the sun of another day was settling into the ocean behind her, and the only thing Kaila had learned about Rohan Frye was that he was quiet possibly the most boring man in Tah'raus. Most days, he didn't even leave his penthouse. Hell, he'd barely left his *desk* long enough to eat a meal today.

Unlike Theron's plan to win the hand of the princess, she had no means of integrating herself into his life. That was just fine by Kaila. Her skin still crawled at the memory of Eamon pressing his lips against hers—and he had only been a minor noble. How much worse must be a prince, with all the privileges afforded to his birth?

Despite his severance with the Magisterium, Rohan lived in one of the most opulent buildings in the merchant quarter. It was a modern tower of concrete, glass and agimet, and his fifth-floor penthouse was the most extravagant of all. It had floor-to-ceiling glass windows and the latest agimet machinery, much of which Kaila could only guess at its purpose. A broad balcony wrapped around the entire floor, though the dome of the Sanctum would mar his view across the harbour.

Her spy nest had been afforded by a building across the street, where an old warehouse stood abandoned. From the soot staining its walls, Kaila thought it had once been a coal store. There were people living inside now, but disguised as a beggar, she had passed amongst them without drawing attention. Rohan's penthouse was two storeys higher than the rooftop of the warehouse, but its enormous windows still afforded her views directly into his study and dining chambers. She had taken up residence in the hope of learning something about his interest in the throne.

Instead, she'd spent a week watching the man *read*. Day after day, night after night, each passing hour more painstaking than the last. The only breaks to her monotony were in the evenings after the prince retired, when she would meet Theron in one of Ambrose's shops. They were using it as a base of operations, since she could hardly show up on the doorstep of the Falkenrath mansion dressed as a vagabond. The shop had a hidden basement where they could practice with her Gift. Moving things. Deflecting projectiles. She was getting better, slowly, though her shoulders ached from last night when Theron had thrown her into a wall. He claimed it had nothing to do with the night before, when they'd gone up to the rooftop to practice lifting each other and she'd accidently launched him into the sky. At least she'd caught him!

Tonight, however, she wouldn't even have the pleasure of his company. After a week spent preparing his credentials and cover story with Quintin and Ambrose, Theron would be attending his first ball at the Sanctum, where he hoped to make his introductions to the princess.

Her stomach twisted, a sick feeling gnawing at her insides. Clenching an old iron bar sticking out of the rooftop, Kaila tried to tell herself it didn't matter. This was all part of the game. Theron was just a character, like she had played with Eamon. And the princess was only a means to an end. Whatever passed between them meant nothing.

Unfortunately, *knowing* that was one thing, convincing the knot of muscles in her chest of that much was something else entirely.

Twisting her fingers in her frazzled hair, Kaila growled and rose to pace the rooftop some more. The prince remained at his desk, reading over a book thick enough to serve as a doorstop. What was on those pages that he found so much more interesting than the delights Tah'raus could provide? The spas and the markets, the shows she had seen plastered on walls outside the theatres, the jesters who performed in the great plazas—or even the less savoury entertainments enjoyed by some amongst the nobility. Rohan Frye could have done *anything*.

Instead, he chose to remain in his apartment all day and *read*. Kaila had enjoyed many of the books Sister Eurador had given her, back when she believed the stories spun by the Magisterium. But this was something else entirely. An obsession.

Settling herself back on the ledge, Kaila removed her dinner from its paper bag. Today she'd brought sandwiches from a vendor down the road, trading a lump of coal for the meal. It was a common currency amongst the disenfranchised in Tah'raus. While merchants and the nobility traded in gold and gemstones, the common folk were given ration chips that could only be used in official offices. Yet another way the Magisterium kept the populace under their thumb.

But for every law in Tah'raus, there were those willing to break it. So long as they didn't make any noise, stalls like the sandwich maker seemed to be tolerated.

The rumble of a carriage in the street below interrupted Kaila's thoughts. She darted back to the edge of the rooftop, but only caught a glimpse of blonde hair before the guards ushered a young woman through the front door. She frowned as the carriage drew away. It was probably nothing, just another resident returning for the evening.

Then she glimpsed movement in the penthouse apartment. The prince had risen from his desk. Rather than stairs, the building had one of the new elevators Kaila had seen in modern buildings, but her vantage point didn't give her a view of the doors.

Her blood began to race. Did the prince actually have a *visitor?* Curious, she watched him move into the dining room, where his personal servant was busy setting two places at the table. He *did*! Though taking his seat, the prince did not wait for their arrival, gesturing for his manservant to fetch his food. By the time the blonde woman stepped into the room, he already had a fork to his lips.

The newcomer froze as she entered the apartment, and even from the awkward angle, Kaila could see her confusion. The distance and the reflection on the glass obscured the young woman's face, but she must have said something, for the prince made a gesture without even looking up from his meal.

Everything from the prince's posture to his discourtesy suggested he wasn't at all happy to have a visitor. Kaila wouldn't have been surprised if the woman simply turned around and walked back into the elevator.

But if the prince was opposed to her presence, the young woman must have been equally determined to make the most of her visit, because after a few seconds hesitation, she slid into her chair. The servant had set the two at opposite ends of the long table, which made for a slightly humorous sight.

As the woman took her place, however, there was something about the way she moved that snagged in Kaila's thoughts. Frowning, she leaned closer, trying to work out what had drawn her attention. The few inches did little to help with her view, but she did catch the glint of gold about the woman's neck.

The breath caught in Kaila's throat.

The prince's visitor was a Daughter of the Magisterium!

She scrambled for the spyglass, which lay forgotten alongside her. Maybe her presence here wouldn't be a complete waste after all! If the prince was treating with a Daughter, did that mean he was making a move for the throne after all?

When she pressed the spyglass to her eye, the apartment appeared blurred. She quickly twisted the cylinders and the lenses inside shifted. It took a few adjustments before she got it right. She focused first on the prince. Her stomach rumbled as she saw the plateful of meat and roast vegetables set before him —the meal put her miserly sandwiches to shame. Though maybe she should spare a thought for the Daughter, who had only been served a sparse plate of what looked to be pea soup. Shifting the lens, Kaila focused on the woman's face…

And felt her heart stop.

For the longest time, she just stared at the building across the street, where the prince of Fresia dined with a Daughter of the Magisterium. The woman was saying something now, though of course Kaila could not hear what was said. She doubted she would have heard even had she been in the room. Blood pulsed in her ears, sucking the sound from the world until only the screaming in her mind remained.

She *knew* this Daughter.

It was Eliza, her old rival from Elgoss.

It shouldn't have come as a surprise. The last thing Sister Eurador had done was send Eliza off to the capital to become a

Daughter. Kaila had even pretended to be the girl just a few days ago, when wooing that fool Eamon.

But seeing Eliza here, in the flesh in Tah'raus, dining at the table of a prince, it struck Kaila like a brick to her face. Even after everything that had happened in Elgoss, a part of Kaila had still preserved an image of the village in her mind. Of a peaceful people, innocents turned slaves by the lies of the Magisterium. It wasn't their fault what had happened to her, no more than it was Theron's or her own. It was the Magisterium. The Sisters and the Wardens and nobility that controlled them all.

But here was the lie to her fantasy; proof that at least *someone* in Elgoss had known what was happening.

Eliza Wrenn was here.

Her anger, always simmering so close to the surface nowadays, *thrummed* in her skull, the embers that had slowly built over the past months roaring into an inferno. It stained Kaila's vision scarlet.

Crack!

She gasped as the spyglass snapped in two and shards of glass sliced her palms. Trembling, she let the device fall and stared at her hands. Blood welled there, the pain following slowly, radiating out through her flesh. The shaking wouldn't stop, the roaring, the anger and the fear and doubt. It was like learning the horrible truth all over again.

Lies upon lies.

Eliza had *known*. She *had* to have known. Her father was the Earl. They controlled the flow of agimet out of the village. How could Eliza have watched while everyone she had ever known sacrificed their lives for a lie?

Kaila couldn't have said how many hours passed while she crouched on that rooftop watching the pair. All she knew was that eventually the dinner ended and the prince returned to his book. Eliza lingered a while, seemingly intent on making conversation despite the prince's obvious disinterest, and then...

...the next Kaila knew, there came a bang of the doors below as the Daughter erupted from the front doors of the apartment building. There she paced, the *tap-tapping* of her heels against the concrete street loud even from the rooftop above. She kept on like that for a few minutes, casting glances up the street on occasion in search of her carriage, until deciding she'd waited long enough.

Kaila blinked the scarlet from her vision as the young woman set off down the street on foot. Eliza Wrenn. Her once upon a time friend. Her enemy.

Suddenly, Kaila was moving. Before she even knew what she planned, she was slipping into the stairwell of the old warehouse and descending to the street. Her heart was racing; Eliza was her last connection to Elgoss. She had to see her, if only this one last time. To look into the eyes of the evil that had consumed her entire life.

Lost souls watched her from the shadows as she dashed through the warehouse, but they made no move to intercept her. And then she was outside.

The street was empty.

No, no, no.

Eliza couldn't be gone. Kaila needed her to *know.* To understand what she had done to her, and her father, and Leonardo, and Caellum, and everyone else in Elgoss.

Eliza needed to pay for the lives she had destroyed.

She spun around, looking one way, then the next—and from the end of the street she caught a glimpse of blonde as someone turned the corner. Kaila didn't hesitate. Fire burned inside her as she reached for her crystal, *atar* filling her veins. The glow of her eyes cast back the darkness, glinting against the shadows.

Heart pulsing, Kaila raced after her nemesis, Theron's instructions and all his words of caution, the entire plan, forgotten.

She couldn't stand by while this ghost from her past slipped through her fingers, while Eliza got to live her dreams and be a

Daughter, to enjoy a life of luxury while everyone else back home suffered.

While *Kaila* suffered.

She still didn't know what she planned to do as she chased her old nemesis down the street—only that she couldn't do nothing.

***

To say Eliza was irritated as she left Prince Rohan's apartment would be an understatement. Her jaw ached from clenching it so tightly and only an imbecile could have missed the rage conveyed by her various *sighs*, *tisks* and clearing of her throat throughout the dinner.

Which meant the prince *must* be an imbecile, for he hadn't picked up on a single signal.

Now as she stalked through the streets of Tah'raus, too irked to wait for her carriage, Eliza was already steeling herself for the wrath of Sister Vera. She should have listened to the other Daughters when they'd tried to warn her off the prince and his frustrations. But Eliza didn't have options like the other Daughters, most of whom hailed from Tah'raus or others of the great cities like Bermish or Rivergate. Their families had real power to trade, while Eliza was from a tiny village in the middle of the Iron Pinnacles that didn't even exist anymore…

Fire burning in her eyes, she came to a stop in the middle of the street. No, she couldn't think about that. She needed an explanation of her failure for Sister Vera. It seemed like nothing she did was ever good enough—not how she ate, or sat, or curtsied. Even how she *spoke* was apparently wrong. She had more marks against her name than all the other newly anointed Daughters combined. The other girls were already calling her *barely* a Daughter—some even to her face.

So when the Matron herself had called on suitors for her son,

Eliza had been one of the few Daughters desperate enough to take a shot. And now…

The breath hissed between her teeth as she started walking again. The First Matron could damn Rohan Frye to the pits of hell for all she cared! Who did he think he *was?* A private dinner with a Daughter was meant to be a *privilege*—and he'd started eating before she even arrived! The nerve! Any other man and she could have had his name forever tainted in the records of the Magisterium.

Instead, it was *her* who must go crawling back to the Sanctum to explain why she had failed to lure the estranged prince back into the fold.

Seriously, who couldn't even take a few minutes to chat about the weather? The ever-changing climate of Tah'raus was endlessly fascinating compared with Elgoss, where the sun shone three hundred and twenty days of the year. Not that Rohan Frye would know anything about that, locked away in that penthouse with his books.

Though that wasn't far from the life Eliza had lived in Elgoss after her parents had decided she should become a Daughter.

Another tremor rippled through Eliza's gut. Her parents. Her home. Elgoss. She'd never thought she would miss it. Her eyes lingered on the lanterns that lit the streets. Agimet. Her parents had explained the truth about the crystals the night before she'd departed Elgoss. How it was used in the great cities to create wonders. How the Magisterium controlled its supply, using it to control the Dominances and maintain the pact that had held humanity together for centuries.

There had been a certain sense to those words, at least at first, when she'd still been high in the mountains of the Iron Pinnacles. But now she had witnessed the miracles performed by the crystals, the life it granted those in the capital, the extravagance and the excess, Eliza couldn't keep a seed of guilt from taking root. There was just so *much.* Surely some could have been spared so those back home didn't go hungry…

I have no home anymore…

She felt a tear streak her cheek and angrily batted it away. Bad enough she would appear before Sister Vera a failure; she would not ruin her mascara as well.

As her legs began to ache, Eliza paused to rest. Back in Elgoss they had walked everywhere and the steep streets had built the strength in her legs—the size of her quads had been yet another complaint by her tutors. But it had only taken a few months with the luxury of agimet powered carriages to lose her fitness.

And of course the high heels didn't help.

Taken by a fit of impatience, she pulled them off and set off down the street again. The act was strangely liberating, even if it was *completely* inappropriate for a Daughter of the Magisterium to walk barefoot through Tah'raus, alone, at night. Too bad. Afterall, she was only *barely* a Daughter.

A sigh slipped from her lips. If only tonight had gone differently. She found her mind returning to the dinner. Maybe if she'd just been a little more attentive, or a little more *forward*, she might have gotten the prince to open up. That would have changed *everything*. To be the Daughter that won him over, brought him back to the Magisterium. There were even rumours—

Crack!

Eliza flinched as something shattered against the wall above her head. She cried out as porcelain scattered across the street, the remains of what looked to have been a vase. She was still trying to work out where it had come from when she sensed movement behind her.

Spinning, she found a dark-cloaked figure rushing towards her. Panic left her no time to think—she hurled her shoes at their face. For once her aim was true and Eliza heard a satisfying *thump* as the ivory stilettos connected with her assailant. She didn't stick around to find out if they'd done any real damage. Shrieking at the top of her lungs, she took off at a sprint in the direction she hoped was the Sanctum…

…only to find herself suddenly airborne.

For a second, she was too surprised to scream. She hung suspended a few feet above the ground.

Then a snarl came from behind her, and suddenly Eliza wasn't just floating, but *hurtling* through the air. This time she did scream as the pavement rose to meet her. Red flashed as she struck and something went *crack*. Agony followed a few seconds later, a terrible rending in her arm and head.

Footsteps approached. Panic welled in her chest and she tried to lift herself, but her stomach heaved. A moan rasped from her lips as she collapsed.

The last vision Eliza had before the darkness claimed her was of silver eyes and an old friend's face.

6

Theron never ceased to be amazed by the places you could go with a finely tailored suit and the proper company. Like right now, here he stood atop the grand balcony of the Sanctum, staring out over the squat concrete buildings of Tah'raus, the enormous dome rising at his back. He was even enjoying the most wonderful cocktail—the bartender had called it a *Midnight Mirage*, and the navy blue concoction had not disappointed with its strangely dark, velvety texture.

Sadly, the company was not half so interesting.

"Isn't it all so beautiful?" the young woman on his arm gushed, gesturing to the lights of the city below. "Your own estate must seem tiny by comparison."

She wasn't wrong—the view at this hour *was* quite lovely. The Sanctum was the tallest building in the capital, affording them views across the sprawling city and the bay beyond, where the setting sun turned the ocean scarlet. The shimmer of agimet streetlights cast the concrete buildings in shadow and concealed their ugliness, though he didn't think his admirer would agree with that last part.

She had found him not long after his arrival. The golden collar marked her as a Daughter, so he had the interest of

87

someone high up in the Magisterium at least. She had probably been sent to investigate the new arrival from the Iron Pinnacles. If he was honest, Ambrose had been right to see the opportunity in his old identity. Theron was only irked he hadn't thought of it sooner for himself.

Sadly, while most noblemen would have swooned to receive just an hours attention from a Daughter, Theron had a far more difficult mountain to climb. The tailor's underworld contacts claimed the princess would be here tonight—she had been somewhat of a recluse like her brother until recently—but so far he'd seen no sign of her. It made him anxious. A part of their plan relied on the novelty of his presence to catch the woman's attention, but if she wasn't here...

His fingers twitched as he felt the familiar hunger creeping over him, like an itch just beneath his skin. His heart beat just a little too hard, and his stomach ached, the need for *atar* gnawing at his insides. The longer he went without it, the worse the withdrawal would get. He had a single crystal sown into the cuff of his tuxedo as backup, in case everything went to hell. Or at least, that's what he'd told Ambrose.

In reality, it was so he could draw on it if the pain grew too great. He wore a pair of spectacles, and in the brilliance of the agimet lanterns, he hoped the silver glow would be mistaken for reflected light. It was a risk he would rather avoid, but the temptation was becoming a primal thing now, the desire so great he struggled not to reach for one of the nearby lanterns and just *take* its power.

It was also getting harder to hide from his companions. Theron could sense Quintin lingering in the shadows, dressed as his personal servant. He knew he should tell the man, but just thinking about the admission filled him with shame and dread, the way they would look at him, the pity and disgust in their eyes...

"Beautiful indeed," he said, forcing down his fears and turning back to his date. "Though I admit, with the loveliness of tonight's company, I find myself quite unable to appreciate the view."

"Oh!"

The compliment took the words right out of his companion's mouth. Her cheeks flushed bright red and she stood gaping at him. It was gratifying to see. He'd been trying all night to poke a hole in her façade. Though when it came to Daughters, you never could be sure. They were almost as impressive actors as Ambrose himself.

The Daughter belatedly raised a hand to cover her embarrassment. "Master Falkenrath!"

He flashed her a roguish grin. "My apologies, Miss Gardner, if my words are crass. We speak plainly in the Iron Pinnacles."

"Well, so long as we are speaking plainly." She placed a hand on his bicep. "Your company is no strain on the eyes either, Master Falkenrath." This time there was no mistaking the gleam in her eyes.

Theron couldn't resist a glance in Quintin's direction. He was laying it on *thick* with this one, cranking up her curiosity. Hovering in the shadows, the Psionic caught his glance and smirked. They'd discussed their strategy beforehand and decided he would play the mysterious stranger to try and draw out the princess. Of course, that would only work if the girl was *actually here*.

"Alas," Theron sighed, abruptly pulling away from the Daughter, "my father has forbidden all distraction while I'm in the capital."

"Iron Hand himself sent you?" his companion asked. She made no effort to conceal her surprise this time. "Why would he do that?"

Theron grimaced. "I cannot say, Miss Gardner."

"I can assure you, Master Falkenrath," she said, taking his hand and looking up at him through long lashes. "Whatever your father has sent you here to do, it will go easier with the aid of a Daughter."

He bowed his head. "Alas, Miss Gardner, it cannot be so."

"Please—"

"I fear I've already said too much," he cut her off sharply. "Please, if you would excuse me…"

He walked away before she had a chance to stop him. Several people glanced in their direction. His stomach twisted in sudden anxiety. Turning her down had been imperative—he couldn't afford his character to be tangled up with another woman—but hopefully the rejection hadn't been *too* sharp. The princess was a Daughter as well so he couldn't afford to get offside with her order.

"That was well done," Quintin murmured, falling into step with Theron as he neared the bar.

"You don't think I overdid it?"

Quintin snorted by way of response, then moved to the bar. Theron hung back, allowing his manservant to order his next drink while he surveyed the crowd. The gala was now in full swing, the enormous balcony packed with noblemen and women from across the kingdom. The appearance of both moons in the Fresian sky marked winter's final swoon. Their twin brilliance made the agimet lanterns mostly unnecessary, especially combined with the braziers set along the edges of the balcony. The vanilla incense they burned kept the scents of the city at bay, while a string quartet covered the general racquet that hung about Tah'raus at all hours of the day.

It didn't take long for Theron to locate his now-former-admirer. She'd wasted no time finding other Daughters—a group were huddled at the edge of the balcony, heads leaned in close to listen.

Content his story was spreading, Theron averted his eyes before they noticed his attention—and found himself face to face with a man he'd only ever seen in paintings. The man was solidly built, his barrel-chest straining against the buttons of his black tunic, while his wiry beard was unshaved. With his grizzled appearance, he could have been mistaken for a common guard or soldier, if not for the crown that perched atop his greying hair.

"Master Falkenrath," Alaric Frye, king of Fresia, said, offering his hand. "Welcome to my city. I am pleased to finally make your acquaintance—I have had the pleasure of knowing Leonardo for many years."

A chill ran down Theron's spine. He stared at the king's extended hand, in a state of shock. They should have foreseen this—*of course* his thrice-cursed-father would be on a first name basis with the king. He searched the man's eyes, seeking some hint of suspicion, but Alaric seemed genuine with his offer of hospitality.

"The pleasure is all mine," Theron said, taking the offered hand after an extended pause. As he did, he cast a glance in the direction of the bar, but there was no sign of Quintin. He was on his own for now. "My father has always spoken highly of you."

"I should hope so," Alaric chuckled. "We fought together in the Brenshield campaign some twenty years ago; saved his behind more times than I can count."

"I have heard the stories," Theron said, ignoring the cold sweat that dripped down his back. The need had returned, clawing at his insides like a living thing, but he couldn't risk drawing on *atar* in front of this man. "You'll have to tell me a few of your own sometime," he added, trying to keep his voice even. "I'm curious to know whether the details match."

Alaric roared with laughter. "If they don't, I promise that my version is the correct one."

"I don't doubt it." Theron grinned back while his heart raced. Depending on how they played it, this could be a disaster...or if he was quick on his feet, maybe this could be the connection they needed. "Actually," Theron added, dropping his voice to a whisper, "I am pleased to see you tonight, Your Majesty. There was a somewhat...delicate matter I wished to discuss with you."

The king raised one eyebrow. "What's this?" he quizzed.

"Don't tell me Leonardo has decided to get involved in politics this late in the game?"

Theron wet his lips, attempting to take on a nervous look. "Not so much my father, as myself, Your Majesty." It might clash a little with the story he'd spread with the Daughters, but knowing the Tah'raus rumour mill, the finer points would be lost anyway by the time any whispers got back to the king.

A second bushy eyebrow joined the first on the king's forehead. "Well, well, well, that *is* interesting!" he said quietly. "I had wondered what might have tempted Leonardo's reclusive son out of hiding. Very good then, Master Falkenrath, I will have my people get in touch with your people. In the meantime, do try to enjoy the joys of the capital. They should be quite the extravagance after Bermish."

Theron bowed his head. "They are indeed," he hesitated then, wondering whether to try his luck. "One more thing, Your Majesty. I wondered if the prince and princess might be in attendance tonight? I would very much like to make their acquaintance."

"My son hasn't stepped foot in this building in three years," the king grunted, before pursing his lips. His eyes scanned the crowd, before letting out a sigh. "As for my dear Jenna, I haven't seen her tonight. She's probably lurking about somewhere, avoiding the hordes of noblemen clamouring for her favour.

Theron swore softly to himself as the man moved away. Still, if the princess wasn't present, at least his interaction with the king meant the night wasn't a complete loss.

"Your drink, sir," Quintin announced, appearing at Theron's shoulder and handing him a tall-rimmed glass filled with what could have been liquified emeralds for all Theron knew.

Theron accepted it with a grunt. "What took you so long?" he added. He took a sip and gasped as the spirits burned his throat. "First Matron be blessed, I could have used this *before* my little chat with the king."

Quintin wrinkled his brow. "Trouble?"

"Potentially. He knows Iron Hand," Theron replied. The shaking in his hands eased as he took another sip of the fiery liquor.

"That's concerning…"

"Or perhaps an opportunity," Theron replied. "We could use him to make contact with the princess."

The words did nothing to budge the frown on the Psionic's face. "I don't like it. If he knows Iron Hands…"

Theron supressed a sigh. He recognised that look in his friend's eyes. Quintin couldn't help but play dad—even years before his girls had arrived, he'd been the one looking out for their crew, making sure they covered their tracks and only used clean agimet—even reminding them to eat when the stress started getting to them.

"Forget about Iron Hands for now," he replied, "did you learn anything from the other servants about the princess?"

Quintin studied Theron for a heartbeat longer, before exhaling. "She was here, but no one's seen her for over an hour." He pursed his lips. "We may have missed her."

Muttering a curse, Theron considered the news. "The king mentioned she might be lurking somewhere," he said at last.

"Okay, well, you can't be seen asking for her. It'll ruin your mysterious persona. But I can have a hunt around."

"What am I meant to do in the meantime?"

"Try not to drink too much?" Quintin said, shooting a meaningful look at Theron's glass—which was almost empty already.

Theron grinned, though inwardly he cursed his own weakness. Quintin eyed him one last time before disappearing into the press of bodies. Assessing the crowd, Theron decided he'd had enough of meaningless banter about court rumours and the weather. Despite Quintin's warning, he snagged another drink from a passing waiter—this one a red wine no doubt of some great vintage—and returned to the balcony in search of a break in the crowd.

There was only one exit from the dome and most revellers

seemed to be gathered around this section of the balcony, but earlier he'd noted it wrapped around the entire circumference of the Sanctum. As he moved around the dome, the racing in his heart slowly subsided, though he still felt the trembling in his hands. He steeled himself against reaching for the hidden crystal. He didn't need it. He'd lived half his life ignorant of his Gift —he could survive a few hours without the magic flowing in his veins.

Even if it felt like razorblades digging through his flesh.

On the far side of the dome, the crowd thinned, the press of bodies and stench of perfume receding. Leaning against the stone balustrade, he savoured the cool night air.

For Trickster's sake, what's wrong with me?

Needles danced across his skin as he finally surrendered to the desire and drew a drop of *atar* from his crystal. Theron was meant to be the one in control, and here he was, barely able to stop himself from draining his crystal dry. But *atar* was the only thing that soothed the ache inside. Even with it, he felt like a drowning man sucking air through a reed stalk. It was never quite enough to sate the need the broken crystal had left inside him.

Just concentrate on the job, a little voice whispered in his ear.

The job. He could have laughed. Pain gave him clarity, and this so-called-job was a fool's errand. The desperate hope of an old man to leave some kind of legacy when he was gone. Not even Ambrose could *really* hope the legends were true. Another world? He could have laughed.

No, there was only one reason this job was worth the risk —*vengeance.* Ambrose could dream of other worlds and Quintin of saving this one, but the chance to destroy his father was the only reason Theron had accepted this suicide mission. He felt guilty involving Kaila, but then, who was he to deny the young woman her own chance at vengeance?

"And here I thought I'd escaped the last of the prancing parakeets," a voice said from behind him. "Tell me, who was it that sold me out? Sister Vera? Or maybe it was one of my ever so lovely fellow Daughters?"

Theron's skin crawled as the clack of heels announced the speaker's approach. *Atar* still burned in his eyes. In this dimly lit section of the balcony, it would be impossible to miss if he turned his head. Panic clawed its way up his throat, screaming for him to draw in the rest of his crystal and flee.

Instead, he exhaled and activated his *atarsight*. As *soullights* danced before his eyes, he could see no immediate target through which to thread his power, so he settled for the balcony beneath him. Constructed of solid concrete, it would take far more than the trickle of *atar* in his veins to shift it—but he could use up what he had trying.

Gritting his teeth, he poured his *atar* into a thread of his Gift and directed it straight down into the concrete beneath his feet. As the energy left him, he felt a slight trembling beneath his feet, before a sheer pain drove through his skull as his body realised it was without *atar* once more.

Thankfully, a cry from the young woman covered his own groan—before a weight slammed into him from behind. Instinctively, he grasped his assailant, before realising it was not an attack at all. As the ground shifted, the young woman had lost her footing and tripped.

"First Matron guard us, was that an earthquake?" she muttered, righting herself before turning to Theron. "Are you okay? Sorry, I swear I don't usually tackle potential suiters I've just met. Well, less than ten percent of the time, anyway," she said the last part with a smile.

Theron hardly heard what she said. He stared at the young woman in his arms. She wore a floor-length black sequin gown with side cutouts that drew the eye to her hips. Auburn hair hung in curls around her shoulders and the golden collar of a Daughter shone proudly around her throat, but that alone was not enough to steal his words.

The princess's emerald eyes glinted in the moonlight as she

reached down and gently removed his hands from around her waist. "I think I've found my feet now, thank you, good sir," she said.

"Sorry," Theron croaked.

"Ha." Her eyes danced as she watched him. The moment stretched out, silent other than the distant chattering of the crowd, until finally she inclined her head to the side. "You really weren't looking for me back here, were you?"

Swallowing, Theron struggled to recover his wits. "Ah…" Where was Quintin when you needed him? "Sorry, I was just… needed a break from the crowd."

To his surprise, the princess threw back her head and laughed. "And instead you've been assaulted by a clumsy princess in high heels. The Nameless works in strange ways at times, does he not?"

"Ah, princess?" Theron asked, deciding it was probably best to continue playing dumb. It wasn't exactly an act at this stage.

"Jenna Frye," the young woman said, offering her hand, "and who might you be, Master…"

Finally regaining some of his composure, Theron swooped down to press his lips to her wrist. "Theron Falkenrath," he murmured as he straightened. "My apologies, Your Highness, I'm new in town and did not recognise you. The portraits truly do not do your beauty justice." For once, the words were not a lie. Jenna Frye was as stunning a specimen as any he'd encountered.

"Falkenrath," she murmured, brushing off the compliment. "I didn't realise Iron Hands *had* a son?"

"I'm his best kept secret."

Her eyes seemed to narrow ever so slightly, before a grin appeared on her lips. "Surely we in the capital can't really be so intimidating to a Falkenrath?"

Theron snorted. "I can tell you with absolute certainty, I'd rather face five Elysian soldiers than spend another minute with that pack of hyenas."

"Is that so?" This time he thought the princess's laughter might have been genuine. "And what about me, Master Falkenrath? Do you not find the princess of those hyenas intimidating?"

"I'll admit, witnessing you tripping over your own feet has sucked some of the fear from the encounter."

"I swear the ground moved," she muttered, before leaning against the balustrade with a sigh. "I'll be honest though, I came back here for the same reason—to escape."

Theron studied the young woman, weighing his next words. This was his chance—Quintin or no, he couldn't waste it.

"I would have thought you were used to it?"

The princess snorted. "Used to it? I may not have been so bold as my brother, but I've done my best to avoid these engagements like an Elysian plague."

"And yet here you are."

"Here I am," she agreed, flashing him a smile. "At my father's behest."

"Oh?"

"Indeed," the princess replied. Refusing to elaborate any further, she promptly changed the subject. "So, what brings the Iron Hand's secret son to the capital then? A crisis on our borders? A secret Elysian plot to destroy the heart of our nation?"

This time it was Theron's turn to chuckle. "Nothing so exciting," he responded—though she'd jokingly guessed the *exact* reason he was there. He spread his arms. "I fear I am not a swordsman like my father, so in his wisdom, he has sent me here to represent his interests in the capital."

The princess arched an eyebrow. "You're to be a politician then?"

Theron sighed. "Correct."

"Arg," she replied, wrinkling her nose like she'd caught a whiff of something foul.

The princess's reaction was so unexpected, Theron couldn't

help himself—he burst into laughter. "Well, I can safely say that was not the reception I would have expected from the daughter of King Alaric Frye," he said after recovering from his amusement.

Rolling her eyes, the princess leaned back against the railings—then as if taken by a bout of recklessness, she boosted herself up onto the balustrade. Theron's heart lodged in his throat as his one shot of pulling off this job perched herself over a four-hundred-foot drop. The princess didn't seem to think anything of it as she kicked off her heels and grinned at him.

"You seem to have lost some of your colour, Master Falkenrath," she remarked, showing a mischievous smile. "Don't tell me you've lost your nerve for politics already?"

Theron swallowed. "Can you blame a man for wondering how your father would react if his daughter were to plummet from this balcony while under my supervision?"

The princess inclined her head. "Oh, I'm under your *supervision* now, am I?" Her eyes never leaving his, she leaned back, auburn hair swirling out over the darkness. "In that case, just how do you plan to keep me safe, Master Falkenrath?"

As his pulse spiked, Theron reacted instinctively, snatching her arm and dragging the princess back from the edge. Her eyes danced as she returned to solid ground, bare feet slapping lightly on the concrete.

"Why Master Falkenrath," she gasped in mock outrage—or at least, he hoped it was mock outrage. "I could have you flogged for assailing a Daughter of the Magisterium in such a manner."

The blood still pounding in his ears, Theron just glared at the young woman, until he could maintain the expression no longer and the crack of a smile appeared.

Trickster's mercy, where did this woman come from?

Chuckling, he released her and dipped into a bow. "What can a humble man do to earn the Daughter's forgiveness?"

Leaning back, the princess eyed him, lips pursed as though in contemplation. "You're an interesting one, you know that, Master Falkenrath?"

"How so?"

She shook her head. "Tell me, can you dance? Or did you inherit the Iron Hands reputation for joyless duty?"

Theron could hardly believe his good fortune as he smiled. "I fear it has never been my strong suit, but to earn your forgiveness, I could make an attempt."

"Very well then, Master Falkenrath," she said, holding out a hand for him to take. "Then why don't we—"

She broke off, stiffening as someone behind them cleared their throat.

"Sir?"

Theron turned to find Quintin hovering in the shadows. The Psionic looked torn as he met Theron's gaze, hesitating just a second longer than was necessary before approaching.

"Sir," Quintin repeated. "I am sorry to interrupt."

"Yes, Quintin," Theron choked out the words. What was the man *thinking?* "What was it?"

"A message, sir. From Lord Ambrose Braider."

At his side, Jenna frowned. "Ambrose Braider…as in the *tailor?*"

"Yes, ma'am," Quintin hesitated, eyes darting to the princess and then back to Theron. "My apologies, sir, but his messenger said it was urgent. A problem with the ah…the custom suit. He requested your presence at your earliest convenience."

What the hell?

Theron hid his confusion with a frown. Whatever was going on, it had to be bad—that was a *terrible* cover story. Stealing himself, he turned to the princess and dipped into a bow.

"My most sincere apologies, princess," he said, "it seems I will have to owe you that dance?"

The princess frowned at him. "You're serious, aren't you?"

"I'm afraid so."

She stared for so long he felt himself shift nervously on his feet. Finally though, she snorted. "You are an odd one." Stepping in close, she lifted herself onto her bare tiptoes and planted a kiss on his check. "Very well though, you may go. I shall hold you to that dance, though," as she spoke, her eyes took on a stony glint, "or maybe we'll have to revisit those repercussions we spoke of."

With that she turned and strode away, that tantalising sequin dress swirling around her thighs as the two men stared after her. Theron had to bite his tongue to keep himself from screaming. Instead, he turned to Quintin with a scowl.

"Whatever it is, Quintin, it better be life or death."

Taking a glass of wine from the tray of a passing waiter, Jenna Frye studied Theron Falkenrath and his manservant as they spoke beside the balustrade. The son of Iron Hand. He intrigued her, though she still had her doubts about the nature of their encounter. Was he really the inoffensive young man he presented himself as, or was he playing the game like every other intolerable nobleman that had tried to win her hand over the years?

He was certainly different from those puffing jays. She'd tried with them, at least in the early days. She'd been made a Daughter when she was just fifteen—before she'd even taken her Trials—so she'd been forced the learn the game early. But most of the nobles at court were just so *boring*. Weak, timid men too afraid of putting a foot out of line to ever grasp a little piece of *excitement*.

Certainly, none of *them* would have grabbed her off the balustrade! She had not expected that—she'd almost struck him in her surprise. She'd played the same game with a few of the more boring suitors that had pestered her over the years, and it always went one of a few ways. Either they grew increasingly distraught in their demands for her to get down, or they marched off to report her outrageous behaviour to someone with more authority than themselves.

None of them had ever simply taken her down themselves.

For some reason, her cheeks flushed at the memory of it.

Ah, but then what had that been at the end? Despite herself, Jenna found her irritation prickling at the sudden dismissal. She watched as the pair finished their conversation and made their way through the crowd. They seemed to be angling for the exit. Frowning, Jenna slipped through the crowd after them.

What was this newcomer's game, leaving her high and dry like that? She had offered him a dance with a *princess?* Any other man in this court would have leapt at the offer. And she hadn't been bluffing—she could have had the guards beat him bloody for laying hands on her. Her lips twisted, wondering how Theron Falkenrath might react in the face of *that* threat. Would he submit, or would he retaliate…

She found herself growing flustered picturing those smouldering eyes watching her, daring her to give the order.

The sensation faded as she considered their interaction from another angle—that their encounter had not been coincidence at all. Her father had made it clear she needed to choose a suitor to preserve his legacy—or risk one of her mother's flunkies ascending. The Matron would like nothing more than to seize control of Fresia's leadership after his death. Her stomach twisted, but she pushed the thought away. She needed to keep her mind clear, objective.

Theron and his attendant had disappeared inside now. The man himself had admitted he was here at the behest of his father. The Iron Hand was a General of Fresia—and so sworn to her father. Had he sent his son at the king's request? She sighed. That would be just like her father. She had promised to find a husband by the Summer Gala, but it would be just like him to get involved where his interference was not required.

Or could Theron be a plant, an agent sent by her mother to engage the princess. The Matron had evidently learned about her husband's illness, because two weeks ago she had sent a Daughter to treat with Rohan. He'd ignored the poor young woman, but another was to dine with him tonight. Her poor brother had no interest in the throne or their parents' games, but others were sure to follow.

Yes, that was probably it. Her mother was trying to play both sides—ensure she had one hand on the throne whichever of her children ascended. Her heart sank as she thought of Theron Falkenrath and that smile. She had enjoyed their interaction, Jenna realised. It hurt to think it had not been genuine.

Though…there might be one way she could know for sure. The pair had certainly high-tailed it out of the gala after receiving the news from the tailor, but they weren't familiar with the Sanctum like she was. They would be slowed by the crowds bogging down the main corridors. If Jenna was quick, she could be waiting to follow them when they left through the front gates.

Her fists tightened into tiny balls. Then she could find out who Theron Falkenrath was *really* meeting.

It had better be a suit maker, or she might have to throw him off the rooftop after all.

7

Heart palpitating, hands slick with sweat, Kaila paced the dimly lit basement until she reached the far wall. Snarling, she spun in frustration and stamped back the way she had come.

Whywhywhywhy!

Stepping over a roll of fabric and piles of discarded silk, she made another lap of the basement, barely taking in her surroundings. Red. All she saw was red. Panic had set in long ago and now her mind whirled from one thought to another, tossing them about like a haybale caught in a whirlwind. She ran her fingers through her hair, tugging at the dark locks until pain prickled her scalp. It did nothing to stop the whirling.

"What were you *thinking?*" the words tore from her, echoing loudly in the empty room.

Well, almost empty.

Eliza Wrenn lay on a pile of scrap material where Kaila had dumped her. Thankfully, the Daughter still hadn't woke. Maybe Kaila had hit her too hard, and she never would.

Not that her old rival's death would solve anything.

Stupid, stupid, stupid!

Kaila *hadn't* been thinking—that was the short of it. For one joyous moment, she'd felt elation as Eliza slammed into that wall.

But her euphoria had been short lived. Even as the Daughter had fallen to the ground, her body crumpling like a ragdoll, Kaila had been struck by a sense of dismay.

She'd watched, horrified, as her former friend and enemy struggled to lift herself. Even then, the rage had warred with her shame. *Atar* bubbling in her veins, Kaila had advanced on the girl, eyes blazing, veins thrumming with the ecstasy of her Gift.

But at her approach, the young woman had looked up. Their eyes met. And the magic had stuttered in Kaila's veins. As the power slipped from her control, she had lowered her hand. Looking down at Eliza Wrenn, she didn't see a Daughter of the Magisterium, or even the girl who had mocked and tormented her for all those years, but another child of Elgoss, lost and alone in this terrible city.

"K…Kaila…" Eliza had rasped, almost managing to rise—before pitching face first into Kaila's arms.

She didn't have a choice. She couldn't just leave the young woman lying in the street. Eliza had seen her face! If the Magisterium knew that Kaila lived, the girl from the mountains, the Elysian that had evaded their Trials, who wielded the power of a Warden…who knew what they would do to hunt her down.

She had to kill her, and yet, she couldn't. Not now. Even if Kaila hated the girl for everything she represented, something inside her balked, some last fragment of affection from her former life.

So instead, Kaila had brought her to the tailor's shop.

Her gaze returned to the pile of discarded linen where Eliza lay unconscious. Fortunately, the shop hadn't been far from her ambush. The sight of an unconscious Daughter being dragged through the streets of Tah'raus would have raised questions. But it also meant the inevitable search wouldn't have to look far to locate the missing Daughter.

Because they *would* come looking. You didn't touch a Daughter of the Magisterium and expect to survive. They would tear apart the city to find Eliza and then those responsible would be hung, drawn and quartered for the whole capital to see.

Little wonder then Ambrose's reaction when she showed up on his doorstep with an unconscious Daughter in her arms. His anger had been something to behold—the burning in his eyes, the way his lips parted, baring his teeth as though he was a hound about to bite her.

But then he had stepped aside and gestured for her to enter.

She wouldn't have blamed him if he'd left her standing in the street. *Idiot!* But seeing Eliza smiling, smirking, enjoying the life of privilege that had been denied to Kaila…it was like being back in Elgoss, suffering the things that had been done to her all over again.

Trembling, Kaila came to a stop over Eliza's body. There was a bruise the size of an egg on her forehead, already turning purple. She must have struck her head when Kaila had launched her into the wall.

First Matron, what was I thinking?

Wrapping her arms around her chest, Kaila resumed her pacing. At least no one had seen her. She hoped. Ambrose was checking into it. Or his man was, the big one with the ugly nose, Garrick. What would happen if she *had* been spotted? Even now, Wardens and soldiers could be surrounding the shop, readying their terrible blades to take her and rescue the Daughter…

She forced the image away and sucked in a breath. Ambrose had been apocalyptic, but bringing Eliza here had been the right choice. She could have hardly brought her anyplace else! The basement was *meant* for eventualities like this, wasn't it? So why was there still a lead weight in Kaila's stomach?

The squeal of hinges sounded from above as someone opened the hidden door. She expected to find Ambrose returning to berate her some more, but instead her heart sank further as Theron, Quintin and Ambrose descended the iron staircase. This was bad. Theron's presence meant she had put not just herself at risk, but the entire plan.

"Theron!" she gasped as they reached the basement. "I can explain!"

The man came to a stop before her, his eyes narrowed. The silence stretched out as he seemed to search her face for something. The others lingered behind him, both flicking glances to the corner where Eliza remained unconscious. At last, Theron raised an eyebrow.

"Well," he said, "I'm waiting."

"Oh!" she said. "Ah—"

"She clearly *wasn't* thinking," a growl came from Ambrose. Light burned in his eyes as he advanced on Kaila. He seemed to grow larger as he did so, teeth enlarging, claws extending from his fingers, his face twisting into an image of horror.

"Ambrose—"

"She kidnapped a *Daughter*, Theron," the monster swung on the thief, waving a fist. "Do you know what she's *done?* They can track those collars, sense where they've been. Once she's reported missing, they'll be all over this place. If they find us, it's *over*."

"I'm sorry…" Kaila tried to speak over the screams.

"Sorry?" Ambrose snarled. "That's all you have to say for yourself? *Sorry?*"

"When I saw Eliza…I just…I just lost it."

She closed her eyes, trembling, but she could still sense Ambrose looming over her, the *roaring* of his anger.

"I told you she would be a liability," the tailor said at last.

Kaila winced. She had no words to defend herself. Strangely, it was Quintin who came to her rescue.

"You know her, don't you, Kaila?" he asked in his soft voice.

Swallowing, she shook her head. She couldn't talk about that, not with these men. She clenched her hands, but nothing would stop the shaking.

Footsteps approached, then a hand settled on her shoulder. "Kaila, look at me."

It was like a cool breeze blew over her soul. All her fear and anger, her hatred and guilt and grief, all of it receded as a soft melody played in her mind, carrying with it a gentle peace. The trembling finally stopped. She opened her eyes. She wasn't surprised to find herself looking up at Quintin.

"Who is she, Kaila?"

She surprised even herself when the words flowed from her. "Her name is Eliza Wrenn. I knew her back in Elgoss."

"An old friend of yours?"

"No," she whispered. "More like an enemy."

"If she's an enemy," the tailor snarled, "why didn't you leave her dying in the street?"

"Ambrose," Quintin said, "let me handle this."

The tailor grumbled a few choice words, but fell silent. Quintin turned back to Kaila. His eyes glinted a soft silver in the gloom of the basement.

He's using his power on me, she realised.

She still had the crystal in her pocket. Her fingers closed around it, drawing on some *atar* of her own. She wanted to see what he was doing. The world shifted with the glow of a thousand *soullights*. For a moment, she saw nothing; then a silver thread shimmered into existence between herself and Quintin, connecting them. She struggled to follow it, to understand *how* he could make her feel like this, like everything didn't hurt. But she could make no sense of the swirling lights of her own soul. It was as Theron had told her—each Elysian could only control one aspect of reality—

Skree!

A sharp screeching filled her mind, like broken glass scraping across a chalkboard. Clapping her hands to her ears, Kaila flinched away, but her foot caught on a loose scrap of fabric and sent her crashing to the ground. The crystal jarred from her hands and the lights of the world flickered out. Groaning, she clutched at her knee where it had slammed into the brick floor.

"Kaila," Theron said, stepping towards her, "are you all —*look out!*"

Her head snapped up at the panic in Theron's voice, but it wasn't some demonic vision that came at her this time.

It was Eliza.

"Murderer!"

Screaming, the Daughter launched herself at Kaila from the pile of linen. She must have woken unnoticed during their argument, for she was on Kaila before anyone could react. A loose brick gripped in one fist, the girl swung it for Kaila's face.

Kaila ducked, but she wasn't fast enough and the blow struck her collar instead. Pain flared in her shoulder as she hit the ground. Then Eliza's weight crashed into her, pinning her to the floor. The others shouted and shadows flickered around the basement as they drew on their power, but the Daughter was already drawing back her fist for another blow. Desperate, Kaila fumbled for the agimet in her pocket. Her fingers closed around the eight-sided crystal as the brick descended. Silver light lit up Eliza's face. Her lips were drawn back in rage and blood dripped from her forehead as she swung.

Then she was hurtling backwards, the brick tumbling from her fingers as Kaila's Gift hurled her across the basement. She landed with a crash amidst the great rolls of silk and did not rise.

Groaning and muttering a few choice words to herself, Kaila climbed to her feet. The others gathered around her to check whether she was alright, but Kaila shrugged them off. Gritting her teeth against the pain in her shoulder, she advanced on the Daughter.

Eliza lay moaning and clutching at her wrist, which judging by the swelling had probably been broken, but she stilled as Kaila approached. There was a moment as the two girls from Elgoss watched one another. Then Eliza's lips drew back in a sneer.

"Do it," she hissed. "Kill me like you killed everyone else."

Her words gave Kaila pause. "What?" she asked, her rage giving way to confusion.

"My parents," Eliza snarled. "Sister Eurador. *Your own father. EVERYONE!"*

To Kaila's utter shock, the girl surged at her again. Eliza had no weapon now, just her tiny fists, but she didn't seem to care. Not even the silver glow of *atar* in Kaila's eyes was enough to deter the Daughter. But she wouldn't catch Kaila off-guard again.

She activated her Gift, more gently this time. Grasping Eliza's *soullight*, she lifted the Daughter off her feet instead of hurling her across the room. Unfortunately, it did nothing to calm Eliza's rage. Screaming and thrashing, she tried to kick out at Kaila with her boots—anything, it seemed, to attack her old enemy from Elgoss.

Only when Quintin approached and laid a hand on the girl did she finally quiet. This time Kaila didn't try to figure out what he was doing—with all Eliza's writhing, it was taking all of her concentration just to keep a grasp on the girls' *soullight*. Only when the Daughter drooped in the air did Kaila feel confident setting her back on the ground.

"What was that all about?" Theron asked as he joined them.

Kaila could only shake her head. "I don't know," she whispered, even as her mind shrank from the possibility and the void inside her trembled.

"How dare you?" Crouched on her knees, there was an emptiness to Eliza's eyes as she lifted her head to stare at them. "You slaughtered our home, and now you won't even admit it?"

"What?" Kaila whispered, shaking her head. "No, Eliza, we left Elgoss. The Warden chased us…"

"You killed them all," Eliza glared at her from the floor, anger shimmering in her eyes. It seemed not even a Psionic's power could keep it bottled. "They told me what happened when I arrived here. The Matron herself came to me and told me everything." Her words were like venom, eating through Kaila's rage, her hatred. "How you butchered them like animals, the people who called you their friend, your *family*. *You killed them all!*"

The accusation rung in Kaila's ears. She stumbled back, unable to face the hatred in Eliza's face. Hatred, so like her own.

She was innocent. She hadn't touched any of the villagers in Elgoss. She and Theron had fled rather than fight. But those words, Eliza *believed* them.

They're all dead.

"No," she whispered. "It wasn't me…"

Eliza looked like she might hurl herself at Kaila again, but Quintin's eyes burned brighter and she slumped to the floor instead, a long sigh whispering from her lips. Kaila stared at her former enemy, trembling, shaking at those final words. They had been rivals for years, but that look in her eyes now, the rage…

"Kaila…" Theron said, resting his hand on her shoulder. "Are you—"

"Did you know?" she asked sharply, spinning on him. The void *roared* and she lashed out with her power, pushing him away from her. He staggered back a step, looking shocked. "*Did you know?*"

"*No!*" he roared, straightening, his own eyes lighting up with *atar*. She felt his power pressing back against hers. "Of course not! How could I have known?"

How could I have known?

The anger went from her as quickly as it had appeared. She sank to the floor and hugged her knees to her chest, still staring at her former friend and rival. Just when she thought the Magisterium couldn't grow any more vile, they found a way to plumb fresh depths of cruelty.

An entire town, destroyed, *butchered*, all so they could keep their secret. So the agimet they used to fuel their vehicles and power their contraptions would continue to flow without cost or interruption. They were beyond evil.

"…dispose of the body."

Theron and the other men were talking again. She barely heard them over the pulsing of blood in her ears, but now she jerked as though stung.

"*No!*" she said sharply.

Three heads turned to stare at her. "No?" Ambrose growled. "*No?* Girl, this isn't your decision to make."

"I don't care," she snapped, defying the Weaver's glare. Rising, she moved to stand between him and the now-unconscious-Eliza. "It's not her fault she's involved in this."

"No, it's *yours*," Ambrose said bluntly.

She swallowed at that, jaw clenching. It was true. But it didn't matter. She couldn't take back what she'd done, however much she might wish to. But she could stop them from doing something worse.

"Please…you can't just kill her." She turned to Theron, desperate. "You don't kill slaves, remember?"

Theron shook his head, looking unconvinced. "She's a Daughter, Kaila. They don't count."

"She's barely been a Daughter for a few months," Kaila croaked, glancing over her shoulder at Eliza. "Maybe…maybe she didn't know the truth, like the rest of us in Elgoss."

"It doesn't matter what she knew," the tailor growled, eyes glinting silver as he advanced. "She can't go back. She knows too much. And she can't stay here. I have protections on this basement to protect against *atarsight*, but if the search goes building to building, they'll find it."

"What if there was no search?" Theron interrupted, stepping between the two, arms extended.

The rest of them frowned. Quintin was the first to speak, sounding hesitant. "A Daughter has been taken, Theron. Of course there'll be a search."

The Mover's eyes shimmered. "But what if a Daughter *hadn't* been taken?" He turned from the others to look at Kaila. "What if in a couple of hours, Eliza Wrenn shows up on the doorstep of the Sanctum, all in one piece?"

Kaila frowned. Why was he looking at her like that? "Ambrose already said she can't go back."

A grin spread across his lips. "I wasn't talking about Eliza."

She blinked. "Then who…"

"Theron…" Quintin said, a hint of warning in his tone, "you cannot seriously be thinking…"

"You're talking about impersonating a Daughter," Ambrose said, shaking his head. "It will never work. There are too many Wardens in the Sanctum. They'll drain any crystal faster than the nexus can recharge it. Why do you think we've never managed to replace one of them before?"

He was right. From what Theron had explained about weaving back at the Falkenrath manor, no crystal could possibly be large enough to maintain an illusion around too many Wardens, not unless…

Kaila's skin crawled as she realised what Theron was getting at.

"Oh ye of little imagination," Theron continued, grinning as he met Kaila's eyes. "Just for a moment, think what we could achieve with someone inside. Someone that could find out everything there is to know about the princess, about the king's illness and what the Sisters might be scheming." He eyed Ambrose. "And most importantly, ensure no one goes around asking questions about one missing Eliza Wrenn."

"Your speculation is pointless—my weaving would fail. You can't simply alter facts, Theron, however much you might wish it."

"The illusion wouldn't fail if you sent someone who can charge agimet crystals," Kaila whispered.

Quintin and Ambrose turned to stare at her, both wearing a frown, while Theron beamed. "Exactly!"

"That's not possible," the others said in unison.

"Unless you're a Warden," she said quietly.

Silence.

"What is this?" Ambrose asked, looking from Kaila to Theron. "What is she saying?"

The Mover shrugged. "We always wondered what the selection criteria for a Warden was," he said. "Kaila has definitively solved that mystery."

Two heads turned to stare at Kaila once more.

"I can charge agimet without waiting for the nexus," she said quietly, lowering her eyes. "I was meant to be a Warden, but a mistake was made during my Trial."

"Theron, you knew about this?" Ambrose demanded.

"I told you she was an asset," he replied. "She also passed her Trials without revealing herself as Elysian."

"*What?*" Ambrose's voice rose above the others. "*How?*"

"I don't know," Kaila croaked.

"How can you *not* know?"

"She never knew her mother, but her father swore she wasn't Elysian."

"You and I both know that doesn't mean much, Theron."

Theron shrugged, but offered nothing more and silence fell over the basement. Nostrils flared, Ambrose turned his gaze back to Kaila, though there was less hostility this time, and more curiosity. Kaila swallowed. It was like he had just seen her for the first time—and was now sizing her up as prey. She preferred the open hostility.

Quintin, on the other hand, was slowly shaking his head. "Forget it, Theron. Whatever strange powers the girl has, she's not ready for something like this."

"What other choice do we have?"

The Psionic pursed his lips, glancing at the unconscious Daughter. "Plan A."

Kaila's stomach clenched. He was talking about killing Eliza. She couldn't let it happen.

"I'll do it."

Even as Kaila spoke the words, she doubted them. The trembling from earlier had returned and the iron band around her gut had only grown tighter.

They killed everyone.

She thought of the townsfolk in Elgoss, the people she had seen every day of her life until Theron had come. The former soldiers, Tomas and Sareen, doing their best to keep their little paradise safe. The men in the mine who had served with her father. Evan the village baker and poor Jacob, just a scared little boy. Now they were all dead, and she and Eliza were the only ones left.

Kaila couldn't let them hurt her. Even if it meant marching into the heart of the Sanctum and taking on the Wardens and the Sisters and Daughters, she couldn't. So when the three men turned to stare at her, she lifted her chin and met their gaze with defiance.

Theron was the first to break. Chuckling, he turned to the other two. "There you have it."

"Are you sure, Kaila?" Quintin asked.

"No," she said quietly, "but Ambrose is right—this was my fault. And if this is the only way to protect Eliza..." Her gaze shifted to the unconscious girl. "Then this is what I have to do."

There was a final silence as Quintin puffed out his cheeks and exhaled, before offering a nod. Together, they looked to Ambrose, who was still studying Kaila with that odd look.

"You can really charge agimet?" he asked, his eyes never leaving hers.

She nodded.

He pursed his lips. "Well then, it's doable. But there's one other problem."

"And what's that, my grouchy friend?" Theron asked with a roll of his eyes.

"The collar. Like I said, they can track those things, and if she shows up outside the gates of the Sanctum without the real thing, she's toast."

"Well, its good thing we have a real one on hand."

"Only if the girl is willing to remove it," Ambrose replied. "We don't exactly have a key."

They all turned to stare at Eliza. Kaila shivered as the smile faded from Theron's lips, a glint appearing in his eyes.

"She will," he said quietly. "I'll make sure of it."

8

"Here, put this on your nose," Ambrose said as Kaila joined him in his workshop upstairs, where he was ostensibly going to use his Gift to disguise her as Eliza. "It'll help with the smell."

Instead, the man held out a wooden peg to her.

"Ahhh, what smell?" she asked, suddenly doubtful. "I thought—"

"It doesn't matter what you thought," he said, cutting her off. "We do not have time for your questions, girl. Any minute now, the Magisterium is going to notice your little friend is missing and send out a search party. If you really want to fix your mistake, you are going to shut up and put this on your nose."

Kaila glared at the man. She didn't like anyone speaking to her like that—least of all a man dressed in a suit fine enough to make even the king feel underdressed. But his words left no leeway for argument, so she took the peg and did as he ordered.

The tailor spent the next few minutes bustling about the workshop. She watched with curiosity as he mixed liquids and various jars and muttered to himself about chemicals and meddling children. The smell must have been terrible, but she noticed Ambrose had a pair of far more comfortable looking nose plugs for himself.

She didn't complain. At the very least, it was fascinating to watch him work. Was all this really needed for one weaving? She hadn't realised there would be so many steps. For her power, all she'd ever needed was a piece of agimet. But this was something else entirely.

Finally, his concoction ready, Ambrose waved for her to lay her head back in a metal sink. She had even more misgivings about *this* instruction, but a glare from the tailor was enough to silence any other offending questions.

When he turned on a tap and poured water over her head, however, it was almost too much. The running water itself wasn't so strange—by now she'd encountered it many times in Tah'raus. Another miracle produced by the stolen agimet. Of course, those like herself who lived in halfway houses and abandoned factories didn't enjoy such luxuries, but more than a few of the manors she and Theron had burgled—and the Falkenrath mansion itself —did.

That he wanted to do something with the foul chemicals and her hair, however, had Kaila ready to demand an explanation. Unfortunately, she had to swallow the words or drown, as the tailor diverted a stream of water over her face. She was still gasping and choking when he turned off the tap and returned with his strange concoction.

"You will want to keep very still for this next part."

Before Kaila could object, he gathered a handful of her hair and applied a brushful of the gelatinous paste. She froze, eying the concoction warily from the corner of her eyes as Ambrose smeared it generously on her long locks. By the time he was finished, she could detect the acrid scent of burning, even with the peg on her nose.

"What exactly is that stuff?" she asked, her heart beginning to pound as she futilely tried to get a better look at her hair.

"Don't move," Ambrose repeated. "The chemical will burn if

it touches your skin. I had to use the quick and nasty stuff, since this is a rush job. Sorry."

He didn't look sorry at all, however. He was already gathering fresh supplies for some other concoction. Glaring at his back, Kaila wished Theron could have joined them. Quintin had ducked out to check for signs the Sanctum might know Eliza was missing. Hopefully he would be back soon with good news.

Theron was downstairs with Eliza.

Her stomach churned. Just thinking about the girl manifested a confusing mess of emotion. So many horrible things had passed between them, yet if what Eliza said was true, they were the only ones left from their village. The only ones who remembered…

She blinked quickly as Ambrose returned, struggling to keep the tears from falling. Absorbed in his work, the tailor didn't seem to notice. She waited patiently as he washed the gel from her hair with fresh water. Only as he offered her a towel did Kaila notice the water draining from the tub.

It was black.

A chill crept over her skin. Her hands went to her hair, grasping a raven-black lock and pulling it in front of her face to see.

But her hair wasn't black anymore—it was blonde.

"What did you do!" she gasped, half-rising from her chair and swinging on Ambrose. Rage drained her face of blood. Kaila wasn't exactly vain about her looks and there was nothing particularly special about her hair. Most of the villagers in Elgoss had the same shade of black—although it was rarer in Tah'raus, where most were brown, blonde, or auburn. But…her father had black hair.

Ambrose didn't care about any of that though. He wore the same impassive look he always favoured, lips pursed tight, studying her.

"It will grow out," he said simply, though his tone carried a note of judgement. "Now, would you like to sit down so we can continue?"

In the end, she acquiesced. What else could she do? The deed was done, and from the collection of chemicals and instruments Ambrose had prepared, the job was far from finished. In fact, the tailor was already puttering around with his equipment, readying his next method of torture. She suspected he was enjoying her suffering.

"I thought you were supposed to be good at weaving," she muttered as she resumed her seat.

"I'm not just good, *girl*," Ambrose replied with a scowl. "I'm the best."

Kaila raised an eyebrow. Was that vanity? The comment had clearly struck a nerve—it gave her an idea.

She snorted. "The best wouldn't need all these…props."

"Only amateurs rely solely on their Gift."

Before she could get another word in, he grabbed a handful of her hair and took to it with a brush, yanking and wrenching at the knots without so much as a ration chip of mercy for her squeals. Kaila was forced to grit her teeth through the torment. By the time he finished, tears of pain were watering in her eyes, but she was ready with her next question.

"I think I get it," she said slyly, "this is in case your magic fails."

"*No*," Ambrose growled, brandishing a pair of scissors. "It's so the magic *doesn't* fail."

Moving behind her, he went to work on her long locks. Eliza had grown out her hair somewhat since arriving in Tah'raus—but it still barely reached her shoulders. Kaila's was almost to her waist.

"So your Gift only works if I look like the person you're copying?" she muttered, more to distract herself than anything else at this point. "What good is that?"

Snip-snip.

"Crafting the perfect illusion is a *process*." Even with her back to him, Kaila could tell the tailor was speaking through his teeth. "It has to be done the right way—like prepping a house to be painted."

Snip-snip.

"Ah *what?*" Kaila grated, trying not to notice the long strands of hair gathering around her feet.

"First," Ambrose continued as if he couldn't hear her distress, "you sand back the wood. Then you dust it down. That way when you start with your primer, you don't get any bubbles or imperfections in the paint."

Snip-snip.

"Primer?" Kaila gasped.

"So the following coats stick. You can have one, two, sometimes even three coats of paint. Always sanding and dusting in between. Do it right, and the job will last a decade or two. Take shortcuts, and you'll be redoing the entire job within a year."

Snip-snip.

Would he leave her with anything?

"What does any of this have to do with *Elysian magic?*"

Lips pursed, Ambrose stepped back from her to appraise his work. Kaila didn't dare ask for a mirror.

"For my weaving to succeed without me around to constantly repair its imperfections," Ambrose said at last, "the target needs to be as similar as possible to the illusion." He nodded to himself a final time. "Yes, almost done now."

"So all this," Kaila murmured as Ambrose wandered into the back of his workshop. "It's preparation to make the final illusion…stick?"

"Exactly." Returning with one of the agimet furnaces the nobility used to heat their chambers, Ambrose set it in front of her. This device looked to have been modified to hold several iron rods, which Ambrose now carefully removed with a gloved hand. "Now don't move—"

"Or something terrible will happen to me," Kaila snapped.

"I get it." Clenching her jaw, she held his gaze, challenging him to reprimand her again.

Ambrose just grunted and set about his business. Taking a handful of her hair, he wrapped it around one of the heated rods. Despite her blustery words, feeling the heat of the burning iron so close to her scalp was almost too much. But Kaila Dwyn had faced Wardens and Elysian assassins; she would survive this as well.

Leaving the irons in her hair, Ambrose moved onto her face, starting with a light brush of makeup, before moving onto more delicate matters. Kaila barely dared breathe as he traced a pencil across her eyelashes, the tip coming far too close to her eyes for her liking. But at least this part didn't involve any horrible chemicals, burning or cutting, so she held her tongue as he finished, and then removed the heated rods from her hair.

Stepping back, he studied her with those cold eyes for several long minutes, until Kaila couldn't hold her tongue any longer.

"Well?" she asked, exasperated. "Am I good enough for your magic to work?"

"See for yourself," Ambrose replied.

The tailor rummaged amongst his things, coming up with a hand mirror. Kaila took it with hesitant fingers, trepidation fluttering in her chest to see what he'd done…

The breath caught in her throat as she found a stranger staring back at her. Her once-wild hair had been tamed, transformed into blonde curls. The makeup was subtle, yet her skin seemed softer, her lips fuller, her cheeks a delicate flush of pink instead of the dirt and grime of her recent appearance. She could have been mistaken for Eliza's sister, though they were both only children.

"Well?" Ambrose asked. Unless she was mistaken, there was a touch of pride in his voice.

"I take back everything I said," she murmured. "Do I even need the weaving?

The elderly tailor snorted. "We still need to fix your eyes."

Kaila's stomach tightened. "How…"

Ambrose was already revealing a small leather case from the drawer of his desk. "Here," he said, handing it to her, "these should do the trick."

Kaila arched an eyebrow as she accepted the offering. Popping open the case, she found a tiny vial of water with a strange pair of glass lenses floating inside. "What are they?"

"Coloured contact lenses. They'll change your eyes to hazel." He hesitated. "They'll also help to hide minor uses of your Gift, though I would recommend against using it inside the Sanctum. Given you're a Mover, I don't have high expectations you'll listen to that advice."

Kaila eyed the lenses warily. "How do they work?"

"Another invention curtesy of the Magisterium and their obsession with agimet," Ambrose replied. "Someone figured out how to concentrate the *atar* from a crystal into a beam fine enough to cut glass. They were designed for vision correction, but with a little added colouring, we've adopted them for our own uses."

"You put these in your *eyes?*"

"Would you rather have a Warden notice they're the wrong colour?"

"No, I suppose not," Kaila muttered.

Following Ambrose's instructions—and a great, *great* deal of cursing—she managed to get them in.

"Trickster's *balls*," she gasped, blinking rapidly. "I feel like my eyes are on fire."

"Did I not mention that part?"

"*No!*" She could have sworn the man was smiling, though it was difficult to tell through the tears.

"You'll get used to them. Though make sure you remove them every few hours and place them back in the water. And *definitely* do not sleep with them—otherwise they could blind you."

"Are they *really* necessary?"

"Yes."

"Fine," she muttered, struggling to hold her temper. The things *burned.* "So what now? Are we ready for this illusion?"

The tailor grunted. "As ready as we're going to get on such short notice."

Returning one final time to his desk, he removed a silver bangle from the drawer. It shone with the light of a dozen agimet crystals, each finely cut and polished so as to stay in their settings. Her skin crawled as he opened the clasp and placed it around her wrist.

"One of the crystals is uncut," he explained. "It's encased in polished glass to disguise it, but you should be able to feel the difference with your Gift." He hesitated. "Your Warden's ability, will you be able to use it through the glass?"

Kaila nodded. She and Theron had conducted a few experiments with her power when they'd first arrived in Tah'raus. So long as the crystal was on her person, she should be able to direct the power of the nexus into the agimet, charging it almost instantly.

"Good," Ambrose grunted. "Your appearance is now similar enough to Eliza's that the weaving should last the twelve hours under normal circumstances, but if you encounter a Warden in that black armour, you will have to use your other ability. I would recommend avoiding them as much as possible."

"No need to tell me twice," Kaila agreed. "When will you do the weaving?"

"It's already done," Ambrose replied, holding up a mirror.

Kaila's face grew cold as she stared into the eyes of her old rival. Eliza Wrenn. She had already changed into the girl's clothing, but while *she* could feel it hanging loose in some places, and too tight in others, in the mirror it now appeared to fit her perfectly. And her face…if before they could have been sisters, now there would be no telling one from the other.

"Ambrose…" she breathed, hardly able to believe her eyes.

"Told you, didn't I?" There was no mistaking the pleasure in his voice this time. "Been doing this longer than you've been alive, girl. How do you think I got where I am now?"

The words resurfaced some of Kaila's earlier doubts. They might not speak about it, but they all knew this plan was a long shot. Even ignoring the fact half their hopes were pinned on what was pretty much myth and legend about the Aegis at this point, the idea they could fool the Magisterium long enough to reach the throne…it was ludicrous if you paused more than one second to think about it.

So what did a man like Ambrose Braider get from a job like this?

"Ambrose," she said quietly, "why are you doing this?"

The tailor had just begun to pack away his equipment, but he paused at the question, glancing up from his desk. "Why do you ask?"

"You have *everything*," she said softly. "Why would you risk it all on a fairy tale?"

"That depends on what you mean by everything."

She frowned. "You have wealth and power," she said. "The nobility accept you—Trickster's own hand, *you're practically one of them*, the way they talk about you. The way they *act* around you."

The tailor's expression did not alter, but she sensed something from him, like the distant blasting of a trumpet.

"If you believe that, girl," he said at last, "then you are even more naïve than I thought."

"What—"

"*Enough*," he snapped, eyes flashing with a hint of *atar*. "Instead of questioning *my* motives, how about you concentrate on your own task. For all our sakes. If you can't replace that girl in the Magisterium, we're all as like to end up swinging in Soul Square, remember?"

Swallowing the lump that had appeared in her throat, Kaila nodded.

"Good," the tailor grunted. "Now, why don't you go and find out if Theron has convinced your friend to part with her collar."

So saying, he went to the bookcase and selected a book with a red spine. As he pulled it, the shelving swung outwards, revealing the hidden staircase which led to the basement. She shuffled past as he waved for her to descend, still struggling with his words. The tailor wasn't a persona for Ambrose the way it was with Theron, a stolen face and borrowed riches. The fruits of his success were all around them, the workshop, the fine clothes, even the way the Falkenrath servant had bowed and scraped before him. And yet his anger when she'd questioned him…

"Ambrose," she said, glancing back from the darkness of the passageway. "Did you really used to paint houses?"

The tailor still stood in the entrance, glaring down at her. "What do you think?"

"I…I don't know what to think."

He grunted and held up his hands. "Do these look like they're used to hard labour?"

Kaila swallowed. His skin was soft and pale, without so much as a callous. "No…"

"No," he agreed. "A client told me the story once. I thought it an appropriate metaphor for my work. Now get moving, the sun will be up in a few hours. If we don't have that collar, my weaving won't get you past the front gate."

9

"**M**y *sweet daughter, I am so sorry, come here.*"
Soft arms embraced Eliza, filling her with warmth…

Eliza resisted as she felt the tug of reality against her consciousness. For the first time in months, there was no pain or sorrow or anger, not even the hatred that had consumed her since she'd learned of Elgoss's destruction. So she clung to the lie of her mother's embrace…

…until a bucket of ice cold water tore away even that scant comfort.

Coughing and choking, Eliza surged upright—only to find her hands and feet bound to a wooden chair. The coarse rope bit into her skin, and the sudden movement sent the chair lurching sideways. The wood groaned as it teetered on one leg, before gravity reasserted itself, settling her back on solid ground with a thud.

"Oh, good, you're awake."

Head pounding, mind still fuzzy, Eliza squinted through watery eyes at the speaker. There was a furry texture in her mouth, like she'd forgotten to brush her teeth the night before, and for the first few seconds, everything appeared dark and blurry.

She struggled to recall where she was, what had happened. There had been a noise in the street…then someone had been standing over her…and later, voices, speaking. She had opened her eyes and seen…

Kaila.

Burning eyes appeared amidst the darkness. A face; not the pale and haggard Kaila Dwyn, but a man. He sat in a chair opposite her, one leg crossed over the other, a piece of agimet held casually between his fingers. Eliza had grown used to seeing the deadly gemstones since arriving in Tah'raus, but this crystal was different. It didn't glow a pure white, but pulsed from one colour to the next, always changing. And as the colours changed, so too did the light that shone in the man's eyes.

Eliza did her best to jerk away from the Elysian, but the bindings held her tight. She opened her mouth to scream—only for an invisible force to clamp tight around her jaw, silencing her.

"Ah, ah, ah, I didn't say you could speak yet."

Panic well and truly taking hold, Eliza tried to scream again, but the pressure only tightened. The man leaned closer, eyes burning brightly with unholy *atar*.

"Are you done?" he asked, lips twisted in a sneer.

Eliza quelled, slumping defeated in the chair. Her entire body trembled as fear spread like acid through her limbs. The enemy had her. Every Daughter knew what foul, horrible things the Elysian did to their human prisoners—especially members of the Magisterium.

And here she was, helpless, unable to so much as speak without the Elysian's permission. Even her thoughts might not be her own—some of these creatures had dark powers over the human mind. So she clung to her hatred, and prayed for the protection of the First Matron.

Nodding, the man leaned back in his chair. "Good," he said quietly. With a gesture, the pressure around her jaw vanished. "Then if you don't mind, I have some questions for you."

"Who are you?" she growled, clinging to her rage like it was her only buoyancy in a storm upon the ocean. "Do you have any idea who I am?"

Her eyes darted around the room. It was the same place she had woken earlier; strewn with discarded cloth and rolls of old silk and offcuts piled high in the corners. There were no windows and only a single iron stairwell for an exit. As far as she could tell though, they were alone.

There was no sign of Kaila. Doubt touched Eliza. Had she ever been there at all—or had that just been another phantom from her past come to mock her, like the dream of her mother.

Leaning forward in his chair, the man steepled his fingers. "Only your name, Eliza," he said quietly. Her skin crawled, hearing her name from his mouth. "And that you're a Daughter of the Magisterium. But I'm glad you mentioned it, cause that is, in fact, why we're here. You see, I want to know everything there is to know about you."

"I'll never tell you anything," Eliza said with more conviction than she felt.

"Are you sure?" Suddenly the pressure was back, only now it closed around her throat, the collar squeezing into her flesh like a vice. She opened her mouth to cry out, but only a squeak emerged. "Never is just so *permanent*, don't you think? Like a Daughter who trips and ends up at the bottom of the harbour, *never* to be seen again."

Cold touched Eliza's heart. Her courage wilted before the stranger's threats. "Please…"

"Oh none of that now." Abruptly, the pressure vanished. Grasping his chair, the man scooted it closer, until their knees were practically touching. He leaned in, so close that Eliza could smell the wine on his breath. "Come on, you're a *Daughter* aren't you? I've never tortured one of your kind before! Where's that famous wit? The iron loyalty to the Magisterium?" Throwing back his head, he howled with laughter.

Eliza shuddered. This man was clearly insane. She strained

against her bindings, desperate to get away, but there was no give in the coarse fibres.

"I won't…" she started, but as she spoke the man's head snapped around, a mad smile stretching his lips.

"That's more like it!" he gasped. With a flourish, a knife appeared in his hand. "Now, let's put that defiance to the test. Where shall we start?"

He leaned in, bringing the blade to within an inch of her face. It crept closer, the cold steel resting against her lips.

"The tongue?" he mused.

Eliza gave a strangled cry and tried to lean away, but his hand shot out and caught her by the chin.

"No, that's no good," he tisked, tapping the flat of the blade against her cheek. "Need you to talk, don't I? Eye, yes, how about the eyes?" He shifted the dagger again, so that it pointed at her eye. "You don't need those to talk."

It was too much. "*No!*" Eliza cried, squeezing her eyes shut, for all the good that would do. "Please, I'll tell you anything you want!"

That laughter again. "Are you sure?" he pressed. Eliza didn't dare open her eyes for fear of what he might do. "Don't you think a Daughter should resist at least *a little* torture before spilling her guts? You know, for reputation's sake?"

"Please…" she sobbed, wits abandoning her entirely now. "Please, just tell me what you want, for the First Matron's sake."

The stranger chuckled. "Let's start with that pretty collar of yours."

A chill crept down Eliza's spine. "What about it?"

"I want it."

Her eyes snapped open, panic gripping her heart. The collar of a Daughter was sacred. It could only be removed by her hand —and she was forbidden. To do so would break her vow to Fresia and the Magisterium, to the Matron herself! And giving it to an Elysian…that would be nothing short of treason.

"Please, I can't…"

The dagger swept back up, its blade shimmering in the *starlight...*

"*Theron!* That's enough!"

Eliza startled as a woman's voice carried from above. Her head jerked up, heart catching in her throat. The point of the knife hovered barely an inch from her eye. But that was not what sent chills burning through her body.

A young woman descended the iron staircase.

It was her.

Her curly blonde locks and rosy cheeks, even her hated button nose. It was almost like looking in a mirror that moved and smiled and walked towards her. Only *this* Eliza's eyes were harsh, and she wore a disapproving frown, as though the real Eliza wasn't good enough to share the same room as her.

"Who are you?" she groaned.

A thin smile stretched the other Eliza's lips. "Why, I'm your conscience, Eliza," she mocked, approaching, "you probably don't recognise me."

Alarm spiked in Eliza's gut. She knew that voice. Not the tone, which was eerily similar to Eliza's, but the way she spoke, the manner of her words. A chill spread down her spine as she stared at her double.

"*Kaila?*" She practically bit the name as she spoke it. "So it *was* you behind all this."

"No, Eliza," the other Eliza said. Then she sighed. "I mean, yes." She shook her head. "This is not the way I wanted this to go."

"I suppose you didn't want to murder everyone in Elgoss either," Eliza spat back.

"I didn't!" Kaila cried, her foul mimicry of Eliza's face twisting in anger.

She leaned down, then stopped, trembling for a second over Eliza's chair. Her eyes slid closed, before she swung on Eliza's tormentor—who had gone silent.

"What the hell was that all about, Theron?"

The stranger stared back at her, unflinching. "I had it handled, Kaila."

"By putting out her *eye?*"

"I wasn't going to *actually* do it! Besides, it was working, wasn't it? She was about to give up!" He turned to Eliza with a look of exasperation. "You were, weren't you?"

Eliza glared at him. Righteous rage burned now in her heart. She knew what they planned to do. They wanted to use her collar and her identity to infiltrate the Sanctum. She couldn't let it happen.

"Never," she snarled.

"That word again," Theron tisked. "Come now, we've already seen how far courage will take you." He paused to glance at Kaila. "I'll give you a hint—not far."

"I don't care," Eliza interrupted before the other her could respond. "I won't help you slaughter any more innocents." Her voice cracked as she thought of her parents, murdered by Kaila's villainous hands.

"Innocents?" Kaila swung on her, fire burning in her false eyes. "You dare talk to *me* about innocents?"

"Kaila…" Hovering nearby, Theron tried to inject himself, but Kaila would not be dissuaded.

"*You*," she snarled, "whose family enslaved all of us in Elgoss." She leaned in close, and now Eliza saw the glint of *atar* burning in the girl's eyes. It was unnerving, to see that on her own face.

"How could you do it?" Kaila continued. "How could you look us in the eye, day after day, knowing what you were doing to us?"

"I *didn't* know!" Eliza snarled. Something in the girl's words struck that little piece of guilt she had harboured all these months.

A long silence followed her words. The other Eliza looked shocked, lips parted as though to refute her. Then she frowned, and the light slowly faded from her eyes.

"You're telling the truth, aren't you?"

"Of course I am."

"I'm telling the truth as well." Kaila looked away as she said it. "About Elgoss. It wasn't me. I ran. I never thought for a moment…" She bowed her head.

Confusion bubbled its way to the surface of Eliza's rage. Why would Kaila lie now, here of all places? What could the denial possibly serve?

"If it wasn't you, then who?"

"The Magisterium," the other her said quietly, "or the Wardens. They're all the same."

"*Liar!*" Her rage came rushing back, flushing away Eliza's doubt. How *dare* she?

Kaila sighed. "It doesn't matter what you think, Eliza," she said, straightening. Resolve hardened her face. "We need your collar."

"I'll never let you take my place."

It was eerie as the other her looked Eliza in the eyes. "You will," Kaila said coldly, "or I will go to Sutton Street wearing your face and use my Gift—and the entire world will see that Eliza Wrenn is one of the Elysian."

"*You wouldn't!*"

But Kaila did not flinch. The faint glow of *atar* appeared again in her eyes, slowly growing brighter. Eliza trembled as she held that iron gaze. The Elysian were the ruthless enemy of humanity, determined to subjugate and destroy their civilisation, to enslave them as they had all those centuries ago. She wanted to be brave, like T'iana the First Matron and all the other heroes who had defied the enemy in the face of certain death…

…but looking into those burning eyes, Eliza's courage crumbled and instead she bowed her head.

"I hate you."

"I don't care," Kaila's voice was cold.

"I'm not even sure I can remove it."

"You'd better hope that's not true," Kaila growled. There

was a moment's pause, before she continued in a softer tone. "Tell me how it works. Maybe we can help you."

Eliza shuddered. That was forbidden knowledge. But she was already doomed—she could not resist Theron's torture or Kaila's threats. The words slipped from her lips as she wilted.

"The Matron brought us into the depths of the Sanctum…" she trailed off, her voice quivering at the betrayal, "and bade us swear a vow before the Aegis."

"What vow?" Kaila pressed.

"To obey the Matron," she croaked. Why was she telling them this? She should have gone to her grave before opening her mouth to the enemy. Yet something nudged her, something Kaila had said, the *way* she had said it.

The Magisterium, or the Wardens. They're all the same.

There had been no anger in Kaila's words, no hatred or defiance. Just…resignation. Goosebumps spread along Eliza's skin. Kaila was telling the truth—or at least, what she *thought* was the truth.

"What happened next?" Kaila pressed.

"I swore the vow," she rasped, "and then the Matron placed the collar around my neck and closed it."

Never to be removed until your death…

She swallowed, recalling the Matron's words.

"What do you think, Theron?" Kaila asked.

"I think she's stalling," the thief growled, rising from his chair. The knife glinted in his hand as he approached—and then lunged towards Eliza.

She cried out, trying to pull away, but the ropes held her tight —until the blade slashed through the bindings. She gasped as her right arm came free, clutching it to her chest.

"No tricks," he said, looming over her. "Remove the collar, *now.*"

There was no mercy in the Elysian's eyes. Hands trembling, Eliza reached for the golden collar. There was a groove on the back—though it looked smooth to the naked eye. She had felt it many times, running her fingers over the barely perceptible lump, wondering what would happen if she pressed it. Her life in the Sanctum, her parents' deaths, nothing had been as she'd expected. But in the end, fear stopped her.

Now it was fear that drove her fingers to find the groove and press it.

For a second, nothing happened.

Then Eliza felt warmth around her neck, gentle at first, but it quickly grew hotter. The breath caught in her throat as she tried —and failed—to scream. It was as though the collar had turned to molten metal. Desperately, she clawed at the golden band, but though she'd pressed the catch, it refused to release. Instead, it seemed to be tightening. She caught the stench of burning smoke, tasted metal on her tongue and choked.

And still it burned hotter, searing into her flesh…

…and then the other Eliza was there, scrambling for the collar. The metal seemed to tighten in response, constricting, trying to kill her. She gasped, but it was like sucking air through a narrow straw. Stars burst before Eliza's eyes, red at first, then black, threatening at the corners of her vision. But Eliza—Kaila—was still there, still clawing for the gold, struggling—

With a cry of triumph, Kaila tore it loose and threw the burning thing to the floor. Eliza gasped, sweet air rushing to fill her lungs, and sagged in her chair. The pain…it was unlike anything she had ever felt. She barely heard the others speak above the ringing in her ears.

"What the hell was that?"

"You didn't think the Magisterium would let its servants betray them without reprisal, did you?"

"You *knew* this would happen?"

Silence.

"*Bastard!* She could have died!"

"She would already be dead if not for you."

A longer silence this time. Pain, searing, agony. Head

dangling in her lap, Eliza clung to consciousness. The darkness receded somewhat, though not the pain.

"Will…will the same thing happen…if I put it on?"

"I…don't think so."

"You don't *think* so?" Kaila gasped. "What the hell does that mean!"

"You haven't sworn any vows to the Aegis," Theron said calmly. "Theoretically, you should be fine." He hesitated. "Of course, no one's ever done this before, either."

"Then…"

"It doesn't matter," Theron said quietly. "Even if I'm wrong, when we have the Aegis, we can use its magic to remove the collar."

"Unless we fail."

"We won't."

The darkness was looming again. Eliza barely held to the light. It hurt so much. But she needed to know, to see. Light drilled into her skull as she forced her eyes to open, her head to lift. Theron and Kaila stood over her, eyes on one another, but with her movement, they turned. Kaila's face—or rather, the fake Eliza's face—softened. A long moment passed as they stared at one another, until Eliza felt the darkness swirl, the abyss rising to sweep her away.

"Kaila…" she whispered, fighting against the pain. "Why…"

The other girl grimaced. "Because it's the right thing to do."

The last thing Eliza saw before the darkness swallowed her up was the collar closing around the throat of her old enemy.

10

"Are you sure you're ready for this?"

Kaila blinked. Her eyes and thoughts had been on Eliza. Her old enemy had finally surrendered to the pain and lost consciousness. They'd moved her to a cot Garrick had set in the corner and brought cold water and ice to cool her burns. Even so, Eliza would be scarred for life.

If she even recovered from her wounds. Kaila shuddered, recalling the sight of Eliza's skin bubbling, and her screams, the terror in her eyes. Despite their past, she couldn't stand back and watch while her enemy suffered, not like that...

...her hand went instinctively to the collar she now wore. The gold was cool to the touch, unmarked by whatever twisted magic the Magisterium had used against its original owner. Yet again they had outdone themselves—except this time, it was against their own followers.

But Theron had asked her something, and blinking she finally tore her gaze from the sleeping Daughter.

"Am I *ready*?" she croaked, fingers tightening around the gold collar. "No?" Her voice cracked, tears springing to her eyes. "Theron, I don't know—"

Theron drew her into a hug.

She was surprised. He had kept her at a distance since that night in Iselador. It hurt—but she accepted it. After learning the truth about agimet, she hardly even cared. All that mattered was revenge. But now…now Kaila hugged him back with a desperation she hadn't known lay inside of her, sobbing, burying her head in his shoulder as all the anger and fear and hatred came rushing out.

"Theron, what am I doing?" she gasped. "Quintin was right. I'm not cut out for any of this!"

"No, Kaila." His arms held her tight. "You're stronger than you think. Believe me, if I didn't know you could do this, I wouldn't have let you put on that collar."

She swallowed, the cold metal pressing against her flesh. It terrified her, recalling what had happened to Eliza. But Theron was right—she had come too far now to turn back. Slowly, painfully, she rose from that empty pit in her heart and found herself clinging to Theron like he was the only thing solid in a world of chaos.

Remembering herself, she released him and stepped back. He wore a little twist on his lips that looked a lot like pity. Thankfully, the squeal of the hidden door saved them from further awkwardness.

"Doesn't look like she's been missed yet," Quintin announced as he descended. "It's getting late though; if she's still doing this, it's time we got moving…" He trailed off as he reached the basement and saw the pair of them.

Or rather, saw Kaila wearing Eliza's face. There was a moment where the Psionic just stood there, lips pursed and sharp eyes watching. Then he gave a grunt.

"Well, I see Ambrose hasn't lost his touch," he muttered. "And that's her real collar?" When they both nodded, the crease in his forehead deepened. "Were the stories…"

"Afraid so," Theron confirmed.

"Trickster be *damned*, Theron," Quintin muttered. "That changes everything—"

"It doesn't change anything," Kaila interrupted, lifting her chin to meet the man's eyes. "I still need to take her place to stop them looking for her."

The Psionic sighed. "Agimet save us all, there's two of them," he said with a roll of his eyes. "Well, come on then, I'll escort you to the gates of the Sanctum."

That gave Kaila pause. "Not Theron?"

"Theron Falkenrath," Quintin grunted, "should already be tucked away safely in his bed. He *definitely* shouldn't be seen wandering the streets with random Daughters that *are not* the princess."

Kaila pursed her lips. The man had a point.

"Remember, all you need to do is pretend to be your friend. That should be enough to keep them off our backs," Theron said, resting a hand on her shoulder. "If you find out any information about the prince or the princess, that's just a bonus." He hesitated. "Don't worry, you'll be fine."

Nodding, Kaila glanced at the cot in the corner. "And Eliza?"

"Ambrose will keep an eye on her."

"I'm sure he's going to love that," Quintin muttered.

<hr>

The Sanctum loomed in the darkness, its enormous dome silhouetted against the night sky. Shadows seemed to stretch and twist around it, as if its very presence was a stain upon the heart of the city. Kaila's steps faltered as they neared the gates, her breath coming in sharp, uneven gasps.

Quintin walked beside her, his face grim. "Almost there."

The words did nothing to calm her nerves. Suddenly her mouth was parched. She could almost see the gates. A tremor shook her. Was she really going through with this? Up until now, it hadn't fully struck her, the magnitude of what she intended to do. Impersonating a Daughter was one thing, but disguising herself as one to sneak into the Sanctum itself…

Suddenly, her entire body was shaking. In her mind, she was back in the Iron Pinnacles, watching the Warden's inexorable climb toward them, feeling the suffocating weight of his magic pressing against her mind. She came to a halt in the street and Quintin glanced back at her with a frown.

"I'm going to mess this up, aren't I?" the words came tumbling out before she could stop them.

Quintin didn't respond. She wondered if he was using his powers on her again. His eyes lacked the glint of *atar*, but she knew now there were ways to mask that, lenses like what Ambrose had given her. But if the Psionic was using his Gift, she didn't feel any different. Rubbing a hand through the stubble on his chin, he studied her before giving a shrug.

"Probably."

Kaila blinked. "Ah…"

"Not what you were expecting to hear?" Quintin asked with a grin.

She jerked her head from side to side, the heat of fear seeping through her limbs, eyes burning. *It's just the lenses*, she told herself.

The older man crossed his arms. "Would you prefer I lied to you?"

Gritting her teeth, Kaila forced herself to meet his gaze. "You don't like me very much, do you?"

This time it was Quintin's turn to blink. "Why do you say that?"

"Because I'm angry," she said, "because I hate them."

To her surprise, Quintin chuckled. "Perhaps I was a little harsh on you earlier," he said. "But it's only because it pains me to see another young Elysian following down that same well-worn path."

Her stomach churned. "Maybe you're right," she whispered, unable to meet his eyes. "When I saw Eliza, all I could *think* about was hurting her. But when the time came…" She swallowed. "I was a fool."

"You'll get no argument from me. But I'm proud of you all the same."

She frowned. "Why?"

"Because even though you had every reason to kill your old enemy, you spared her instead." He offered a wistful smile. "It makes me think there might be hope for the rest of us as well."

Kaila hung her head. "But I still screwed up."

"We *all* screw up at times—even Theron."

"Sure he does."

"*He does*," Quintin said, surprising her with the vehemence in his tone. "He just *expects it*, is all. That's the secret to this profession, you see. You can't just stroll through this world thinking you're never going to make a mistake."

"Why would I want to make a mistake?"

"It's not a matter of *want*, it's a matter of *fact*. It will happen."

"Not if I plan—"

"For everything?" Quintin smirked. "Believe me, smarter men and women have stood where you are now and said the same thing. Do you know what happened to them?"

She shook her head.

"They froze," he said softly, "they became too afraid of their mistakes to make an actual decision."

"So, what?" Kaila pressed. "I just make mistakes on purpose?"

"Now you're being purposely dense." His eyes shone with amusement. "My oldest is like that. No, you don't make mistakes on *purpose*, but you accept you will never be perfect. You prepare for when you do inevitably mess up. Like painting a wall—you know you're going to make mistakes. Eventually, you'll get paint somewhere the paint shouldn't go. But if you have a damp cloth on hand, you can wipe those mistakes away without ruining the entire job."

Kaila frowned. "Ambrose told me a metaphor about painting earlier as well."

"That's how we all met," Quintin explained, "didn't you know? Before Ambrose was…well, Ambrose, he was like the rest of us—bowing and scraping for coin, hoping to save up enough one day for a piece of agimet on the black market."

"So you painted houses as a cover?"

"Sometimes. Sometimes we just needed food."

Do these hands look like they're used to hard labour?

She swallowed, grappling to reconcile the image of the impeccably dressed tailor with that of a common labourer.

"So…" she said at last, forcing the conversation back to more pressing matters. "You're saying I need to be ready for things to go wrong."

Quintin offered a warm smile. "Exactly. And realise it doesn't have to be the end of the world."

She sighed. Given her circumstances, the end of the world wasn't exactly outside the scope of possibilities, but she took the point. If she let those worries consume her, how could she possibly move forward?

"Alright," she breathed. The trembling receded.

More out of habit than anything, she reached into her pocket to check the compartment Ambrose had added. Her fingers brushed against the hidden crystal. Normally she would have feared just to touch it while in public, but the tailor had assured her the weaving and lenses combined would hide the faint glow in her eyes, and she needed the reassurance of its *atar*.

Instead, she froze as her hand closed around the crystal and she felt…nothing. The shaking returned a hundred-fold as she looked up at Quintin. He must have seen the sudden terror in her eyes, for he frowned and drew her into the shadows of a nearby alleyway.

"What is it?"

"My agimet," she whispered, drawing out the crystal and holding it in her palm. "I can't use it!"

"*What?*" Quintin hissed.

"The *atar* inside, I can sense it, *feel it,* but I can't draw from it. It's like my Gift is—"

She broke off as realisation dawned on her. It must have come to Quintin as well, for they each stood staring at each other as the seconds ticked past.

The collar.

Her hand went to the cold metal around her throat. "It's blocking my Gift," she whispered. "How is that possible?"

"Eliza said the Aegis was involved…" Quintin rasped, then shook his head. "It doesn't matter. We have to call this off."

"What?"

"Kaila, we can't send you in there alone without your power!"

"I don't have a choice!" she replied desperately, fingers closing around the collar. "If it can block my Gift…"

The panic built inside her as she followed that trail of thought. If it could block her Gift, did that mean the protections were also in place? The collar tightened like a noose around her throat as she remembered Eliza's screams.

"We'll find another way, Kaila," Quintin whispered. "When we take the Aegis—"

"There won't *be* a heist if they come looking for Eliza," she replied. Lifting her chin, she met the Psionic's eyes. "I have to do this, Quintin."

He pursed his lips, looking doubtful. "What about the weaving? It'll fail without your power."

Her skin crawled. He was right. Gritting her teeth, she turned her vision inwards and called upon her Warden's power. The nexus flickered into sight, curls of power drifting through the city. Trembling, she reached for one—and was surprised when it responded to her command, swirling down to touch the crystal in her hand.

"It works," she breathed, relief washing through her. Her head lifted. A frown still creased Quintin's brow. She forced a smile. "Be ready for things to go wrong, right?" she repeated his words back to him.

Shaking his head, the Psionic let out a sigh. "Theron is going to be apocalyptic when he finds out."

Kaila exhaled her relief. "Thank you, Quintin," she said quietly, "for believing in me."

He nodded. "Don't make me regret it." Then he hesitated, his gaze lingering on her face. "Incredible. There's not a hint of *atar…*" he trailed off, lips twisted as though in thought.

Goosebumps tickled Kaila's scalp. "I'll manage," she whispered and slipped the crystal back into her pocket. "I survived most of my life without it."

"You know what they'll do if they catch you."

Almost as one, their eyes drifted to the dome that loomed above the alleyway. They were almost there. Kaila's legs began to shake again. She swallowed. She needed to go now, or she would never do it."

"I think it's time I went on alone," she whispered.

The Psionic opened his mouth as though to say something, then closed it again and nodded. She reached out and squeezed his hand, then turned and headed for the street.

"Anything you'd like me to pass on to Theron?"

She froze as the question chased after her. Warmth flushed her cheeks as she recalled Theron holding her, comforting her. *My rock amidst the storm.*

Then she remembered his own part in all this, imagined him with the auburn beauty of the princess, the pair of them close, and Theron leaning down to kiss her…

"No," she said quietly, not daring to look back. "He knows what he's doing. I'll see you again when all this is over, I hope."

Without another word, she turned the corner and started up the street towards the gates of the Sanctum.

―――――

Lingering in the shadows across the street, Jenna Frye watched the Daughter that had met with Theron in the tailor's shop re-emerge from the alleyway. Theron's servant appeared a short while later and headed in the direction of the Falkenrath mansion.

She lingered, even after both had disappeared from her sight, considering what she had learnt. It wasn't much, if she was honest. Clearly, *something* was going on—but then, that wasn't altogether surprising with a family like the Falkenraths. Much as Iron Hands might protest at the inference, he was still a powerful man and thus as much involved in the politics of the realm as any other noble.

But whose game was he playing—her father's or the Matron's? Or perhaps the elder Falkenrath had some other agenda all of his own on the books.

Jenna pursed her lips, considering her options. She could do the diplomatic thing and demand answers from her father and the general. But the king was just as stubborn as his daughter and would likely spend days evading the question, and it could be weeks before she received a response by pigeon from the frontier.

What's a girl to do?

There was another option of course—go straight to the source. Smiling, she reached into her bodice and drew out the dagger concealed in the cleavage. The razor point shimmered in the moonlight. Most of the court might think the princess was just another pretty face, but she hadn't always wanted to be a Daughter. There had been a warrior woman in her father's court when Jenna had been just a child. Years ago she'd disappeared, but not before mentoring the young princess in the way of the blade. Even now, Jenna kept up her lessons with her tutors maybe that was why her mother so despised her.

But now it was time to put them to some use—and pay Theron Falkenrath a home visit.

11

"**D**aughter Wrenn. What do you have to say for yourself?"

Kaila startled awake as a voice boomed through the little stone room in which she had been locked the past however-many-hours.

Things had not gotten off to a great start.

The guards on the gates of the Sanctum had greeted her cordially enough, and while there'd been a Warden present, he had barely glanced up from his seat in the guard booth long enough to check she was a Daughter, before returning to his nap. The trouble had come when she tried to actually *enter*.

"Miss, you'll have to wait for the Sister to attend you."

"Excuse me?" Kaila tried to summon the edge of authority to her voice she had used previously while pretending to be a Daughter, but standing in the shadow of the Sanctum, she found it would not come.

"Sorry, miss, standard protocol for a Daughter out past curfew. She will only be a minute."

Kaila's skin crawled at the words. Eliza hadn't said anything about a curfew. Why hadn't they thought to ask her more before removing the collar? Kaila had known Eliza all her life, but she wasn't prepared for a lengthy questioning, especially not from a

Sister. They were the teachers and judges of Fresia, trained to hunt out the enemy wherever they might find them. But with a Warden waiting in the wings and her Gift blocked, Kaila had had no choice but to wait for the woman.

The Sister, when she arrived, took one look at Kaila and bid her to follow.

From there, she'd been led deep into the Sanctum, down beneath the earth where the endless corridors quickly rendered the scant knowledge she'd gleaned from Ambrose's maps useless. By the time the Sister had led her into this room, Kaila was completely at the woman's mercy. She had no idea how she would find her way back to the gates, or the dormitories where unpartnered Daughters slept for that matter.

The room itself was empty and windowless, without so much as a stool to sit. The only source of light came from a candle stick set in the centre of the room. It flickered in the draft from the door, casting shadows dancing across the circular walls. When Kaila had turned back to the door, she'd found the Sister barring the exit.

"What is this?"

"As the First Matron suffered the enemy's punishments," the Sister replied. "So must our errant Daughters."

"What, *wait*—" Too late, Kaila had realised what the woman was going to do.

The door had slammed in her face, sealing Kaila inside. And so she'd been left shivering alone in the dark, watching her light slowly die with only the vague hope she would eventually be released. When her legs had begun to ache, she'd laid down on the concrete floor and tried to rest. Little good it had done her—in her dreams she had been stalked by soldiers garbed in black armour.

Now, as Kaila rose trembling from the floor, she found the silhouette of a woman darkening the entrance. Light still glinted from her candle, which had burned to the nub. Heels tapped against the hard floor as the newcomer approached.

"Well?" the voice pressed. "I'm waiting for an answer, Daughter Wrenn."

As the candlelight caught on her face, Kaila realised it was not the same woman from the night before. Had there been a change in shift? It probably didn't matter. This Sister was just as cold and intimidating as the last. Her dark hair was threaded with silver, catching in the flickering glow of the candle, and she wore long robes of royal violet.

Carefully, Kaila pulled herself to her feet and bowed her head. "My apologies, I have no excuse," she said, hoping it sounded sufficiently demure. "I did not notice the hour."

Silence answered her remarks. Kaila kept her head bowed, hardly daring to breathe. These were powerful people and she was currently powerless. She couldn't afford to put a single foot out of place.

"Sister Vera tells me you were with my son last night," the woman said at last. "Yet you returned well after curfew. I would like an explanation."

The words brought a frown to Kaila's brow, though she kept her head bowed. A son? Sisters didn't have children. And the only person Eliza had met with last night was the prince...

A chill crept over Kaila as she realised who she was talking too. Carefully lifting her head, she found herself pinned by the grey, compassionless eyes of the Matron. For a second she just stood there, struggling to think.

Accept that things will go wrong.

Grasping at Quintin's advice like the lip of a cliff-face, she drew herself up. It was easier said than done.

"I was...I was with the prince," she managed at last.

The Matron slowly began to circle the chamber. She was surprisingly tall, towering over Kaila at almost six feet. "Over the years," the woman spoke slowly, as though speaking to a child, "my son has typically dismissed my suitors well before the strike of midnight. Or they have retired themselves, upset at his flagrant disregard for etiquette." She came to a stop, leaning in close. "And you wish to tell me you simply *lost track of time?*"

Sheknowssheknowssheknows!

Kaila bit her lip—it was the only thing she could do to keep herself from squealing. Blood pulsed in her skull and she realised she was holding her breath. Air whistled through her clenched teeth as she exhaled. Heart racing, she forced herself to think rationally. Ambrose's illusion was impeccable; she even had Eliza's real collar. What reason could the Matron have to think an Elysian stood before her, and not the same woman she had sent that afternoon to treat with her son?

"I…ah…" she paused, wetting her lips. "He and I…ah…we both like…books?"

It was about as pathetic an explanation as Kaila could have imagined—but after a week observing the prince, it was also the only thing she could thing to fit. Drawing in a breath, she matched eyes with the Matron, and prayed they couldn't pierce her mask and see the frightened little girl inside…

"I see," the woman said. "So, you wish to tell me, Daughter Wrenn, that you arrived four hours past curfew because you were busy *reading with my son?*"

Heat rushed to Kaila's cheeks as she realised how it sounded. "No!" she gasped. "I mean, ah, nothing happened…"

"Nothing?" the Matron scoffed, her forehead folding in a frown. "That *is* a shame. Sister Vera tells me you made many great promises to be granted this appointment."

Damnit, what the hell is going on here? And why exactly was the Matron sending Daughters to dine with the prince in the first place? That should have been the first question they asked of Eliza, but in the rush to put together their new plan, none of them had thought to question it. It was too late, however, and now Kaila was knee deep in her own mess.

"Well, not *nothing*," she said, hoping it was the right direction to take. She could feel her cheeks growing hot. Hopefully the

Matron would mistake it for embarrassment. Swallowing, she pressed on. "Like I said, we were…I lost track of time…"

"But nothing happened?" The woman's face remained impassive, but her eyes had taken on a glint.

"The prince," Kaila breathed, leaning into her gamble, "was *wonderful*. But…" She lifted her chin. "I fear he was the perfect gentleman."

The Matron held her gaze. Kaila prayed to whatever fickle god watched over her kind that the woman wouldn't call her bluff. She almost sagged where she stood when the smile finally crept across the Matron's lips. Unfortunately, it was almost as terrifying as her frown—like a lizard attempting to smile.

"A gentleman?" she said with a snort. "Well, he certainly didn't get that from his father." Her eyes lingered on Kaila, before she wrinkled her nose. "Nor my husband's good taste, mores the pity. Maybe he thinks your plainness will offend me."

Kaila bristled at the insult, but common sense prevailed and she clamped her mouth shut. The woman wasn't even talking about *her*, but Eliza. Although to call Eliza plain…she had been the most beautiful woman in Elgoss!

"No matter," the Matron continued, waving a hand. "I suppose your *rustic* charm got you further than any of the others."

"Ah, thank you, ma'am," Kaila choked out the words.

"You will see the prince again—tonight," the woman added.

Kaila had been about to relax, but now all her anxiety came rushing back. That wasn't part of the plan! She was meant to lay low, ensure no one came looking for the real Eliza—not go on another date with the prince. Would seeing him be good for their plans, or a distraction?

"Ah…thank you ma'am," she said. After all, it didn't matter what *she* wanted. She was a Daughter of the Magisterium now— slave once more to duty.

The Matron nodded and dismissed Kaila with a wave.

Letting out a sigh, she started towards the door, but a voice called her back.

"Oh, one last thing, Daughter Wrenn," the Matron said, her voice cold once more.

"Yes, ma'am?"

Approaching, the woman reached out with a wrinkled finger to lift Kaila's chin, forcing her to meet that concrete gaze.

"You will not fail me, understood?"

Kaila's eyebrows lifted, but she nodded. "Yes, ma'am."

"You will be the perfect Daughter for my son, yes?"

Again, she nodded.

"And if he should decide to be…ungentlemanly, you will be a good little Daughter and comply, now won't you?"

A chill ran down Kaila's spine. She stared at the Matron, her lips parted, not quite sure how to respond. "But…" she stammered. "That's not—*ow!*"

Kaila cried out as the Matron's nails sliced into her chin. She tried to pull away, but the woman's fingers were like iron, holding her fast.

"This is why you don't send a girl to do a woman's work," the Matron muttered, "but very well, if you need a reminder of your place, Eliza…"

The Matron drew back the sleeve of her robes, revealing a golden bracer imbued with dozens upon dozens of agimet crystals. Their fiery glow lit up the chamber, casting back the dark. They weren't cut either, for the way they shone, shifting from red to blue to green, and a thousand other colours, spoke of the raw power of the earth.

"You remember this?" the Matron whispered. "The vow you swore?"

The Aegis!

Kaila swallowed. She didn't know the words that Eliza had spoken, but she knew what the bracer was. For a moment she experienced wonder, looking down upon the fabled device. Then the Matron spoke again.

"Kneel."

And Kaila knelt.

There was no chance to resist, no moment of struggle as she fought whatever compulsion the Aegis placed upon her. Submission came instantly, before Kaila could even comprehend it had happened. Suddenly, she was on her knees staring up at the Matron.

"What—"

"Silence."

Fear sank its hooks into Kaila's gut as the words left her mouth. Theron's theory about the collar had clearly been wrong. It was more than just a block on her power, or a safeguard against treason. She strained against the compulsion, the muscles in her jaw burning as she tried to force her mouth to open, to scream and rage against the woman.

Nothing.

A sad smile twisted the old woman's lips. "It's always the quiet ones who fight the most," she said, "but I have found pain to be a great teacher." Leaning down, her lips brushed against Kaila's ear. "Now, suffocate."

Her breath stopped. Fear became terror, then panic. Red burst across Kaila's vision as she strained against whatever spell had stolen control of her body, but no matter how hard she fought, it would not respond. The Matron's command had locked her lungs in a vice, unable to inhale the dank air. A burning started in her chest, growing slowly, spreading until her entire body was aflame and red spots danced in her eyes. She looked at the old woman with desperation, pleading.

The Matron stared back, a cruel smile on her lips

The darkness rose to claim Kaila.

She was in that other place again. Down in the grey beyond the world, trapped between life and death. Without pain, or fear, or warmth, there was no need for breath in this place. No need for anything, just the stillness of nothing.

Nothing, and the king.

Oberon. Strangely, he did not seem to have noticed her. Perhaps because she was no longer in Iselador, or maybe she only lingered on the edge of death this time. He seemed farther away, a shadow amongst the shadows, rather than the burning light he had once been. Sitting at a great desk, his powerful hands fiddled with one of his contraptions—the great cubes of shadow. As she stepped closer, Kaila thought it looked familiar, like one of the agimet heaters they used in Tah'raus.

Her movement finally seemed to alert the king. His head lifted, surprise showing on his noble face. His mouth moved, but Kaila did not hear the words. She thought his lips formed the word 'child'.

Then hooks of fire slashed into her spirit, binding her in flame, and dragged her back…

Kaila gasped, waking on the concrete floor of the chamber. The Matron loomed above her, the Aegis still shining on her arm.

"You cannot escape your duty, Daughter Wrenn. Not even in death," she whispered.

Fire burned all through Kaila's body, sinking into her limbs, her muscles, her flesh and bone. But she could breathe. It was all that mattered just now.

"Yes, ma'am," she sobbed, uncaring for the tears spilling down her cheeks. "I understand."

"Good girl," the Matron said. "Though to be sure you have learnt the lesson, you will remain in this cell until Sister Vera comes to prepare you for tonight."

"Please, no—" Kaila choked, but the Matron cut her off.

"*Stand.*"

She stood.

"Good," the woman grunted. "Remember, Daughter Wrenn, do not fail me—or this chamber will be the last thing you see for the rest of your sorry life." She studied Kaila, before offering a curt nod. "I will speak to you when you return."

With that, she turned and strode from the chamber. As the door slammed closed behind her, the candle flickered and died, leaving Kaila alone in the darkness.

But that was not the worst of it.

With growing horror, Kaila realised even with the Matron gone, she still could not move. Frozen in the black cell, she felt the cold creeping upon her, then as the seconds turned to minutes, the pain. It began in her feet, but it soon radiated up through her legs, before gathering in a fiery ball around the base of her spine. Her body began to tremble as little gasps tore from her lips. The sobs were soon to follow, then the moans, and finally the screams as she cried out for mercy.

No one came.

12

Light was just beginning to show on the horizon by the time Theron stumbled through the front doors of the Falkenrath mansion. He'd taken the carriage home—with Garrick acting as his servant for the moment—but even so, fatigue weighed heavily on his mind. He could *feel* the withdrawal in his veins, like barbed wire dragging through his flesh. He'd had Kaila restore his crystal before the interrogation with Eliza, but in the privacy of the carriage he'd almost drained it dry already. The need was primal, the temptation of the agimet lanterns so very, very great.

His fingers twitched as he saw one that had been left unshuttered. Just a touch, and the pain would go away, and the very world would shake at his power…

…Theron actually took a step towards it before he caught himself. Groaning, he tore his gaze from the light and stomped up the stairs. He needed rest. The withdrawal was easier to manage after a full night's sleep. Hopefully Quintin would be merciful enough to leave him sleeping when he returned. Dawn couldn't be far away and if Theron had anything to say about it, he would spend half the day in his bed.

It was a struggle just to remove his tunic, and in the end he collapsed onto his bed without removing his pants. The room spun like he was drunk and the splitting pain in his skull redoubled. Letting out a groan, he reached for his agimet. Hopefully its remaining *atar* could banish the pain long enough for him to sleep.

Before he could find it, however, a weight fell on him and cold steel pressed against his throat.

"Ah, ah, ah, no sudden movements, Master Falkenrath," a woman's voice whispered in his ear, "or I'll be sending you back to your father in pieces."

For just a second, Theron thought sleep must have already carried him away to the land of dreams. Because he recognised that voice. It just wasn't possible that she could be here.

Yet as he opened his eyes—there she was. The princess straddled him, knees pinning his arms to the soft woollen mattress, fierce emerald eyes glaring down at him. She still wore the tight-fitting dress from the balcony, but her fiery hair had been tied back in a knot and the dagger at his throat was held by a practiced hand.

"Princess," he spoke with more calm than he felt. "This wasn't exactly the dance I had in mind. I don't suppose we can talk about this?"

"That depends on how you answer my questions," she said, smiling dangerously. "I don't like liars, you understand?"

Theron stifled a curse as the dagger bit his skin and he felt a trickle of hot blood streak down his neck. "Seems fair."

"Then you'd best tell me who you're working for."

"I'm not working—" Theron broke off with a yelp as the knife cut deeper.

"How about we try that again, Master Falkenrath?" the princess said, her voice far too sweet for Theron's liking.

He held his breath, blood pulsing in his ears. If the princess pressed any harder, she was likely to sever something important. Just what the *hell* was happening? The Trickster must have decided Theron's life wasn't quite interesting enough yet. At least she was still calling him *Master Falkenrath*—and not Elysian.

"I'm still waiting for an answer," she growled. "Please don't test my patience." She actually sounded angry about that. It gave Theron something to work with.

"Okay, okay!" he gasped. "Please, just let me up and I can explain."

"I knew it," her voice became a snarl. "It's my mother, isn't it? She put you up to this? I swear on the First Matron—"

"Your mother?" Theron gasped. "What's she got to do with any of this?"

A frown creased the princess's brow as she stilled. "You're telling the truth, aren't you?" she said, before her eyes narrowed, the blade firming against his throat. "Or are you just that good of a liar?"

"I can honestly say your mother has nothing to do with any of this," he replied quietly, unflinching beneath the princess's emerald glare. "It *was* my father who sent me, like I told you on the balcony." He paused, considering his options. "Only it wasn't to become a politician."

"Why then?"

Drawing in a breath, Theron decided to roll the dice. "He knows about your father's illness," he said quickly. "He wants a union between our houses—the Fryes and the Falkenraths. He sent me to win your hand in marriage."

The princess's eyes widened as he spoke, but now they narrowed again. "Our encounter on the balcony, it wasn't a coincidence, was it?"

"Actually, it was—" Theron hissed as the blade cut him again. His fingers twitched towards the agimet in his pocket, but he resisted. "It's true, I swear! I was looking for you, okay, but I had no idea you were there."

She studied him for a long moment, before leaning in close, so their faces were separated by barely an inch. "Why should I believe anything you've said?" she whispered. "When the first thing you did after our encounter was run straight to my mother's little lacky at the tailor's shop?"

After passing by Ambrose with some supplies for the basement, Quintin did not reach the Falkenrath mansion until the sun was just peaking above the horizon. He'd lingered after farewelling Kaila, wondering at what he'd seen. An Elysian holding uncut agimet, without so much as a hint of *atar* in her eyes. It made him wonder…

…but no, they had seen what the collars could do to those who crossed the Magisterium. Peace wasn't worth giving up their liberty.

Was it?

The thoughts continued to circle in his mind as he stepped through the front doors, until a *thump* from somewhere above snapped his attention back to the present. Frowning, he climbed the marble stairwell to the upper storeys, ears, eyes and Gift alert for intruders.

It was with some surprise when, through his *atarsight*, he detected the presence of a man and a woman in Theron's chambers. Their *soullights* were close, practically overlapping, each vibrating with a sharp concordance. Slowing his pace, he crept closer, attempting to untangle the emotions, to separate excitement from anxiety, fear from passion.

It was difficult through the stone walls. They forced him to narrow his *atarsight*, concentrating only on the pair of intruders. Only then did he breathe a sigh of relief as he recognised Theron. But who in the Trickster's name was the woman?

Hesitating, he approached another step, taking care not to disturb the woollen rug in the hall. The music of the two *soullights* finally began to separate, growing clearer in the silence of the waking dawn. Warmth flushed his cheeks as he saw why they had been overlapping. The pair were more than just close—they were entwined in the vicinity of the bed.

Embarrassment brought him to a halt. Theron was with a woman. The who and why were entirely different matters, but this was clearly no business of his. He was about to retreat down the hall, when he caught the murmur of voices from behind the mahogany doors. They brought a frown back to his lips. The woman's voice sounded familiar.

He wavered, caught in the indecision he'd earlier warned Kaila of, but in the end caution won out. If Theron wanted private time with whatever lady of the night he'd picked up en route to the mansion, he should have taken her elsewhere. *Atarsight* extended, he crept closer.

"Our encounter on the balcony, it wasn't a coincidence, was it?"

Pinpricks raced across Quintin's scalp. That voice, he *did* recognise it. That was no lady of the night—it was the princess. What was she doing *here?*

"It's true, I swear! I was looking for you, okay, but I had no idea you were there."

Quintin pursed his lips. Theron sounded panicked. He studied the pair again, his *atarsight* allowing him to see their *soullights* through the walls of the room. Now he was closer—and no longer under the false impression the pair were up to something inappropriate—he caught a truer sense of their emotions.

Theron's *soullight* was unusually open and what Quintin sensed, what he *heard*, disturbed him. The Mover's soul was in disarray, the music broken and jagged, like shards of broken glass scraping against the pavement. He was angry—that much was no surprise—but he was afraid as well. Terrified, in fact, but excited also, ecstatic even.

The more Quintin studied his friend, the more worried he became. Something was happening with Theron, something that had nothing to do with the woman in his room or this heist. Something that was tearing his emotions in every direction, fragmenting his *soullight* to the point Quintin found himself wondering how his friend was functional at all.

"Why should I believe anything you've said?"

Quintin gritted his teeth. There was no time to worry over

his friend now. He had a job to do. Hesitantly, he focused his Gift on the princess. From her, in contrast, he could sense only one, all-powerful emotion—suspicion. It cut deep as well, not a shallow, recent thing, but a note that sounded from the depths of her soul, singular, powerful. This was a woman who trusted nothing and no one.

"Why should I believe anything you've said," the princess's voice was hard, "when the first thing you did after our encounter was run straight to my mother's little lacky at the tailor's shop?"

Quintin supressed a sigh. Of course Theron would end up in this situation. It wouldn't be the same working with the blasted man if he didn't find himself in mortal peril *at least* once during the job.

He and Kaila were quite alike in that way.

Crap, crap, crap...

So that was the reason for this dawn visit. They'd been spotted at the tailor's shop. Theron added several choice words to his string of curses as he struggled to produce an explanation that would explain why he had just been with Eliza Wrenn in the shop of Ambrose Braider.

"Well, Master Falkenrath," the princess growled, "I'm waiting—"

Tap, tap, tap.

She broke off as a knock came from the door. She was on her feet in an instant, blade poised to strike the first person to enter. *Hell, this one's jumpy.* Thankfully, she hesitated when the door swung open. Quintin stood on the other side.

"What are you doing here?" the princess growled, advancing on the man.

"My apologies, princess," the Psionic murmured, bowing low, "but I could not help but overhear your altercation."

"Mr Gaines," Theron croaked, using Ambrose's cover name, "please, return to your quarters…"

"If you would, sir," Quintin interrupted, "I cannot allow you to bear the burden of my…dalliance." He turned to the princess and bowed his head. "I fear I am to blame for what you witnessed. The good Daughter Wrenn and I have been, ahem, engaged in an unsanctioned courtship…"

He trailed off under the piercing gaze of the princess. Theron sat frozen, shocked both at his friend's appearance and the story he'd spun. Quintin may as well have thrown himself in front of a carriage—a man of his apparent station partaking in a relationship with a Daughter was akin to a capital offence.

Slowly, his gaze shifted to the princess. She hadn't moved from where she stood, midway between the bed and the door. Back stiff, blade raised as though to hurl herself at the intruder, Theron couldn't tell if she was buying the Psionic's lie or if Quintin had just given them *both* away with his outrageous tale— until at last, the hint of a smile appeared on her lips.

"Well, well, well, *Eliza!*" she exclaimed. "So the little country lass finally found herself a *lover.* Didn't think the girl had it in her!"

Relief swept through Theron as the young woman burst into laughter. He allowed a smile of his own as he waved to Quintin, dismissing the man.

"So you see, princess," Theron said, smiling as the servant departed. "No insidious plans here."

Emerald eyes flickered in his direction. "Except the part where your father is conspiring to put you on the Fresian throne."

"Right, yes, well that was before you tried to slit my throat." Sitting up, he rubbed his neck where the knife had bit. His fingers came away streaked with blood. Privately, he was impressed—not many people could get the jump on him, even if he *was* exhausted.

The princess rolled her eyes. "Don't be so dramatic, it's barely a scratch."

"That wasn't exactly my point."

"What was your point then, exactly?"

Theron frowned, eying the woman. Had her demeanour changed since Quintin's visit? This job wasn't exactly going to plan, but if the Psionic was doing his part in all this, he would be outside even now, using his power to subtly tone down the princess's fears and suspicions. The effects wouldn't last, but played right, they could give Theron the opening he needed.

So far though, the princess didn't seem to be biting—if anything, all this talk of politics was hardening her stance towards him. They were a long way now from the easy conversation they'd shared on the balcony. What was it she had said about him—that he was different?

"My point, princess," Theron said, deciding to take a stab at something cheeky, "is its usually customary to take a man out for a drink before climbing into his bed."

A stubbornly extended pause followed his words as the princess stared at him, seemingly in disbelief. Then, inexplicably, the young woman burst into laughter.

"Oh my," she replied, "is that really the best you can do?"

Theron raised an eyebrow. "I considered something to do with roughhousing."

"Probably would have been a better direction," the princess remarked. Her tone remained short, but Theron couldn't help but note the touch of a smile on her lips.

"I'm working on about two minutes sleep at this point."

It was true. The night had been long and every so often his withdrawal would flare, sending lances of white fire searing through his skull. He had to grit his teeth each time until it passed.

"You poor thing," the princess shot back.

Silence fell. They stood for a moment, watching each other.

"Can I get you something to drink?" Theron asked, moving

to the liquor cabinet and pulling out a bottle of brandy. He poured himself a measure, before lifting his gaze to the princess. She pursed her lips, before giving a nod. Preparing a second glass, Theron passed it to the princess before seating himself on the side of the bed.

She eyed her glass before letting out a sigh and sitting alongside him. "I knew there had to be an ulterior motive."

"Is that really so bad?" he asked, offering his drink to cheers.

"I suppose not." Glass clinked as the princess's tapped her own against his, though her eyes never left his face. "So, what now?"

Theron swallowed, suddenly aware of her closeness. Her auburn hair glinted in the dawn light and he found his pulse quickening as he breathed in the heady scent of her perfume. His hands began to shake again, though this time he could no longer discern whether it was from the withdrawal or the woman at his side. To cover his nerves, he drank deeply, the cool liquid doing little to calm the heat rising in his chest.

"How about this?" he croaked, his mouth inexplicably parched. "Why don't we pretend for a moment that I am *not* the son of Iron Hands, and you aren't a princess?"

"Oh?" She arched one eyebrow. "And what good would that do?"

"We could speak more freely, for starters."

The princess pursed her lips, seeming to consider his words, before nodding. "Very well." She held out her hand. "Jenna," she said, inclining her head. "And who might you be, noble stranger?"

Theron chuckled despite himself. "Theron." A grin tugged at his lips. "Though I fear there is nothing noble about me."

She'd said she wanted someone authentic, different from the hordes of noblemen that surrounded her at court. He was pleased to see the answering smile that appeared in response to his words.

"Oh?" she asked. "And what might you be, if not noble, Theron?"

He eyed her, taking in the faint flush of her cheeks, the glint in her eyes. A strand of hair had fallen across her face and his fingers twitched, resisting the urge to brush it aside. Nothing about tonight had gone the way he had expected—the way he'd *planned*. Yet here he was, sitting alongside the princess, exactly where he had wanted to be.

"A scoundrel," he rasped. Then, despite the pain and the exhaustion, he rose and offered her a hand. "One, if I'm not mistaken, who owes you a dance."

Her eyes widened at the gesture, but her lips twitched. Clasping his hand, she allowed him to lift her to her feet.

There was no music. Even if there was, Theron wasn't sure he would have heard it over the thumping of his heart. Her eyes never left his as he placed a hand on her hip, while hers went around his waist.

"So, a scoundrel, are you?" Jenna murmured. Her eyes danced with amusement. "I'm not sure I buy it."

"No?" Theron quizzed as they moved about the room.

"Growing up in that frontier city of yours, coddled by your father…"

"You've clearly never met Iron Hands," Theron murmured. "The man is a *monster*." The words came out harsher than he intended as an image flickered before his eyes, the memory of a tree and two lengths of rope…

A frown touched Jenna's forehead as they paused. "You're shaking," she said, lifting her eyes to meet his. "Something you'd like to share, Theron?"

Exhaling the pain in his chest, Theron forced a smile. "Not tonight," he replied, taking her hand again and sending her through a spin. "What about you? Your mother must be quite the piece of work, judging by your, ah, entrance?"

"You have no idea," Jenna muttered. "They say when I was

just a babe, she tried to drown me in a bucket. Only my father's bodyguard stopped her."

Stumbling to a stop, Theron gaped at the princess. "You're not serious?" He shook his head. "Maybe we *should* exchange stories sometime."

A smile touched Jenna's lips. "Like you said—not tonight."

Smiling, Theron took a firmer hold of the princess and dipped her over his hip. "Very well," he said, suspending her there a second, "so where were we before we got distracted by the princess and the general's son?"

"I believe you were telling me how much of a scoundrel you are."

"And you were not convinced?"

"I was not," Jenna replied, her eyes shimmering in the dawn light.

"Well then," Theron breathed, "how about I show you?"

He held her gaze for a heartbeat, then slowly, deliberately, he leaned down and kissed her. For just a moment, he felt her stiffen and wondered if he'd made an error—then her grip around his waist firmed, and she was kissing him back. A growl rumbled from his chest as he felt her pressing herself against him, her tongue tasting him—

And then abruptly, she was pushing him away, pulling back. He stumbled slightly, caught off-balance by the sudden shift.

"What…"

"The sun is up, Master Falkenrath," she said, her voice light, "I am a princess once more."

Theron groaned. "You can't be serious…"

A smile stretched Jenna's lips. "Deadly," she said, though she stepped forward and took his hand in hers to take the bite from her words. "Look, Theron, about your proposal…" she trailed off, seeming uncertain. "This has been entertaining. You're certainly different, but I'm not sure you understand what you're getting yourself into. The last coronation left a trail of bodies.

Even with a direct claim, there's no guarantees someone won't…interfere."

"My father commands the armies of Fresia," he replied softly, "I can handle myself, Jenna."

Her lips twisted in a frown. "I thought you said you *didn't* inherit your father's talent with a blade."

He made a vague gesture in the direction of the front gate. "I have guards."

"You have *one* servant who's too busy running around with his lover to notice an assassin sneaking into his master's bedroom."

"Ah, but I'm still alive, aren't I?"

Jenna smiled. She didn't seem to be able to help herself.

"Come on, it'll be interesting, won't it?" he pressed, grinning. "Let's see where this goes. Besides, if you want to be Matron you're going to need a partner, and I didn't see any of the other men in court dragging you down from that ledge.

Snorting, the princess burst into laughter at that. He laughed with her, until at last she sighed and shook her head.

"Alright, Master Falkenrath," she muttered, "you've convinced me. With my father's blessing, you may have my hand in marriage."

"Glad to hear it," Theron said, grinning. "I promise—wait, what was that about your father's blessing?"

The princess inclined her head, eyes dancing. "You didn't think you could marry me without speaking to the king, did you?"

"Ah…"

"Oh relax," she laughed. "He doesn't bite. My mother, however…well, the First Matron help us both if she decides to get involved."

QUINTIN KEPT HIMSELF BUSY AROUND THE HOUSE WITH CHORES that would normally be attended to by the family servants.

However, since Leonardo Falkenrath rarely left the frontier, the mansion had been maintained by only a single manservant—who Theron had apparently fired as his first act in charge of the house.

It had created a suitable cover for Quintin to remain close, with the unfortunate consequence that he actually had to keep the place liveable to maintain appearances. And Theron wasn't exactly what you'd call 'neat'. A trail of discarded boots had been left in the entranceway, along with a rumpled coat and an array of empty glasses left everywhere from the banisters to the dining table.

At least Quintin's talents had been useful. His Gift couldn't *create* emotions that weren't there—another common misconception amongst humans, though one the Magisterium was happy to spread. But rather he *could* massage things, mute certain emotions as he'd done with the couple in the square. Take away their anger for a moment, or their fear or distrust. Without those, other emotions like love and passion and excitement, the ones so many tried to suppress nowadays, were free to sprout.

They all knew her story; Ambrose had made them read the file. Princess Jenna had been anointed a Daughter at just fifteen, younger than almost any Daughter before her, and once you wore that golden collar, there was no going back. After so many years within the Magisterium, Ambrose had expected to find a dark soul, an equal to the parents that had raised her.

Instead, beneath the fear and the doubt, Ambrose had found a woman who wanted to *live*. It was by no means a perfect tune, the music of her *soullight*. Even without the cloud of her darker emotions, there was still anger, and greed, and far too much pride. But there was a softness too that surprised him, an intensity of warmth that said this was a woman who would defend her own to her dying breath.

It made Quintin wonder the kind of woman the princess might become if she were not bound to the Magisterium. Well, he couldn't free her from her physical chains, but he could at least liberate her from the psychological ones, the yolk of circumstance and duty, of a past stained with cruelty and betrayal.

Yet even as he'd worked, as he felt the woman she had hidden within emerge to smile on a new day, Ambrose felt an ache deep in his soul. Because he knew it was all in service to a lie. He wasn't doing this for Jenna, but so that Theron could dangle another world in front of her—only to snatch it away in the cruellest of manners.

Think of your girls, he reminded himself, *think of their future. This is the only way.*

And so he'd persevered, done his part, until he felt the soft tunes echoing from the princess's *soullight,* the low notes of warm affection, the high, bright tunes of excitement. Only then had he walked away, knowing his part was done. Theron's silver tongue would do the rest.

By the time the princess left, the sun had reached its zenith and Quintin had made the mansion presentable—at least on the surface. Theron found him in the great terrace at the rare of the house, sitting on the edge of the pool and looking out over the harbour. He enjoyed listening to the ocean, the way its sound would shift from gentle whispers to a thunderous roar as the tides rolled in and out. Unpredictable, ever changing, it had a way of grounding him when the emotions of this city grew too much to bear.

"It would seem your first gala was a success after all," Quintin said as the man joined him.

He kept his eyes on the distant waters, even as he reached out with his Gift. Theron's walls had been restored and all he sensed from his friend was a roiling excitement.

Nodding, the man took a seat on the ledge next to Quintin. "The jobs halfway done," he agreed.

Quintin frowned at Theron. He didn't seem overly joyed by the announcement. "Halfway done?"

"She wants her father's approval before things go any further."

"The king," Quintin grimaced. "We knew that was likely."

Theron nodded. "Thank you for coming to my rescue in there," he said. "I'm not confident things would have gone the way they did without your story."

Quintin snorted. "That, and no small amount of *atar*. That girl might just be suffering from the worst case of paranoia I've ever seen."

Theron said nothing, and in the silence Quintin finally glanced at the Mover. Despite their success, his lips were pressed in a thin line and his eyes were distant, his brow creased.

"She spoke about her mother," he replied at last. "There's something about her, something I can't quite put a finger on." His eyes flickered to Quintin. "Did you sense anything else from her?"

Quintin hesitated. "Not from her." He eyed the other man, his friend of more than a decade. "But from you...Theron, what I sensed from you, before I arrived..." he trailed off, not sure what to say next, what to ask.

But Theron surprised him, for once, with the truth. "I did something bad, Quintin," he whispered. His eyes returned to his hands, which lay in his lap. They were shaking. "I used cut crystal, Quintin."

"*What?*"

Heart suddenly pounding, Quintin half-rose from where he sat, but Theron looked across at him, his eyes pleading. "Please, let me explain before you explode on me."

Quintin's fists were clenched so hard around the marble ledge he feared his fingernails would tear. Exhaling slowly, he forced his body to relax and sank back to the cold stone.

"Speak," he said shortly, unable to keep the anger from his voice.

"It happened in Iselador," the Mover whispered, holding Quintin's gaze. "In the Black Tower. We were fighting a Warden, Kaila and I. My last crystal broke..."

"Theron..."

"I wouldn't have used it," he interrupted. "Not to save myself. Not to beat the monstrous bastard. But Kaila…" He closed his eyes. "She fell. I couldn't…I couldn't let her…"

As Quintin watched the other man, understanding finally dawned. Why Theron had pushed her away, why he still saw the longing in the girl's eyes—and in his friend. Theron had destroyed himself to save her and now…

"She doesn't know, does she?"

Theron shook his head.

"And Ambrose?"

"You think he would have begun this job if he'd known?"

"Theron…" Quintin started, then trailed off. A grimace stretched his lips. "Is it bad?"

"The withdrawal?" He grimaced. "Worse than you can imagine."

Momentarily lost for words, Quintin stared at his friend. Now Theron had admitted the truth, it was like a veil had been drawn back. Only now did he see the exhaustion that lined the Mover's face, the red dots in his eyes and the way his shoulders slumped like they bore the weight of the world.

"Theron, what the hell are we doing here?" he said at last. "You can't go on in this condition."

"That's just it, Quintin," Theron replied. "I can't stop. I *have* to go on."

"But why—"

"Because it's all I have left!" Theron snarled, swinging on him. Teeth bared, *atar* flickered in his eyes, and belatedly Quintin saw that he'd drawn a piece of agimet from his pocket. He felt a tug, only gentle, but unmistakably the touch of the Mover's Gift.

"Theron…" he said carefully.

The Mover blinked, before the light faded and he was himself again. His shoulders slumped as he lowered his eyes to the water.

"It's all I have left, Quintin," he repeated, quiet now, voice barely raised above a whisper. "It's like there's a tiger inside me, clawing to get out, and this…this *thing* we're doing is the only way I can sate its hunger."

A shiver ran down Quintin's spine. It was eerie, hearing the pain in Theron's voice, yet through his *atarsight* there was only the same excitement he always felt from Theron. Except, was that true? There were hints amidst the music, maybe, places where it faltered, where he thought something else might be poking through.

"If Ambrose finds out about this," he whispered.

"Please, you cannot tell him, Quintin," Theron insisted. He drew in a breath, and when his eyes met Quintin's they were clear once more. "I have it under control, I swear. I wouldn't…I wouldn't risk all of this if I didn't, okay?"

Exhaling, Quintin allowed his eyes to flutter closed. Of all the things he'd expected to hear from his friend, this possibility hadn't even crossed his mind. But now he'd admitted it…

"Okay, Theron," he said, "I won't tell Ambrose." He paused, unsure how to approach what he'd witnessed with Kaila's collar.

Truth was, Quintin wasn't sure what to make of it himself. The implications for Kaila were terrifying, but what did it mean for the rest of them? Could the effect be replicated, used on their children so they could pass the Trial of Agimet without risking discovery from a failed weaving? His stomach churned at the possibilities…

…but first, Theron deserved the truth.

"There's something you should know," he said softly. "Kaila, before she entered the Sanctum, she tested her Gift. It was blocked."

"What?" Theron froze, his eyes suddenly wide and staring.

"It has to be the collar. It blocks the Elysian Gift."

"And you still let her go in there?" Theron snarled. Suddenly he was on his feet, eyes simmering once more with pure *atar*.

Quintin rose more slowly. "She didn't leave me much choice, Theron," he said, maintaining his calm.

Snarling, Theron advanced on him and for just a second,

Quintin thought his friend would strike him. He tensed, preparing his own suite of abilities to combat the Mover. Perhaps he'd misjudged Theron, and the addiction was even worse than he thought. But then the Mover halted. Jaw clenched, his entire body trembling…

He exhaled, and the tension went from his body.

"No, she wouldn't have," Theron said quietly, turning away, "she's like that sometimes."

Quintin hesitated, then spoke: "You should have told her the truth, Theron." He wasn't sure it was his place, but he had seen the looks the two flashed each other, when they thought the other wasn't looking.

The Mover grimaced. "Probably."

Quintin exhaled. "It's been a long night." He eyed the Mover. "We'll speak more about your…condition later. I'm going to get some sleep." With that he turned and moved inside the house, leaving his old friend alone with the sounds of the ocean. From the distant rumbling off the waters, a storm was on its way.

13

K aila was in trouble.

An hour into her first dinner with the prince—second for Eliza—and she had yet to exchange more than a single sentence with the damnable man. Every minute that ticked past brought her one minute closer to that terrible room. Just the memory of the darkness, the sensation of being unable to move, while the pain came creeping up her legs and spine…it was enough to set Kaila to shaking all over again. By the time a sister had come and released her from the spell, there had been no strength left in her legs. She'd collapsed to the ground, twitching as her muscles spasmed, burning like they'd been stabbed by hot pokers.

But even worse than the pain was the dread; the knowledge that the Matron could turn Kaila's own body against her—and there was nothing she could do about it. She couldn't even run— tonight, the Magisterium had sent guards to escort her to the prince's tower, as though they feared she might try to run. Even if she could slip from their sight, there was still the collar. The memory of Eliza screaming and writhing on the floor of Ambrose's shop was seared into her mind.

She was in a trap of her own making, and the only one

capable of saving her couldn't even be bothered looking up from his book long enough to eat his own dinner—let alone *converse* with her. Prince Rohan sat at the opposite end of the long table, his nose practically swallowed by an enormous tomb while his plate of steak and potatoes sat untouched beside him.

Letting out an accentuated sigh, Kaila took a swig from her wine glass. It was a red of some kind and it burned a little going down, but the flavour was pleasant enough on her tongue. She was already on her second glass, the prince's servant having recently topped her up. Wrinkling her nose, she considered her plate. It amounted to a handful of peas and carrots, with a sliver of beef on the side. The whole plate could barely be considered a mouthful. Her stomach rumbled. She hadn't eaten since her sandwich the night before—she hadn't been offered so much as a piece of bread before the sisters bundled her up in a fresh dress and shoved her into the carriage bound for here.

She gritted her teeth, glancing again at the disinterested prince. *Bastard!* She sat here starving for his pleasure, and he didn't even have the good grace to finish his own Trickster-cursed meal. Blood pulsed at her temples. It was too much. Here she was, surrounded by wealth and power, in a station elevated far above anything she could ever have imagined as Kaila of Elgoss, and *still* the Magisterium conspired to starve her!

Abruptly, Kaila rose, her chair scraping loudly on the porcelain floor. Across the long table, the prince looked up from his book. A frown creased his forehead at the interruption, before his eyes returned to the page. Kaila clenched her jaw so hard she was sure her teeth made an audible grating noise. Her fingers twitched towards her hidden crystal, but that would do her no good now.

Instead, Kaila set her eyes on a different prize. He obviously thought she'd grown tired of him already and was about to leave. Well, that wasn't happening. Instead, she marched the length of the table and swiped the plate from under the prince's nose.

"There are children starving in the Dominances, you know," she said, a little too sharply.

His head jerked up, blue eyes widening as his mouth made an *oh* of surprise. Kaila sniffed, then strode back to the other end of the table, taking the plate with her. Her stomach gave an embarrassingly loud rumble as she set it before her. Still pointedly ignoring the prince, she took up her knife and fork and attacked the meat with a vengeance.

She almost moaned when the first morsel touched her tongue. After a day of torture, hardship and starvation, the meat was like honey in her mouth.

She didn't have to look up to know the prince was staring at her like she was some foreign animal in a cage. She tried to ignore the attention, but despite her best efforts, her cheeks warmed. Really, he chose *now* not to return to his book?

When she could take it no more, she looked up and caught him with a glare.

"You know, it's rude to stare."

The prince blinked. "Ah…I'm a little rusty on my etiquette, but I'm pretty sure its ruder to steal another person's food."

Her scowl deepened. "Oh *sorry*, were you going to eat this?" As she spoke, she cut another chunk of steak and shoved it into her mouth. Meeting his eyes, she chewed. *Violently.*

His eyebrows lifted, his lips parting, but no words came out. He looked like a startled rabbit caught in the lanternlight. She almost felt sorry for him, finding a wild, untamed creature in place of the lovely, obedient Daughter she was meant to be. Except, this bastard's lack of manners was very likely going to condemn her to a dungeon. Somehow her heart just wasn't in the mood for pity.

"You know…what else…is rude…" she continued between bites. "Ignoring…your dinner…companion!" She jabbed the knife in his direction.

Across the table, the prince's cheeks were steadily progressing through several shades of red. "I…ah…didn't mean…"

"Two days," she spat, talking over the top of him. Cursed man, if she was going to choke to death in a dark cell because of him, he could at least feel bad about it. *"Two days* I've sat across this table from you, and you haven't so much as asked me where I'm from!" She was just guessing on that last part, but it hadn't seemed like much conversation had gone on between him and Eliza last night either.

"You're…ah…the same one as last night?" the prince stammered.

Kaila stared in disbelief. "You…you didn't even…" It was her turn to be left speechless. She felt a sudden, burning desire to bury her knife in the blasted man's chest.

The prince rubbed his head, looking sheepish. "I didn't really…I thought…why would my mother send you *twice?*"

"Because—" Kaila broke off as she realised she didn't really have an answer to that question—at least, not one that would make sense to the prince. "And I…ah…" Flustered, she scrambled for a lie. "I…may have said something…to the Matron that…implied you liked me."

The prince's eyebrows lifted into his mop of dark brown hair. "Really?" He paused, looking thoughtful. "Err, why?"

Kaila snorted. "Not for your delightful company, that's for sure."

The prince actually managed to look abashed. "Then I'm confused, why would you lie?"

Well, she'd put her foot in the wolf trap now. At least he was talking to her. She wasn't sure that was an improvement if it ended up blowing her cover.

"Tell you what," she breathed, deciding to take a gamble. Setting aside her plate, she steepled her hands. "You tell me why you've been blowing me—and every other Daughter of the Magisterium—off, and I'll tell you why I lied."

To her surprise, the prince chuckled. "Have you *met* my mother?"

Her eyebrows lifted. "The Matron?"

"Unless there was a serious mix-up around my birthday."

Kaila frowned. "She's a woman with an…indomitable will," she said charitably, unsure where he was going with this. "What about her?"

"She wants me to succeed the throne instead of my sister," he replied with a shrug. "Who knows why, but she's always had it out for Jenna. But for the Magisterium to overlook my sister's claim, *I* would have to marry a Daughter." He shrugged. "Not that it matters. I've never wanted anything to do with the Magisterium or the throne." He gestured at the apartment around them. "That's why I left the first chance I got."

Looking around at the luxury of the penthouse, with its enormous windows and sprawling sofas and personal servant, Kaila couldn't help but think his idea of 'leaving' the Magisterium was quite different from her own. Hells, the dining table was almost the size of the flat she had once shared with her father.

But Kaila could say none of that, only nod along sympathetically. The other part of his tale, however, was significant. If the Matron didn't want the princess to succeed her, it could put a serious wrench in Ambrose's plan. She would need to find a way to get word to the tailor—if she survived another night in the Magisterium, at least.

"The Matron is a hard taskmaster," she said diplomatically.

"Is that a Daughter's way of saying she's an outright witch?" the prince asked with a snort, his eyes dancing.

Feeling her cheeks grow warm, Kaila looked away. "You shouldn't say things like that," she said softly, feeling the cold touch of the collar around her throat. "She is a powerful woman."

"Ay, that's all your order cares about, isn't it?"

She looked up sharply at the accusation. Gone was the gentleness that had momentarily come over his face, as though something in her words had reminded him who he was speaking with.

"I didn't…"

She trailed off as the prince rose abruptly. Without another word, he strode to the grand bookcase that filled most of the interior wall. Setting his tomb back on the shelf, he scanned the titles, then selected another, before returning to his desk in the corner. There he slumped into a chair and practically tore the cover open.

Silence followed as Kaila sat, lips parted, still not quite able to formulate a response. Her blood was racing again, her fickle hope teetering on the edge. *What happened?* It had seemed like she was getting through to him. She licked her lips. Somewhere behind her, the prince's personal servant cleared his throat. This was obviously a dismissal, but until he said the words, Kaila wasn't going anywhere. She couldn't.

"You're being rude again," she said instead, rising carefully from her chair. Her muscles screamed and it took an effort of will to keep the pain from her face. Wandering across to join him, she peered over his shoulder and tried to get a glimpse of the book title, but he was holding it so close to his face it might as well have been a mask.

"You are welcome to leave."

She gritted her teeth. This wasn't going well. Inhaling, she felt the weight of the collar around her throat. Blood pulsed in her skull and she longed to draw on her crystal and tear her way through the problem, but that wasn't an option this time.

"Your name is Rohan, isn't it?" Kaila said instead, sliding into the chair alongside the prince. Steeling herself against the memories of Eamon, she placed a hand on his wrist. "Can I call you that?"

The prince didn't respond, but she noticed his eyes were no longer moving across the page. His hand was warm beneath her fingers.

"What are you so afraid of, Rohan?" she pressed. "That you'll enjoy my company?"

Slowly, his gaze lifted to meet hers. "I know what you're doing."

"Do you?"

"You work for my mother." He bared his teeth. "I won't come back. Call me Rohan all you like, I won't be the next tyrant of Fresia."

Kaila's eyes widened. "What do you mean?" No noble she'd ever met in this hellhole of a capital had ever thought of themselves as tyrants.

"Taking from the Dominances, crushing our citizens beneath the burden of duty…" he paused, then shook his head. "You wouldn't understand. People from Tah'raus never do." His eyes returned to his book.

"I'm not from Tah'raus."

His head jerked up. "You're not?"

"No," she said with a frown. "I come from a small mining village in the Iron Pinnacles." At least her cover story was the same as Eliza's, except… "My father was the Earl of Elgoss."

"Elgoss?" His eyes widened. "Then the attack…"

Her jaw clenched and all Kaila could manage was a sharp nod.

"I'm sorry," he whispered, though he couldn't possibly know how much that memory truly hurt for Kaila. The real Eliza had lost her parents that day in Elgoss, but Kaila had lost her entire world. "But then you of all people should understand why I can't go back."

Kaila forced herself to swallow the lump that choked her throat. "I'm not sure I follow."

"Everyone in Elgoss, they died…" His voice cracked and it seemed he would not be able to continue. "They all died so the nobility can enjoy a life of luxury." He gestured around the room, as though to encompass the entire city, before his eyes returned to hers. "So you must understand, why I can't…"

Despite her peril, Kaila found herself nodding. She did know, better than anyone, better than he could ever understand. And oh how it hurt to understand, to feel that familiar void within, the rage for all the injustices of the world, and know she could do nothing about it.

Which really, *really* sucked—because now the Matron was going to lock her in the dark for the rest of her miserable life. As she started to shake, the hand around hers gave a squeeze. She swallowed, drawing reassurance from the touch—before she remembered it was the prince's hand she was holding. Jerking her arm away, she came to her feet in a rush.

"My Lady, are you okay?" Rohan asked.

There was concern in his voice as he rose with her. She flinched as his hand touched her shoulder.

"I'm fine," she said, pulling away. "And my name…" Distantly, a voice called out in warning. "My name is Eliza…" she finished, remembering herself at the last second.

The worry on the prince's face didn't flicker. "Was it something I said?" he asked, reaching out again before seeming to catch himself.

Plan for things to go wrong…

Drawing in a breath, she steadied herself. This conversation…had not gone in the direction she had expected. And yet here she was, standing in the middle of the prince's apartment, having got more words from the prince than she'd seen in a week of spying on him. She knew now why he had defied his mother and the Magisterium, why he would *never* accept a Daughter's hand, however many his mother sent to harass him…

A tingling crept across her scalp as an idea came to her. "I'm fine," she said softly, her voice suddenly calm again. "It's just, your mother. Remember how I told her you liked me?"

He nodded. "You never did say why."

She exhaled. "Because I don't fit in here, Rohan," she replied. "I'm the orphan girl from Elgoss—the Daughter without a title. So when I heard the Matron wanted fresh candidates to present to her son…I leapt at the opportunity to stand out." It was more or less the truth, from what Kaila had gleaned from interaction with the Matron. "So when our first encounter went so terribly…I just panicked and lied." She shrugged. "I'm an idiot," she added, eyeing the young man across from her, "but now…"

"Eliza…" There was definite pity in the prince's eyes. "You seem nice enough, but I'm sorry, like I told you, I don't want any part of the Magisterium or my mother's games."

"But you're already a part of them, aren't you?" she pressed. "Whether you like it or not, she's going to keep sending Daughters to harass you—and you obviously don't have the power to stop them."

He shrugged. "I know how to handle them."

"By locking yourself away up here with your books?"

"It's worked so far."

"Has it?" Kaila asked, arching one eyebrow and gesturing to herself. "I'm the *least* qualified of our order, and I've wasted half your night in pointless conversation. Imagine the lengths some of the *qualified* ones will go through to catch your attention."

"Somehow I doubt they'll be so bold as to *steal my food*," Rohan muttered.

"I wouldn't put it past them," Kaila replied, before waving a hand, as though to wipe the conversation clean. "That's not my point. What if there was a *better* way of avoiding all this mess with your mother?"

That brought a frown to Rohan's brow. "What did you have in mind?"

"Announce that you've decided to court me."

Rohan blinked. "So your solution to my mother's harassment is to *completely capitulate* to her demands?"

"I didn't say *marry me*," Kaila said with a scowl. "I'm saying we *pretend* to be courting."

It was, in a way, the perfect solution. She wouldn't return to the Sanctum emptyhanded, and so long as there was an official courtship between them, the Matron wouldn't feel the need to send any other Daughters to harass the prince. It might irk Ambrose, but the distraction would ultimately serve to further his plans with Theron as well, since the prince would remain out of the game.

"That's redic…" the prince began, before trailing off, a frown wrinkling his brow.

Kaila smiled back. Rohan scratched his chin, seeming to consider the proposal, before their eyes met in the dim glow of the agimet lantern.

"You really aren't playing some game here, are you?"

Biting her tongue, Kaila shook her head. She *was* playing a game—just not the one he thought.

"I have no interest in playing her games," he continued, "or marrying any of her little minions—no offence."

"None taken," Kaila muttered, "but if I leave here empty-handed, she's going to keep sending them until you marry one."

"I know," Rohan said, eyeing her, "what I still don't understand is: what's in it for you?"

"Well, that part's easy," Kaila replied with a shrug. "I'll be the Daughter that won the attentions of the prince, won't I? Even when our courtship inevitably ends, I'll be *someone* then." Or at least, she *hoped* that was how it worked…

Rohan nodded, either proving her right or that he was just as naïve in the politics of Tah'raus as she was. "Alright then, Eliza…"

"Wrenn."

"Eliza Wrenn," Rohan repeated with a nod.

Returning to his desk, he flipped open the book he'd placed there and tore out the front page. Despite everything that had passed since her classes with Sister Eurador, Kaila let out a little gasp at the sight. Books were sacred in a place like Elgoss, where supplies of coal and food were few and far between—let alone *paper*.

Rohan didn't seem to notice her discomfort, however, as taking up a quill he scribbled furiously across the page. Curious, Kaila tried to peek over his shoulder, but his handwriting was almost as poor as her own.

"Here," he said finally, scratching something that might have been his name at the bottom. "This is a formal letter of courtship." Straightening, he made to offer it to her, before pausing. "Are you sure about this, Eliza? Once you present this to my mother..."

It's this or a cold, dark cell, Kaila thought to herself, even as outwardly she reached for the paper. She was proud the only sign of her nerves was a slight trembling in her fingers.

"I'm sure," she said with a smile. "And thank you, for trusting me."

He shrugged. "It's not me who's taking much of a risk," he replied. "Like you said, I'm not *marrying* you. If we break it off, my mother will be irritated, but she still needs me if she wants to have any chance of keeping my sister off the throne." He grimaced. "I imagine she'll be somewhat miffed at you though."

The words formed as a cold block of ice in Kaila's stomach. *Out of the campfire, into the furnace.* He was right, of course. If their deception was discovered before Theron got his hands on the Aegis, the Matron would do more than just lock her away in the dark—she might very well string Kaila from the walls of the Sanctum as an example to the other Daughters.

But she would deal with that eventuality if and when she came to it. In the meantime, this piece of paper gave her breathing space.

"Thank you, Rohan," she said quietly, "you're a better person than your mother."

He grinned at that. "And you're not like the rest of those awful Daughters."

She arched an eyebrow. "Thanks, I guess."

14

Theron whistled a gentle tune to himself as he meandered through the bustling night market. Quintin followed a step behind, as befit the attendant of a nobleman. His friend had made no more mention of their argument, but guilt touched him as he looked around and found the man's eyes on him. He could sense Quintin's tension, even if he wasn't a Psionic himself.

Still, he'd told the man the truth, or at least most of it. He really did need this job. It was just…it wasn't *only* about the addiction, or making a difference. It wasn't even mostly about those things.

The real reason he'd accepted it, why he would see it through to the end, was his father. Whatever happened before the end came, he wanted to see the man destroyed. So long as that objective aligned with the plan, he didn't see the need to share it with the Psionic.

Thankfully, the job was giving him the chance to do just that. A smile came to his lips as he recalled the princess. He had to admit, Jenna was nothing like he'd expected—quick witted and unpredictable, she would keep any man on his toes. No wonder the other noblemen in the court had taken to giving her a wide birth, crown or no.

Unfortunately, he still had to convince her *father* he was the right man to sit the throne—a dangerous task, given the man's very real connection with his own estranged father. Fortunately, he'd already laid the groundwork for that at the gala. It had only been a matter of a few messages back and forth to secure a private meeting with the man—though his choice of venue had been somewhat peculiar. Soul Square. Usually home to vagabonds, the condemned and ladies of the night, it wasn't the kind of place you expected a noble to linger—let alone a monarch.

The sun had just slipped beneath the horizon, painting the sky in dusky hues. A few more twists and turns through the bustling night market, and they reached the plaza. There, the pair were greeted by the roaring of a crowd. Soul Square was packed with men and women of every stripe and shade. They stood shoulder to shoulder, hundreds, thousands even, pushing and jostling to get closer to a temporary stage raised in the centre.

Theron and Quintin exchanged a glance. The atmosphere was charged, voices raised and banners waving. The motley clothing marked most as commoners, but Theron noticed several sections of the crowd adorned in finer garments.

"What in the name—"

The words died in Theron's throat as a man in black armour stepped onto the stage. His blood ran cold as he recognised the Warden. Cased from head to toe in steel, the man studied the crowd from behind a black visor. All around the plaza, the mob went wild.

As Theron shared another look with Quintin, a brilliant light flashed across the square. Years of instinct drove both to duck as they saw the Warden holding a crystal high in one fist. As they watched, the light within the piece of agimet grew brighter, swirling, rippling, flashing. Theron grimaced, bracing himself. That was a massive crystal, and the bastard was using the Gift of a Binder on it—changing its state, energising it until…

Boom!

Even knowing it was coming, Theron winced as the crystal exploded, the shriek of its destruction echoing through the plaza. A hushed silence fell over the crowd in its aftermath.

"Goddamnit," Quintin muttered, "that crystal must have been worth more than I could steal in a year."

"More than *you* could steal in a year," Theron said with a quiet grin.

"Every year our enemy grow more cunning," the Warden's voice carried across the plaza, harsh and metallic from within the helm. "Even now, they hide amongst us, creeping into our cities, enticing those weak of will with their magic, luring our children with promises of easy power and lives free of duty." In his black armour, the Warden cut quite the heroic figure. "And in their greed, our leaders in the Magisterium allow it."

A lump lodged in Theron's throat. What the hell was this? He cast a gaze around the plaza, but the crowd was jostling them again, while others raised fists and booed. He could see no sign of the king. Why had the man invited him here, of all places?

"Agimet," the Warden continued, holding up the broken shards, "is the tool of the enemy. Only those pure of heart can withstand its corrupting nature. For centuries, the Wardens have born this burden gladly, in the knowledge others will be spared its evil."

Cheers rose from the crowd. A scan of their faces offered an easy explanation for their support. The last few decades had seen agimet machinery go from a luxury used exclusively by the nobility, to something almost commonplace amongst even the lowliest of merchants. And not just for lighting—heating and clocks and carriages; even cooling boxes and elevators. It was everywhere and in everything, at least for those whose labour wasn't paid in ration chips.

But for the common men and women who thronged to the plaza, agimet had been the systematic destruction of their livelihoods. From coachmen to chimney sweeps to lamplighters; vocations that had been passed down for generations had vanished, leaving thousands destitute.

And in Tah'raus, those who didn't work didn't eat. The fortunate might be reassigned new employment by the Sisters, but in a city undergoing so much upheaval, there weren't enough empty positions to go around. And the Magisterium knew the peril of idle hands. Whenever beggars in the plazas grew too numerous, soldiers were sent to clear the streets. Anyone they deemed a layabout or a drifter was bound in chains and dispatched elsewhere in the kingdom, where their labour might go wanting. Those deemed most offensive might even lose their tongues, so they could be sent to those secret places like Elgoss, where the Magisterium mined their agimet.

Of course, none of this was particularly *new*. Even before the current regime, Tah'raus had undergone cleansings when the population grew too large for the likings of the Magisterium. But then the numbers had been small; affording the majority the luxury of ignorance. Only now, as the needy spread like roaches through the streets and the Magisterium came for *them*, did these citizens take note.

Not for the first time, it made Theron wonder if he and the other Elysian simply did nothing, humanity would tear itself to pieces on its own. But of course, Theron didn't have that kind of patience.

"…only a few months ago, one of our agimet mines was infiltrated by the enemy and attacked." Theron's ears picked up. The Warden was talking about Kaila's village. "Elgoss, it was called. Your fellows burned so a lucky few in our capital could enjoy a hot bath!"

Theron's scalp prickled. So Eliza had been telling the truth. Five hundred men, women and children, dead so the Magisterium could keep their secrets—and now this man was using the tragedy for his own cause. It had the desired effect too, as the crowd roared their disapproval.

"The king and his Matron have ruled unchecked for long

enough," the Warden continued. "Their folly has drawn the enemy to our gates. The agimet they hoard will be the ruin of us all. The crystals must be returned to the Wardens. Only we, the true soldiers of the people, are fit for the responsibility!"

Theron frowned. The man's words bordered on the edge of outright treason.

"What does he think he'll win out of all this?"

"More power for his Wardens?" Quintin replied.

"I doubt it," Theron muttered. "The Sisters are the real power in Fresia. An angry mob in Tah'raus isn't going to change that."

The Warden on the stage had finished gesticulating and was now shaking hands with some men and women who had joined him on the platform. Nobles, from the look of their clothing.

"I'm not so sure," Quintin was saying, "the Sisters might keep the populace in check elsewhere, but the nobility support the Magisterium because of the comforts they're afforded in the capital." He hesitated. "If that were to be upended by civil unrest…"

"Humans, standing up to the Magisterium?" Theron muttered while he scanned the crowd for signs of disturbance. It didn't make any sense. How could the man so openly debate treason? "Seems like a longshot to me."

Of all the times and places the king could have chosen, why had he bade Theron meet *here?*

His eyes returned to the Warden. He looked to have finished his speech and was now descending the stage, arms outstretched towards the crowd. Theron didn't recognise the man—why would he? His kind all looked the same inside that terrible armour. But he had done something rare in Fresian society—he had raised a mob.

The square was a tinderbox, filled with the snarl of angry voices and heaving bodies. All it would take was a match and this mob would tear apart half the city.

His skin grew chill as another thought occurred to Theron—

this would be the perfect chance for the authorities to crack down on their political enemies.

"Come on," he grunted to Quintin, "I don't know what's happening here, but I don't think we're going to find the king in all this."

"Agreed." His old friend wore his worry like a mask.

Together, they threaded through the crowd back the way they had come, but the push and shove of the mass drove them back towards the churning centre. With each passing moment, Theron's fear grew. Teeth bared, he let out a growl of frustration. They couldn't use their Gifts—if they were spotted, no amount of magic would stop this mob from tearing them apart. But if they couldn't get out, he could feel the tension growing, like a storm of two nights hence before it broke upon the city.

His fingers twitched towards the crystal in his pocket. Maybe if he just used a dab of *atar*, enough to move a few bodies between themselves and the entrance to the plaza…

…his hand had just closed around the crystal when a dozen soldiers suddenly appeared in front of him. The crowd parted for the scarlet uniforms. They might be angry, but they were not yet in the maddened state of a riot.

"Master Falkenrath, thank the First Matron we found you. Please, come with us."

Heart thundering, a cold sweat upon his brow, Theron's cheek twitched with the effort it took to release his *agimet*. Nodding, he gestured for Quintin to follow, while the soldiers formed an honour guard, several taking up position on either side, while others took point and forced their way through the press of bodies.

Escorted from Soul Square, they were led to a nearby building, where they climbed four storeys of old-fashioned stairs to the rooftop. There, seated at a table draped in a silk cloth and laden with wine and several choices of cheese and cured meats, sat the king of Fresia.

"Master Falkenrath, at last, don't tell me you got lost!" Alaric

Frye exclaimed. Wine glass in hand, he rose to his feet, a smile wrinkling his aging face. "Come, please, sit and join me for a drink."

Standing in the doorway of the rooftop, Theron exchanged a glance with Quintin. The Psionic gave the slightest of nods before clasping his hands behind his back and moving to stand in the corner where his master could call for him should a need arise. Swallowing, Theron returned his gaze to Alaric. The Psionic would work his magic behind the scenes, but ultimately convincing this man to give his daughter's hand in marriage to an Elysian imposter came down to Theron.

The man with the silver tongue, he thought to himself, before he started towards the table.

He had only taken a few steps when the sounds of the crowd in the plaza below changed. The shouting changed in pitch, becoming screams. Theron's stride faltered as he recognised the unmistakable notes of fear. Adrenaline racing in his veins, he crossed to the ledge. Below, the familiar scarlet uniforms of the Fresian army now blocked the roads into Soul Square. Steel blades glittering in the light of agimet lanterns, they advanced on the helpless crowd.

"Tell me, Master Falkenrath, have you ever made a mistake you could not undo?"

"It was a trap," Theron muttered, hardly hearing the king's words.

He turned away as the line of scarlet soldiers met with the mob. Fear turned to outright panic as the helpless crowd realised death approached. Chaos descended over the plaza as they tried in desperation to escape, but at every exit they found the same wall of scarlet blades approaching.

Theron could feel his heart palpitating in his chest, but he forced his face to remain neutral. Carefully, he approached the table and took his seat opposite the king.

"A mistake?" he asked, clearing his throat. A servant poured wine into his glass as a blood-curdling scream echoed up from below. He pursed his lips, as though to consider the question. "There was a vase my mother was fond of."

Alaric chuckled. "And a certain young Falkenrath was less than careful around it?"

Theron shrugged. He still remembered his mother's wrath when she'd found him standing amidst the shards of porcelain. How meaningless it must have seemed a few days later, when the soldiers placed the noose around her neck.

"I hadn't thought to find such treason on the streets of our fine capital," he said, gesturing with his glass to encompass the chaos below.

"Fresia is not as united as it appears, as your father very well knows."

"Of course," Theron agreed, "but even so, a Warden? Or was he one of yours?"

As he spoke, a roar came from the square. Both men turned as a figure garbed all in black tore into the soldiers stationed at the exit farthest from their vantage point. Theron winced as he saw the black blade carve into their ranks. Several men went down before the others broke. The way clear, the Warden didn't hesitate, but bolted into the nearest alleyway, leaving the rest of his followers for dead.

"So, *not* one of yours?" Theron corrected his statement as he took a sip of wine. It was a red, its flavour rich and full bodied, though a little warm. He waved for the king's servants to add a cube of ice to his glass. "So, why haven't you dealt with him yet?" he continued, turning back to his dining companion.

Alaric grimaced. "Do you know who that was?"

Theron shook his head.

"Nor do I," the king muttered. "That's the crux of it—we don't know who of the order is raising these disturbances. I've tried to take him several times now, but regular soldiers cannot stand against his kind, as you just saw."

"What about the Wardens themselves?" Theron offered. "Surely they——"

"*They* refuse to move against one of their own kind," Alaric said bitterly. "As it is, they barely submit to my authority nowadays. If not for *this*…" The king drew back his embroidered sleeve, revealing the golden band that encompassed his forearm. "I believe they would have had my head on a stake long ago."

The breath caught in Theron's throat as he realised he was in the presence of the Aegis—or half of it at least. The other half would be in the hands of the Matron. His skin crawled as he watched the *atar* shimmer through the agimet embedded in the soft metal, each uncut but perfectly symmetrical. *Power.* He could sense it, *feel* it radiating from the talisman, calling to him like the uncut gemstones called. Withdrawal swelled in his chest, that desperate yearning to hold a crystal in his hands and breathe its power—

He stifled a groan as the king drew his sleeve back into place. "As it is, we are in a stalemate," he grunted. "They cannot move against the Aegis, while I will not cave to their demands and put the agimet machines back in the box." He eyed Theron. "Such are the dilemmas of kings."

Pursing his lips, Theron turned from the king to observe the plaza. Bodies were piled high around the entrances of Soul Square now. Those still living no longer tried to escape, but rather huddled in clusters, waiting for their fates. The killing seemed to have stopped, however, and now soldiers were rounding up survivors and binding their hands.

"They will hang," Alaric explained. "An example, so others know to think twice before questioning the crown."

Theron's scalp prickled, but he kept his thoughts to himself as he turned back to the king.

"Jenna told you of my proposal," he said. That much was obvious from the king's behaviour.

"She did." He arched an eyebrow. "I'll admit, I was surprised your father had changed his mind on the matter."

Theron's heart did a little summersault. "How so?"

Busy cutting himself a piece of cheese, the king did not respond for a few heartbeats. Theron counted each one, hands tight around the arms of his chair. If the king had spoken with his father…

"I floated the idea myself a few years back," Alaric murmured. "My daughter has ever been…wilful, unsuited to the suitors of the capital. I thought a man from a military family might suit her better." He shrugged. "At the time, your father refused to even contemplate the idea."

Theron exhaled, relieved the communication had not been more recent. "Yes, well you know how my father can be."

"Stubborn to the core? That's true." The king chuckled. Taking the piece of cheese, he placed it on a cracker and popped it in his mouth. "Though in this case, it seems his delay may have cost you the chance at the throne," he finished between bites. Somewhere below, a woman was wailing.

"How so?" Theron asked, trying to keep his voice calm as his stomach churned. "I thought you said your local suitors were unsuited to your daughter's temperament?"

"Oh, not from those vermin, goodness no," Alaric said with a wave of hand. "You can blame my wife. It seems that one of her little blood suckers has finally managed to latch itself onto my son."

"Prince Rohan is engaged to a Daughter?" Theron exhaled the words, his voice bordering on panic.

"*Formally courting,*" the king's voice carried an air of disgust. "Poor kid, finally capitulated to his mother. He always was too soft for this business. I told her to leave him be, but she's insistent that he be the one to succeed us."

What's this? Theron thought with alarm, even as he maintained an outward calm. "I see," he mused. "And what are your thoughts on the matter?"

Reclining in his chair, the king regarded Theron with icy blue eyes. Nothing moved now in the square below, and a haunting silence had fallen over the evening. Even the city seemed quiet, the distant rumble of carriages and shouting of hawkers almost absent. Clouds covered the sky, so that only the shimmer of silver agimet lit the rooftop.

"I think he's soft," the king repeated at last, leaning forward to rest his arms against the table. "I think the Wardens will chew him up and spit him out. If that happens, they will undo all the progress our kingdom has made over the past two decades. And then it won't be the commoners rioting in our streets, but the nobility. Fresia will splinter, centuries of unity cast aside for one old woman's superstitions. And the Elysian would come." He pursed his lips. "But what of you, Master Falkenrath? What manner of king would you be?"

Despite the silence, Theron managed a laugh. "You don't set the stakes high, do you?"

"As I said, such is the duty of a king."

Theron's smile faded. His eyes were drawn back to the plaza, where the soft rumble of agimet engines covered the approach of prison carriages. A shiver ran down his spine as an idea came to him. A terrible, pitiless plan. The Fresian king would love it.

"You said they would hang?"

"Please, do not tell me you would offer clemency?"

"Not at all," Theron replied, forcing a smile. "Only, an example has already been made for the citizens of the capital." He gestured to the bodies still lying where they had fallen. "It is the Wardens you need to send a message to."

"What did you have in mind?"

"That you will not be diverted from your path," Theron replied. Bile burned in his throat for what he was about to suggest, but the king wanted to know the kind of man he was. And Theron…he could still feel that burning within, that need for the power he had sensed from the Aegis. He wanted it for himself. "There is an agimet mine lying abandoned in Elgoss, no?" he rasped. "It would seem you have found yourself a work crew to get it functioning again."

Silence fell with his words. Theron could feel Quintin's eyes drilling into the back of his skull, and he could only imagine what Kaila would say if she ever found out what he'd done. The king, however, smiled.

"Well, Master Falkenrath, that would indeed be a unique form of justice," he murmured, scratching his wiry beard. Then he waved a hand. A woman emerged from the shadows and offered a salute. "Lieutenant Sareen, you know those mines. How long do you think it would be for you to get them operational again, with the workforce you see below?"

Theron's attention snapped to the woman, alarm tingling down his spine. He hadn't recognised her, not at first, but with the king's words he realised he knew her. She was a guard from the mine in Elgoss—one of those he'd taken hostage while searching for agimet.

Trickster's blasted balls, he cursed silently.

His heart palpitated. Of all the villagers that could have survived…teeth clenched, he forced his gaze to return to the king. So far, the woman hadn't spared him a second glance. And why would she? He was the son of a powerful general—what possible reason would she have to connect him with the Elysian thief that had brought ruin to her village?

"It won't be quick," the lieutenant was saying, "we lost a generation of knowledge in the attack. If Overseer Dwyn hadn't been…" she seemed to catch herself, before drawing back her shoulders and turning to the king. "I'll see it done, Your Majesty."

"See that you do, Lieutenant," the king grunted, waving a hand in dismissal, before returning his gaze to Theron. He studied the Elysian a moment, those crystal eyes glinting in the light of the lanterns below. "I had feared isolation might have made you weak, like my own son," he said at last, "but the boiling water that softens the potato, hardens the egg. Perhaps my daughter has chosen well."

Theron inclined his head. "I would like to believe so."

"Very well then, Theron Falkenrath, let us see if you and Jenna can't make a competition of it with my darling wife."

"I hope so, Your Majesty," he replied, before pausing. Something about this entire situation was bugging him. It was too coincidental, the prince announcing a relationship the same week they began their job. "If I may ask, who is the Daughter your son has chosen to court?"

"Another lass from Elgoss, actually," he replied with a snort. "Likely the boy heard her sob story and decided to take pity on the poor thing." He rolled his eyes. "Should have shipped the kid off to your father when he was young. But his mother was afraid the Elysian might get him. Shoulda realised the witch would ruin him worse than any of those foul creatures."

Theron hardly heard the rest of what the man said over the roar of blood in his ears. Kaila. He was talking about Kaila. There couldn't be any other orphans from that tiny town, surely. Disguised as Eliza Wrenn, Kaila had begun a courtship with the prince of Fresia.

And in doing so, she might have brought them all to ruin.

THERE WERE DAYS WHEN QUINTIN WISHED HE'D NEVER BEEN BORN with the Gift of a Psionic. But today was the first he'd found himself wishing he'd never been born at all. It had begun when he'd first used his power on the king. That was his part in all this, after all.

Just brushing against the man's mind had been enough to set Quintin's stomach to churning. Whatever his outwards appearance, there was something terribly wrong with the man's *soullight*, a wrenching, twisted music that whispered of death and corruption. At first, he thought it might be a defence like Theron's. But as he delved deeper, the sensation only expanded, and he felt icy tendrils reaching back to grasp him.

He had withdrawn then, troubled by just what it was he had touched.

Then the massacre began. Even now, hours afterwards, Quintin could still hear their *soullights*, the reverberations of their terror and dread. A thousand souls had been crammed into the plaza—and at least half had been extinguished while he stood on the rooftop and listened to Theron speak. He had thought that would be the worst of it.

Until Theron made his proposal.

It had taken all of Quintin's self-control not to act, right there on that rooftop. As it was, he managed to hold his tongue until the pair completed their meal and Theron took his leave. Only when they were safely in the privacy of their carriage did he finally speak.

"*How could you?*" The words came out in a rush. He had to grip the leather seat beneath him so as to not physically lay hands on Theron.

Seated across from him, the Mover didn't immediately respond. Instead, he reached into his pocket. His hands were shaking as he drew out the agimet hidden there. Quintin watched as the crystal's glow dimmed, then dawned in the eyes of Theron.

"How could I do *what* exactly, Quintin?" he said at last, leaning back in his seat with a sigh.

"You just condemned hundreds of lives to die in darkness."

"No, Quintin," Theron replied, his tone soft. "I just bought them a few more months of life." He shook his head, brow creasing in the gloom. "Besides, they were only humans."

"Human *slaves!*" Quintin all but exploded. "And those *few more months* will be filled with hardship and agony."

"As opposed to the alternative, where they lived happily ever after with a pardon from the crown," Theron's voice dripped sarcasm.

"You could have at least *tried* to save them."

"No, Quintin," Theron snapped. Leaning forward, his eyes

shimmered strangely with the *atar* he'd consumed. "I couldn't—because that's not the job."

"And what exactly *is* the job, Theron?" Quintin snarled. "To steal the Aegis, no matter the cost?"

"*Yes!*" Nostrils flaring, eyes burning, the Mover stared at him with what Quintin could only believe was desperation.

"Why, Theron?" he whispered. "Help me understand. Why is this so important—and don't give me that crap about a debt to Ambrose."

The energy went out of Theron like a switch had been flicked. His shoulders slumped, eyes falling to the mahogany flooring. "Because maybe it could fix me."

A tingle began in Quintin's stomach. "You can't think…"

"Why not?" he rasped. "We've seen what it can do."

"Theron—"

"I know. I'm pitiful, scrambling in the muck for a miracle that doesn't exist." Slowly he lifted his eyes to meet Quintin's. "But it's all I have."

Quintin shuddered; red streaked the Mover's sapphire eyes and the whites were stained yellow. But it was the desperation he saw that twisted in his soul. He'd never seen his friend wear a look of such defeat.

"So where does it all end, Theron?" he asked quietly. "How many people will you sacrifice for your miracle?"

Something shimmered in Theron's eyes, a glint he didn't recognise. It was gone in an instant, so quickly Quintin wondered if he had even really seen it.

"You're right," the Mover whispered. His fingers clenched around the stone in his hand. "I've been a fool."

Watching his friend, Quintin drew on his own crystal, listening for some hint of Theron's true emotion. But he sensed only pain from the Mover, a steady, mournful tune that blotted out all else. He studied the man for a heartbeat longer. What was Theron hiding? But there was no piercing that veil, so eventually he let out a sigh.

"Do you wonder sometimes," he said softly, gazing out the window at the passersby in the street, "if any of what we're doing is right?"

The words seemed to catch Theron off-guard, for there was a pause before he replied. "Of course what we're doing is right. Just because we—"

"Really?" Quintin interrupted, turning to stare at the man. "Since we started this job, I've watched you torture an innocent girl and send an Elysian that can barely control her Gift into the Sanctum alone. And now…this. Does *any* of this sound like the actions of the good guys to you?"

This time when Theron met his gaze, there was a hint of defiance there. "Sometimes doing the right thing requires sacrifice."

"Spoken like a true believer of the Magisterium."

"That's not…" A scowl twisted Theron's lips. "What's gotten into you? Since when did *you*, of all people, care about doing the *right thing*? Last I checked, we just needed to make the bastards pay."

"What's gotten into me?" *A dark night. A dozen screaming soldiers. And then…fire.* "That attitude is what cost me everything, Theron."

Theron opened his mouth to reply, before seeming to think better of it. His brow furrowed and reaching into his pocket he drew out another crystal. Quintin was alarmed to realise the first was already empty. His withdrawal was getting worse. Theron let out a sigh as fresh light shimmered in his eyes.

"I know you miss her," the Mover said at last, "but don't forget why *you're* doing this." He leaned forward in his seat. "Your girls will have the chance at a normal life."

"Will they?" Quintin pressed. "Or will all this only lead to more violence? Stealing the Aegis isn't going to change their minds about us, Theron. The people of Tah'raus will still fear us. Hate us. And without their talisman, without a king, what happens to the Magisterium?"

"They collapse," Theron replied, his voice cold. "That's half the point."

"And then what?" Quintin asked quietly. "Chaos? Anarchy?"

"We would be *free*," Theron hissed.

"Is our freedom worth setting the world on fire, Theron?"

As he spoke, the carriage rumbled to a halt. They had arrived at the mansion. The pair sat staring at each other in silence, the gloom lit by the eerie glow of *atar*. Quintin was the first to break the tableau. Rising with a grunt and pulling open the carriage door, he stepped out into the chill night.

"What would you have us do instead, Quintin?" Theron's voice chased after him. "Lay down and surrender?"

He glanced back, stomach churning. "No, Theron," he said. "It's just…" He trailed off, unable to complete the thought.

They stayed like that for a long moment, before shaking his head, Quintin turned and climbed the marble steps to the Falkenrath mansion. As he walked, however, his mind remained with Theron's question, turning it over and over in his head. His entire life had been spent fighting the Magisterium, chipping away at their invisibility, undermining their power, anything that might one day shift the balance towards his people.

It had cost him everything.

Now the years were catching up with him, and more and more Quintin found himself thinking about the future, about his girls and what it held for them. A life of struggle, and pain, and loss. In truth, it was no life at all. So as his mind returned again to Theron's question, he found another answer lingering there. One inconceivable, unimaginable, and yet…

Maybe?

THERON WAITED UNTIL QUINTIN HAD ENTERED THE MANSION before following him up the steps. He didn't feel any guilt about what had happened in the square. It was a tragedy, but Quintin was wrong—there was nothing he could have done to save those men and women. His suggestion, cruel though it might be, was only a practical response to an impossible situation.

He *did* feel bad, however, about lying to the man.

I'm pitiful, scrambling in the muck for a miracle that doesn't exist.

That, at least, had been an invention. He didn't really believe the Aegis could help him. The pain was everything now, a burning radiance that spread from his *soullight* through every bone and muscle in his body. It was a wonder he could think straight at all—let alone fool the king of Fresia himself. But it wasn't a potential cure that kept him moving.

Vengeance.

The only thing that kept him going now was the thought of Leonardo Falkenrath hanging for his crimes; just as he had hanged his mother and sister. How sweet the thought seemed now, as he faced the end. Theron just prayed the Trickster would bless him with the chance to see it for himself.

But Quintin would never understand.

How many people will you sacrifice for your miracle?

It had been the right question—just the wrong context. Theron pursed his lips. How many people would he sacrifice to bring down his father?

In his mind's eye, he saw the soldiers leading his sister to the tree, and the noose being prepared. And he heard again her voice in his head, telling him to run. *Freya.* Even all these years later, he still heard her at times, when he was at his most desperate, when the darkness came for him.

How many people will you sacrifice?

Standing on the steps, Theron looked up at the great doors, the gilded walls of his father's mansion. He listened to the rumble of waves against the coast, breathed the fresh ocean air, and exhaled.

"I'm sorry, old friend," he whispered to the night. "I never should have gotten you involved with all this."

Somewhere far to the east was his father. Would word of his

son have reached the general yet? How would old Iron Hands react to the news the exiled Elysian had returned, and claimed a seat for himself in the capital. A smile touched Theron's lips. There was only one answer—the general would fight. He knew nothing else.

I would watch this world burn.

15

"Did you *really* use lace edging for that frock?"

Bent over his workbench, Ambrose closed his eyes and prayed for patience. If only he could close his ears as well. It had been less than a week since Theron's latest plaything had thrown the whole plan in jeopardy, and Ambrose was quickly reevaluating his entire life's choices that had led to this moment. He inhaled, fingers tightening around the needle in his hand.

Chains rattled as Eliza dragged them over the metal railings of the makeshift bed he'd had Garrick carry down to the basement for her. He'd thought a show of kindness might finally shut the girl up. It…had not.

Gritting his teeth, Ambrose did his stolid best to ignore her and continue his work. His upstairs workshop was for traditional tailor work—suits and dresses for the nobility and occasional merchant with enough social heft to command his services.

The basement, however, was reserved for the Elysian side of his business. He worked down here with his Gift, weaving illusions into the very fabric of his clothes and shaping containers to camouflage the agimet crystals that would power them. It was delicate work, and the kind he couldn't risk being seen by idle eyes.

Which made his current companion all the more grating.

"Seriously," the Daughter continued, "even *I* know that went out of style five years ago—and I'm from a backwater in the middle of a mud pit!"

"By the cursed queen," he snarled. "Would you *shut up!*"

Immediately, Ambrose regretted the outburst. He *knew* Eliza was only trying to get under his skin. Sprawled on her bed with her head tilted to the side, the girl wore a grin like a cat that had just caught a mouse in its claws.

"I really can't," she replied in a mocking tone. "If I let such a crime against fashion out into the world, I would have to renounce my title as a Daughter of the Magisterium."

A fiery rage took the tailor as he slammed the frock down on his benchtop and swung on the girl. "*I* decide what is and what is not fashionable!" he snapped. "And *I* decide when it is time for a style to return." Honestly, just who did the little minx think she *was?*

"If you say so," Eliza sniffed, "personally, I think your style is just a little too...*dated*, Ambrose. Have you seen some of Marriat's latest? Maybe you could get some inspirati—"

"*Marriat?*" Ambrose spluttered, truly indignant now. "That hack couldn't come up with an original design if T'iana herself was his muse."

"I dunno, some of the Daughters are calling his stuff *timeless*." She paused. "And those who conspire with Elysian should not defile the First Matron's good name."

Ambrose snorted. "As far as I'm concerned, she did that to herself a long time ago."

Her eyes widened, lips parting as though to object, then apparently she thought better of it. Gritting his teeth, Ambrose returned to his work, though not without muttering a few choice words to himself. How had it come to this? He was meant to be the man in the shadows pulling the strings—instead, he found himself babysitting a Trickster cursed *Daughter of the Magisterium* while the men and women in his employment did their honest best to bring the plan he had spent years preparing down around his ears.

The latest news from Theron was that his brilliant apprentice may have inadvertently put the prince in competition for the throne. Theron insisted she was not a traitor, but with her sequestered in the Sanctum there was no way of verifying that. And if she *had* betrayed them…

…a growl slipped from Ambrose's lips as he glared at the frock. The lace cuffs were meant to house a dozen tiny balls of agimet—one of which would be a natural crystal—but the more he considered the picture, the more her words needled him. Snarling, he set the dress back on the table.

"Oh thank the First Matron," Eliza muttered from the corner.

This time Ambrose managed to ignore her—barely. Digging around in his supplies, he removed several options and set them on the table. Unfortunately, not all were to his unwilling companion's liking.

"*Sequins?* Okay, I was half-joking before, but that is outright *garish.*"

Lowering his hands, the tailor turned to glare at her. "I'd like to see you do any better."

Arching one eyebrow, the Daughter jerked her head in the direction of her foot. "If only I wasn't *chained to this bed…*"

They glared at each other for several long seconds. Then abruptly Ambrose rose and stalked towards her. He was pleased to see the girl flinch.

"Please," she gasped, "I didn't mean…"

She trailed off as Ambrose produced a key. Crouching beside the bed, he unlocked the shackle from around her ankle. It was almost worth the days of torment to watch her reaction. For a moment, all the girl could do was stare at her liberated foot. Only as he rose did she seem to remember he was there. He watched the change come over her face, the calculations taking place in those hazel eyes. They were alone in the basement. Ambrose was an old man, well past his prime, while she was young and strong.

"Don't get any ideas, girl," he said, drawing a trickle of *atar* from one of the many crystals hidden on his person.

"You're one of *them?*" she croaked, scrambling backwards across the sheets in an effort to put space between herself and the monster.

A familiar pain twisted deep inside Ambrose as he watched her reaction, but he didn't let it show. Supressing a sigh, he leaned across the bed towards her. "Why don't you say the name, Ms Wrenn," he murmured. "Your First Matron won't strike you down for it."

"Elysian," the girl whispered. "You're Elysian."

"Yes."

"But…but how? The Trials…"

Letting out a sigh, Ambrose tapped into his Gift and reached for the girl's *soullight.* As he had explained to Kaila, his power didn't manipulate light or change anything real in the world, but rather what others saw when they looked at him. From Eliza's perspective, his body rippled, melting and reforming into a gaunt man with sunken cheeks and a cruel smile.

"I'm a Weaver, my dear," he murmured. "Once I discovered my abilities, I could become anyone I wanted."

He was already changing again before she had a chance to react, becoming a plump woman with a powdered face. Next was a soldier wearing the uniform of Fresia, muscles pressing against a torn shirt, face scarred from battle.

"Though at heart," Ambrose continued. "I am what I have always been, Ms Wrenn."

He watched the fear and bewilderment play out across Eliza's face as he became himself again. Whether they'd known him a day or a lifetime, the reaction was always the same. Why wouldn't it be? Humans spent their entire lives believing Elysian to be monsters, dark creatures that hid in the shadows, awaiting their chance to strike.

He let out a sigh and turned away. What had he been thinking, seeking her advice? Her kind were all the same, unable to see past their own eyes. He made to return to his work, before realising his heart wasn't in it. He started for the stairs instead.

"Wait, please don't go."

Frowning, he glanced back to find Eliza standing beside her bed, fists clenched at her side, eyes wide and…shimmering? *Oh Trickster no*, he thought, *she's about to cry.*

"Please," she stuttered, "I didn't mean to be cruel. Just, don't leave me alone." Her lower lip trembled as she spoke. At any moment it looked like she would burst into tears.

Pursing his lips, Ambrose removed his foot from the step and turned back to face the basement. This was certainly a surprise. But perhaps it shouldn't have been. The poor thing had been locked down here for a week with only her fear and a grumpy old tailor for company. The burns from her collar had improved, helped along by the best ointments gold could buy, but the flesh around her throat was still an angry red. He could only imagine what she had suffered.

Wordlessly, he gestured towards his workbench. Her eyes shimmered for a second, before she swallowed her terror and offered a nod.

"I'm sorry," he said as she joined him in the work area, "I did not mean to scare you—only warn you there is no point trying to escape."

"I wasn't…" Eliza trailed off as he glanced at her. "I mean, I'm not…"

"Good," he grunted. "Then let that be an end to it. Now come, how are we going to fix this dress?" He held up a handful of crystals. "So these don't seem so…how did you put it, garish?"

A red hue appeared in the girl's cheeks and she quickly lowered her eyes, but her embarrassment only lasted a moment. Her gaze settled on the dress, her lips drawing into a thin line.

"What do we have to work with?"

Arching one eyebrow, Ambrose reached under the bench and drew out a large box containing his samples and hefted it onto the table.

"Take your pick."

Eliza's eyes widened as she peered over the rim. Hesitantly, she began removing the samples, considering them one by one. Ambrose watched first with amusement, then curiosity, and finally some admiration as she went through the various options, until finally…

"What about satin?"

He considered the picture before him. The silver satin would catch the light of the agimet, accentuating the lavender-dyed-wool of the frock. No one would even take a second glance at the gemstones.

"I think that's it," he said, nodding his approval. He hesitated, glancing sidelong at the Daughter. "Thank you for your help. You've got a good eye for this. Well, for someone who likes Marriat's work, anyway."

Her cheeks grew bright again at the praise. "I don't really think Marriat is better," she muttered, lowering her eyes. "I mean, some of the other Daughters do. The princess and the like, but not me. His work is just so…" She wrinkled her nose. "*Crude.*"

Ambrose chuckled despite himself. "You should have seen the dress he made for the princess at the last gala," Ambrose grunted. "*Crude* doesn't begin to describe it."

"Oh I *did*," she gasped. "I saw her before I left the Sanctum. I thought it was just me!"

A strange kind of silence settled between them, amiable at first, but Ambrose noticed the girl's shoulders drooping as the seconds stretched out.

"Ambrose, have you heard…I mean, I was wondering if you had news…"

Ambrose exhaled. He'd been waiting for that question. "You

weren't meant to be a part of this, you know," he said quietly, keeping his eyes fixed on the dress in his hands. "I had it all planned out—Theron, the princess, even the king and Matron. It was all so simple—until that *girl* lost control of her emotions."

"You're talking about Kaila?" Eliza whispered. "About what she did?"

"Did," Ambrose muttered, "and *continues* to do." He gave a cold laugh. "You know what she's gone and done now? She's officially courting the damned *prince!* The Trickster must enjoy watching my plans fall to pieces."

"The prince…" Eliza stared at him, her mouth practically on the floor. "The prince, as in, *prince Rohan?*"

"I know, I can hardly believe it myself," Ambrose said with a scowl. "Must be something about the girls from Elgoss." He shook his head. "And now…well, now we don't know *what* she's planning."

Letting out a sigh, he rose with the dress in hand. He was about to store it away with the rest of his Elysian works, when Eliza spoke again.

"Ambrose, am I ever leaving this place?"

He froze, halfway to the closet. A lump rose in his throat as he turned and saw Eliza had that look in her eyes again. He swallowed, trying again to imagine her situation. Attacked, abducted, locked away for days on end by a group of monsters intent on destroying her kingdom. All that, and she was still barely a woman grown.

It would have been easy to lie to her. Tell her everything would be okay, that when all this was over they would let her go back to her real life.

"I don't know, Miss Wrenn," he said instead. "That's the truth of it."

He watched the cracks appear in her mask, the twitching of her cheek, the shimmer in her eyes and the way her fists clenched into tiny balls. A tremor shook her and for a second he thought she might shatter right there and then.

"Thank you," she croaked, barely managing to get out the words, "for being honest."

The silence stretched out between them. Ambrose didn't know what to do now. Eliza seemed similarly lost, swaying on her feet, midway between the workbench and her bed. Closing his fists around the dress in his hands, he silently cursed Kaila and her meddling.

"Here," he said, an idea coming to him. He held out the dress they had created together. "Why don't you try it on and we can see if it works?"

Eliza's eyes widened at the offer. "Are you sure…"

"Sure, you earned it."

Eliza's lips twisted as she glanced around the basement. "Where…"

Ambrose muttered a silent curse to himself. "Let me see what I can do."

It took a bit of rigging, but he managed to raise some curtains around Eliza's bed in the corner. He probably should have done it earlier, but in all honesty he'd been too angry at the entire situation to consider his unwilling guest's comfort. Now he found guilt lingering in his stomach as he waited for Eliza to change in her newly constructed privacy. He liked to pretend Elysian were better than humans and their Magisterium, but when it came down to it, he and his people could be just as cruel as their enemies.

There was a smile on Eliza's face as she emerged from behind the curtains. It brightened when she stepped up to the mirror and saw herself. Smoothing a line in the dress, she turned slowly so that the light of the crystals shimmered across the fabric.

"It's *perfect*," she gushed, doing a little spin on her heel. "Who's it for anyway?"

"No one yet," he murmured, moving forward with his pins. A few of the seams needed to be adjusted if they were to fit Eliza to court standards. "I like to have a few options…"

He trailed off as an idea came to him, leaving a seam still halfway pinned. Noticing the pause, Eliza glanced at him.

"What is it?"

Straightening, Ambrose swallowed the lump that had caught in his throat. "Just…an idea for who might wear this dress?"

"Oh?" Eliza asked, grinning. "So who's the lucky woman?"

"You."

16

"What do you think they're like?"

Kaila looked up from the sofa where she'd been reading—or allegedly reading, since she'd just about fallen asleep from boredom trying to decipher the dense wall of text that was *Soren's Comprehensive Exploration of Consequentialism.*

"Who?" she asked.

Blinking sleep from her eyes, she struggled to concentrate on Rohan, seated as usual at his desk. He had been studying some other leather-bound tomb that was somehow even larger than her own, but now she found him watching her with those soft blue eyes of his.

"The Elysian," he said quietly. "What do you think they're like?"

"You've never met one?" Kaila asked, surprised despite herself.

"You *have?*" Rohan exclaimed. Rising from his chair, he darted over to the sofa and sat next to her. "*When?*"

She hesitated, wondering how much to tell him. How much might the Magisterium know about Eliza's day to day life in Elgoss? Then again, Rohan was more or less excommunicated…

"There was a boy in my class," she said quietly. Then, before good sense could stop her, she pressed on. "His name was Caellum. He was my friend, actually, before we found out…"

She looked away, struggling to keep the tears from her eyes. She had thought about Caellum just about every day since discovering her Gift, weighed down with guilt for what had happened. Why had *she* been able to pass her Trial, while he had been discovered? She'd discussed it with Theron a thousand times and they still didn't have an answer.

"Tell me about him," Rohan asked, surprising her with the softness of his voice. When she looked up, instead of disgust or hatred, she found curiosity in his eyes. It was…unnerving.

"He…he wasn't…" She swallowed. "Or at least, I never suspected. He was never cruel or harsh, and his parents…they were kind to me. Fed me, even when they barely had enough for themselves."

"Why?" Rohan breathed, "why would they do that, if they were only there for the agimet?"

Kaila shrugged. "You tell me."

He pursed his lips. "What about the girl. The one that…did it. Did you know her?"

"Kaila," she spoke her own name like it was a prayer. Ropes of fire wrapped about her insides, burning with the beginnings of alarm. "I did," she whispered. "We were friends when we were younger, before…" She still didn't know why Eliza had started to avoid her. "Before we grew apart."

The prince nodded. "Even as a child, you must have sensed the monster she would become." Kaila flinched at the words. They should have meant nothing, coming from him, and yet they were like a blade through her gut.

"Eliza…"

Seeing her discomfort, the prince reached out to rub her shoulder. It was meant as a comforting gesture, but Kaila suddenly found herself shuddering, struggling to breathe. Shards of ice trickled through her veins, setting her head to spinning.

They're all the same, a voice whispered in her mind.

"Are you alright?" he asked softly.

"I'm…fine," she said shortly, trying to focus on the book she was holding.

She had hoped he would take the hint—but Rohan possessed the social intelligence of a hamster and he just kept sitting there, watching her with those damned eyes of his.

"I'm sorry," he said at last, shifting awkwardly in his seat, "you probably don't want to be reminded of what…happened." Finally, he rose.

"It's not that," the words burst from her lips in a rush. He paused, frowning down at her, clearly waiting for her to continue. Inwardly cursing her lack of impulse control, Kaila scrambled for something else to say. "It's just…" she was too afraid to continue.

"What is it, Eliza?" Rohan whispered. Crouching beside the couch, he took her hand in his. "I know I'm not exactly the best listener…but you can talk to me." He managed a sheepish smile. "After all, we're co-conspirators, aren't we?"

Despite herself, Kaila found herself smiling back.

"We are…" she said quietly, "but…there's things…things we're not meant to talk about."

"About the Daughters?"

"About Elgoss."

The prince's frown deepened. "I don't understand. Elgoss is gone. What could it matter if you speak about it now?"

Her stomach twisted, but all she could do was shake her head. Rohan studied her for a long time. Twisting on the sofa, Kaila tucked her legs beneath her and tried to look anywhere else. The suite was much larger than her room back in the Sanctum, and would have dwarfed the apartment she had shared with her father in Elgoss. Yet despite its size, there was a homely feeling to the place. Eventually though, her eyes found their way back to the prince.

"Please, Eliza," he murmured as their eyes met. He laid a hand on her knee. "You can trust me with this."

Damnit, why is he so sincere?

It was too much. Closing her eyes, she felt the hot tear streak her cheek. Her skin tingled where his hand rested. She wanted to tell him to remove it, to get away from her, but she couldn't. Instead, she exhaled.

You can trust me with this…

She believed him.

But where to start?

"We were *slaves*, Rohan," she breathed.

Panic immediately followed the words.

Trickster take me, why did I say that?

And yet, once she started, the words just kept coming.

"The Sisters raised us on tales of duty and responsibility," she rasped. "They told us how important our work was, that everything we produced went to our soldiers on the frontier." Her eyes burned as she opened them, anger giving her strength. "How we had to starve and work ourselves to the bone to protect our kingdom." She drew in a trembling breath and met his eyes. "And all the while, those crystals were going to Tah'raus to power your machines."

"Eliza…" Rohan seemed struck dumb by her words.

"Some winters, we went weeks without coal," she continued, her voice growing sharp. "No agimet heaters for poor Elgoss. No agimet at all. Just our blood and our sweat. But we did our duty with a smile on our faces because we knew it meant something." She stared at him through blurry eyes. "I never wanted anything more than to serve the Magisterium. I would have gladly given my life for them. If not for Th—" she cut herself off. She'd gotten a little too close to the truth. Sucking in a breath, she continued in a calmer voice, "and then I came here and saw the truth."

The prince's hand twitched on her knee. Glancing at him, she saw the anger dawning in his eyes and braced herself. *Fool, fool, fool.* She never should have spoken. He wouldn't believe her. How could he? Someone like him, living in this glass palace, he could never understand what had been done to her and so many others.

"Eliza," Rohan's voice was hoarse, "I'm so, so sorry."

For a moment, Kaila didn't think she'd heard the words right. She blinked, trying to understand what Rohan had said. The silence stretched out between them, until finally Rohan rose and gestured for her to follow. Swallowing her grief, Kaila obeyed, and together they stepped out onto the balcony. All of Tah'raus spread out before them, the streets lit red by the setting sun. And above it all, the hulking shadow of the Sanctum.

"When my parents rose to the throne," Rohan said quietly, "they were granted a vision by the Aegis. It showed them a Tah'raus transformed by the promise of agimet and the machines it could power."

"Rohan," Kaila interrupted, "what—"

"Please, just let me speak," Rohan rasped. Kaila looked around at the pain she heard in his voice. "From that day forth," he continued, "the only thing that has mattered to them is building that eutopia."

Kaila shivered, her fingers tightening around the railing of the balcony. "You're saying...all the men and women who died down in the dark, searching for agimet..."

"A small price to pay for a new world," Rohan whispered. He lifted his eyes to the emerging stars. "Everything you just told me, that is *exactly* why I left the Magisterium."

"Rohan..."

There were no words. The wind swirled around them, tugging at her thin clothing. Ignoring the cold, she turned to the Sanctum, the dark thing that cast them all in its shadow. How she longed to draw on her Gift and hurl it at the distant building, to tear it apart brick by brick if she had to, until there was nothing left.

It surprised her when a hand touched her shoulder. Rohan looked down at her, a sad little frown on his lips. It seemed he would say something more, but as their eyes met, he must have thought better of it. Instead, he opened his arms, and despite her fears, Kaila sank into his embrace. A sob tore from her lips as he wrapped her in his warmth. For a second, she could almost imagine herself safe; forget that in an hour or two she would have to return to the Sanctum and its Wardens and Sisters. They stood like that for a long time, the light slowly fading, until at last she felt strong enough to pull away.

"Thank you," she whispered as they separated.

"I didn't do much," he said, his voice sad.

"You listened when I needed a friend."

"We're friends?" Rohan actually looked surprised.

"Why not?"

"Well, I guess I just thought…with our arrangement, all you really wanted was to impress my mother."

A smile tugged at Kaila's lips as she leaned against the balustrade. "A girl can multitask."

"I've never really had friends."

Kaila lifted her head at the note in Rohan's voice. It had been an offhand comment, so she was surprised to see the intensity in his eyes. The teasing smile left her lips as she looked up at him.

"It's lonely up here in the sky, isn't it?" she whispered, reaching out to take his hand in hers. His fingers were warm as they closed around her own. "It's the same…in the Sanctum, I mean," she continued, not quite sure why she was saying these things, but unable to contain the words.

"You don't have friends among the other Daughters?"

She didn't—or at least, Eliza didn't. It was one of the things that had surprised her most about the Sanctum. The sheer, cut-throated nature of the Daughters, even the Sisters…

"What was it you said about me and them: *you're not like the rest of those awful Daughters.*" She snorted. "Well, you weren't wrong. We're only friends so far as we can offer each other something. And being from a town that doesn't even exist anymore…"

His fingers tightened around her hand, then entwined with hers. "That sounds lonely as well," Rohan said quietly.

Kaila swallowed as she looked into his eyes. There was something more there now, a glint that had nothing to do with the last glow of the setting sun. Suddenly, she was distinctly aware of how close they stood. In that moment, she couldn't help but think how different he was from Theron. Rohan was soft and nurturing, where Theron was heat and flame, demanding. Two men had never been so different, and yet…

The breath caught in her throat as he leaned towards her, but she didn't pull away, just lifted her chin and allowed her eyes to flutter closed, to let the warmth, the need carry her…

Ding!

Startled, the pair of them sprung apart as the elevator doors inside the apartment rattled open. A man in the uniform of the Magisterium stepped out—one of Kaila's guards from below.

"Excuse me, Daughter Wrenn," the guard announced, seemingly unaware of the intrusion. "This man claims to have an urgent message for you."

Kaila struggled to control the pounding of her heart as she stared at the guard. Why did she feel like they'd been caught doing something…forbidden? Belatedly, she turned as a second man emerged from the elevator.

"Who would send a messenger at this hour?" she asked, frowning at the intruder.

The second man was dressed in a fine suit and tie, and wore his hair slicked back with grease.

"Apologies, My Lady," he said, dipping into a bow that brought his nose almost to the floor, "but my employer only recently learned of your news." He straightened with a sweep of his arm and beamed at the pair of them. "He wished to convey his congratulations to yourself and the prince."

Kaila's heart pounded faster. There was something familiar about the man and his mannerisms. "And who exactly is your employer?" she asked, narrowing her eyes.

"Why, Ambrose Braider, of course," the man replied with a

smile. "In fact, he wishes to offer you a personal gift—a dress of his own design."

"Oh my," she said, blood pulsing in her ears. "Isn't that generous of Mr Braider. When might the famed tailor like to see me?"

"At your earliest convenience, of course," the messenger replied, bowing low once again. "Tomorrow morning, perhaps?"

Kaila shared a glance with Rohan, who wore an expression somewhere between a frown and a smile. He knew nothing of what was going on of course, but already the rush of anxiety had returned to her sorry heart. Unfortunately, there was no avoiding this confrontation. She had known it would come eventually. She had just hoped…

…looking at Rohan, Kaila realised she wasn't sure what she had hoped for. All she could do was turn to the messenger and nod.

"Tomorrow morning it is."

17

"What were you *thinking?*"

Kaila had braced herself for Ambrose's anger, but the sheer *fury* she encountered upon entering the workshop was unlike anything she could have prepared for. The tailor was apocalyptic, and she meant that quite literally, as the world begin to collapse around her. The walls of the shop warped, melting inwards, and the air grew unbearably hot, suffocating like in the deep places beneath the earth where agimet crystals formed. It clawed at her lungs, strangling her with panic.

Except this time, somewhere buried beneath the terror, a piece of Kaila resisted, a voice that whispered this wasn't right. It wasn't real. She bit her tongue and the sharp stinging grounded her. The air still rippled and the darkness closed in, but she forced herself to ignore it, to remember she was still in the shop. This was all in her mind, a horror summoned by the Weaver to frighten her. But Kaila had seen real power now, felt it from the Aegis and its absolute control over her body—and this was not that.

"Stop. This. *NOW!*" she shrieked, throwing out a hand.

To her surprise, she actually connected with somethings soft and fleshy. There was a crash, then abruptly the darkness shimmered and vanished, the walls returning to their normal state. The shop's interior snapped into focus, though the boiling rage of Ambrose still simmered in the air. Ambrose wore a thunderous expression as, rubbing his cheek, he picked himself off the ground and started towards her again.

As his eyes began to glow, however, the door to the shopfront opened and Garrick, still wearing the weaving with the broken nose, poked his head through.

"Ah, boss—" he began, but a second man—one of Kaila's own guards—pushed through after him.

"Everything okay in here, Daughter Wrenn?" he demanded, looking from Kaila to the tailor, who's eyes had returned to their usual obsidian.

She nodded quickly. "Yes, the good tailor just dropped something while retrieving my dress!"

"See!" Garrick exclaimed, taking the guard's arm, "everything's okay in here. Come on, let's give the good Daughter her privacy."

Her guard eyed them suspiciously, before allowing Garrick to show him back out. Exhaling, she turned to find the Weaver's expression had become thunderous once more.

"Do you have any idea how long I've been planning this?" he growled. "What exactly is at stake? If this all falls apart because of some foolish girl's crush—"

"That's not what happened!" Kaila protested.

"You expect me to believe all this was just a coincidence?" Ambrose demanded. "You spent all that time watching the boy— now next thing I know, the *Matron herself* is announcing your courtship with the brat!"

"You don't understand!" Kaila gasped. "The Aegis—"

She broke off as her collar suddenly tightened about her throat. Staggering, tears sprung to her eyes while she strained for breath. *What the hell?* Terror crawled across her scalp and she looked to Ambrose for aid. The tailor, however, didn't seem to have noticed her distress.

"Oh, is that it?" he growled, eyes glowing menacingly. "You thought you could make a move on the Aegis?" His hand closed like a vice around her wrist. "*With my own weaving?*"

"*No!*" The words burst from her lips as the pressure relented. "It's not like that," she continued, panting, "please, where's Theron? He knows I would never…"

"*Theron* is doing his job—the *real* job—cleaning up the mess you made—"

"Ambrose, that's enough," Quintin spoke over the Weaver's deluge. Emerging from the rear of the store, he laid a hand on Ambrose's shoulder. "Can't you see she's upset?"

Nostrils flaring, Ambrose glared up at the Psionic. "Don't."

"I'm not."

The tailor's eyes lingered on Quintin a second before he shrugged him off. Swinging back to Kaila, he grabbed her by the arm and dragged her towards the changing booth in the corner. "Come on."

"What—" Kaila tried to protest as Ambrose shoved her through the curtains.

"Try this on," he snapped, thrusting a dress in after her. "It'll bring out Eliza's eyes."

Kaila blinked, momentarily stunned. "You mean…"

"I mean nothing," Ambrose replied, "but you still have to leave this shop with a dress. You can explain exactly what you were thinking while you change."

The dress was beautiful, the lavender dyed wool running easily through her fingers, yet still heavy enough to keep off the chill of spring nights. The stitching was simple, but as she pulled it on, Kaila was surprised to find the fit perfect, the bodice flowing with her own curves. It was sensual in a subtle way, with long sleeves and a flowing skirt that would allow a full range of movement. The satin trimmings had been studded with tiny crystals of agimet. She ran her fingers over them, eventually picking out the uncut gem on one of her sleeves. It roiled with potential *atar*, but just as it had every other time she tried to draw from a crystal since putting on the collar, it remained just outside of her reach.

"I didn't have a choice," she said, returning to the conversation with Ambrose. She had to tread carefully—clearly there were some things the collar wouldn't let her discuss. "The Matron thought something had happened between Eliza and the prince when I returned late. I had to improvise."

"Sounds like you had a choice to me," Ambrose grumbled.

"She…" Kaila swallowed, recalling the dark cell and the choking pressure of the Aegis, the long night she had stood paralysed in the dark. Instinctively though, she sensed the collar would harm her if she talked about its power over her. "She threatened to kill me."

There was silence, before Quintin spoke up. "Why didn't you run, Kaila?"

Kaila bit her lip. "I couldn't." The collar was heavy. "You saw…what happened to Eliza." She didn't dare explain any further. Even now, she could feel the blood pulsing around her throat, like a warning.

On the other side of the curtain, she sensed the men exchanging glances. Part of her longed for them to say everything would be alright. That her part in all of this was over and she could stay here in the shop, safe from the Matron and her Aegis. To have Theron put his arms around her like he had done that night by the pool…

Stupid girl, he doesn't care about you. He never did.

Blinking back tears, Kaila busied herself with the dress, smoothing out the curves and studying herself in the mirror. Ambrose was right—the lavender did bring out the hazel in her —*Eliza's*—eyes. Rohan would like it.

"We could try to remove the collar," Quintin suggested eventually.

"*No*," she said sharply, jerking back the curtain. The two men stood on the other side, faces creased with concern. Struggling for calm, she softened her tone. "At least, not yet. Not unless it's our only option."

"What about the prince?" Ambrose muttered. "I won't let him ruin this for me."

"For you?" she snapped. "I'm the one with my neck on the line—believe me, I want Theron to take the Aegis more than anyone." She hesitated. "Look, Rohan has no interest in the crown, alright? We just realised this arrangement would have… mutual benefits."

"You didn't tell him…"

"Of course not," Kaila said, "but he wanted to stop the suitors his mother was sending, and I…" she shrugged, unable to say more.

Ambrose grumbled something unintelligible beneath his breath. When he didn't say anything further, Kaila took it as her opportunity to leave the booth. Striding into the centre of the dressing room, she held out her hands and raised an eyebrow at the two men. Lounging in a sofa now, Quintin grinned and gave two thumbs up. His face still a shade of scarlet, Ambrose moved his finger in a circle. Matching his scowl, Kaila turned slowly on the spot.

"It fits well," she said, figuring some praise might soften the touchy tailor.

"Of course it does," Ambrose grunted, circling her with a frown. "Eliza tried it on first." He prodded a seam and tugged several others into line. Finally he stepped back, his eyes returning to Kaila's. "So, you're telling me the job is still on? The prince won't be an issue?"

She shrugged. "Consider me your secret weapon," she replied, attempting to inject some levity into the gloom of the tailor's shop. "The Matron…is determined to bring her son back into the fold. If it hadn't been me, chances are a *real* Daughter would have worn him down eventually. This way, she *thinks* she's won, and we don't have to worry about the prince spoiling your plans."

Quintin chuckled. "You have to admit, Ambrose, it makes a certain amount of sense."

"I don't have to admit anything," the tailor grumbled, his eyes glinting. "I still say the prince is only on the board because of her meddling."

Kaila tried not to wilt under his stony gaze. She didn't like the way he looked at her, as if she was nothing—*worse* than nothing—a speck of dirt that had ruined one of his dresses. All she could manage was a nod.

Thankfully, Quintin came to her rescue. "Oh give the girl a break, Ambrose," he said, rising with a sigh. "She's done more than any of us ever managed—infiltrated the Daughters of the Magisterium. Come on, I'll help her get this dress boxed up. Why don't you go make sure those guards remain up front."

The tailor snorted. "Just make sure she doesn't rip it," he muttered, before doing as suggested and returning to the front of the shop.

Kaila hesitated, staring after the tailor. She tried to imagine him as a common labourer, painting houses alongside Quintin and Theron, but it was difficult to see him as anything other than the tailor to the nobility of Tah'raus. Powerful, dangerous, untouchable.

"Are you sure we can trust him?" The words tumbled from her lips as she turned to Quintin.

"Who, Ambrose?" the Psionic asked, frowning.

She nodded. "I don't understand, he already walks in the same circles as the nobility. Acting against the Magisterium puts all of that at risk.. So what does *he* get out of all this?"

"Have you asked him?"

"I tried!" she gasped. "He didn't give me a straight answer."

Quintin let out a sigh. "Ambrose may present himself as the swanky nobleman, but deep down he's a good man."

"How can you be so sure?"

"Because I've known him a long time," the Psionic replied,

before pursing his lips. "Just now though, it's *you* that I'm worried about." He paused. "Are you okay?"

With the question, Kaila realised she was shaking again. "Fine," she replied, forcing a smile. Stepping into the cubicle, she pulled the blinds and began to undress. "I'm…sorry if what I did…made life difficult for you…and Theron."

Quintin sighed. "Right, Ambrose didn't explain." He hesitated, and Kaila's heart gave a little pulse. Had something happened? "You were seen," the Psionic continued. "The night we delivered you to the Sanctum."

"*What?*"

"Relax, I covered for you," Quintin said, a smile twitching at his lips. "If anyone asks, you and I were once engaged in a tepid affair."

Kaila blinked. "We…*what?*" She was starting to sound like a broken record.

"That's why Theron couldn't risk coming this morning," Quintin continued. "It would have looked too suspect, him showing up at the shop at the same time as you—*again.*" He paused, eyeing her closely. "But forget about Theron. What was all that about the prince?"

She frowned. "What about him?"

"You called him Rohan."

"That's his name. What about it?" she said, a defensive anger creeping into her voice. Free of the dress, she set it aside and set about donning her original clothing.

"Just…be careful," the Psionic said after a pause, "I know you did a few of these jobs with Theron, but this is different. Dangerous."

"I know it's dangerous," she snapped. Pulling on the last of her clothing, she stepped into the backroom and tugged at her collar. "I've got this to remind me, remember?"

"I wasn't talking about physical danger," he replied. "I'm… worried you may be letting your personal feelings get in the way with the prince."

"You're worried about *my* personal feelings?" Kaila could hardly believe what she was hearing. Here she was, risking her life in the belly of the beast, and Quintin was accusing her of letting *feelings* get in the way? "What about Theron?"

A frown touched the Psionic's brow. "What about him?"

"His entire *reason* for taking on this job was to destroy his father."

"His…father?" Quintin asked, a puzzled look on his face.

Too late, Kaila realised the truth. "He didn't tell you," she whispered.

The Psionic slowly shook his head. "Tell me what, Kaila?" he asked, ice creeping into his voice.

She swallowed. "I…it's not really for me…"

"Tell me, Kaila."

Her shoulders slumped. *Sorry, Theron.* "He's not playing a role this time," she rasped. "His father *really is* Leonardo Falkenrath. I thought you knew."

"I didn't."

A harsh silence fell between them then, one Kaila couldn't begin to fill. What had Theron been thinking, keeping that from Quintin? Hadn't he been the one to say they needed to trust one another if they were to have any chance of succeeding?

"I'm sorry…"

Quintin waved a hand. "It's not your fault," he murmured. "I should have known there was something else." He eyed Kaila, and she thought he was going to say something, but finally he sighed. "Come on, let's get that packed up for you." He gestured to the dress Kaila held.

Swallowing, she handed it over. Accepting the dress, Quintin held it in his hands, looking momentarily lost. "Tell me, Kaila" he said suddenly, "do you still hate them?"

The question took her by surprise. She thought back to their conversation in the park, then everything she had seen since. The bad—and the good.

"I don't know."

He nodded. "Just remember, it's not real. At the end of all this…you can't stay with him. You can't pretend to be Eliza forever."

"I know." She should have been angry. He was patronising her again. But after what he'd just learned…all she felt was sadness. Drawing in a breath, she tried to inject a bit of levity into the conversation. "I just want all this to be over already, so I don't have to wear anymore of these fancy dresses."

"Are you sure?" Quintin said with a smile. "They look quite fine on you."

"They look fine on *Eliza*…" she trailed off, her throat growing tight. "Is she…"

Quintin pursed his lips. "Would you like to see her?"

"Please."

Nodding, Quintin showed her to the stairwell hidden behind the bookcase. "Be quick," he said, "I'll say here, in case those guards come looking."

A kind of panic gripped Kaila as she descended, the pressure of it growing with each step until it felt as though her heart might burst through her ribcage. She had played a role the past week, but now she would confront the reality of her failure. Gloom swallowed her as she reached the basement and her eyes struggled to adjust. As the stars faded, she found a pair of eyes watching her. The iron joints of the bed creaked as Eliza rose and started towards Kaila.

"So, you're still alive," she said, her voice sharp.

Lingering in the shadows, Kaila opened her mouth, and then closed it again. She could see the anger in Eliza's eyes, the desperation.

"What, nothing to say?" Eliza demanded when Kaila didn't speak.

The Daughter took another step, only for the chain around her ankle to bring her up short. Kaila's stomach crawled as the lantern lit Eliza's face. The burns around her neck had begun to heal, but the flesh was still a terrible, scarlet red. She must be in incredible pain, yet her face showed none of it.

"Come on, Kaila," Eliza continued, her voice dripping venom. "Tell me what it's like walking in my shoes? It has to be nice, living a life you stole from someone else."

Watching her twin, hearing the pain in her voice, the fear, Kaila felt something breaking inside.

"It's lonely," she gasped. When the other girl's eyes only widened, Kaila went on in a rush. "I didn't…I didn't know what it was really like. The games you play with each other. Not until…" she trailed off, struggling to free the words lodged in her throat. "I…I'm sorry I ruined it…ruined it all. I never meant for any of this."

Standing in the flickering light, Eliza stared at her, hazel eyes shifting in the gloom. Her lips were parted as though to unleash some fresh insult, but instead only silence stretched out between them, until suddenly, Eliza gave a little whimper. The mask she wore cracked, her face twisting with grief as she slid to the ground and hugged her knees to her chest. Tears slid down her cheeks.

"I'm not leaving this place alive, am I, Kaila?"

Kaila opened her mouth to deny it, but found the words wouldn't leave her lips. Looking at Eliza, for the first time in over a decade, she saw the girl from their childhood. Her friend, scared and alone, lost, out of her depth.

She took one hesitant step towards Eliza, then another, then knelt on the floor alongside her. "It…it doesn't have to be like that," she said quietly. "Theron and Ambrose, I know you're afraid of them, that they're…*we're* Elysian, …" she swallowed, recalling the words Theron had told her all those weeks ago. "We don't kill slaves, Eliza."

"But I'm not a slave, am I?" Eliza looked at her through teary eyes. "Not like your father and the others in Elgoss. Not even like the commoners here in Tah'raus. I'm a Daughter of the Magisterium. I'm one of *them*."

Kaila shivered. Her old enemy was right. Theron and the others might stay their wrath against commoners, but the Magisterium was another story. Why would Eliza be any different—especially given everything she knew. And yet…

"Why did you stop talking to me, all those years ago?" she asked without thinking.

"My parents," Eliza replied, clearly surprised by the question. "They decided the other children in Elgoss weren't appropriate playmates for a future Daughter."

Kaila blinked as her eyes stung. "But…we were friends," she croaked, surprised at the weight of that pain.

Eliza looked away. "I know," she whispered, and Kaila saw that she was blinking too. "I'm…I'm sorry, Kaila."

Somehow, it helped. "I'm sorry I dragged you into all of this."

The silence returned, but this time it did not hold the same weight. After a moment, a wry smile appeared on Eliza's lips. "I heard you seduced Prince Rohan," she said, chuckling. "Maybe you're a better match for the Daughters than my parents gave you credit. Please, *you have to* tell me what you did to manage that?"

Kaila snorted. "I stole his dinner."

"You…*what?*"

Somehow, despite the fear and pain and terror of the past few weeks, Kaila found herself grinning. "He was ignoring me. And those damned servants seem to think we don't need to eat—"

"*Right?*"

"Exactly!" Kaila exclaimed. "And he wasn't eating anything on his plate anyway, so…I took it."

Utter disbelief shone in Eliza's eyes. "*You took his plate?*"

Grinning, Kaila nodded.

"And *that* is how you ended up…" she trailed off, shaking her head. "First Matron be damned, they don't teach that one in seduction class."

The pair of them laughed then, long and loud. When the sound faded and the silence returned, the darkness that hung over Kaila no longer seemed so great. She watched her old enemy and realised she understood Eliza a little better now, having lived her life for a few weeks.

"You really didn't know about the agimet, did you?" she said finally.

The smile faded from Eliza's lips. "No, Kaila. I swear, they never told me. Not until that last night."

Kaila nodded. It was a relief, to know they hadn't been in it alone, that even some amongst the powerful were ignorant to the evils of the Magisterium.

"I won't let them hurt you, Eliza," she said softly, and was surprised to find she meant it. "When this is all over, I'll make sure you go free."

A tear streaked Eliza's cheek. Before Kaila could react, the other girl reached out and grabbed her. She tensed, readying herself, but this time Eliza wasn't looking for a fight.

"Thank you, Kaila," Eliza whispered as she hugged Kaila.

Kaila was surprised when the tears spilt from her own eyes. She was even more surprised when she found herself hugging the girl back with all the strength she had.

18

Leaning against a pillar, Theron watched as Jenna paced up and down the hall, her high heels tapping loudly against the concrete floor. Tonight she wore a mini dress of cobalt blue and the sway of her hips had the uneven hemline riding up her thighs, flashing more skin than was technically considered civil in Tah'raus, but he wasn't about to complain. In fact, under other circumstances he might have spent a little more time appreciating the view.

Unfortunately, they were currently lingering in the entrance chamber of the Sanctum. It was meant to be a simple dinner engagement with some of the major players in court, after which the king would announce their engagement and ceremony at the Summer Gala in two weeks' time. Instead, upon Theron's arrival, Jenna had informed him there would be an unexpected guest at the table.

Eliana Frye, the Matron of Fresia herself, was to be in attendance.

Just the thought of the woman set his pulse racing—a sensation made all the more unpleasant by his withdrawal. The Matron was a force unto herself, representing the political power of the Daughters and Sisters of the Magisterium. In a few moments, he would sit at her table and break bread with the woman responsible for the torment of his people. If he survived the night, Theron would surely be the only Elysian in history to boast he had dined with a monarch of Fresia, let alone *both*.

If he survived.

He cast a glance out of the corner of his eye. Quintin lingered in the shadows, his eyes locked on Theron with a strange intensity. There hadn't been time to talk after he and Ambrose had met with Kaila. Hopefully the girl was alright. They needed Quintin on his game if something more was afoot tonight, which judging from Jenna's reaction, was *exactly* what they could expect.

The clack of heels announced Jenna's approach. "I don't understand why it's taking this long," she hissed, striding up to Theron and placing her hands on her hips.

Still reclining against the pillar, Theron drummed his fingers against the stone. Technically, being the son of a soldier, Theron Falkenrath fell under the authority of the king, but that didn't mean the woman couldn't make ripples.

"You really think she's plotting something?" he asked.

"She has hated me for as long as I can remember," Jenna replied with a shrug.

She rejects one child, while the other spurns her, Theron kept the thought to himself. *Truly, mother of the year here.*

Still, he sensed they were missing something. The Matron's motivations were all wrong. Jenna still hadn't explained what the cause of the rift between herself and her mother, but it was seeming more and more likely it could be a problem.

"We have the support of your father and mine," he lied, doing his best to reassure her. "Not even your mother would dare to defy the both of them."

Lips pressed in a thin line, Jenna hesitated. "You don't know my mother like I do—"

She was interrupted by the whisper of the entrance hall

doors swinging open. Theron expected to find a servant beckoning them into the dining chambers; instead, the Matron herself strode through the doorway, grey dress swirling about her generous form. The woman wore a scowl as she marched up to her daughter.

"There you are," she snapped, "what are you doing loitering out here while your dinner guests wait on you?"

"Mother." Caught off-guard, Jenna took a moment to compose herself. "We told…"

"Never mind, the damage is done. Come." She spun on her heel before either of them had the chance to reply—or Theron to introduce himself—and disappeared through the open doors.

Theron shared a glance with Jenna. "I'm beginning to see where you get your charm from," he said as they started after the Matron.

She narrowed her eyes. "Say that again."

"I mean, the first time we met you did threaten to cut my throat."

"Technically, that was the *second* time we met," Jenna paused, "and that knife is currently in my boot, if you'd like to keep talking."

Theron smiled despite himself. "You know, I think I'll let you do the talking."

Jenna snorted but did not reply.

As promised, the dining room was already full. At least fifty guests stood about an enormous table draped in pristine white silk. Tall ceilings met massive arched windows of stained glass, which shimmered with hues of crimson, gold and cerulean in the light of an enormous agimet chandelier. The low hum of conversation from the guests grew muted as they entered, all eyes drawn to the princess and her soon to be fiancé. Plastering a reconciliatory smile on her lips, Jenna murmured her apologies and began to mingle with the crowd.

Theron started after her, only for a hand of iron to grasp him by the arm. Startled, he turned to find the concrete eyes of the Matron on him.

"Master Falkenrath, a word, if you would?" the woman said, her voice firm.

"Ah…" Theron glanced around in search of Jenna, but she had disappeared, "I think the princess—"

"Please, Master Falkenrath, it will only take a moment."

He pursed his lips, but he was talking to one of the most powerful individuals in the entire kingdom. He could hardly refuse. There was a shimmer in the Matron's eyes, as though she understood quite well his predicament. Gesturing for him to follow, she led him through the crowd into a small antechamber that branched off the main dining hall.

Cursing beneath his breath, Theron paused in the entrance and cast a glance over his shoulder. It took a moment to find Quintin. The Psionic's eyes lingered on Theron, though he hadn't followed them. Theron frowned. What was the man *doing*? He needed his Psionic close. He nodded towards the room with as much subtly as he could, then disappeared inside, leaving the door open a crack as he did so. Hopefully Quintin would be able to overhear the conversation and intervene with his Gift.

"Very well, ma'am," Theron said, keeping his voice jovial as he spread his arms and offered the semblance of a bow. "You have me. What was it you wished to discuss?"

The frosty look the Matron returned suggested she did not share in his cheer. "I must say, I am impressed at your father's nerve. I had not thought he held any interest in matters of politics."

"Let us say it is a recent pursuit."

"I should think so," the Matron replied. "Given the impetuous manner in which you have imposed yourself on my court."

Theron blinked. "Sorry?"

"How else might I interpret the persistent, late-night excursions of a certain Daughter?"

"I can assure you, ma'am," Theron responded quickly, "Jenna and I have been quite proper—"

"Knowing Jenna Frye, I'm not sure I believe you, Master Falkenrath," the Matron replied. Arms clasped behind her back, she studied him with those concrete eyes. Finally though, she let out a sigh. "It is a shame your father did not contact me before enacting his plan. Uniting the Falkenraths with the royal line would be an excellent consolidation of power. Unfortunately, it cannot be."

"What, *why?*" Theron was so startled by the statement, the words just burst out of him.

"The boy from the Dominances shows his true manners at last." A smirk twisted the Matron's lips, before she let out a long-suffering sigh. "But if you must know, it is because Jenna is not fit to be Matron."

"Sorry?"

"Fear not, you can be forgiven your ignorance, Master Falkenrath. You have only recently met the girl, and are no doubt quite intoxicated by her…outward nature. You must trust me, however, when I tell you she does not have the temperament to be Matron."

"Temperament…" Theron could only stare at the woman in confusion.

"I'm saying, Master Falkenrath," the Matron said slowly, as though speaking to a fool, "you may not marry Jenna Frye. At least, not until my foolish husband has taken his leave of this world and a new successor has been chosen."

"A successor?"

"My son, should the First Matron be kind and grant Daughter Wrenn the perseverance to endure his company until a marriage can be procured."

There was a terrible ringing in Theron's ears as he stared at the woman. This couldn't be happening. They were already at the finish line. The king was to announce their engagement tonight. In just two weeks, on the night of the Summer Gala, this would all be over.

And now…

He drew in a breath, eyes flicking towards the door. Quintin would be there—*he had to be*. This wasn't over yet. Finally recovering his wits, Theron unleashed his best smile.

"Come now, Your Majesty," he said lightly, "surely we can discuss this."

The concrete eyes studied him in the light of the agimet chandelier. "There is nothing to discuss, Master Falkenrath."

His heart gave a little pulse of panic. "Ma'am, I understand you and Jenna have had your differences, but cannot this be a chance for reconciliation?"

"No," she replied coldly. "I fear it cannot."

Trickster be damned, what are you doing *out there, Quintin?*

Had something happened to the Psionic, or was the Matron simply this obstinate? Regardless, there was obviously going to be no bargaining here. His jaw hardened. Time for a change of tact.

"And if I refuse?" he asked, allowing some anger to creep into his voice.

She glared down her thin nose at him. "I am the Matron of Fresia, Master Falkenrath. My word carries the authority of the Magisterium. It is not to be refused."

"That may be true," he said softly, inclining his head. "However, we Falkenraths are soldiers. We answer to the will of the king."

"And Jenna bears a collar of the Magisterium," the Matron replied, drawing her lips back in a sneer. "Though she would do well to remember it more often." She leaned in close, until Theron could smell the aged liquor on her breath. "I could make both of your lives very difficult, Master Falkenrath. Understood?"

Looking into those eyes, Theron found that he believed her.

Silently, he cursed himself for a fool. Jenna had warned him from the start that she had enemies, that her mother loathed her. He had just never considered the possibility she might try to stand between her own daughter and the throne. It didn't make any sense—and even less so that she preferred the prince, given *he* had withdrawn himself completely from the Magisterium. No, there was something more going on here; he just didn't know *what*.

Fortunately, by the Trickster's fickle blessings, their plan now had a failsafe. Kaila. He clenched his fists, thinking it through. It was a terrible risk, placing the entire plan on her shoulders. If she stumbled, if her weaving so much as flickered or the prince tired of her, there would be no second chances…

"Okay…" he whispered, so quietly he wondered if she would even hear him. He bowed his head, hoping to appear defeated.

"Good," the woman grunted. "If you still wish to marry the little hussy *after* my son is wed, you may have at it. Though I suspect by then you will be long gone." She paused, then gave a sniff. "Come then, let us return to your meal. I imagine you will have to speak with my dear husband before he goes and makes a fool of himself."

Speechless, Theron followed the woman back into the hall. He looked around for Quintin, but he was nowhere near the door of the antechamber. Instead, the Psionic had not moved from his earlier spot. A questioning frown touched Theron's brow as their eyes met, but the Psionic gave no indication of a response.

A bell chimed before he could approach his friend and ask what had happened. It was the signal for the diners to sit. Jenna must have noticed his absence, for as he made his way listlessly to the dining table, she appeared at his side.

"What in the *Elysian* was that about?" she hissed. "I told you to *avoid* my mother—not go off with the witch alone."

"Sorry," he murmured.

He shook himself as they took their place among the host of diners. They'd been given pride of place, with Jenna directly to the king's right and he alongside her. It also placed them both, thankfully, about as far as they could get from the Matron, who was seated at the opposite end of the table from the king. Supposedly this was to represent the separation of state and Magisterium—but Theron suspected there was more than just physical distance between the king and Matron nowadays. The way the woman had spoken of her husband implied there was little love lost between them.

"Well," Jenna growled as the servants began to circle with the first plates, "what did she want?"

To destroy you, he thought to himself, but he couldn't say it out loud.

"Not here," he said quietly. "I'll tell you later."

Even as he spoke though, he glanced at the king. How was he going to play this? How was he going to explain it to *Ambrose?* The tailor was going to be apocalyptic—but he at least would see the reasoning. Eventually. Once Theron explained he would still get the Aegis, just not the way he'd envisioned.

But the king and Jenna…if he backed down now there would be no coming back. There would be consequences. Within hours, pigeons would be winging their way towards the Iron Pinnacles to inform Iron Hands of his son's conduct…

He'll escape.

The realisation sent a chill running down Theron's spine. Leonardo Falkenrath possessed the same silver tongue that had been getting Theron out of sticky situations for the better part of two decades. If he was given *any* wiggle room, the man would slip free of the noose—especially if they gave him an easy scapegoat in the form of a newly crowned Matron disappearing along with the Aegis.

No, if Theron wanted his revenge, his marriage to Jenna had to continue.

Pinpricks raced across his skin as his eyes travelled the table, settling on the Matron. He wasn't surprised to find her watching him, a strange intensity in those slate grey eyes. It made him wonder. Why *hadn't* she simply made a public announcement, denouncing their engagement. Or given Jenna an official order, for that matter?

His frown deepened. Even now, she was waiting for *him* to inform the king. For *him* to call off the engagement. Why?

I could make both of your lives very difficult, Master Falkenrath.

She could, that much was certainly true. Defying her would put him in a perilous situation. His every movement would be watched by members of the Magisterium, all of them searching for something that could destroy him. And well, there were plenty of those, with his addiction. Could he do it?

The honest answer was no. He would slip at some point—the desire was too great. Even now, just the thought of going without *atar* for days, weeks even, had his hands shaking. No, the smart decision, the best decision for the job, was to hand over the reins to Kaila. Give her a clear shot to the throne and the Aegis, and forget about his father.

Instead, Theron found himself rising. All eyes in the room turned to stare at him as he tapped his wine glass with his spoon. Most were on their second course by now, and many held forks halfway to their mouths. This was most definitely not the point in dinner one stood to make an announcement. Even the king wore a look of irritation on his face. The Matron looked like the cat who'd just stolen the cream.

Well, she was in for a nasty surprise.

"Excuse the interruptions, my friends, but I fear I would burst if I keep this news to myself a moment longer." Theron took a certain amount of satisfaction watching the Matron's smile falter. Turning, he beamed down at Jenna. "You see, these past weeks, princess Jenna and I have been courting."

A murmur went around the table as the guests exchanged glances. Most seemed merely irritated—they'd likely already heard the rumours floating about the court. He flicked a glance in Quintin's direction, but the Psionic steadfastly ignored his gaze now. He clenched his teeth. *What the hell is going on with him?*

Whatever it was, it would have to wait. For now, if the Psionic wouldn't get the excitement around the table flowing, maybe what came next would.

"Recently, her father, granted me his blessing that we might be married," he continued, nodding in the direction of the king, who continued to watch Theron with suspicion. Grinning, he turned to the other end of the table. "However, due to familial rifts, I had feared our dear Matron might withhold that honour for her only daughter."

He paused, allowing the words to sink in. The whispers died to silence as every eye around the table steadfastly avoided looking in the direction of the steely woman. Even Jenna tensed, her hand shooting out to catch Theron by the wrist.

"Gladly, not ten minutes ago, our esteemed Matron took me aside," he said quietly. "We spoke of the princess and the love shared between us. And finally…" Theron was the only one watching the Matron as he continued—and so was the only one to enjoy the true heat of her fury. "She agreed to grant us her blessing."

A collective intake of breath carried around the table as the guests turned as one from Theron to the woman in question. She quickly concealed her rage behind a mask of ice, even as her eyes continued to bore holes into Theron's skull. He had made an enemy today, one that would see him bound in chains and dragged to the depths of hell if he was ever within her power, but what did the condemned care about future threats? If he was lucky, she would take it out on his father, when the man's decades long deception was finally uncovered.

For now though, he raised his glass in a toast.

"To the future of Fresia and its rulers," he said, his eyes never leaving the Matron. "May we live long in defiance of our enemy."

"WHAT IN THE *NAMELESS* WAS THAT ALL ABOUT WITH MY mother?" Jenna demanded.

They had barely taken two steps through the front door of the Falkenrath mansion before she spun on him. Theron stifled a sigh. Exhaustion weighed heavily on his shoulders and he wanted nothing more than to drain an entire crystal and attempt to sleep. She should have remained at the Sanctum after dinner—he certainly would have preferred it—but of course Jenna was having none of that. His only victory had been to delay her questions until they reached the mansion.

Now he attempted to summon one last bout of strength and gestured her into the privacy of his study. As he did so, Quintin brushed past without saying a word. He glanced after the Psionic, a frown crossing his lips. There hadn't been a private moment for them to speak since the dinner. Yet another mystery that needed solving before he slept.

But for now, Jenna was wearing her look that said if he didn't start talking *immediately*, he would be reintroduced on a much more intimate level to her dagger, so entering the study, he closed the doors behind them.

"Well?" she said, swinging on him immediately. "What did my mother *really* say to you?"

For just a moment, he considered lying and sparing the girl the indignity of what her mother had done. But one glance in Jenna's eyes and Theron knew he couldn't do it. He let out a sigh.

"You know what she said, Jenna."

He saw something in her eyes as he said the words, a flicker of hurt, as though even though she *knew* what her mother was, a part of her had still hoped, or maybe just wanted to believe that Eliana Frye could have changed. That just once, the Matron of Fresia could be her mother first, ruler of the Magisterium second.

"Of course," her voice cracked. Stumbling across the study, she slumped into a sofa. "Of course she wouldn't…"

Theron was surprised to see tears spill from the princess's eyes. A sharp pain twisted in his heart that was only partly his withdrawal. He actually felt sorry for Jenna. And why not? They had both suffered at the hands of terrible parents—though he, of course, would be the victor in a head on pity contest. Still, he understood her pain, perhaps better than anybody.

Crossing to the liquor cabinet—apparently old Iron Hands had one in just about every room—he returned with a bottle of the Cascade's finest whiskey and two glasses. Wordlessly, he handed one to Jenna, then splashed the amber liquid inside when she accepted.

"To terrible parents," he murmured, raising his own beverage.

They chinked glasses. Jenna knocked her entire glass back in one gulp. Raising an eyebrow, Theron followed suit. The liquor burned on its way down, bringing tears to his eyes. With mascara already running down her cheeks, Jenna didn't seem to care if a few more streaks were added to the mix. She held out her glass for a second round and he filled it without rebuke.

Sitting himself on the sofa alongside her, Theron poured a second glass of his own. The first still had a fire burning in his stomach, and he found it helped to distract from the cravings. There was a crystal hidden in the cabinet—they had a sizeable store from Ambrose in case of emergencies, but he resisted the urge to go and claim it. His friends were relying on him to see this job through now—he'd seen to that.

"You know what the worst of it is?" Jenna surprised him when she finally spoke. "I don't even know why she hates me."

He turned to look at her. She sat alongside him, eyes fixed on her second glass of spirits, as though the alcohol might somehow held the answers to her questions.

"Sometimes…" Theron trailed off, wishing suddenly he could tell her the truth. About his father, the terrible things he'd done. "Sometimes it's better not knowing." Afterall, there was no doubting why Leonardo Falkenrath hated his son.

"You really think that?" she asked, before shaking her head. "Half my life, the only thing I wanted was to please her. To make her proud of me. Why do you think I became a Daughter in the first place?" Fresh tears spilt down her cheeks. "I was younger than any Daughter in a century when she came and offered me that collar. I foolishly thought she had finally accepted me." She snorted. "What a fool I was."

"What happened?"

"After the ceremony, she sent me to the Daughters quarters without so much as a backwards glance. I hardly saw her again after that, and only then it was to admonish me."

His stomach churned as he watched the young woman grieve. For some reason, Jenna's pain moved him more than all the lost lives in Soul Square, more than Eliza's agony and Quintin's pleadings. He had thought he would find in the princess just another selfish, egotistical noble. But here was a young woman who had been used her entire life, manipulated by those who should have cared about her.

And here he was doing it all again.

"Jenna, I—"

Theron started to speak, to let the truth flow from him, but before he could get the words out, Jenna was there, her soft body folding into him, her hot lips pressed against his own. Her urgency consumed him, the soft sounds she made between gasps lighting a fire inside he hadn't even realised had been there. His hands moved of their own accord, finding her hair, her neck, the soft fabric of her dress as they ran along her waist. Forgotten was his own pain, the burning of his withdrawal; for the sweetest of moments, it was all washed away by the flames of their shared grief and longing.

Then Theron felt her fumbling at his belt and knew he had to stop.

"Jenna, wait," he gasped, then groaned as the withdrawal threatened to wash him away. His entire body trembling, he managed—barely—to catch her hands and hold her away from him. "Wait," he managed when he saw the confusion in her eyes.

"Why?" she hissed. Her emerald eyes were wild, her hair a mess. "You don't understand, Theron. She's coming for us now, my mother. You made an enemy of her and now she won't stop until she destroys us both."

"I won't let that happen," he growled, still holding her wrists. He could feel her trembling. "But you're hurting, upset. This isn't the way…" he trailed off, unsure of his next words. "It isn't…proper."

She stared at him with a look of utter mystification, as though Theron had been speaking in the lost language of the Elysian.

"You just defied the Matron of Fresia," she said quietly. "Have probably set *the entire Magisterium* against us—and you're worried about what's *proper?*"

Tearing herself from his grip, the princess burst into laughter. It annoyed Theron at first, the hint of a glare creeping into his brow. It didn't help, of course, that he *burned*. The withdrawal was more than just physical, and the guilt about what he was doing, he could feel it splitting him open, a chisel working at the cracks in his mind, prising them apart. The agimet lanterns were so bright, he wanted to close his eyes against their brilliance—*no, he wanted to consume it…*

…instead there was a princess *laughing at him*.

"Stop." The growl ripped from his throat as he rose to his feet.

"Why?" she hissed, advancing on him.

Her eyes shimmered in the agimet light. There was something eerily familiar about them. Maybe it was the rage that burned inside those emerald depths, built upon a life of pain and servitude and frustration. He knew it well, could feel it burning through his body now, the frustrated desire—though for *atar*, or the princess, he couldn't say.

All he knew was the inferno within him would consume anything it touched.

"I don't want to hurt you."

"You really think you could?" Jenna murmured. She took another step. He loomed over her, but she did not flinch from his gaze. "How cute."

Rage washed through Theron, filling him, mixing with the need, until he no longer knew where one began and the other ended. A snarl slid from his lips as his hand closed around her pale throat. The golden collar was cold to his touch, her flesh warm. Jenna's eyes widened, but still she refused to look away.

"Enough games," he growled.

To his surprise, Jenna grinned. "There he is. *That's* the man I need."

Theron's anger spluttered. "What?"

"I don't need *Master Falkenrath*—or whoever that was just now —to take on my mother," Jenna hissed. Her eyes burned as she pressed herself into his grasp. "I need the man who was willing to gamble everything to call my mother's bluff." She bared her teeth. "I need Theron Falkenrath."

Theron was taken aback by the words. No one…no one had ever *needed* him. Not like this. They looked for the prince of thieves or the Elysian with the special talents. Jenna…Jenna just wanted him to be…him.

Even if that wasn't who she thought it was.

"I could destroy you," he whispered. It was the truth, after all.

Jenna didn't care. Those strangely familiar eyes just kept watching him, shining with the light of agimet, and something more. Not fear, or anger now, but a need of her own, a desire only he could fulfil.

"Show me," she whispered.

QUINTIN SAT BY THE POOL, HIS GAZE ON THE STARS SCATTERED across the velvet sky. Memories swirled through his mind like ripples upon the water, weighing on his soul. Claire. She would have loved what they'd set out to do here. Always the dreamer, she'd believed they would one day change the world. Make it better.

That's what a job like this should have been about.

Instead, one selfish man had turned it into a game of revenge.

He should have known better. It was always about Theron, even when the plan bore another man's name. And yet, Quintin had let himself believe—again—that the Mover could be better. That foolish hope had already cost him his beloved.

His father is Leonardo Falkenrath.

Quintin closed his eyes. He should have walked away the moment Kaila told him the truth. Instead, he remained, helping Theron, clinging to the man like a merchant to fool's gold.

Footsteps on stone broke his reverie. He looked over his shoulder. Theron approached, his tunic askew, his hair in disarray. His heart sank. He hadn't, surely?

"The princess?" he whispered.

Theron looked away, but Quintin glimpsed the shame in the man's eyes. "I didn't mean…"

Quintin lowered his head. He shouldn't be surprised; the man's depravity knew no limits. "I'm done, Theron."

"What?" There was disbelief in Theron's voice. "Quintin, come on. We're so close. And it's not like I used your power—"

"Leonardo Falkenrath is your father."

Theron stilled, frozen in the moonlight. Quintin could see him weighing his next words. Would he deny it?

"Ah, I see," the Mover murmured instead. Stepping up to the edge of the pool, he took a seat. "How…"

"Kaila let it slip," Quintin replied flatly.

Theron nodded. "Understandable."

Silence stretched between them, filled only by the faint rustle of leaves in the night breeze.

"You lied to me, Theron" Quintin said at last. "Again."

"I know. I'm sorry."

"No, you're not."

Theron didn't respond. Quintin looked at his friend. He wasn't looking at Quintin, but the reflection of the twin moons in the water. It set a spark amidst the kindling of Quintin's rage.

"You don't care about anyone but yourself, do you?"

Theron flinched. "Of course I care. It's just…the addiction—"

"*Enough*," Quintin snapped, rising to his feet. "Enough with the excuses! You were like this long before that shard, Theron. Otherwise, Claire would still be with us, and you know it!"

He loomed over Theron, fists clenched, rage spilling from him with every word. He saw the flicker of hurt in Theron's eyes as he rose more slowly.

"That's not fair. She was my friend too."

"Was she? Or was she just another body to send to her doom so *Theron Falkenrath* could have what he wanted?"

Theron just stared at him, unable to reply. Quintin knew he wasn't being fair. They'd chosen the job together: a raid against a merchant's villa they knew held a small fortune in gold and jewellery—enough to buy them each several years supply of agimet.

But the target hadn't been random. Theron had orchestrated the con, disguising himself as a nobleman from Brensheld with ore and timber to trade. They had met the merchant in his villa outside the city to arrange the trade, though of course their side of the transaction had never existed.

Unfortunately, they hadn't planned for the illegal militia of sellswords their mark kept on the take. The merchant had caught them in the act and called his guards before they could make a clean escape. Cornered in the upper storeys of the villa, Claire had stayed at the stairs to hold them off. She had been what

Theron called a Binder—able to change the natural state of matter—and she had used her Gift to good effect, hurling makeshift explosives down on the sellswords.

But there had only been a few crystals between them and their store of *atar* had depleted quickly. Theron's agimet gave out as he lowered them from the upper windows of the villa. Quintin had broken his leg on the landing, while Claire…

…Claire had never made it to the window.

"I can't change what happened, Quintin," Theron said softly.

"But you could change what you are now. You just don't want to."

"You think I haven't changed?" Theron snarled. "I cursed myself to save Kaila. I had Ambrose make weavings to protect your girls—"

"Don't bring them into this!" Quintin barked. "You're not doing any of this for them."

"I'm doing it *all* for them!" Theron roared, his voice raw. "For them, for Claire and my sister, for my mother. Even for those sorry bastards in Soul Square. Every single person who has suffered under the Magisterium and the monsters it empowers."

Quintin shook his head. "Words," he rasped. "Do they even mean anything to you anymore? You'd see the whole world burn if that's what it took to destroy your father, wouldn't you?"

Theron looked away, his shoulders sagging. He didn't deny the accusation.

"Exactly," Quintin said, his voice softening. "And then what would be left for my girls?" He turned to leave.

"Hope," Theron whispered.

Quintin frowned, glancing back. "What?"

"There would be hope," Theron repeated. He gestured across the bay to the shadow of the Sanctum. "The Magisterium *might* be better than anarchy. *Might*. But even if everything you say is true, it still must be destroyed."

"Why? Because your petty—"

"No," Theron interrupted, lifting his head to meet his friend's eyes. "It's because men like the king, *like my father*, they won't go quietly, Quintin. And so long as they rule, there will never be hope for anything better. There will only be…this."

For a long moment, Quintin held Theron's gaze. He wanted to believe his old friend, but there had already been so many lies. And this was no longer just about him. He had his girls, their futures to think about. He couldn't afford to follow Claire's dreams any longer. Even if it meant giving up on hope.

"Words," he whispered, and this time his voice cracked.

Then turning, Quintin walked away, leaving Theron alone beneath the twin moons of Fresia.

19

There were dark places beneath the Sanctum, Kaila had discovered in her time there, darker even than the chamber where she'd been locked that first night. Black cells where the enemies of the Magisterium could scream and scream and never be heard by another living soul, and hidden rooms where the very stones were stained black with the blood of its victims.

So when the Matron appeared at the door of her private chambers in the Daughter's quarter, Kaila had feared the worst. A voice inside had screamed for her to attack, to take her chances with the collar and try and make her escape. If her Gift had not been blocked, she might have tried just that.

But of course, resistance was futile so long as the Aegis shone around the Matron's wrist. So Kaila had submitted instead, allowing the old woman to lead her into the depths with only the vague hope she would ever see the light of day again.

Word had reached the Sanctum within hours of the dinner —Jenna Frye would marry Theron Falkenrath in less than two weeks, on the night of the Summer Gala. Kaila had caught glimpses of the Matron since, her face twisted as though she'd been forced to swallow a lemon, rage simmering in her eyes.

Whatever her plans for Rohan, they obviously hadn't involved Jenna upstaging the prince with a relationship of her own.

So Kaila had failed, and now the Matron was leading her into the dark. Within minutes, the concrete passageways swallowed them up. The deeper they went, the more Kaila felt the weight of the Sanctum above. It was oppressive, knowing all that stone and concrete stood between her and the light. Not even the agimet hidden in her dress could comfort her, blocked as she was by the golden collar.

"I am sorry I couldn't be of more service, Matron," she said after long minutes had gone by without a word passing between them. She struggled to keep the tremor from her voice. "I…I still hope to return the prince to the Magisterium's embrace one day."

"I should hope so," the Matron said without looking back. "If you are to take my place as Matron, you'll need my son at your side as king."

Kaila blinked. "Sorry…am I missing something?" she asked. "With Jenna's marriage, she will be first in line, won't she?"

The older woman snorted. "Jenna couldn't keep a man to save her life," she replied. "Which, on this occasion…" she didn't finish, though laughter rasped from her throat.

They continued into the depths, until even the walls changed, grey concrete giving way to jet-black glass. *Obsidian.* Kaila's skin crawled and a chill crept down her spine. The same as the Black Tower. It couldn't be a coincidence, could it? She came to a stop, reaching out to touch the wall.

"Where are you taking me?" she whispered, unable to hold her tongue any longer.

"Not far now," the Matron evaded the question.

A few minutes later, they stood before a great stone door. Again Kaila's scalp tingled as she recognised the runes carved into the surface—they were the Elysian script. What was this place? She said nothing though, hardly dared speak, least she give herself away. Reaching out her hand, the Matron pressed the Aegis against one of the runes.

Light flashed and the stone door rumbled open as if gripped by a will of its own. Within, a fresh light shimmered strangely against the black walls—not the artificial, haunting brilliance of broken crystals, but the ever-changing colour of pure agimet.

Kaila was trembling as she followed the old woman inside. Could the Matron know who she was, *what* she was? Why else would she have led her to this place, this secret shrine to the Elysian. Just stepping into the chamber, Kaila could sense the power in the room, the strength of the ambient *atar*. There must be hundreds of crystals inside, though in the brilliance she was momentarily blinded.

The door slid closed with a harsh *thud,* sealing them inside. It was almost too much for Kaila. Her panic had become a wild thing by now, a screaming animal demanding it be released. Only the cold pressure of the collar kept it tamed.

When her eyes finally adjusted, Kaila found herself at a loss for words. She'd been mistaken. The light didn't come from multiple crystals—but a single stone, the largest she had ever seen. It sat on a pedestal in the centre of the room, as large as a skull, larger even, maybe. And its glow…she could *feel* it. Even without touching the stone, she could sense the *atar* inside, shining with enough power to match a nexus. In fact…

…she looked deeper into the dimension beyond their world and found the looping energies of the nexus. They concentrated in this room, so intense she could hardly bear to look at them. As she'd suspected, like the high chamber of the Black Tower, this room sat at the centre of the Tah'raus nexus.

What Kaila didn't understand was *why?* The ambient energy *anywhere* in the city was more than strong enough to power the crystals of even the largest machines created by the Magisterium. What possible need could there be for someone to dig down all this way.

Her eyes travelled the room. There were differences from the

Black Tower. The floor here was polished metal, and there were other chambers as well, side passageways through which she glimpsed the shimmer of glass and metal and other crystals. This place was larger than it appeared, like a building within a building—or maybe…someone had built the Sanctum around it.

"What is this place?" she whispered.

"This is the heart of the Sanctum," the Matron said quietly. "Our legends say that T'iana herself built it after she first set humanity on our path of liberation."

"T'iana built this?"

Exhaling, Kaila began to wander around the circumference of the chamber—ignoring the other passageways for now. Closer to the obsidian walls, she saw these too had been carved with Elysian runes. Except, these were different from the ones outside. Those had been chiselled with precision, while these…they were shallow, like they'd been etched by an unpractised hand. How she wished she could read them. Maybe…

"What do these words say?" she whispered.

"We do not know," the Matron replied. "It is in the language of the enemy."

Kaila looked around, her heart suddenly racing. The Matron was watching her; not with suspicion, but curiosity. She exhaled and asked the question that was obviously expected.

"Why would T'iana have left writings in the language of the Elysian?"

"Because," the Matron said quietly, "the First Matron was one of them."

She had known that already, from Theron and the ruins of Iselador. But it was a secret the Magisterium had closely guarded for centuries, a truth their Sisters fought to supress. Why would the Matron be telling her it now?

"What?" Kaila whispered, hoping she appeared stunned. It wasn't a difficult part to play.

The Matron nodded. "She was their queen."

"Then why…"

"Because people are simple creatures. The uncivilised would not understand. Eventually, some would begin to question, if one of them could change, maybe others can as well. There would be calls for a ceasefire. *Peace.*" She studied Kaila, eyes like chipped granite. "They would not see the truth."

"What truth?" Kaila croaked. Blood pulsed in her ears. She stared at the woman, hardly daring to breathe. This was it, the answers she had longed for since the day she'd first learned about her powers, the day her old life had ended.

The Matron's expression was unreadable as she approached the podium and its enormous crystal. "T'iana knew," she murmured, "that it doesn't matter what their intentions are or where they come from; the Elysian are dangerous. They cannot be controlled—their *power* cannot be controlled." She turned suddenly from the crystal, her eyes finding Kaila. "So it falls to *us* to destroy them."

Standing there in that room, surrounded by the power of the nexus, by the heat of that shining crystal, Kaila found she could not breathe. She stared at the Matron, that terrible, brutal truth ringing in her ears.

It wasn't an accident. There had always been a piece of her that wondered, if only Sister Eurador had believed her, that she was faithful to humanity, all of this could have been avoided. Her life could have gone on, her Gift dedicated to the Magisterium and her duty.

But her loyalty had never mattered. All that mattered was that she was dangerous.

Kaila could feel her pulse in her stomach. "I still don't understand what this place is."

"It is T'iana's last gift to us," the Matron replied.

Approaching the podium, she held out her hand towards the crystal. Intrigued despite herself, Kaila crept closer. As the Matron's hand approached the agimet, the light shifted, and she realised there were wires around the crystal, looping, crisscrossing to form a web of steel and gold and silver that encased the stone.

As the Matron rested her hand on the cage, the Aegis began to glow.

"The First Matron used her cursed magics to imprint herself on this chamber," the Matron explained, "with the Aegis, the rulers of Fresia have been able to commune with her remnant." She pursed her lips, considering Kaila. "She has a warning for those who hold the Aegis."

"What…what warning?"

"I will show you."

Alarm shot down Kaila's spine as the Matron offered her hand. She didn't want to go anywhere near that crystal or the infernal device around the Matron's wrist, nor anything else T'iana had created for that matter. The more she learned of the woman, the more she understood why the Elysian called her the Great Betrayer and the cursed queen. Even a thousand years after her death, T'iana still influenced events in the world today. But the Matron was watching her, brow furrowed, eyes shining in the glow of that great crystal. Kaila needed a way out, but she wasn't going to find one down here. She turned to the crystal, trying to keep the fear from her face.

"Do not be afraid, child," the Matron said. "The First Matron is kind to her chosen."

Kaila shivered. The way the Matron spoke, it was like the woman still lived. What exactly had she left behind in this dark place? Had she been a weaver, like Ambrose? Was this remnant an illusion, cast into the minds of each Matron that had followed her, or was it something more?

She was about to find out. Bracing herself, Kaila accepted the Matron's hand. To her alarm, the older woman dragged her forward, toward the crystal itself. For a moment, she resisted, thinking of the *atar* she would absorb and reveal herself—but for once the collar was a boon there. So steeling herself, Kaila let the fight go from her. Reaching out together, Kaila and the Matron touched their hands to the shimmering wires surrounding the crystal.

Everything went dark.

She was in that other place again, the realm between life and death. It was almost growing familiar, though it also seemed to change in subtle ways, as if each visit she touched a different part of it.

"Welcome, my daughter."

Kaila spun as the voice spoke from behind her. A woman had appeared in the darkness. Suddenly her heart was racing as she looked upon the familiar face. T'iana, First Matron of Fresia, had not aged a day since they had carved the great statue of her in Iselador. If anything, in the flesh—if this realm could be called that—she seemed younger, more vibrant as her hazel eyes looked upon the void. She was still the most beautiful woman Kaila had ever seen—and that was saying something after brushing shoulders with the likes of Jenna Frye.

"T'iana, T…T'iana, I'm…honoured—"

"It pleases me to know my legacy continues." The remnant spoke over the top of Kaila, her voice strangely metallic, like it echoed from the depths of a pit. The image flickered as the First Matron continued. "Though our kingdom was born in blood, it is my hope…" The voice crackled and it seemed as though several words were lost, "shall build something better… grander…in our wisdom. Or perhaps…"

Acting on a hunch, Kaila stepped towards the apparition. The image spluttered, but the eyes of the queen did not follow her. Instead, T'iana stared at the empty space where Kaila had just been standing.

She's not really here, Kaila realised. The Matron was right, this was only a shadow left behind by the ancient queen.

"…be warned, my daughter. The enemy…cunning. Be watchful for… return…I sought to cleanse…children will seek…possess the Aegis."

Her heart pounding, Kaila approached another step as the shade fell silent. Was this the threat the Matron had spoken of? A warning against the Elysian ever regaining the Aegis. Her heart pulsed as she remembered her conversation with Theron and Ambrose, about another world. Could it actu-ally be true?

Kaila had felt the power of the Aegis. In both human and Elysian histo-ries, its loss had been a great blow to the enemy. But could it truly tear open the fabric of reality?

Her heart pulsed as the spirit spoke again. This time, however, the message was scrambled beyond all recognition. "…gain…power…contain…darkness return—"

Abruptly, the remnant of T'iana froze, cutting off her final words.

The nether world shifted.

And suddenly Kaila was no longer in the presence of T'iana, but her long lost king.

Oberon sat at an enormous workbench, head bent over a contraption like the ones Kaila had seen those times she had almost died. This one lay in pieces, little gears and levers and nuts spread out over the table, tiny in his massive hands. He did not seem to notice her presence, even when she approached the workbench. Alarm prickled her scalp when she saw the device. It looked familiar somehow, yet Kaila was sure it hadn't been in the king's chamber the last time she had visited.

"Oberon, what's going on?" she whispered.

The king didn't move or even raise his head. He couldn't see her either. Yet she sensed this image was different to the last. While the remnant of T'iana felt empty, its very fabric stuttering, Oberon was solid. Despite the emptiness of this place, there was a power about the man, like the heat from a furnace, contained, controlled, yet capable of incinerating her in an instant.

Trembling, she reached out a hand. Maybe if she touched him—

With a jolt, Kaila returned to the real world. Heart pounding, a sharp pain driving through her temples, she staggered back from the enormous crystal. The room spun, shimmering as stars filled her vision—no, not stars, *atarlights.* For one glorious second, she rejoiced at the feeling of *atar* once more rushing through her blood.

But joy soon turned to panic—the power of the crystal had torn past the block placed on her Gift. Now she had far too much power boiling inside. It was bound to shine through both Ambrose's illusion and the lenses, revealing her as Elysian.

Thinking quickly, Kaila cried out and fell to one knee, squeezing her eyes closed as she did so. At the same time, she turned her gaze inwards, seeking the *atar* filling her soul. She couldn't use her Gift to consume it—the Matron would notice that for sure—but she still had her Warden's ability to channel *atar*. Carefully, Kaila channelled the excess *atar* into her hidden crystals and prayed they could contain that much energy.

A second later, a hand rested on her shoulder.

"Easy, Daughter Wrenn," came the Matron's voice, "the transfer can be difficult for those inexperienced in the magics of the enemy."

Trembling, Kaila nodded, though she didn't dare lift her eyes from the floor. The gushing of *atar* in her veins had slowed to a trickle, but she couldn't risk it until the last drops had left her soul.

"What was that?" she rasped instead, still unsure what the woman had meant to show her. Or why.

"You heard the warning of the First Matron?"

Mouth parched, Kaila could only manage another nod. The last *atar* had left her now, so she opened her eyes and found the Matron leaning over her. Was that actual concern in the old woman's eyes?

"I did," she said carefully, "but it was broken, incomplete."

"The fragment has become corrupted over time, but its meaning remains clear."

Did it? Kaila wasn't so sure, but based on the conviction in the Matron's voice, she wasn't about to say as much out loud. With the woman's help, she carefully regathered her feet. Her legs remained unsteady. What was it the First Matron had said, a warning against…an enemy?

Her blood chilled as she remembered the second vision. "There was…something else."

The old woman nodded sagely, lips pursed in a thin line. "So the First Matron blessed you with a vision too," she murmured. "Good. It means my faith in you is not misplaced. Tell me what you saw."

Kaila swallowed. This was dangerous ground. Carefully, she recounted what she had glimpsed: a great man in the darkness, seated at a workbench, tinkering with some strange device.

"I understand all of this is difficult to take in, Daughter Wrenn," the Matron said when she finished, "but what you saw was no man, but the most vile and hated of our enemies. He was called Oberon in his day. He ruled the Elysian as their king before the First Matron used the power of the Aegis against him."

A cold breath blew across the nape of Kaila's neck. "But he…that didn't…*he* didn't seem like a remnant."

"Because he is not," the Matron said, "even with the power of the Aegis, T'iana was not strong enough to slay Oberon. Instead, she trapped him." The woman loomed over Kaila. "*He* is the reason the Magisterium was created. Why there must always be a Matron and a King to hold the two pieces of the Aegis. We keep watch over the Dark King, that he may never escape to terrorise our people again."

Needles prickled Kaila's skin. The words of the ancient king came to her from all that time ago, when she had spoken to him in the nether world between life and death. She had asked him why he was still there.

I wait…

That had been his answer. She had thought it strange at the time, that his spirit lingered in that place. She had thought maybe T'iana…but now she knew the truth. He was not lingering in the other realm—he was trapped there. Hope swelled in her heart as she recalled the power of his presence, the strength of his gaze…

…and then died as she realised what this meant. The Aegis *wasn't* a gateway to another world where the Elysian would find allies against the Magisterium. It was a prison, built to hold one man.

And one man, however powerful, couldn't save them. Though…she frowned, recalling again the object on Oberon's workbench. A machine…her skin tingled as Kaila realised she *did* recognise it, dismantled though it had been. It was one of the agimet heaters she had seen dotted all about Tah'raus.

"The…Dark King," she whispered, using the name the Matron had given Oberon, "the device he was working on…"

"In his boredom, he creates machines."

"But I *recognised* it."

The woman smirked. "Yes, my husband and I have used the Aegis these past two decades to spy on the Dark King. His inventions have helped fuel our revolution."

Blood pulsing in her ears, Kaila slowly shifted her gaze to the Matron. Did she dare ask for the truth? "Is that why you oppose your daughter's succession? Because she would not follow your path?"

"No," the woman said. Her nose wrinkled, as though disgusted at just the mention of Jenna. "I oppose her succession because Jenna must never hold the Aegis."

"But *why?*" Kaila pressed, trying to sound earnest. If she could learn the woman's motivation for keeping Jenna from the throne, then she might also know how far the woman would go to prevent it happening. "She's your own flesh and blood. Surely…"

"That's just it, Eliza," the Matron replied, "Jenna is *not* my flesh and blood. She never was." Those granite eyes held her gaze. "She is one of *them*. One of the enemy."

"*What?*" Kaila rocked back as though struck.

That wasn't possible. *It wasn't.*

Her kind couldn't…

The Magisterium wouldn't…

The Elysian were…

The words buzzed in her ears, *searing* into her skull until it throbbed with the madness of it all.

"Jenna was—*is*—the result of my husband's shame," the Matron said quietly. She wandered around the pedestal, Aegis held out towards the crystal. Something was happening between the two; *atar* flowed between them, draining the enormous crystal, charging the device.

"But…her Trials," it was all Kaila could think about.

Elysian. Jenna was Elysian, like her. Kaila couldn't bring herself to believe it. Why would the Matron do such a thing, an act of treason, when so many others had been hunted and tortured and killed for the very same crime.

"That's why I made her a Daughter so young," the Matron replied. "The collars block the power of the enemy. I know, the Nameless will judge me for my sins. If I had a chance to do it all again, perhaps I would have done it differently. Drowned the brat before she could take her first mewling breaths." Her granite eyes watched Kaila, unflinching. "But my *beloved* wouldn't allow it. He had lain with the cursed creature, but he would not accept the cost of his actions. So I was forced to clean up after him; to rewrite my own histories, expunge and exile those Sisters who suspected the truth, so no one would ever know."

Oh how Kaila loathed this woman! That she and so many others had suffered because of who and what they were, the cursed *Elysian,* and this woman, the most powerful in the kingdom, had hidden one in her own house.

"Why?" she needed to know. Needed to understand what could have made a woman of such convictions commit this hypocrisy.

"At first, it was because the child was convenient." A sneer stretched the Matron's lips. "She was an assassin, an Elysian who went by the name of Reaper."

Kaila's skin tingled at the name. She recalled the stuffed rabbit the woman in the ruins of Iselador had kept. A child's.

"She was a powerful tool when it came to the succession," the Matron continued, unaware of Kaila's revelation. "It was different in my age. My predecessor had no children. Things got…messy." She pressed her lips in a thin line. "The Reaper was useful, but difficult to control—until my fool of a husband decided to get the witch pregnant."

By now Kaila's heart was pounding so hard she feared it would burst from her chest. *Jenna was the Reaper's daughter!* Her hands balled into fists. Did the girl know? Did she even *suspect?*

"She tried to hide the child, of course, but I found it. After that, the witch did whatever I told her."

"What…what happened to her?"

"Eventually, she became a liability. I had her taken care of…" the woman trailed off. "My assassins never returned, but nor did the Reaper."

"And Jenna?"

"Why do I still protect her?" The Matron's voice was bitter. "Ungrateful child, much as I would like to be rid of her, my husband would never allow it. And were I to expose her…" She bared her teeth, her frustration evident. "I would hang alongside her for aiding the enemy."

A shiver ran down Kaila's spine. So that was it. Despite all her ideals and claims of a higher meaning, it all came down to protecting her own life.

"I understand your loathing, Daughter Wrenn." Kaila swallowed at the words. Had she really let her expression slip? "Perhaps one day, you will understand what it is to make a difficult choice. However, know this, I am not so far gone that I would risk my kingdom. So long as it is within my power, Jenna will never possess the Aegis." She raised her hand, the light of the recharged Aegis shimmering strangely across her face. "Whatever it might cost."

A part of Kaila longed to call the woman's bluff, to show the world once and for all the selfish monster she really was. But looking into those terrible eyes, she found herself believing the words instead. Whatever terrible things the Matron was capable of, the lives she had taken, the depravity she had committed to rise above the muck, sacrificing her kingdom was the one line she would not cross.

Kaila could almost respect her for it. Almost.

Instead, she felt a powerful anger building within her, a rage that yet again her life, her decisions had been taken from her. This secret would destroy everyone it touched. When the rest of the Magisterium discovered what she'd done, they wouldn't just come for the Matron and Jenna, they would come for *everyone*. The king, of course, but Theron as well; even Rohan, even the real *Eliza* might not be safe from their vengeance.

And so Kaila didn't have a choice. She had to do what the Matron asked; had to convince—*force*—Rohan to marry her, to do whatever it took to stop Jenna's secret coming out. Otherwise, Rohan, Theron, *the entire plan*, would all be doomed.

Though, there was *something* left. The king. Was the warning even true? Would an Elysian using the device really break Oberon's cage? A tremor ran down her spine; not of fear or anger, but *excitement*. She had stood in the presence of the king, sensed his power when she was a spirit lost in the nether world. Now she had a chance to free him.

She clung to the thought. Let the others keep their schemes, *that* would be her true purpose. She would marry Rohan, not because the Matron commanded it, but to free the man that had saved her life. And maybe, just maybe, the Elysian would gain an ally against their terrible enemy.

"What do you need me to do, Matron?" she whispered.

If the warning was true, it didn't matter whether Jenna and Theron claimed the throne, or herself. A part of her wanted to throw back her head and howl at the mockery of it all. Here was the Matron, scheming to keep one Elysian from the Aegis, and inadvertently gifting it to another. They had already won. The woman just didn't know it yet.

"My son is…soft," she murmured, and for a moment Kaila thought she actually saw something in those empty eyes, "but he is the tool I must use. You and Rohan must exchange your vows alongside Jenna and Theron, at the Summer Gala."

Kaila frowned. That was unusual. Why the same night? Surely if Rohan was to supplant his older sister as heir to the throne, they needed to be married *first*. But she had learned not to question the Matron, so only gave a nod.

"Good. I will arrange the rest," the Matron said with a smile. Reaching out the arm that held the Aegis, she rested it on Kaila's shoulder. The breath caught in her throat as her collar tightened. "Your only priority now is my son, understood?"

Kaila nodded quickly as stars danced across her vision. The pressure vanished as quickly as it had started. Struggling to keep her calm, she sucked in a long breath of air and dipped her head.

"Thank you for trusting me with this, Matron," she said. "I won't let you down."

"I know you won't, Eliza," the Matron replied, then hesitated. "You will speak to no one of this, understood?"

The Aegis pulsed once more, and Kaila felt the collar pulsate. It didn't tighten this time, but seemed more like a threat—a promise of violence if she broke her word. Fortunately, she didn't intend to fail. Lifting her head, she met those concrete eyes.

"Yes, Matron," Kaila said. "Understood."

20

One day later, Kaila stood in the whirring, agimet-powered elevator as it lifted her the seven stories to the princes apartment. It made her skin crawl just to stand inside the thing, feeling all the corrupted crystals around her.

Unfortunately, a Daughter using the stairs would have immediately drawn attention, so she had forced herself to grow accustomed to this ritual. Today, however, was different. She couldn't have slept for more than a few hours after the Matron's visit. Her body felt strangely energised, as though she could *almost* access her blocked Gift. Touching the crystal in her pocket, she tried yet again to draw out the *atar*.

Nothing.

Her shoulders sank. Though she had only possessed it a short time, she had grown accustomed to that power, reassured by its presence. For what she was about to do…

Ambrose had warned her not to meddle with his plans—but that didn't matter now. Their plan had a fatal flaw and she couldn't even tell them about it. Hopefully they would trust her.

Hopefully *Rohan* would trust her.

Her stomach twisted uncomfortably at the thought of the prince. He had been nothing but kind to her, welcoming her into his home, trusting her with his secrets, even listening to her own painful story.

And now she must make him accept a burden he had run from his entire life—or his mother would destroy them all.

She had already decided on her strategy. Rohan would never submit to the Matron's demands. He had only agreed to this arrangement to stop her pestering. Marriage would turn their charade into something real, confirm his place in the line of succession. From there, it was just a hop and a skip and he would find himself king—with all the terrible responsibilities that came with it.

No, he would never agree. But there had been something between them on her last visit, a budding fondness. Attraction, even. Exactly what Kaila needed; a weakness she could exploit, like she had done with Eamon Stadwit all those weeks ago.

She didn't want to manipulate Rohan, but this was the path she had chosen. Kaila would no longer be the pawn others used in their games. And if that meant others were hurt in the process—

Ding.

Kaila winced as the bell announced her arrival. The doors slid open with a rattle of iron wheels. Drawing in a breath, she straightened her shoulders and stepped from the elevator. She paused in the foyer, glancing at the great mirrors that lined the wall. Until today, she had remained conservative with her pick of outfits from Eliza's closet. Full bodied gowns, flattering for sure, but nothing too revealing.

Tonight, just looking at herself, Kaila could feel her cheeks growing red. She had spent the day at Marriats, a designer known for his somewhat *controversial* outfits. The slip-dress she was wearing now had to be some of his best work. The scarlet silk— what little there was of it—clung to her skin, while thin straps left her back almost entirely exposed. The fabric gathered at the base of her spine and cascaded into a skirt that was altogether too short for the brisk Tah'raus nights or her own comfort. Each time she took a step, Kaila had to stop herself from tugging the hem back down, as the fabric rode up the curve of her hips.

Footsteps carried from the kitchen as Rohan emerged, lips parted to offer a greeting. Instead, he froze and for a full second just stood in the doorway, mouth hanging open, eyes so wide they were at risk of falling out of their sockets. Despite her discomfort a moment ago, Kaila felt a little fluttering of butterflies in her stomach. Rohan's reaction almost made the embarrassment of finding the dress worth the effort.

Almost.

"Eliza…" the words finally tumbled from Rohan's lips. "What…"

Plastering a smile on her lips, Kaila stepped forward and quickly took his hand. "I thought…after our last conversation, I might surprise you, my prince," she said. Silently, she cursed her overly formal tone. Her tongue felt heavy and it was a struggle not to trip over her words. "That is, ah, I guess, I thought a thank you was in order…"

She adjusted the strap of her dress, feeling the weight of the collar around her throat.

"You didn't have to do that," he said with a frown. "You don't have to do anything for me or my mother."

Kaila forced a smile. "I know," she replied, her voice faltering. She wanted to tell him the truth, but… "I…I wanted to."

Rohan's eyes softened, though his brow remained furrowed. "Eliza…"

Heart pounding, Kaila stepped in close and placed a hand on Rohan's chest before he could finish whatever he'd been about to say. "I want this," she whispered, the words like bile on her tongue.

His face flushed, Rohan swallowed visibly. "I don't know, Eliza…I mean…" He didn't seem quite able to meet her eyes.

"The other night on the balcony." Her voice was barely a whisper as she reached up to stroke his cheek. "You seemed to know then."

"Maybe I was wrong."

Kaila felt sick. The butterflies had died, replaced by a cold lump that settled in the pit of her stomach. But it was too late to turn back. Tilting her head to the side, she forced a little smile.

"Why don't you kiss me and find out?"

There was a pounding in her ears as his eyes found hers again. Suddenly, he was watching her with a powerful intensity. It should have filled her with warmth like it had that other night. Instead she found herself struggling to breathe.

Wrong, wrong, wrong!

Before there had been warmth and hope and friendship—now all Kaila could think about was her betrayal, how she was manipulating him to save her own skin, how all he'd ever done was help her.

She almost choked when Rohan leaned in, almost pushed him away and confessed everything. But fear and the cold metal around her throat stopped her, and so she stood frozen as their lips met.

The kiss was everything she had dreamed it would be—soft, tender, his arms around her, his lips against hers, the taste of him on her tongue. All she wanted was to lose herself in this moment, in the racing of his heart against her chest and the heat of his breath, the strength of his body beneath her fingers…

…yet all she could feel was the hollow in her chest and how it was nothing like what she wanted.

Wrong.

There was a sound crashing inside her head, discordant and broken melodies—one beautiful and sweet, the other harsh, tearing at her soul. Goosebumps ran down her spine as Rohan's fingers traced lines across her exposed back. His touch was light, but his fingers burned as they explored her skin, slowly growing more adventurous as she drew him deeper into the kiss, finding the slits in the sides of her dress, the deep neckline, the short skirt—

Gasping, she pulled away, grabbing his hands to push them between them, creating space.

"We can't," she said, her voice trembling.

Rohan's pupils were enormous, his face flushed. "What?" he rasped, hoarse. "Sorry, I didn't mean—"

"No, no, I want to," she whispered, the lie burning on her tongue. She stepped in close again, fingers entwining with his own. "But…we can't. It's not real, right?" The blood was pulsing in her ears again. "And if we did…I can't lie to the Matron. She would know. And then…" She swallowed hard. "Then she would make us…"

Rohan frowned. "Eliza, I don't understand. What are you saying?"

She looked away, unable to meet the sincerity in his eyes. "She would force us to marry," she whispered. It took an effort to keep the tears from falling. "But that's not what you want, is it?" Her voice cracked, and her head jerked up to look at him, eyes wide as her breath quickened. "Unless you've changed your mind…"

She watched him for a response, but he just stared at her, brow furrowed. Her scalp crawled as sudden doubt rose in her chest. She raised a hand to stroke his cheek. "Maybe it wouldn't be so bad?" she wondered, voice wavering. "If we really did? I know—"

She broke off as Rohan took a quick step back and released her hands. His expression had changed. A scowl now darkened his lips.

"Eliza, what is this?"

Bile rose in Kaila's throat. He knew. The Trickster had damned her and now all her lies were set to unravel. She opened her mouth to let the truth spill out—about the Matron, about his sister, about everything—but instead, the collar tightened, cutting off her words.

Her heart lurched and she gagged, stumbling back from Rohan as stars burst across her vision. Legs buckling, she crashed to the ground, clawing at the cold metal band around her throat.

"Eliza?" Rohan shouted, his anger turning to alarm. "Eliza!"

She barely heard him through the ringing. Her vision began to tunnel and her limbs grew weak, uncooperative. The room faded towards darkness, like she was being dragged far beneath the surface of the harbour waters.

I can't tell him. I can never tell him. Never!

Abruptly, the collar loosened. She gasped, sucking in a ragged breath. Fresh oxygen filled her lungs, but the darkness still circled, filling her body with a trembling. She could hear Rohan's voice, distant, panicked.

"Eliza, are you okay? Speak to me!"

Her chest ached as if bound in steel, and as the darkness retreated, the world felt too bright, too loud. A cold sweat beaded her skin. Slowly, Rohan's face resolved from the haze. He knelt beside her, hands hovering over her body, as if afraid to touch her again. His face softened as their eyes met.

"Come on, Eliza, breathe."

She shook her head weakly, trying to clear the last of the stars from her eyes. Her temples throbbed as she sat up and her fingers twitched, but finally her body stilled. She let the prince help her stand and stumble to the sofa. The fear and panic lingered like a nasty aftertaste as she sank into the cushions. Almost instinctively, she reached for Rohan, but he drew away, retreating to the other sofa instead.

"Eliza, what's going on?" His tone was soft, but she could see steel in his eyes.

She swallowed. She couldn't tell him the truth, not the *real* truth, at least, but maybe there was another way…

"This isn't going to work, Rohan."

The creases in the prince's brow deepened. "Eliza, you're scaring me. What's not going to work?"

"*This,*" she said, gesturing to the pair of them, "this little… game we decided to play. The dinners and the quiet evenings and *moments*, they're all *nice*," with each word, her voice grew harder, "but it's not going to be enough for your mother. It never was."

"It doesn't have to be!" he cried. Leaning towards her, he clasped his hands, almost like in prayer. "Not for much longer. Soon Jenna will be married and it'll be done. We'll both be…free."

A lump lodged in Kaila's throat. There was such earnestness in Rohan's eyes. He *needed* what he was saying to be true. But she knew it would never come to pass. The Matron had made that abundantly clear.

"No, Rohan," she rasped, hating herself for the words. "*You* will be free. I'll just be…gone."

His smile faltered. "Eliza…what are you saying?"

Kaila rose on trembling legs to move around the coffee table. Sinking to her knees beside his sofa, she reached out and placed a hand on his leg.

"I'm saying if you care about me at all, Rohan, you'll marry me alongside your sister at the Summer Gala."

The words had the expected effect. Rohan jerked away from her like he'd been stung. It was a fresh dagger carving into Kaila's heart, but she forced her face to remain unchanged.

"That wasn't the deal!" he snarled.

Guilt writhed in her stomach, but steeling herself, Kaila rose so she stood over him.

"You know I'm right, Rohan." She placed a hand on his shoulder. "This is the only way to keep her placated."

"*Placated?*" Snarling, he tore himself away from her and rose so they stood face to face. The air trembled, vibrating with his anger. "Was this your game all along?" he hissed. "Gain my sympathy, become friends, make me believe…" His voice cracked. "Or was this my mother's plan? This has her fingers all over it."

Trembling, Kaila let her hands fall to her side. "That's not fair," she snapped, anger creeping into her voice.

"Life's not fair," he shot back. Then he turned and stalked

towards his bedroom. "I thought you were different, but you're just like all the rest. I trust you'll see yourself out."

Terror rose in her throat as she watched him walk away. She couldn't fail. Failure meant a dark room and a terrible agony for the rest of her life. But fear wouldn't help her now. She needed to get through to him, to convince him things would be better if they did this together. That he didn't have to be like his mother and father before him.

"Please, Rohan," she croaked. "I can't go back."

There must have been something in her voice, because he paused, glancing back at her with a frown. "What do you mean?"

"If I go back..." Kaila trailed off. How much would the Matron's command allow her to say? Well, she was doomed anyway, what did she have to lose? "If I go back and admit I failed, she'll kill me—or worse."

She held her breath, but there was no response from the collar.

The lines on Rohan's brow deepened. "She wouldn't—"

"She would." Her head jerked up to catch his stare. "She promised, in fact, when this all began. *That's* why I was so desperate to make our deal."

"Eliza..." Rohan whispered, horror dawning on his face. "Why would you..."

Kaila looked away. She couldn't face the judgement in his eyes. "We don't all have the luxury of ignoring the Magisterium," she said harshly. "Just...just forget it."

She turned suddenly, intent on fleeing the penthouse, but ran into a chair instead. It crashed to the ground, wood splintering as it struck the concrete floor. Recovering, she marched towards the elevator, her entire body shaking, eyes burning as tears spilt from her eyes.

"Wait, what are you doing?" Rohan's voice chased after her.

"Leaving, like you said," she snapped.

"You said you couldn't go back."

"This is my mess. I'll figure out how to clean it up," she replied.

Reaching the elevator doors, she bashed the button to call for the machine. *Stupid, stupid, stupid!* Why had she thought this plan would work? That she could be anything *other* than someone else's pawn? She didn't dare look back for fear of what she might see in the prince's eyes. Loathing, anger, *pity.* She clenched her teeth. *Fool, fool, fool.*

Ding.

"Wait."

Ignoring him, Kaila stepped into the metal contraption, but suddenly the prince was there, holding out a hand to keep the doors from closing. She was surprised to see concern in his eyes instead of anger.

"Wait," he said again. "Let's talk about this."

"What is there to talk about, Rohan?"

"You were different tonight," he said softly. "Why?"

"Because…" she trailed off, shaking her head. "What does it matter?"

"Because the things you told me…that night on the balcony…it wasn't all just an act for you, was it?"

Kaila looked away, unable to meet his eyes.

"Please, Kaila, I need to know."

She swallowed. How could she even begin to answer that question after everything that had happened? Between Theron, and the plan, the Matron and *Eliza*…how could she know what she really felt.

"I don't know, Rohan," she whispered, squeezing her eyes closed. "I'm sorry, I don't…"

"I understand," he said quietly. A pause followed and she could sense him watching her, judging her again. "Eliza, would you please get out of the lift?"

She stared at him. Part of her just wanted to flee, to run as far as her feet would carry her. But downstairs were the guards, waiting to bring her back to the Sanctum and the Matron. So instead, she let out a breath and stepped back into the apartment.

Rohan let the doors slide shut behind her and gestured toward the sofas. "Sit."

Her legs trembling, Kaila did as she was told, sinking gratefully into soft cushions while Rohan crossed to the liquor cabinet. He poured two glasses of whiskey, handing her one before seating himself at the opposite end of the sofa. They drank in silence, the tension building slowly between them. The warmth of the fiery liquor helped to steady Kaila's nerves, though it didn't erase the void in her chest.

Finally, Rohan let out a sigh. "What are we going to do?"

"We?"

He shrugged. "She's my mother."

"I got myself into this mess."

"Sure, but a wife's problems become the husband's, right?"

Kaila's head jerked up. Rohan was watching her again. "What are you saying?"

"I'm saying maybe it's time I stopped running away from my responsibilities."

"You…you *want* to be king?"

"Not really." He offered a wry smile. "But we don't always get what we want, do we?"

Wasn't *that* the truth? "I suppose not."

Rohan nodded, a distant look in his eyes. "My mother clearly thought to use your past against me," he said quietly, "but maybe we can beat her at her own game." Blinking, he focused suddenly on her. "I want to change things, Eliza. Really change things." He gestured in the direction of his desk. "That's why I spend so much time in my books. So one day, I might have the knowledge to make this kingdom better for everyone. But…but I can't do it alone."

Goosebumps rippled along Kaila's skin. He was asking for her help. For her to take his hand in marriage, not because of his mother, or Ambrose, or some ancient prophecy, but so *they* could change things. Not some ancient king, but Rohan Frye and Kaila Dwyn. Together.

For just a moment, Kaila allowed herself to believe it, to imagine holding the prince's hand as they spoke their vows, a world where fear and hatred were no longer allowed to rule…

"Maybe…" she found herself saying, "maybe you won't have too."

A light appeared in his eyes as he slid across the couch to take her hands in his. "Maybe your right," he breathed.

She shivered as their fingers entwined. A smile tugged at her lips. "I have an annoying habit like that."

"Oh really?" he asked, nodding to the dress. "Then what was all this?"

Heat bloomed in her cheeks. "I…ah…" she coughed. "I can also be an idiot at times."

The prince chuckled. "That makes two of us."

They shared a look then, and Kaila was surprised to find the awful feeling in her stomach had relented. "So what now?"

Rohan puffed out his cheeks and exhaled, then extended his hand. "Now, Eliza Wrenn, I suppose you go and tell my mother we're engaged."

Kaila froze at the words. They rung in her ears, screaming, *shrieking.* It took all her strength not to pull away. Why? They shouldn't have bothered her. Those words were perfect. Exactly what she needed to placate the Matron and still advance with her own plan.

Rohan frowned at her silence. "Everything okay?"

"Of course!" she exclaimed, plastering a smile on her face. "It's just…really, *that's* how you propose? A *handshake?*"

"Ah…" the prince stuttered, a terrible fear appearing in his eyes.

Kaila laughed. What else could she do? It was all just so… messy. Rohan and Eliza, Theron and Jenna, the Matron and Ambrose. She had already betrayed so many people by coming here. But right now, alone with this gentle man, she could allow herself to believe it was real, couldn't she? To pretend the void in her chest had been healed. That things could be…better.

"It's okay, Rohan," she said quietly, almost shyly. Entwining her fingers with his, she leaned in and kissed him on the cheek. "But if we're to be married, maybe we need to practice a little more than just handshakes."

She was pleased to see the flush creep into Rohan's cheeks. "What did you have in mind?"

21

The shadow of the Sanctum loomed in the scarlet sky as Kaila and Rohan approached along the main avenue of Tah'raus. Bells rung in the growing darkness, calling the powerful home to their masters. The night of the Summer Gala had arrived all too quickly.

Which was perhaps fortunate. Her collar and the Matron's command made it impossible for Kaila to explain her plan to Theron and the others, so she had chosen to ignore the increasingly insistent invitations from Ambrose to attend him in his shop. After their last encounter, she couldn't risk the tailor cutting her loose and ruining everything.

Her heart pulsed. Had that been the right decision? With the Matron's reputation on the line, Theron could be in mortal peril. But surely the Matron wouldn't dare harm him? He was the son of Leonardo Falkenrath, Iron Hands himself. And so long as he lived, the king still protected Jenna.

She should be worrying more about herself. The Matron could kill her with a snap of her fingers. One misplaced step, one slip of the tongue, and she was done.

"Are you okay, Eliza?"

Blinking, Kaila snapped out of her spiralling thoughts.

Rohan walked hand and hand alongside her, a look of concern on his lips.

No, she wanted to say. Instead, she leaned in to press a kiss against his cheek. "Of course," she said, "I'm just…nervous."

They had only grown closer over the past week. It plagued Kaila sometimes at night, when she lay awake in her bed back in the Sanctum. They had avoided speaking of this night, but it was always in the back of her mind, a darkness that crept into her soul, stealing the warmth and the simple joy of Rohan's company.

"Don't be," Rohan replied, giving her fingers a squeeze. "We're in this together, remember? Besides." He grinned. "Did I mention how beautiful you are tonight?"

She snorted, though the hint of a real smile tugged at her lips. She *was* beautiful tonight. How could she not be, wearing the dress Ambrose and Eliza herself had prepared? She traced her hands over the lavender wool. The pair had outdone themselves. It was a great deal more modest than the slip of a thing she had worn for her ill-fated attempt at seducing the prince, but there was a beauty in its simpleness. The neckline was higher and the long sleeves were hemmed with satin. It shimmered in the glow of the agimet fastened to the cuffs—one of which was an uncut crystal she could have used, if not for her collar.

"Thank you," she murmured, returning the gesture. "You look quite handsome yourself, my prince."

He really did. Rohan had replaced his usual trackpants and baggy shirt with a fine woollen suit, complete with embroidered cuffs and lapels and tailored cut. He too had embraced the illuminating fashion of agimet—gold and agimet cufflinks, along with a silver timepiece on his wrist, one of the modern ones powered by a fragment of crystal. Warmth fluttered in her chest as she looked into his eyes and saw that same heat returned.

It's not real. You're not her. It can't last.

Kaila steeled herself against her doubts. She couldn't allow doubts to stop her from what needed to be done. "We had better hurry," she said, nodding to his timepiece. "Don't want to be late to our own party."

With that, Kaila dragged him towards the gates where the usual guards had been bolstered with a half dozen extra soldiers and three Wardens. Half the nobility of Fresia and no small number of wealthy merchants were expected to attend tonight, so the precautions were prudent. Yet Kaila's heart still beat faster as they approached. The Matron had *something* planned—Kaila just wished she knew *what*.

Her skin crawled as they neared the front of the queue and she came into view of the Wardens. Surreptitiously, she laid a finger on the band Ambrose had given her—the one containing his weaving. She had been through this ritual plenty of times over the past weeks, but under the gaze of three Wardens it was alarming the rate at which she sensed its *atar* depleting. Quickly turning her mind's eye outwards, she grasped a handful of shining whisps that was the nexus and drew them into the crystal. To her relief, its power stabilized. Making sure the smile didn't slip from her face, she nodded to the familiar faces she knew on the gates and led Rohan inside.

"We should find Jenna," Rohan said as they wandered through the entrance hall. "I tried to speak to her earlier, but my mother's minions wouldn't let me anywhere near the Sanctum." He snorted. "She wants to deny my sister the throne and make me king, but she doesn't even *trust* me."

Kaila knew exactly why the Matron wouldn't want the two colluding. Likely, the announcement of their marriage for the same night would appear like a coup to Theron and Jenna. Maybe that was the Matron's plan—to force a wedge between the siblings?

A sigh slipped from her lips. She was grasping at straw. The truth was, there was no knowing what the woman was planning. She just had to hope her own plan would be enough to thwart it.

Oberon.

Would the Aegis really restore the ancient king to the physical world if she wielded it? He had lived a thousand years ago—surely his body had perished. Or had the netherworld preserved him? There was only one way to find out.

Through the long corridors and up winding stairwells they marched, until they reached the ballroom beneath the dome. They were not the first to arrive—already, dozens of revellers moved about the three-hundred-foot chamber. The entire structure was a marvel of engineering, though its brutal architecture could never match the majesty of the Black Tower in Iselador. The Sanctum might impose itself upon the skyline of Tah'raus, but beside the pure obsidian and carved runes of the lost city, it was a plain, ugly thing. Even the ballroom, lit up as it was by a thousand shards of agimet and decorated in silk and velvet tapestries, could not conceal the fortress-like air of the exposed beams and plain concrete walls.

They had hardly stepped foot on the dancefloor when a voice called out to them. Kaila's stomach lurched when she saw the Matron approaching.

"Eliza, Rohan." The woman was beaming. "I am so glad you decided to take this step, my son." Stepping up to the prince, she place a hand to his cheek. "I know you will do me proud."

"You don't have to sound so surprised, mother," Rohan replied. There was no warmth in his voice, but to his credit, he kept his words polite. "Eliza is a wonderful woman."

"She is, isn't she?" the Matron mused. Kaila's stomach churned as the granite eyes turned on her. "She will make a wonderful wife, standing at your side. Now, if you don't mind, I would have a word with Daughter Wrenn before the ceremony."

Suddenly Kaila's heart was thundering in her ears. Her fingers tightened around Rohan's hand as the dread returned, coiling its sickly tendrils around her stomach. Rohan looked like he might object, but she couldn't let that happen. If the Matron had plans to harm Theron, or even Jenna, this might be her chance to wheedle that information from her.

"It's okay, Rohan," Kaila said before he could open his mouth. She gave his hand a squeeze. "I'll be right back."

Releasing him, she allowed the Matron to lead her through the crowd. The hour was still early and the music of the band was low, leaving the nobles to gather in little groups to gossip. Several looked up at the Matron's approach, curiosity showing on their faces. But neither Eliana Frye nor Kaila paused long enough to be drawn into conversation.

A brisk wind whipped across the night sky as they stepped from the ballroom onto the enormous balcony that ringed the dome. The Matron crossed to the balustrade, her gaze sweeping over the city. The twin moons shone tonight, as they did every year to herald in the summer, filling the night with light.

"You have done well, Daughter Wrenn," she said, turning to regard Kaila, "better than I dared hope."

"Thank you, Matron," Kaila said, dipping her head, before straightening to meet the woman's eyes. "Might I ask now, how...how you plan to grant Rohan the throne?"

The woman smiled. Reaching out, she brushed a lock of golden hair from Kaila's eyes. She shuddered as the woman's finger brushed her skin.

"Ah, my sweet child," she murmured. "I would not stain your soul with that knowledge. You will understand with time the dark deeds needed to protect our kingdom. For now, let us preserve your innocence, if only one night longer."

Needles prickled Kaila's spine. So it *would* happen tonight. The Matron was wasting no time. *I need to find a way to warn them!*

But just the thought brought a tightening around her throat. Frustration bubbled up inside her. *Helpless!* She had come all this way, gained magic and mighty allies, fooled the most powerful family in the kingdom, yet she was still unable to help her friends. All she could do was smile and nod as the Matron drew her back into the ballroom.

"When the time comes, you will be ready," was the last thing the woman said before she walked away.

Kaila was left standing in the doorway looking over the swelling crowd, wondering if she had the strength to return. To find Rohan and complete the lie, to hold his hand and swear a vow to protect him with her life, even as he would protect hers.

I would not stain your soul with that knowledge.

It was far too late for that.

"Eliza!"

She winced as the prince's cry carried over the murmur of voices. Closing her eyes, she drew in a breath.

You can do this, Kaila.

She caught sight of Rohan approaching through the crowd. The worry on his face brought a smile to her lips, though it didn't last as she remembered the Matron's words. She gave a little wave to show she was alright—even as her stomach twisted with dread.

Oberon will save us.

She had to believe it. He had saved her once before, in the nether world when she'd used her body's own energy to fuel a crystal instead of the nexus. He would help her again, once she wielded the Aegis.

"Everything okay?" Rohan panted as he reached her. He held a glass of wine in each hand. "What did my mother want?"

To kill your sister, Kaila thought to herself. Outwardly, all she could do was shrug. "Oh just..." she trailed off as a thought occurred to her.

She couldn't warn Theron or Jenna, but Rohan could. There was no doubt in her mind that the collar would throttle the life from her if she said anything about Jenna. But Rohan was no fool. He already suspected his mother was up to something nefarious with all her scheming. He just needed a nudge to put him on the right path.

Buying herself time, she took the offered wine and downed half the glass in one gulp—then gasped as she was reminded of her own inexperience with liquor. There was a bite to this one— and the colour was lighter. She studied it with narrowed eyes.

"It's fortified," Rohan explained, the creases on his brow deepening. "Kaila, what happened? You look like you just saw an Elysian."

She looked up at the prince's question. What should she tell him? How much *could* she tell him? The Matron's silent threat hung over her head, but there had to be something she could say…

"It's nothing," she said, puffing out her cheeks and exhaling. "She just wanted to congratulate me. She thinks I will make a fine Matron."

Kaila tensed as she spoke the words, readying herself for agony and death, but to her relief, the collar did not tighten or grow hot.

Rohan's reaction, however, was everything she'd hoped. His brow furrowed, his lips twisting like he'd just licked something distasteful.

"I don't like this," he muttered, glancing around as though to check for people who might overhear them. "What's her plan? If she wants to make me king, where does that leave Jenna?" He turned to Kaila. "I'm worried. Somethings going on, isn't it?"

He stared at her, waiting, but even considering a response, Kaila felt the noose tighten. She swallowed, holding Rohan's gaze, *willing* him to understand, to connect the dots.

"You're afraid, aren't you?" he breathed.

Kaila could have wilted. Her knees trembled, but still she held his eyes. Normally so gentle, they were suddenly hard like his mothers. His jaw grew tight, the veins in his neck bulging.

"You are." He nodded, more to himself than Kaila. "Eliza, it's going to be alright," he whispered. Glancing at his timepiece, his lips thinned. "We still have time. Come on, we have to find my sister."

He must have spotted Jenna, for suddenly Rohan was dragging her across the ballroom. Sure enough, a second later she glimpsed for herself Jenna's flaming hair through the mass of bodies. They might have time, but not much. The hour was growing late and the crowd had swollen to pack the ballroom wall to wall with nobility. Any moment now the Matron would call on them for the ceremony.

And then Theron was standing in front of Kaila.

They hadn't seen each other in weeks. It was odd, even dressed in that fancy suit with his wild hair cropped short and his beard groomed, Theron *still* managed to look like himself—that is, ever-so-slightly dishevelled. It was the way he stood, hands in his pockets, a grin tugging at his lips—the one that said he knew something no one else did. Kaila felt like she could have picked him from a crowd whatever face he wore.

So it made her heart twist when the smile faded from his lips.

"Master Falkenrath!" Rohan exclaimed before either could speak. "Where—"

He broke off as Jenna emerged from the crowd, sliding an arm through Theron's. Suddenly the twist in Kaila's heart became a gaping wound.

"Brother!" the princess exclaimed, before her eyes slid to Kaila, "and my soon to be sister, well met. Are you excited for the ceremony?" Her eyes glimmered as they lingered on Kaila. "Or perhaps you're more excited for *after* the ceremony?"

Kaila clenched her teeth, but was unable to keep the heat from her cheeks. It didn't help that Jenna sported her usual immodest style of dress. Tonight was another scarlet number, with a split down the middle that had any number of men—and no small number of women—stealing glances in her direction.

Theron, however, had eyes only for Kaila. She could *feel* the rage hidden there, the anger at what she had done. She longed to explain herself, but whenever she even thought about the words, the collar tightened. So instead she was the first to look away, turning her gaze to Rohan.

"Ahem." Holding a hand to his mouth, Rohan coughed awkwardly. She was pleased to see his cheeks were as red as her own were hot. "Actually, Jenna, I wanted to talk to you in private before the ceremony."

Jenna's eyebrows lifted into her mop of fiery hair. "Mysterious much, brother?" she asked, before letting out a little laugh. "Very well, let's find out what's got you all hot and bothered on our big day."

Looping her arm through Rohan's, Jenna led him into an alcove between the great concrete pillars.

Leaving Kaila alone with Theron.

"So, *Eliza Wrenn*," he hissed, his voice like uncut iron, "care to explain what in the name of the Trickster you're doing here?"

"So, *Eliza Wrenn*, care to explain what in the name of the Trickster you're doing here?"

Blood pounding in his ears, Theron stared down at Kaila Dwyn. No one had seen her in over a week and suddenly, here she was. She wore the lavender dress Ambrose had prepared for her, a long, flowing piece with a hem she had to lift to keep from dragging on the floor. Her appearance was still that of Eliza Wrenn, with her pale skin and short blonde hair. But Theron saw the girl beneath. She might wear another's face, but she was still the girl from the mountains, impulsive, inexperienced, naïve. Quintin had been right—she wasn't ready for a job like this. He should never have put that weight on her shoulders.

But never in a million years would he have expected *this* from her.

For days after the dinner with the Matron, they had waited for the woman's reprisal. She would strike back, of that Jenna had been certain. You did not cross the Matron of Fresia and expect to walk away untouched.

But when her reckoning finally arrived, it was in a form neither of them had expected. After all, Kaila had assured Ambrose their relationship was as false as a promise from the Trickster god. The prince had no interest in the crown, and would be all too happy to see his sister replace their parents on the throne.

Until he'd met the girl from the mountains.

They had tried to get her back to the shop to explain. Kaila had ignored each entreaty, avoided every attempt to contact her. Until now. Until tonight. Now here she was, staring up at him with those eyes…

Were the lights growing brighter? Theron could feel their heat on his skin. The corrupted agimet was everywhere, pulsing, shimmering, filling the air with tainted *atar*. His body screamed for it, burned with the need to feel it in his veins once again, to be a *god*. Every second of every day of the past two weeks had been an agony. He dared only draw the tiniest drops from his hidden crystals, and only then when he knew he was alone.

Alone.

Why did everyone leave? First Quintin, now Kaila. They left, and he was in *pain*. His vision shimmered. There was a heat inside him, like someone had kindled a flame in his chest that now threatened to consume him whole.

One more night.

His body shook with desire, but he clenched his fists, forcing his mind back on track. He just had to get through one more night. Try as she might to interfere, Kaila couldn't stop him now. He would have his revenge, and the Aegis too. The pulsing power of the device still lingered in his mind, perhaps the only thing that could come close to the pure *atar* he'd taken from the shard.

Kaila still hadn't answered. She was staring at him, a strange mix of worry and fear creasing her brow. It finally cut through the pain of his withdrawal.

"Well?" he demanded. "Nothing to say for yourself, after what you've done?"

That finally seemed to shake the girl out of her stupor. "Theron, I can't…" she trailed off.

"Can't what?" he hissed, drawing her into another alcove.

"Betray your friends? Betray your *species?* What, *Kaila*, what can't you say?" He bit out the words, frustration boiling over.

But Kaila just stood there, eyes wide, lips parted as though ready to scream. Theron couldn't understand it. She was trembling in his arms. Was that fear in her eyes, or something else? When she finally spoke, it was the last thing he could have expected to come from her lips.

"Please, Theron, you can't marry her."

"Kaila…" he frowned, momentarily taken aback, "I don't know what game you're playing—"

"It's not a game!" she gasped. "Please, you don't understand…"

"You're right, I don't," he snapped. Anger returning, he shook her. "Because you *won't talk to me!*"

"Because I can't!" Kaila hissed back.

Her fire finally showing through, she tore herself from his grasp. They stood there glaring at each other, each posed as though for a fight. Finally though, Theron exhaled and lowered his hands. He could still feel the shards tearing through his insides, but somehow, this hurt even worse.

"Why, Kaila?" he whispered. "Why betray us like this? Is it the prince?"

Her eyes widened. "I'm not," she croaked. "I wouldn't." Again that strange emotion flickered across her face. "Please, Theron, you need to believe me. I would never do anything to hurt you."

He swallowed. Gods, looking into those eyes, he wanted to. But…slowly, he shook his head. "Kaila, if this is about us…I know things are complicated with Jenna, but…" He swallowed. "But what happened in the mountains…I'm sorry if I gave you the wrong idea…"

She stared at him for the longest time, until Theron began to think that, just maybe, he had gotten through to her, that she would stop—

"I couldn't give a donkey's *ass* what kind of *complicated* relationship you have with Jenna," she snarled, practically spitting the words. "Do whatever you want with that red-haired whore, just *do not marry her!*"

Theron's eyes widened at the venom in her words, but before he could respond, a voice carried from over his shoulder.

"Eliza?"

He cursed beneath his breath as Rohan approached, Jenna following a step behind. She wore a strange look on her face, which only became stranger when she saw the two of them standing there. Too late, he remembered her suspicions that first night they'd met.

"We will talk about this tomorrow," Theron said quietly.

Then quickly, he drew back from Kaila and moved to Jenna's side, where he leaned down and kissed her scarlet lips. He wasn't surprised to hear a slightly strangled noise from Kaila's throat.

"Eliza." Coming up from the kiss, he overheard the prince speaking. "I'm sorry, I couldn't—"

"I know," Kaila cut him off. "Come on, let's find some more of that fortified wine. I think I'm going to need it."

When Theron looked around, the pair were already moving away. Despite the woman in his arms, his heart twisted. What the hell was going on?

It didn't make any sense. Could Kaila really be in love with the prince, as Quintin had originally feared, or was something else going on? Just a few days ago everything had been fine—so what had changed?

"Careful, my dear," Jenna interrupted his thoughts, "any other woman might think their soon-to-be-husband was having second thoughts if she caught him staring at another woman like that."

Shaking himself, Theron turned to the princess. Her words were light, but there was a glint behind her emerald gaze that hadn't been there before. He cursed silently. What ideas had the prince been planting in her mind?

"Apologies, my princess," he said quickly, presenting his most charming smile. "It's just…I had the most disconcerting conversation with Daughter Wrenn."

Jenna arched one eyebrow. "Don't you think it's curious," she said quietly, drawing him into the shadows. "That the same Daughter I caught frolicking with your personal servant would end up engaged to my brother not a few weeks later."

A lump lodged in Theron's throat. He swallowed it quickly. "What are you saying, dear?"

"I'm saying its curious," She eyed him. "Where *is* your personal servant, anyway? He hasn't been around."

"I had to let him go."

"Because…"

"*Enough*, Theron," she snapped. "I'm not a fool. I saw the way she looked at you. You weren't covering for your servant that night—you were covering for *yourself*. Now, tell me the truth."

Theron's blood grew cold. In that moment, he saw all their carefully laid plans falling to pieces around him.

Damn you Kaila!

He wouldn't let it happen. He needed this; Jenna and the Aegis, *atar*, to destroy his father. He would have it all. And one spoilt brat from the mountains wasn't going to stop him.

"Very well," he said, quickly cobbling together a story, "if you must know, Eliza and I arrived in Tah'raus on the same merchant train." That lie would barely last the night—Eliza Wrenn had arrived weeks before Theron—but it would have to do. "During our journey, we may have, that is to say…" he trailed off, recalling those long nights in the mountains, alone with Kaila. He let out a sigh. "When we arrived in the capital, I ended it." He studied her. "My father had greater plans for me than a simple Daughter from our own Dominance."

"And that night at the tailors?" Jenna's eyes had narrowed as he spoke.

"She wanted to talk. I made it clear her continued attention was unwelcome. I had Quintin escort her back to the Sanctum…"

He trailed off. The princess still watched him with naked suspicion, but she seemed to at least be considering his story. Finally, she gave a curt nod.

"Very well, let's say I believe you," she said, before her eyes narrowed again, this time in the direction Kaila and the prince had taken. "But it still doesn't explain where this relationship between her and my brother came from."

And right there, Theron saw his opportunity. *Two can play at this game, Kaila*, he thought with an inward smile. If Jenna was busy worrying over her brother, she wouldn't think to dig into his own fabrication.

"She *is* one of your mothers," he said softly. "Eliza may have convinced your brother she's not, but she is *very much* working for the Matron."

The breath hissed between Jenna's teeth. "And there my brother was warning *me* about our mother's plotting."

His heart pulsed. "Oh, I'm sure she is." He paused, besieged by sudden doubt. Could Kaila know the rest of the Matron's plan? Was that what she was trying to warn him about. If so, why not just come out and *say it*?

Do whatever you want with that red-haired whore, just do not marry her!

Theron clenched his fists, frustration bubbling in his veins. Was she jealous? That had to be it. Jealous he dared touch another woman. Jealous he had power and she did not. Jealous he would be the one to claim the Aegis.

Trickster be damned, Kaila, you forced me to do this.

"Don't let her simple appearance deceive you, Eliza Wrenn is cunning. She likely has your brother wrapped around her little finger."

Jenna's frown deepened. "Rohan wanted us to leave. I told him there was no way in a thousand years I would give my mother *that* satisfaction."

"Good," he said. "Then she knows her plan has failed."

"In that case," Jenna murmured, arching an eyebrow. "What do you think will—"

Dong! Dong! Dong!

She broke off as the great bell began to sound. Silence followed in its wake, as one by one, faces turned to look in their direction. Others found the prince and Kaila. His heart pulsed once again as women in the habits of Sisters moved towards them, the crowd parting in their wake.

Theron turned to Jenna as the sisters approached. "I believe we're about to find out."

22

Kaila's heart beat hard in her chest as she followed the sister up the stairs. Hidden within the walls of the great dome, the passageway was dark and narrow and seemingly unending. She could hear Rohan panting behind her—no elevators here—while Theron and the princess and yet more sisters came after.

The knot in her stomach tightened. Whatever the Matron had planned, it must take place before the ceremony, surely? Otherwise, there would be nothing to prevent the king standing aside and allowing Jenna and Theron to claim the throne.

Her fingers crept to the crystal concealed in her sleeve, but the agimet was scant comfort. The only weapon she had left was her mind. But she had run out of options, run out of allies, run out of *time*.

The light of the twin moons shone bright in the sky as they emerged onto a little platform at the peak of the Sanctum. The entire thing was only about fifty feet wide, though the sides did not so much as end, as they did slope gradually away from them, the gradient growing steeper before reaching the vertical curve of the dome. The only adornment on the platform was a simple black altar—obsidian again—alongside which stood the king and

Matron. There weren't even any railings to prevent people from sliding over the sides.

Kaila was normally fine with heights, but she felt a moment of vertigo as she turned on the spot. They were so far above the other buildings of Tah'raus—a hundred feet at least—she felt alone in the sky, teetering on the edge of a precipice.

Then a warm hand found hers and she looked around to see Rohan alongside her. He still wore his concern from earlier, but the squeeze he gave her fingers was reassuring. Kaila managed a smile for him, before the fear drove it from her lips.

"Come, children, approach the altar."

Together, they turned to meet the pair of monarchs. It was almost strange to see the Matron in the presence of the king— even more so to see both with smiles on their faces. Clearly, each thought they were about to get exactly what they wanted. From what she had seen of the Matron, Kaila didn't like the king's chances.

Though if she had her way, both their nights would end with disappointment.

Her heart pulsed and almost unconsciously, Kaila found her feet shifting into one of the old fighting stances her father had taught her. With an effort of will, she forced herself to relax and straighten again. She couldn't give herself away, not now. If she was really going to free Oberon from his prison and protect Theron, she needed to be the one to claim the Matron's portion of the Aegis.

Her eyes returned to the pair, heart suddenly hammering in her ears. They each wore a familiar golden bracer on their arm, agimet shimmering brighter than the stars above. *The Aegis.* The *complete* Aegis—both halves of the ancient device stolen by T'iana.

Her heart lurched at a sudden thought. Would she need both, or was only one required to free Oberon? If it was both, maybe it *should* be Theron and Jenna who claimed it. A string of curses streamed through her mind. She glanced at Rohan, then back to the monarchs. It was too late to change paths now. Besides, maybe she was wrong and the Matron was out of tricks?

Her breath quickened as she and Rohan approached the altar. As they did, Jenna and Theron drew alongside them. She cast them a glance out of the corner of her eye. Theron steadfastly avoided her gaze, but Jenna was watching her, eyes hard as emeralds.

"Welcome," the Matron greeted. "It joys me to witness two children of the realm come to celebrate their union on this sacred night." She nodded to each of them in turn—even Jenna—before turning to the ring of woman that had accompanied them up the stairs. "Thank you, sisters, you may return to the gathering below. My husband and I will serve as witnesses to this ceremony."

Kaila's eyebrows lifted as several of the sisters exchanged glances. That wasn't a normal part of the ritual—a Sister of the Magisterium was present in all official unions. Murmurs passed between them, before one Kaila recognised stepped forward.

"Matron, this is a most unusual request."

Eliana Frye maintained her smile. "This is a most unusual ceremony, Sister Vera. It is not often two heirs come before the Magisterium on the same night."

"All the more reason for our presence, Matron Frye," Vera argued. "We must be allowed to judge the worthiness of the prince and princess, if we are to decide our future."

"That may be so, Sister," the Matron replied, smile sliding from her lips, "but tonight, my husband and I have agreed to allow the Aegis to guide us in selecting a heir."

That really got the whispers going amongst the sisters. Kaila's blood chilled. How exactly did the Matron intend to usc the Aegis?

A cold, dark room, a dwindling candle, her entire body screaming with agony...

"So, my mother got to you after all."

Kaila startled as a voice interrupted her living nightmare.

Swinging around, she was surprised to find Jenna Frye had snuck up on her unawares. A chill spread down her spine when she saw the glint in the woman's eyes. Hatred.

"Princess Jenna," she murmured, attempting a smile, "it's nice to finally meet you."

"Don't give me that bull," the princess hissed, her lips twisting in a sneer. "I know your game. What was it my mother promised you? Power? Riches? Or maybe a new dress from that washed up fart Braider is all the good lady Eliza needs to spread her legs?"

"What?" Kaila was taken aback by the words. "No, Jenna, it's not—"

"No?" The princess snorted. "It must be spite then. That's it, isn't it? You couldn't satisfy Theron Falkenrath, so you decided to get back at me for taking him from you?"

"Theron?" Kaila gaped at the woman. "How…"

Her eyes widened as she remembered. They'd been seen the night she left Ambrose's shop. Quintin had told the princess a story about secret love to cover for them—but apparently she hadn't bought it. And now their little conversation below, when she'd tried and failed to warn Theron about the Matron's plans, had set the woman on her tail.

"Stupid girl," Jenna spat, "you really thought I'd buy that story about you and the servant? Please, you might be a tramp, but no Daughter would stoop so low as a *commoner*."

Kaila's ears were ringing. Elsewhere, the sisters were still arguing with the Matron, while the king stood calmly by. Distracted by the dispute, Rohan and Theron hadn't noticed their conversation. She was on her own.

"It's not like that, I swear!" she gasped. "It's—"

The words died in her throat as the collar tightened.

The princess laughed. "Oh, no? So you're *not* jealous I took your man?" She stepped in close. "That every night, I satisfy him in ways you never could?"

Blood was pounding in Kaila's ears, but it couldn't block out the princess's words. They burrowed into her soul, carving out the little bits of warmth she had found these past few weeks, turning heat to lead and ice in her chest. She saw again and again Theron kissing Jenna on the dancefloor below, the pair arm and arm, the way his hands crept over her body.

Suddenly she was trembling, shaking, and it had nothing to do with her fear any longer. She was *angry*. Here Theron was, accusing *her* of allowing emotions to cloud her judgement, of betraying the job because of some attachment to Rohan, and *he was doing that exact thing with Jenna.*

"What, nothing to say for yourself, *Eliza?*" the princess spat her name like a curse. "Good, in that case, you can listen. If you hurt my brother, I *will* come for you, and I *will* kill you. Understood?"

Kaila gaped at the woman, unable to string together the words of a response. Fortunately, the sisters chose that moment to finally capitulate to the Matron's demands, for one by one, they began to stream past them and disappear into the passageway.

Watching them go, Kaila tried to find some slither of hope in her heart. She had wondered if the Matron planned to contract another assassin—in which case, the habit of a sister would have been the perfect place to conceal a weapon. Now though, the woman had unwittingly removed her only allies on the rooftop.

"Finally," a groan came from the king as the last sister departed, "now those old windbags have retired, are you sure you wouldn't like to do us all a favour and skip this farce, my dear wife?" His eyes shifted to Kaila. "I'm sure the Daughter you've tricked our son into marrying is nice enough, but just once, can't you spare the poor boy your meddling?"

Despite the truth hidden in those words, Kaila bristled. To her surprise though, Rohan came to her defence before anyone else could speak.

"There was no trickery involved, Father," he said, his voice like ice. "I have simply decided to embrace my responsibilities."

The king arched an eyebrow at that, while the Matron curled her lips. "You see, husband." There was a glimmer in her eyes as they met Kaila's. "Rohan makes his own decisions."

"Very well," the king sighed, gesturing to the altar, "can we get on with it then?"

"We may," the Matron replied, before her cold eyes shifted to Jenna and Theron. "Though first I would *also* offer the princess one last chance to step from this path."

It was Jenna's turn to snort. "I won't let your puppet take what's rightfully mine, Mother."

The Matron said nothing, only stood atop the platform, her purple robes shimmering in the moonlight. Her lips were pursed, the skin around her eyes creased as she studied the princess. Finally she shook her head.

"My dear Jenna, all I have ever done is try to protect you." Spreading her hands, she gestured to the altar. "But if you insist on marrying this man, I will not stand between you."

A cold wind blew across the rooftop, bringing with it the distant sounds of gulls in the harbour. Whatever Jenna had been expecting, it had not been this. The words seemed to have thrown her. She stood watching her mother with narrowed eyes.

Kaila could sense it too. There was a trap here, something that tugged at her, *shrieked* at her a warning. Breath held, she watched Jenna, waiting to see what the princess would choose.

"Very well," Jenna said at last. Taking Theron's hand, she stepped toward the altar, the hem of her scarlet dress whipping in the wind. "Let it be done."

Her mother's smirk was very much one of a hunter who's prey had just stepped into their trap. "As you will."

There was a thundering in Kaila's ears. Something was very wrong, but what? Her eyes darted around the rooftop, but they found nothing. They were alone up here, safe from any outside interference. Weren't they? Either Theron would win, or she would...wouldn't she?

"Approach the altar, children," the king barked impatiently.

"You too Rohan and whatever-your-name-is—let's get this over with."

Kaila and Rohan exchanged uneasy glances, then took their places around the altar. The Matron smiled at each of them, and Kaila was reminded again of a predator toying with its prey. Then she held out her arm over the altar—the one with the Aegis. The king did the same with his own, before shifting his gaze to them.

"As my darling wife has already told the Sisters, tonight you will swear your vows on the Aegis," he paused then, eyes lingering on Jenna, then Rohan. "It is not…the most pleasant of sensations. But I can assure you, it is quite harmless."

A tingling crept across Kaila's skull as she heard those words. Again, she was plunged into darkness, into the pit the Matron had condemned her to in that chamber. She felt herself begin to shake. The lights of the Aegis shimmered as the monarchs held the twin parts over the altar. For just a second, Kaila felt as though *she* were on that altar; the Aegis an axe poised to bring down on her skull.

I can't do this!

Then Rohan's fingers tightened around her own. She found his eyes on hers, and there was no longer any fear or worry or even anger there, but warmth, one that reminded her of that night on his balcony and all the times they had shared since, of the friendship they had built between them.

And suddenly, Kaila knew that she *could* do it. That whatever happened, this man would be at her side. She didn't know what came next, whether the Matron really had a plan or if it was all just bluster. She didn't even know what she felt about Theron anymore.

But she wanted this.

Hand clasped with Rohan, they reached out and placed their palms on the ancient artefact of the Elysian. Jenna and Theron had already grasped the golden bracers. Across the altar, Jenna met her eyes, and smirked.

"Speak the vow," the Matron intoned.

"By the name of T'iana, First Matron of Fresia…"

As the ancient words echoed around the circle, Kaila turned her eyes from Jenna and the Matron and found Rohan's instead. They were watching her already, warm and full of life. He smiled as their gaze met. There was so much hope there. Kaila hoped, somehow, she might find a way to live up to that.

"I swear my life to this man," she finished, "let our fate, our future, our life and our death, be as one."

"So it is sworn," the Matron whispered, "let no power on this world break asunder."

With that, the Aegis suddenly grew warm beneath Kaila's fingers. Before she could snatch her hand away, something at once cold and burning sliced into her. *Atar,* forged into a terrible blade, struck her *soullight.* A numbness spread through her body, but to Kaila's surprise, she did not splutter and die.

Instead, a piece of her sheared away, vanishing from her *sight.*

For a second, she stared at her broken soul.

Then a fresh warmth filled her. *Atar,* unlike any she had felt before, burst into life within her. It grafted onto her *soullight,* merging, shifting so that two became one.

And just like that, she was whole again. Whole, but *different.* She blinked as her vision returned and she found Rohan staring at her, his eyes wide, lips parted as though he too had been about to cry out. Slowly, she removed her fingers from the Aegis. They tingled as she lifted them before her face. Nothing had changed outwardly, but inwardly she felt…different, like a part of her *soullight* had been changed by the Aegis.

Her eyes fluttering closed, Kaila allowed herself to believe for a moment that was it. That they'd won.

Then the screams began.

Kaila's eyes snapped open. She turned to Rohan first, thinking the Aegis had done something to him, that its power had harmed him in some way. The prince didn't seem to be injured, but there was horror on his face as he looked across the altar at his sister.

No, not his sister.

Theron.

The breath caught in Kaila's throat as she saw her friend. The brilliance in his eyes outshone the twin moons, casting back the night atop the rooftop.

For a moment, she couldn't understand what she was seeing. *Why* she was seeing it. The Aegis had done something to her—but she hadn't been able to use the *atar* that had touched her *soullight*. It had been like a weapon wielded against her, too sharp and fast to grasp, unlike the still depths of power in agimet. And if Jenna was really Elysian, why hadn't it affected her either…

The collars!

The realisation struck her like a blow. The collars had kept herself and Jenna from absorbing that power, but with Theron, it had been like taking the Trial of Agimet all over again. His shining eyes declared to everyone he was Elysian.

Slowly, Kaila's gaze shifted to the Matron. The old woman wore a cold smile. Blood pulsed in Kaila's skull. *She knew!* Somehow, the Matron had known what Theron was. Known, *and deliberately allowed Jenna to marry him.* Why? She had told Kaila she wouldn't let an Elysian anywhere near the Aegis.

Her answer came quickly enough. Light pulsed once more from the Matron's bracer. Kaila felt a strange *pulling* sensation on her *soullight.* It was different from before, and at first she didn't realise what was happening.

Until she heard the groan from Theron. Again, the light atop the platform flickered. The *atar* in her friend's eyes spluttered and with horror, Kaila realised what was happening. She had seen the Matron do this same thing with the enormous agimet crystal in the basement—she was using the Aegis to drain the *atar* from Theron.

There was one final flash of brilliance from Theron's eyes as he raised a hand towards the old woman—then without so much as a crackling of power, the light died.

23

From the moment Theron laid his hand on the Aegis, he knew he was in trouble. *Fool, fool, fool!* The words rung in his skull as *atar* flooded through his veins. This wasn't like holding agimet, where a small amount of *atar* crept into your soul, or even the corrupted crystals, which an Elysian *could* hold and choose not to connect.

The Aegis was a flood. It filled his body with *atar*, but it did not come for his *soullight*—at least not at first. Maybe another Elysian, one that hadn't used a broken crystal, could have resisted the temptation. But after weeks surviving off only the barest of scrapes, all that *atar*, all that power, it was too much for Theron.

The Aegis contained far more *atar* that any regular piece of agimet. Its power was not unlike the broken crystals, enormous, untameable. Unlike the broken crystals, however, Theron did not *need* to take it all in. He could take only a portion, if he chose.

His addiction chose otherwise.

Theron's *soullight* trembled as he took everything the Aegis would give him and turned it to his command.

Ecstasy.

The world shimmered, changed. For one fleeting moment, he was a god again.

And then, to his horror, Theron felt the energy slipping away. Bliss turned to panic as he clung to the *atar*, scrambling to consume it, to hold it, anything that would keep him complete. But it didn't matter how much he struggled—the power was not his own, and now it returned to its rightful owner.

He shuddered as the last drips of *atar* fled from him, a cry rasping from his lips. He knew what followed now, as sure as night followed day.

Pain.

No creeping agony or shards slowly tearing through his flesh this time. It struck Theron like a hammer to the face. He crumpled, gasping, to the concrete terrace. In desperation, he fumbled for the crystal hidden on his belt, tearing it loose—only to stare in horror at the empty facets. *Drained.* How? It had been full just a few minutes ago, before…

Laughter rang in his ears. Red spots danced in his eyes as he looked up into the cruel eyes of the Matron. Understanding followed. The woman hadn't just taken the *atar* the Aegis had lent him. She had taken it *all.*

A fresh wave of pain rolled through his soul. He screamed. It was not blood that flowed through his veins, but molten stone, burning, searing, *destroying.*

Fool, fool, fool!

He could feel Kaila's eyes on him. This was what she had been so desperately trying to warn him about. He should have listened to the girl, just like he should have listened to Quintin. He'd been blinded by hatred for his father, and pain, and need…

…and now he'd doomed them all.

But that wasn't the worst of it. The worst of it was that *he didn't know how?* Where had he gone wrong? It had to have been the dinner. He'd pushed the Matron too far and she'd gone to his father. Except, how could word have reached the frontlines so quickly? It didn't make sense.

And yet here he was.

Theron supposed it didn't really matter, not in the end. He was done. It was all over.

"Well, well, well." Distantly, he heard the Matron speaking in a mocking voice. "It seems the enemy has crept into our dear princess's bedsheets."

Fresh agony wove a net of fire about his soul. *Jenna*. She didn't deserve this, but now he'd doomed her as well.

Everyone you touch dies, brother. Why can't you understand that?

No, not now. He clenched his eyes closed against the voices. He couldn't afford to hear Freya *now*.

"How…?" the king's voice was strained.

"The Nameless is cruel to the unfaithful and the blasphemous," the Matron mocked. "The princess has only received that which she sowed."

Trembling, Theron forced his head to lift. Jenna's eyes were wide and a vein pulsed in her neck as she stared at him, as though still not quite able to process what she had seen. The monarchs faced one another across the altar; the Matron with a smirk of satisfaction, the king demoralised, defeated.

Kaila and the prince were nearest him. His eyes lingered briefly on Kaila. Why hadn't her eyes brightened with the magic of the Aegis? Then he remembered—the collar blocked her Gift. His chest tightened. There might still be a chance, for her at least.

"So what now?" the king asked. "Will you have them strung up in Soul Square for the commoners to revile?"

"It need not go so far." The Matron tilted her head in mock thoughtfulness. "Declare Rohan your true heir, and I will allow Jenna to become a sister. She can be sent away, somewhere far from the capital, where her corruption can do no harm."

"And the Elysian?"

"He will be locked in the dungeons," the Matron replied. "Evidence, in case your *daughter* ever decides to go back on her word."

"I see," the king spoke softly, but the wind had died atop the dome and no one failed to hear his words. There was a pause as they all looked to him, into which he began to laugh. Lifting his head, he met the Matron's gaze with a smile. "So this was your grand plan? All this scheming to keep Jenna from taking my place? To preserve your so-called honour, and it comes down to *this?*" His nose wrinkled as he glared down at Theron.

"Mock me all you like, husband," the Matron replied coldly. "You've lost. Jenna will never be Matron now."

"Why not?" he replied, arching one eyebrow. "If we can hide one, why not two?" His gaze drifted to Theron. "Or perhaps Master Falkenrath suffers an unfortunate accident tonight." He turned to Jenna and smiled. "What do you think, daughter?"

Jenna looked from one of them to the other, then back down to Theron. "I…I don't understand," she whispered. "He can't be one of them…"

"I'm afraid he very much is," the Matron replied, her tone venomous. "You've bound yourself to the enemy, child. You will forever be unclean."

"No, wife," the king growled. "Jenna is loyal. She has always been loyal—you were just too bigoted to see it. But I've had enough of your foolish superstition. I won't let you destroy our children."

"Rohan is my only child here!" the Matron snarled, eyes flashing.

For a moment, the pair glared at one another. Then abruptly, the Matron sighed. Closing her eyes, she shook her head.

"I feared you would do something like this," she whispered. Her eyes shifted to Jenna, and Theron thought he saw actual remorse in the woman's eyes. "You won't step aside?"

Eyes wide, Jenna stood fixed in place, her entire body trembling. Theron understood her pain, the agony of a parent's betrayal. She didn't deserve this fate. No one did. Despite everything he'd done, a piece of him longed to help her, but the pain, the agony of his withdrawal-racked body…

"Why are you doing this to me?" At last, Jenna seemed to

find her voice. Her eyes shimmered with unspilt tears. "Please, at least tell me that."

The Matron's face softened at the princess's entreaty. "I only do what I must, girl."

Jenna's eyes slid closed, her hands clenched into fists. "Then I will do what I must as well."

"So be it."

In one swift motion, a dagger appeared in the Matron's hand. For a heartbeat, it seemed as though she would plunge it into Jenna—instead, she turned and drove it through the king's chest.

"*No!*" Jenna's scream pierced the calm night.

The king hissed as the Matron stepped away from him, leaving the dagger in place. Blood coated his fingers as he clawed at the blade, but his strength was already failing. Groaning, he pitched face first to the ground.

Jenna was at his side in an instant. Theron watched as she heaved the body over, but he already knew she was too late. There was a stillness that came over the dead, an emptiness he could see even without *atar*, that his *soullight* had changed. His gaze shifted to the Matron. The woman stood calmly over her victim. There was triumph in her eyes as she looked at him.

"An Elysian has slain our king!" she declared. "Let all here today stand in witness—"

"No." The Matron broke off as Rohan—the last person Theron would have expected—broke the circle and advanced on his mother. "No more, mother. I won't let you do this, not this time. Jenna is the rightful heir, not me. *I don't want it!*" He all but screamed the final words as he came to a stop and stood panting before his mother.

She, by contrast, looked calmly back at him. "Are you done?"

Rohan blinked. "No, I…" he trailed off, suddenly seeming unsure of himself.

"Good," the Matron said, her tone matter-of-fact, "because you have a choice to make, Rohan Frye. Either you embrace your duty and become king, or…" she trailed off, eyes shifting to Jenna. "Or your sister hangs alongside the Elysian."

The prince opened his mouth to defy her again, but the words died in his throat. His eyes darted back to Kaila. Still knelt at their feet, Theron followed his gaze. The girl stood frozen, lips parted, eyes shining with fear. Even wearing Eliza's face, she was beautiful.

Theron's heart ached and he struggled to keep the agony from his face. This was his fault. He should have listened to her, believed in her, *trusted her.* And he should have told her the truth about that night in the mountains. And what he'd done to save her life. About everything.

Instead he'd dragged her and Jenna to disaster. Now they would pay for his failures, and there was nothing Theron could do about it. His entire body was in agony, like he'd been skewered by a thousand tiny needles. He was too weak to move.

The prince seemed to realise the situation too. His shoulders slumped and the fight went out of his eyes. It enraged Theron. How could he *not* fight back? How could he not *resist…*

I told you to run, brother.

His stomach twisted with the memory of his sister's voice. She had told him to run, and he had. It had never stopped hurting, knowing that he had left her, that he had fled instead of fighting for her life. It didn't matter that he'd just been a boy with no knowledge of the Gift or agimet or Elysian inheritance. All that mattered was that he had failed Freya.

And now it was happening all over again.

"That's what I thought," the Matron sneered, "so as I was saying before I was so rudely interrupted, Rohan will be king."

Trickster save me, Theron prayed for the first time in his life, *give me a weapon.*

But of course, the Trickster god of the Elysian didn't work that way. Dragging in a ragged breath, he opened his eyes. The Matron wasn't even looking at Theron or the prince anymore, but at Kaila. Raw terror shone from her eyes. Her face twitched, and Theron could tell she wanted to lash out.

He couldn't let that happen. He'd felt the power of the Aegis —Kaila didn't stand a chance. Especially not with her Gift blocked by the collar. His gaze returned to Rohan. The prince was their only hope, but he was just a boy; even his suit was a size too large, and the timepiece hung awkwardly from his wrist…

Theron's scalp tingled as his eyes settled on the device, the breath catching in his throat. Rohan was wearing a timepiece— one of the modern, agimet powered devices that had become popular amongst the nobility. They were so common now, no one had even given it a second thought. Besides, as far as anyone knew, Elysian couldn't use the modified crystals from humanity's devices.

Unless they had already broken that taboo.

A sense of peace came over Theron as the pain receded and he looked at the world with fresh eyes. This was it; he had reached the end. But if he was doomed, he would not make the journey through the netherworld alone. The least he could do was spare this world another second under the yolk of the Matron.

Snarling, Theron launched himself upright and snatched at the device around Rohan's wrist. It parted easily, his practiced fingers making quick work of the clasp. He sensed the crystal immediately, even through the gears and the metal casing, he could feel it there, a twisted, unnatural thing, burning with the brilliance of the nexus.

He didn't care. Theron had resisted this temptation for weeks. He burned with the need for it, to consume that delicious, pure *atar*. But while he had fought and fought and fought, in the end…

I lost.

Atar washed through him. Pure and unfiltered, it swelled in his veins, spread to every muscle and sinew, filling him with a joyous ecstasy. The crystal in the device was tiny, but that didn't matter, not when it had been broken. It was attuned to the unlimited power of the nexus. Already it was replenishing, fresh *atar* swirling into its facets.

So Theron drew more. And more, and more, until the entire rooftop shone with the brilliance of his eyes. Shadows in the dark cowered back from him. Somewhere in the distance, he could hear a voice crying, *screaming.* Mortals. Weak. Frail. They were all fools, too afraid to touch true power. They would bow before him.

Or they would perish.

Reaching out with his Gift, Theron touched the stars.

24

Kaila was still reeling from the Matron's victory when the new light began to shine from Theron's eyes. At first, it had given her hope. She had seen Theron fight with his Gift. His skill was unmatched, and even a device as powerful as the Aegis must surely have its limits.

But that hope had been fleeting. The light Theron held was wrong; not the swirling vortex of colour that was true *atar*, but an eerie, unnatural white, almost like…

…a chill crept down her spine as she saw what Theron had done, what he had snatched from Rohan. His timepiece. Clasping it in his hand like a blade, Theron rose.

No!

She wanted to scream at him. He had warned her to never draw from the broken crystals. That it would destroy her if she did. And now there he stood, his own taboo broken, eyes ablaze with the unnatural light of modified *agimet*. She didn't need her *atarsight* to know what was happening, how the crystal would draw more and more *atar* from the nexus as it was emptied, and how that power would burn until it consumed him…

The night turned a brilliant white as Theron lashed out with his Gift. Kaila's gut wrenched as the power hurled her backwards. Without her own Gift to anchor herself, she was as helpless as a human before Theron's power. Screaming, she went tumbling across the concrete, only coming to rest a few inches from the edge of the platform. Her heart crashed against her ribcage as she looked at the arch of the dome sloping away from her, down into…nothing.

The others were in a similar state, Rohan and Jenna landing nearby. Only the Matron seemed unaffected. Aegis raised before her face, she seemed immune to the power of Theron's Gift.

Though as Kaila knew from the battle atop the Black Tower, immunity from being Moved didn't mean you were protected against *other* objects being moved into you.

Lips drawn back in a snarl, eyes blazing like the twin moons, Theron stretched out a hand towards the Matron—but this time she was not the target of his power. A terrible *crack* tore the night as the altar tore free of the platform. The Matron cried out as it struck her from behind, smashing her from her feet.

A vice clenched around Kaila's chest as the woman went down, but then the Aegis flashed and Theron cried out, falling to one knee. The altar crashed down as the light in his eyes faltered. It split in two as it struck, sending reverberations across the platform.

A moment later, the light in Theron's eyes returned. A dozen pieces of rubble buzzed into the air as he rose once more. Hissing, they slashed at the Matron, forcing her to raise the Aegis against the attack. Without her *atarsight*, Kaila couldn't tell what happened next. The woman didn't seem to have the powers of a Mover, but each bit of rubble that came within reach would suddenly drop from the air, as though drained of the forces holding them aloft.

A few got through though, tearing at her gown and flesh, forcing her back towards the edge.

Theron was winning. But the effort was also having an effect on the man. She could see it in his face, in his bared teeth and the tendons straining in his neck. Kaila's fingers found the crystal in her belt. She could give it to Theron, but would that even help him now? It was only a tiny fragment—miniscule in comparison to the power he was channelling. And against it…

Crack.

A scream of pain drew her eyes back to the altar. Blood sprayed from the Matron's lips as a shard of concrete struck her across the face. She went down like a sack of gravel. This time she didn't get back up.

Debris continued to swirl as Theron approached—in fact, more seemed to be gathering as the last pieces of the altar were picked up in the vortex. *Atar* shone not just from Theron's eyes now, but glowed beneath his skin, lighting up his veins like the glowsticks sold by hawkers in Soul Square. His face was twisted in a grimace, his lips parted as though he was in pain, though no sound emerged.

Kaila knew what was happening to him though. Theron couldn't fight the crystal, couldn't stop the flow of *atar*, even as it burned him up from the inside. He was dying in agony—and he had done it to save them.

On the ground, the Matron managed to push herself to her knees. She looked up at Theron not with anger or fear, but a grudging acceptance, as though impressed someone actually had the strength to stand up to her.

"Go ahead then," she rasped, "do—Rohan, *no!*" At the last minute, the woman's expression changed, and real terror bloomed there.

Too late, Kaila saw it happen. She had been so focused on Theron and the Matron, she'd forgotten the others. Forgotten Rohan. Apparently, everyone had, as unnoticed he had crept back into the centre of the platform, to his father's body. Now, bloody blade clutched in his hand, he leapt at Theron. Even as the Matron's warning echoed across the night, he struck—not at Theron's skull or chest, for he was no warrior, but at the one target that could make a difference against an Elysian.

He swung for Theron's outstretched hand.

A heavy silence followed, as though the world held its breath to see what came next.

Thump.

The sound Theron's hand made as it struck the ground broke the spell. Kaila stared in shock and horror as her friend staggered, clutching at the bloody stump that had been a whole limb just a second ago. A scream pierced the darkness, and it was not just one of pain, but unbearable loss. The light flickered in Theron's eyes as he turned on Rohan, already fading as the source of *atar* was quite literally cut off.

But not yet dead.

Even without her Gift, Kaila felt the attack coming. But there was nothing she could do to stop it.

Roaring, Theron lashed out with the last of his power, catching Rohan and hurling him backwards into the night. The prince cried out, the blade spinning from his hands as he tumbled across the platform, bouncing once, twice—only on the third did the light finally vanish from Theron's eyes.

Yet even as the Mover collapsed, overwhelmed by the injury done to his body by so much *atar*, Rohan's momentum carried him beyond the level of the platform—out onto the slope of the dome.

"No!"

Screaming, Kaila hurled herself after him. No longer under the effects of Theron's Gift, Rohan had come to a rest at the point where the dome began to curve towards the vertical. And the concrete was slick with the night's dew. He groaned as he started to rise, then cried out as his feet slipped from underneath him. Alarm appeared in his eyes as he saw where he was, twenty feet below the platform.

And growing.

Blood pounded in Kaila's ears as she watched him slip away. She needed to reach him and stop his descent. She scanned the concrete dome for cracks or some imperfection her desperate fingers could use for purchase.

But there was nothing.

Rohan continued his inevitable slide towards the precipice. Somewhere behind her, Jenna was screaming, and the Matron shouted, but Kaila ignored the both of them and stepped from the platform onto the slope of the dome. The ground quickly grew slick beneath her feet. Her stomach lurched as she felt herself slipping, before she dropped to her knees and began to crawl.

But Rohan was picking up speed now as he began to thrash desperately for purchase. She would never reach him in time.

He was going to die. Unless…

There was no more time to think.

Kaila had seen how Eliza had released her collar. If her friend was to be believed, it could only be removed by the one who placed it there. And Kaila knew the cost of that decision.

But what else could she do? Rohan hadn't asked for any of this. He was an innocent she had thrown to the wolves. She would not allow any harm to come to him.

Her fingers found the tiny, almost imperceptible clasp, and pressed it. Immediately, she felt the golden band grow warm against her flesh. Terror filled her, but there was nothing she could do now but wait. Clenching her teeth against the growing heat, she reached for her hidden agimet—

Suddenly, the warmth became a blazing furnace. She *felt* her flesh start to melt, smelt the burning in her nostrils, tasted it on her tongue. She would have screamed, but such was the pain, she couldn't even bare to draw breath. The world turned a terrible white, then red, then creeping black, until all that remained was a tiny dot. She could feel the call of the netherworld and knew this time there would be no coming back.

Then she saw his face. Rohan's. The raw terror in his eyes as he fell. If she failed, if she slipped into the nether now, he would perish with her.

Ding.

Distantly, she heard a ring, like metal striking stone. And

then a spark. A shimmer of something more. A star in the darkness. First one, then another and another and another, until the world was filled with them.

Soullights.

Kaila's skin tingled as the world slowly returned. She was still awash with agony, but against it now came the soothing touch of *atar* in her veins. Her fingers shook as they grasped the agimet concealed in her cuffs. *Her Gift. She had her Gift.*

Amidst a world lit with light, one shining point stood out amongst the others, a *soullight* at once unknown, but also strangely familiar, as though…as though she were somehow connected to it.

Rohan.

Despite the weeks without practice, the threads of *atar* spun easily from Kaila's soul, as though recognising the urgency of her need. She sent them streaking towards the prince, one after another, until she was sure it would be enough. Gritting her teeth, she reached out to draw him back—

Screeee!

Kaila flinched as a thrumming, high-pitched shriek filled her mind, like someone had just struck a violin against the concrete columns below. Her concentration wavered and the threads began to slip from her control. She didn't know what was going on with her Gift, but she recalled the sound. She'd heard it once, the night she'd taken Eliza. She'd never had a chance to ask Theron what it had been.

But as another cry came from below, Kaila forced herself to harden. Rohan needed her. Firming her hold on his *soullight*, she drew them taut. Below, Rohan's headward plunge towards the city came to a sudden halt. He gasped, eyes clenched closed as he hugged the concrete dome, though by now the angle was so steep the bare stone would never hold him.

Fresh agony washed over Kaila like a wildfire in the summer mountain steeps. She gritted her teeth as spots danced before her eyes, then sent several more threads to wrap around Rohan, just in case the sound came again and the others frayed. Then she began to reel them in.

Rohan's head jerked up, his eyes widening in shock. Around the curve of the dome, the others wouldn't be able to see what was happening. But it didn't matter what they saw. There was no hiding for Kaila on the bare rooftop. Rohan could feel the impossible force lifting him back to the platform.

And he could see the silver light in her eyes.

She watched as realisation came to him. Fear was quick to follow. Even as she used the Gift of the Elysian to save him, she could see his face twisting. His hands clawed at the stone—no longer avoid the fall below, but to resist the pull of her magic. To escape *her*.

"Rohan, *stop!*" she hissed, gritting her teeth as his movements shook her frail grasp on his *soullight*. She was glad she'd tied his soul with extra bands of *atar*. "Please, I don't want to drop you."

Maybe it was her voice, or perhaps it was just the reminder of the precipice, but he stilled. Exhaling, Kaila redoubled her efforts. His eyes never left her, however, and she found herself quivering at what she saw there. Gone was the warmth, the friendship and whatever else they had shared. Rohan's blue eyes glinted in the darkness, no longer soft, but hard and unyielding.

Finally, the slope became gentle enough for Rohan to find some purchase. Kaila exhaled as the pressure went off her Gift. She let the power slip away as the prince clambered up the last few feet on his hands and knees. Then she closed her eyes and sank to the stone. Without the adrenaline of losing Rohan, it took all her effort not to cry out as fresh pain swept through her body.

Rohan.

She could hear him nearby, panting in the cold night air. He had angled himself away from her, but apparently he was as spent as her, for he did not attempt to complete the climb to the platform. She could *sense* his eyes on her, not so much as any physical attention, but as a ringing in her soul, a pulsing, almost like music.

Harsh, angry music.

"Rohan," she choked, barely managing to squeeze out the words, "are you—"

"Who are you?" he hissed. "You're with him, aren't you?"

The words bore such a venom that they cut through Kaila's pain. Her eyes snapped open, finding his sapphire eyes.

"Please, Rohan, it's still me, its…its…" But the name caught in her burning throat. She wasn't Eliza. The anger she saw in his eyes, the fear and the hurt, it was real. Even if it had always been *her*, she had still betrayed him. "I was trying to…trying to help you."

Bringing himself to his knees, Rohan crouched as though preparing to launch himself at her and send them both plunging to their deaths. Which, after his act of courage above, wasn't entirely impossible. His mouth opened, and then closed. There was no warmth in his eyes when he finally spoke, only a cold, harsh accusation.

"What have you done with the real Eliza?" he growled. "I swear on the Nameless, if you've harmed her…"

It was like a slap to her face. Lips parted, she stared at him for the longest time, before she slowly shook her head. Heart aching, she reached out a hand for him. "Please, let me explain—"

"Get away from me!"

She flinched as Rohan came to his feet. After a moment, she allowed her hand to fall, then rose as well. They stood facing each other on the edge of the dome. A terrible ache filled her chest. She recognised Rohan's fear. How many times had she seen it in the face of those she loved now? Sister Eurador and Sareen and Tomas and so many others in Elgoss. It was the same look she had given Caellum, her only friend, when his Elysian blood had been exposed to the world.

It hurt worse than the burns around her throat.

"It's aways been me, Rohan," she whispered. Tears blurred her vision. "I'm sorry I lied, but that's the truth."

Then, because Kaila couldn't stand to see that look in his eyes one second longer, she turned and walked back towards the platform. She expected Rohan to leap after her, or shout a warning to the others, but instead there was nothing. She didn't look back, nor watch where she placed her feet. Everything hurt. What did it matter if she slipped and fell? What did *anything* matter now?

Yet her steps were true and still Rohan did not come after her.

Atop the dome, her senses finally began to return. Theron was injured, but he lived. Maybe the pair of them could at least escape this disaster with their lives. But as she topped the rise, her eyes found the Matron. She knelt beside the ruin of the altar, Aegis glowing brightly on her arm. Fear wormed its way into Kaila's heart, but there was nowhere else to go but up.

Her mind raced as she approached. The body of the king lay amidst the wreckage, and while his blood had ceased to flow, it pooled now on the concrete, leaving the ground sticky beneath her boots.

As for Theron…Kaila's heart clenched when she saw him. He had collapsed alongside the monarch, his face a shade of grey she had never seen on a living man. For a moment, she thought his body must have succumbed to the damage done by the uncut agimet—then she saw his chest rise. A little squeak of relief slipped from her lips. He was alive—though that might not last long. For either of them. Any moment now, Rohan would overcome his shock and reveal her to all of them.

"Eliza!" It was Jenna who noticed Kaila first. Slumped against the altar, the princess jerked upright at her approach. Regaining her feet, she darted towards Kaila, then hesitated. Her eyes shone with unspilt tears. "My brother…is he…"

"He's alive," Kaila croaked, stumbling to a stop.

"Thank the First Matron," Jenna whispered.

Kaila flinched at the blessing. She stared at the young woman, thinking of everything that had been done to Jenna. The things the Matron had done to hide Jenna's past were almost as bad as what Theron's father had done to him.

At least she's alive, she thought to herself.

"The First Matron had nothing to do with it," Kaila said harshly. She studied the other woman, wondering if what she was about to do was the right thing, or if it would doom the woman to a worse fate. In the end, the truth won out. "The Matrons are the ones that ruined your life. T'iana, and all the others after, right down to your supposed mother."

Then quietly, she drew *atar* from the crystal in her hand.

The princess's eyes widened at the sight. But this night had already been filled with so many shocks, that was the extent of her reaction.

"I don't understand," she said softly.

Kaila ignored the question. "Earlier, you asked your mother why she has conspired all this time to keep you from her throne," she said instead. "It's because you're Elysian, Jenna. Like me, and Theron. Your father had you with a woman known as the Reaper —and then your mother took you to use against her." She fell silent, waiting for the princess to respond.

The colour drained from Jenna's face, until she stood ghost-like in the moonlight. For a moment she swayed, and Kaila thought she would fall, before she seemed to right herself. Her eyes narrowed, jaw hardening.

"You're one of them. How can I believe you?"

"I saved your brother," Kaila replied.

Jenna's face twitched. "But I've never…I don't…"

"Had the Gift?" Kaila swallowed, her hand going instinctively to her throat. The flesh burned, but the *atar* in her veins helped to cool its sting. It felt good to hold its power again. "Your collar blocks it," she rasped. "Your mother knew. That's why she made you a Daughter so early." She paused, studying the woman. "But she also knew if you took the Aegis, you would be free. And she would have rather seen you destroyed than allow her hypocrisy to come to light."

"All my life…" Jenna glanced back at the dais, slowly shaking her head. "And Theron…he was working with her?"

"No, we were playing our own game."

Jenna's face hardened. "So that's all we were to you, my brother and I, a game?"

Kaila's lips trembled. She remembered the warmth of Rohan's hand in hers…

…and the pain of seeing fear in his eyes.

"I'm sorry." She bowed her head.

Silence followed as the wind swirled across the rooftop. Somewhere in the distance, a bell began to toll. Midnight had come. Summer had finally arrived.

"Go."

Kaila's head jerked up. Jenna stood watching her, face hard, fists clenched. She frowned. "What—"

"For saving my brother's life, I'm giving you one chance to run."

Kaila stared at the princess, not sure if she was hearing right. "But Theron—"

"I said *go!*" Jenna snarled. Red rushed to her face as she advanced a step. "Before I change my mind."

Kaila's heart pulsed. She clenched her fists, eyes darting past the princess to where Theron lay. His *soullight* was so dim she could barely see its shimmer amidst the rubble. And that look on his face, before Rohan had attacked him, the madness in his eyes…

…then she saw movement alongside him. The Matron swayed on her knees, then began to rise, Aegis burning in the night.

"You can't help him."

Her gaze returned to Jenna. The princess stood defiant. Kaila knew the truth then. Even if she could make it to Theron, even if she had the strength and *atar* to carry him downstairs, there was a ballroom full of nobles and soldiers and Wardens waiting there. She would never make it to safety with his burden, not before the Matron sounded the alarm.

Even so, she was tempted. All this pain and suffering, and it had been for nothing. They would never defeat the Magisterium now, never take the Aegis or free the ancient king Oberon. Nothing would change.

Yes, she was tempted.

Then she recalled the dark blades of the Wardens, and the awful power of the Aegis, the suffering of the prisoners in the depths of the Sanctum…

…and then she was turning, running, fleeing down the dark stairs, away from the Matron, and Jenna, and Rohan and Theron and the nightmare that had consumed her life.

Away from everything.

———

ATOP THE DOME OF THE SANCTUM, JENNA WATCHED THE ELYSIAN flee. She didn't know why she'd let it go, why she hadn't tried to stop it. They had ruined everything. Destroyed her entire life. And besides, it was the duty of every good Fresian citizen to confront the enemy wherever they found it.

It's because you're Elysian, Jenna. Like me.

She shivered as the words echoed in her mind. She wanted to deny them, to hurl them from her for the lies they must surely be. The enemy knew only how to corrupt, wasn't that what the Sisters claimed?

But Jenna couldn't bring herself to do it. Because as she turned to look at her mother, slowly rising to her feet, Jenna couldn't deny they had the ring of truth about them.

Her hand went to her collar. She had worn it half her life, since she had become a Daughter all those years ago. She would never know the truth, not for sure, so long as she wore it. But the only way to remove it without risking her own life was for her mother to use the Aegis. And if the Elysian was telling the truth, that was something Eliana Frye would never do.

I will allow Jenna to become a sister. She can be sent away, somewhere far from the capital, where her corruption can do no harm

Jenna clenched her fists as her mother regained her feet and looked around. As she did so, Rohan appeared, edging up the dome to reach the platform.

"Where is she?" he rasped, looking from Jenna to his mother.

"Gone," Jenna croaked.

He swallowed. "You saw?"

Pursing her lips, Jenna nodded.

"Saw what?" the Matron demanded.

"Eliza…" Rohan trailed off, squeezing his eyes closed. "She was…an imposter. An Elysian had taken her place."

"And you didn't *stop her?*" the Matron demanded. Nostrils flaring, she looked from one of them to another.

Jenna twisted her lips into a sneer. "We couldn't. She was too powerful."

It felt good to see that rage in her mother's eyes. Ignoring Jenna and Rohan and the murdered king, Eliana Frye marched to the passageway and disappeared into the stairwell. Jenna could hear her bellows from below as she called for the Wardens. Despite the girl's treachery, she found herself hoping Eliza had made it out of the Sanctum.

"Was it really her?" Rohan croaked. His face was twisted in pain and grief. "What she really was?"

She would have rather seen you destroyed than allow her hypocrisy to come to light.

Jenna nodded, even as she considered what she must do next. There was one way to learn the truth that didn't involve removing her collar and suffering a terrible fate. She could make her mother confess. But for that…

"I'm sorry, Rohan," she whispered. "It was really her."

25

Kaila reached the entrance of the Sanctum just as the alarm bells began to sound. Instantly, the soldiers on the gate came alert. Steel rattled as swords and spears were lifted and shields readied, though it was clear they didn't yet know whether the danger came from inside or without.

Heart pounding, Kaila raced towards them. She still wore Eliza's face, and though she no longer had the terrible collar, many on the gates would recognise her. If only she had a coat or something to hide the burns left by its removal—not to mention the tears in her clothes left by her scuffle on the rooftop.

Fortunately, the soldiers were expecting the burning glow of Elysian magic, not a soft-faced young woman that had passed this way many times before. She would work with what she could.

"Elysian!" she cried, staggering towards them. "In the Sanctum! You must help the Matron!"

Whether it was her state of dress or the panic in her eyes or the tolling of the bells, it was enough. The men and women guarding the great doors of the Sanctum exchanged glances, a ripple of indecision passing through their ranks—so they paid little attention to the marked Daughter that raced past.

"Stop that woman!"

Until someone behind Kaila pointed it out. She already had one hand on the heavy iron-panelled door when the shout came. She could have slipped through, out into the streets of Tah'raus. Could have run. Again. Fled the soldiers of the Magisterium and their masters.

Instead, Kaila found herself turning back as the rattle of boots filled the courtyard. Soldiers piled from their barracks, spreading out in a half-circle around the gate. She gritted her teeth, feeling the ache in her body from the bruises she had taken, the strain of using her Gift after so long being denied its power.

But she also felt the rage inside her. Rage at herself, for believing Rohan could be different, that the *world* could be different. That for a few, blissful days, Kaila had actually thought she could change things.

But things would never change. Men and women would continue to obey the Magisterium, spreading its evil through this city, through the hearts and minds of the entire kingdom.

It was satisfying to see fear in the eyes of the soldiers when Kaila reached into her pocket and drew out the crystal she had stashed there. It shone with the brilliance of the nexus, freshly filled by her power. Drawing on its *atar*, she watched the men stumble back, terror replacing the hesitation of a moment earlier.

"Fear not, soldiers of Fresia," a voice bellowed from within the Sanctum. Iron footsteps approached, before the shining light of a Warden's armour brightened the doorway. "We will take her together."

A familiar fear fluttered in Kaila's heart at the sight of the monster. She stood facing them, outnumbered, outmatched. So many times now she had run from the Wardens, fled because of their power. She couldn't touch him, couldn't harm him, and the soldiers knew it.

"For Fresia!" A rallying cry rose from their ranks. Their line straightening, hands firming on sword grips. Together, they began to advance.

It would be their last mistake.

Burning *atar* joined the rage in Kaila's veins as she spun out a dozen threads of power. The Warden might be immune, but his soldiers were not. And if they wanted to die for Fresia, she was only too happy to oblige them. The threads shot from her, piercing half a dozen of their *soullights*. Kaila held nothing back.

The soldiers made wet, squelching noises as they struck the walls of the Sanctum. Others screamed as they crashed into the Warden, flesh crunching against black armour. She couldn't touch the man's *soullight* directly, so she used the bodies to pound him into submission.

Even as the *atar* in her blood stuttered, she used her own Warden's power to draw more power from the nexus, feeding her crystal, and by extension, her own Gift. She would suffer for it later—already she could feel the burning in her veins, like acid after a footrace—but in that moment Kaila didn't care.

Only when there was not a single soldier left standing did she retreat. By then, every muscle, every cord and sinew in her body shrieked with the power she had channelled. She all but lurched out the open gates into the night and was met by the brilliance of Tah'raus. All that corrupted agimet was like a flame against her skin after what she'd just done, but Kaila had no choice but to flee through those streets.

Behind, the screams of the dying and the silence of the dead chased after her.

The night was strangely empty for Tah'raus, as though upon hearing the bells, its citizens had chosen to hide behind their doors rather than race to the aid of their Magisterium. *Cowards.* By the light of day they might claim to believe, but in this hour of need, the Magisterium found itself alone. Maybe there was some hope for them yet.

Her leg spasmed, almost sending Kaila crashing to the ground. Pain radiated from her throat, robbing her of strength.

The *atar* no longer helped—not after what she'd done with her Gift. That had been like adding fresh fire to her already scorched soul. As spots danced across her vision, she staggered into an alleyway. She had to get away from the Sanctum, back to the safe house…

…but in the chaos, Kaila had lost all sense of direction. The sounds of boots on stone echoed from the street. Gritting her teeth, she pressed herself against the wall. A second later, a platoon raced past, led by two Wardens.

A piece of her screamed to attack. To make them pay for what had happened. But as Kaila tried to draw more power from her crystal, a rush of dizziness washed over her. Straining to breathe, she slumped to her knees. Pain spread from her throat into her chest, radiating through her skull.

Run, Kaila. You need to get away.

Easier said than done. But she had no choice. Footsteps reeling, she staggered into the darkness. The pain swelled, threatening to drag her into unconsciousness. She clung on, staggering through the back streets, desperate for some sense of direction. She couldn't stop. If she stopped they would find her. If only she could reach Ambrose's shop. She had to keep going…

…Kaila startled awake, suddenly aware she was on her knees, that time had passed and the darkness had grown deeper. She stayed like that for a while, sucking in breath after breath, willing herself to move but unable to find the strength.

Crunch.

The hairs on her scalp prickled at the sound of a boot on gravel. She lifted her head, but saw nothing in the darkness. Her fingers scrambled for the agimet in her pocket, but Kaila was so weak, she couldn't find it. Even if she could, she was in no condition now to use her Gift. She was going to die in this alley.

Her hand fell from her pocket as a silhouette emerged from the shadows. She wanted to fight, tried to stand, even made it halfway to her feet before her strength gave out. She fell…

...and the darkness embraced her with the welcoming arms of an old friend.

EPILOGUE

E liana Frye regarded the dimly lit room, her gaze lingering on the wounded man in the bed. Only a few hours had passed since the events on the rooftop. Rohan had agreed to remain in the Sanctum while they hunted the vile creature that had seduced him. There was no sign of the impostor—she had escaped out the northern gates, leaving a trail of destruction in her wake. Eliana had only just finished cleaning up that mess.

She still didn't know how it had all gone so wrong. When the stranger had come to her with the truth about Theron Falkenrath, it had seemed like an answer to her prayers. The plan had been so simple. Allow the marriage to proceed and then reveal the vile creature for what it was. Jenna would be ruined, without exposing Eliana's own shame. Rohan would be free to claim his rightful place on the throne. And all it had cost was a pair of Daughterships for the children of her benefactor.

Except in the end, it had not been the First Matron who had answered her prayers, but the Trickster god of the Elysian. Eliana clenched her fists, fingernails biting into her palms. There hadn't been just one of the creatures, but *two*, and now she was left scrambling to repair the wreckage they had left in their wake.

Next, she had to deal with the wilful creature she called her daughter. Her eyes moved to the young woman dozing on the sofa. Jenna hadn't changed out of her dress from the ceremony—if you could call the perverse mockery the two Elysian had made of the union a real ceremony. The girl's eyes snapped open as Eliana closed the door of the chamber behind her.

"Mother, how nice of you to visit," Jenna greeted, her voice carrying an edge.

"It's alive then?" Eliana asked, approaching the bed.

Jenna waved a hand. "For now."

Pursing her lips, Eliana stared down at the creature. They had bound it in chains, and she noted that Jenna had removed all trace of agimet powered devices from the room. Even the lanterns had been replaced with the old oil-fuelled variety.

"It should be in the dungeons," she said, moving to the lounger opposite her daughter and taking a seat.

With the mess the impostor had made of her plans with Rohan, she had lost some of her negotiating power with Jenna. She still held the Aegis, but the challenges to her power would soon come with her husband's death. The strain of the device would start to take its toll. She needed to work quickly to repair the damage the Elysian traitor had done.

"You'd like that, wouldn't you, mother," Jenna replied. Letting out a sigh, she rose and crossed to the cabinet in the corner. Removing a pair of glasses, she glanced at the Matron. "A drink?"

Eliana studied the girl. "Is this really the time?"

Jenna snorted. "I cannot think of a better moment to muddle the senses."

Letting out a breath, Eliana waved a hand. Taking it as agreement, Jenna removed a bottle of gin and carried it back to the loungers along with the glasses, then poured them each a measure.

"Tonic?" Eliana asked as the girl slid the glass towards her. She wrinkled her nose. How the girl could drink her liquor straight was beyond her. She must have inherited the habit from her junkie mother.

Jenna rolled her eyes, but returned to the cabinet and retrieved a second bottle. Topping up her mother's glass, she left the bottle on the table and sat, then raised her glass in a salute.

"Long live the Magisterium," she murmured.

Eliana repeated the words and they clinked glasses, though she had to hold back a sneer. Long live the Magisterium indeed. She sipped her drink, considering her next move carefully. It pained her to admit, but the disaster with Eliza left her little choice—Jenna needed to be dealt with. The survival of the Magisterium, of her *legacy*, was more important than one child. At least her fool of a husband was no longer around to meddle with her plans.

Jenna knocked back her glass in a single swig. "So what's the plan, mother?" she asked, reaching for the bottle. "Will you let the truth about the Falkenraths come out? Try to throw me under the bus and make my brother the grieving widower so he can still be king?" She pursed her lips. "I don't think so," she said at last, "you know I won't stay quiet."

"Not even to spare your brother the humiliation?"

Jenna said nothing for the longest time, just sat in her lounger, slowly sipping her gin. "This was never about him though, was it?" she said at last.

Her eyes found Eliana's, and despite herself, she shivered. Their emerald green was so like the Reaper's.

"I could never understand why you hated me," Jenna whispered. "How any mother could treat her only daughter like a stranger."

"My dear Daughter," Eliana said, unable to keep the sneer from her lips this time. "Still you insist with this. If I have treated you harshly, it is only for your betterment."

"You never treated Rohan harshly," Jenna replied. "Even now, after he committed the same blasphemy as my own, you protect him." Her voice caught, a raw emotion entering her words. Eliana was surprised to find actual anger in the girl's eyes.

"Rohan was not the heir," the Matron replied. Her glass was almost empty and her head was pounding. Damn cursed liquor. She reached for the tonic and topped off her drink.

"That's the part I could never understand," Jenna whispered. "Until now."

"Oh?" Watching the girl, her heart pulsed with a thrill of fear. She stilled it with a thought. She was the Matron of Fresia. She wielded the Aegis. There was no danger for her here. Instead, she allowed a smile to touch her lips. "What do you think you understand, Daughter?"

Those emerald eyes found hers. "I'm one of them, aren't I?" she rasped. "One of the Elysian."

"Don't be ridiculous."

"Ridiculous?" Jenna murmured, her eyes falling to the drink in her hands. She took another sip. "Ridiculous would be the lengths you've gone through to keep me from the throne if it *wasn't* true. You knowingly let an Elysian walk the corridors of the Sanctum, all so you could destroy me. Rohan almost *died* because of your folly. And for what? Because I'm not good enough to be Matron?" She shook her head. "No, it has to be something more than that."

Rising, Jenna crossed to the bed where the creature lay and picked up something Eliana hadn't noticed. Her eyebrows lifted when she saw the crystal. It was still dark, drained by the Aegis back on that rooftop, but in a few hours it would shine with the unnatural light of the nexus. She managed to keep the surprise from her face, however, silently reassuring herself. Jenna still wore the collar of a Daughter. It would prevent her from absorbing the crystal's energy.

"How long do you think it's been now?" Jenna whispered. "A few more hours, and I'll know the truth." She eyed her mother, before letting her hand drop to her side. "Except I won't, will I? Because you trapped me with this collar when I was too young to even understand what it meant. And now it doesn't matter if I hold agimet or not. That's why I was made a Daughter so young. That's why I could pass my Trials."

She stepped towards the sofa. "Everything you've done, my entire life, it's all been to keep this secret from me."

Eliana opened her mouth to deny it, but she could see the truth in the girl's eyes. Nothing she said or did now would sway Jenna from it. The lie was over. In a way, it was a relief.

"That girl told you, didn't she?" she said with a scowl. "Twisted, treacherous creatures, all of you."

It was gratifying, seeing the colour drain from Jenna's face, the arrogance wilt and crumble away. She sank into the sofa, her face a mask of pain.

"So it really is true," Jenna croaked. She clenched her fist around the crystal, her hand trembling. "Why?"

The Matron let out a sigh and reached for the gin bottle. She needed something stiffer for this conversation. "I suppose I owe you the truth," she said, topping off her glass.

"That would be nice for a change."

She laughed. "You were never meant to exist." Her lips drew back in a snarl. "You were the product of a…mutually beneficial arrangement."

"Meaning?"

"Meaning your mother worked for your father and I. Unfortunately, your father being a man of…certain appetites, couldn't keep his hands to himself. Your appearance was an unwanted complication."

"What do you mean, *worked for you?*"

"She was an assassin," Eliana explained. "The Reaper, she was called. We favoured her services during our rise to the throne."

The last of the colour drained from Jenna's face. "So it's true —you had your rivals assassinated? And with an *Elysian?*"

"That's politics, dear," the Matron dismissed the girl's words with a wave. "You should know that better than anyone by now.

Your mother served a valuable purpose—but she was also dangerous. So when I found out about you…" The Matron shrugged. "I took you and held you within the Sanctum, where even the Reaper could not reach."

"And my mother…" Jenna rasped. It seemed to take an effort for her to speak. "What…what happened to her…"

"Her services were no longer required," Eliana said with a shrug.

"Then why keep me around all these years?"

"Your father had already taken to bouncing you on his knee and calling you his daughter." She wrinkled her nose at the memory. "The man was a fool when it came to his children."

"You killed him."

She shrugged. "He was already dying." Her eyes found Jenna's. "At least this way, his death served a purpose."

"Except that Eliza ruined it all for you." Drawing in a breath, Jenna exhaled. "So what now?"

"I should have smothered you in your sleep years ago," Eliana sighed. "Still, better late than never, I guess."

"You intend to kill me?"

"Did you think this conversation would go any other way, Jenna?"

"Truthfully?" Jenna whispered. Clutching the crystal, she watched the dark facets, as though waiting for the light to appear. "No, I didn't."

The Matron laughed. "You still wear the collar of a Daughter. You cannot defy me, even with that crystal. Come now, let us put an end to this."

Smiling, she reached for the Aegis…

…or rather, she *tried* to reach for it. But her limbs refused the command. A tingling horror crept across her scalp as she found the same immobility had come over her legs. Her entire body was paralysed.

"What…what have you…"

"Your tonic," Jenna said. "Really, you should have learnt to embrace at least *some* vices, Eliana. They might have saved your life." Rising, she loomed over the Matron. "I knew only one of us would survive this discussion, like you said." A predatory smile appeared on her lips. "So I decided it was time to take fate into my own hands."

True terror took root in the Matron's heart now. "Jenna, please," she rasped, "please, you have to understand. Everything I have done was for our people. Please, my daughter—"

"Oh, now I'm your daughter, am I?" Jenna's emerald eyes glinted in the lanternlight. She knew that look. It was the same one the Reaper had worn all those years ago when Eliana had taken her daughter. Murder.

"How did you say you'd have done it?" Turning, Jenna strode to the bed and snatched up a pillow. "Smothered in my sleep?"

"Please, Jenna, have mercy—"

Before Eliana could finish her plea, Jenna pressed the pillow against her face. Desperately, she strained against the drug, strained to *fight*, but there was nothing to be done. Finally, the Matron of Fresia felt the helplessness of all the wretched Daughters she had sent to the grave over the years.

"You just lay there and relax, mother," Eliana almost thought she heard Jenna's voice break, "it will all be over soon."

"Again, my child? Truly, you are a girl in love with death."

Kaila shuddered as she opened her eyes and found herself in a familiar darkness. For once, it didn't bring her sadness. In fact, she felt nothing at all. Closing her eyes, she tried to ignore the voice, the one that had saved her last time she'd woken in the dark.

This time, she didn't want to be saved.

Let the darkness take her. What was left for Kaila Dwyn in the world but pain? To be hurt, again and again, and see everything and everyone she loved turn away from her in disgust. Or destroyed by a Magisterium that had spent a thousand years perfecting their cruelty?

"Ah, my child. I am sorry to see you suffer," the voice of Oberon rumbled, "but that is life in the light, to suffer. It has always been so."

"Then I don't want it!"

Suddenly she was back in that strange room, in the darkness and the gloom, surrounded by the arcane machines and devices. The ancient king of Iselador stood before her wearing a gentle smile. Raising a hand, he rested it on her shoulder.

"Then you would choose the dark?"

She shuddered. Once more she lay on the boundary between life and death. How often had she come here now? Yet no other time had she suffered like this, teetering on the precipice of surrender.

"What is it like?" she whispered.

There was silence as the granite face studied her. "It is empty," he said at last. "Believe me, my child, it is a poor replacement for all that fills the world above—ay, even the pain."

"But it's too much," she croaked. "I can't bear it anymore."

He studied her again before he spoke: "Come, let us walk through my realm. Then you shall see."

Kaila didn't want to. She didn't want to go anywhere, see anything, be anyone. But as Oberon said, this was his domain, and she felt the tendrils of darkness lift her up, carrying her as the ancient king wandered. The world shifted, the walls fading, but the dark remained. Eternal. Unchanging.

"This is what the end looks like," the king said softly.

Despite herself, Kaila shivered. "What about that place we were before?"

"No more real than a shadow at twilight. This place is eternal, undying, unchanging. It is a prison."

"Someone trapped you here, didn't they?"

Oberon looked surprised. "Yes," he admitted, "long ago, I was betrayed."

"By T'iana?"

He grunted. "So our tale has not entirely vanished from the world."

Kaila swallowed but said nothing. Her eyes returned to the darkness. "You said once this is only the world between, that you did not know what lies beyond."

"Ay, that is true," he murmured, "but this is not your time, child. You are still needed."

He waved a hand and the darkness shifted. Her skin crawled as images appeared; the face of Theron laughing, Quintin and his kind smile, Rohan in his books and even Eliza, watching her with those suspicious eyes.

"They need you," Oberon said. "Without you, they will fail. They will never claim the Aegis. The world will remain as it is. The Magisterium will rule for another thousand years."

"Why me?" she croaked, squeezing her eyes closed against the images.

"Because of all my children, you alone are free," Oberon said, resting his hand on her shoulder.

"Me?" she asked, frowning, "but the Elysian..." she trailed off, eyes widening as she heard T'iana's message again.

"...be warned, my child. The enemy...cunning. Be watchful for...return...I sought to cleanse...children will seek...possess the Aegis."

The enemy. T'iana had never mentioned the Elysian. Could she mean...
"The Wardens?"

The ancient king inclined his head. "When you take the Aegis, the world will change. That I promise you." His fingers tightened on her shoulder. "Now, my child, are you ready to return to the sunlight?"

A shudder ran through Kaila's soul. She didn't want to go. Didn't want to face what it meant to live. But despite the pain, despite the anger that had dragged her back to this terrible place, deep in her soul a spark remained. A flicker of life, a warmth reminding her that despite the dark days, there was still hope. So long as she lived, she could be something more, things could always get better.

So closing her eyes, Kaila sought the silver thread that led upwards through the void, back towards the light, towards the pain, and grasped it with all her soul.

She woke to a pounding headache. Webs of fiery agony burnt trails around her throat, like someone had caught her in a noose of molten led—which probably wasn't far from the truth. Groaning, she tried to roll over, only for the movement to send a wave of fresh agony radiating through her body.

Sucking in a breath, she forced her eyes to open. The world spun, but then she felt the tingling of *atar* in her veins and some of the dizziness faded. She glanced at her hand and found a crystal there. Panic followed as she realised what she was doing. She fumbled, trying to shove the stone into her pocket—only to realise she wasn't wearing her usual nightclothes, but a single silk onesie. Reaching a hand to her throat, she found a bandage.

The memories struck her like a blow. The rooftop. The king murdered. Theron and Jenna. The Warden and the soldiers.

And Rohan, the horror in his eyes as he saw the truth.

She squeezed her eyes closed. The truth? What even *was* the truth anymore? She wasn't the real Eliza. But it was Kaila the prince had fallen for, her stories, her past, even if he didn't know it...

It didn't matter.

She sank back to the bed as hot tears streaked her cheeks.

"So, you're awake."

Startled, she looked around and found him. Ambrose. Belatedly, Kaila realised where she was. The basement. The tailor sat at a nearby desk, working on a piece of fabric, which he now set aside. Her eyes finished their traverse around the basement before returning to the Weaver.

"Where..."

"Upstairs," Ambrose grunted. "She knows she can't go back now."

Her stomach twisted. Guilt. Kaila had hated Eliza for the longest time—but she'd never meant to destroy the young woman's life. And yet...something else was wrong. Ambrose was gruff, but he should have been furious, enraged by her failure. The beginnings of fear needled her stomach.

"What's happened?" she asked, trying to push herself up.

Approaching the stretcher, Ambrose laid a hand on her shoulder. "Easy," he said quietly, "why don't you start with your part? There are still...pieces missing in our story."

She swallowed. Ambrose's kindness did nothing to ease her panic, but she had no choice.

"It was a trap," she croaked. "I tried to warn Theron, but..."

Her hand crept to her throat. She felt almost naked without the collar. "I couldn't…" Swallowing, she recounted what had happened on the rooftop with Theron and the others.

"That calculating witch…" Ambrose muttered. "But how did she know…" Shaking his head, he looked back at Kaila. "And then what happened?"

"She drained Theron's crystals…" Squeezing her hands into fists, she told Ambrose the rest. How the Matron had killed the king, how Theron had used the corrupted crystal and attacked the Matron, and then how Rohan had stopped him.

The moment she had revealed herself.

Her voice cracked as she reached that final part. Her eyes slid closed. "I thought…I thought he was different."

To her surprise, the tailor sighed. "Now you know the pain we all feel," he said, his voice gentle. "It doesn't matter who you are to them, Kaila. What you do. You are still the enemy."

She was surprised to hear the depth of sadness in the old man's voice. Why would he care that Rohan feared her? Ambrose was untouchable, the famed tailor of the nobility, most powerful Elysian in the city…

The most powerful *Elysian*…

"That's why you did it," she whispered. "Why you were willing to risk everything taking on the Magisterium."

Ambrose nodded. "It's a hard lesson, but one we all learn eventually. Powerful or powerless, famous or forgettable, loved or hated. None of it matters, because so long as the Magisterium rules, tomorrow it can become nothing. That's why I fight, girl, why I am ready to risk everything. So that one day I no longer have to wear the mask."

"So what now?"

"Now?" Ambrose pursed his lips. "Now we get back up and fight again another day."

"Just like that?"

Ambrose's eyes were hard as he looked at her. "What other choice do we have?"

Consciousness came slowly to Theron. He fought against it, clinging to the darkness, the emptiness of the void, but life was not done with him just yet. Bit by bit, the pain returned, needles digging into his flesh, driving deeper, hacking and stabbing until his very skin seemed alive.

Finally, the last remnants of oblivion fell away and the agony of withdrawal returned with all its searing heat. Desperately, he thrashed where he lay, the fingers of his remaining hand clawing at the stone floor, reaching for something, *anything*, that would sate his need…

…only for the chains that bound his arm to pull tight.

A cry whispered from his lips, desperate, pathetic, torn from the depths of his despair.

In response, a voice spoke.

"So, you're awake."

A tremor shook Theron. He recognised the speaker, though his mind was still sluggish. For a moment all he felt was a burning need. Then he remembered how his body worked. His eyelids rasped like sandpaper as he opened them and looked upon the face of Jenna.

"Princess," he croaked, trying and failing to maintain his composure. "How…"

"Oh yes, I would like to know how you managed it as well," she murmured. Crouched alongside him, a smile twisted her lips. "And why. I want to know all about what you and your little friend were planning."

Another tremor shook him. Theron's mouth was parched, and his heart palpitated with a wild rhythm. But this was Jenna. He knew her. He could turn this around, manipulate her into releasing him.

"Of course—" he started, but Jenna held up a finger to interrupt him.

Carefully, she reached into her pocket and drew out a piece

of agimet. It shone with the burning power of *atar*. Driven by a mindless desperation, Theron strained against his bindings— even reached for it with his bloody stump. Chains rattled, but did not give so much as an inch.

"Please, give it to me," he groaned. He needed that crystal, needed the *atar* more than he needed breath in his lungs. Without it he was drowning.

The princess only laughed. "All in good time, *husband*," she jeered. Her fingers tightened around the crystal, and to Theron's horror, her eyes glowed silver. "But, first I want you to tell me all about how your magic works."

Enjoyed Rogue's Gambit? Follow the Kickstarter to grab yourself the Limited Edition Hardcover!

A NOTE FROM THE AUTHOR

Wow did this book make me work for it! I've had this little heist fantasy story fermenting in my head for over a year now, so it was amazing to finally get it on the page and out to all you loyal readers—although to say it came out a little differently than I originally planned would be a massive understatement! In fact, book one of this series was originally meant to be about the first three chapters of this book, before it grew into a complete 80k word chase story.

As for Rogue's Gambit, well after blowing out to over 100k (I keep saying I'm not going to do that anymore, but here we are!), I ALSO had to split off a part of the story I originally wanted to have in this book. I still like where we ended up for the end of book 2, but some of these characters really did just demand more page time than I'd originally planned—chief amongst them being Jenna and Rohan. Now I'm excited to see where their characters go in book 3. I hope you all are as well!!! Until then…

Write on!
Aaron Hodges

FOLLOW AARON HODGES…
And receive TWO FREE novels and a short story!
https://aaronhodgesauthor.com/newsletter

ALSO BY AARON HODGES

Trials of the Aegis

Book 1: Warden's Justice

Book 2: Rogue's Gambit

The Sword of Light

Book 1: Stormwielder

Book 2: Firestorm

Book 3: Soul Blade

The Legend of the Gods

Book 1: Oathbreaker

Book 2: Shield of Winter

Book 3: Dawn of War

The Knights of Alana

Book 1: Daughter of Fate

Book 2: Queen of Vengeance

Book 3: Crown of Chaos

The Evolution Gene

Book 1: Reborn

Book 2: Havoc

Book 3: Carnage

Descendants of the Fall

Book 1: Warbringer

Book 2: Wrath of the Forgotten

Book 3: Age of Gods

Book 4: Dreams of Fury

The Alfurian Chronicles

Book 1: Defiant

Book 2: Guardian

Book 3: Conquest

The Swords of Heaven and Hell

Book 1: Darkstrider

Book 2: Voidlight

The Four Circles

Book 1: Help! My Wizard Mentor Had A Heart Attack And Now I'm
Being Chased By A Horde Of Giant Spiders!

The Untamed Isles

The Path Awakens